AUG   2021

WHAT DOESN'T KILL US

WHAT DOESN'T KILL US

David Housewright

MINOTAUR
BOOKS
NEW YORK

First published in the United States by Minotaur Books, an imprint of St. Martin's Publishing Group

WHAT DOESN'T KILL US. Copyright © 2021 by David Housewright. All rights reserved. Printed in the United States of America. For information, address St. Martin's Publishing Group, 120 Broadway, New York, NY 10271.

www.minotaurbooks.com

Library of Congress Cataloging-in-Publication Data

Names: Housewright, David, 1955– author.
Title: What doesn't kill us / David Housewright.
Other titles: What does not kill us
Description: First Edition. I New York : Minotaur Books, 2021. I
    Series: Twin cities P.I. Mac Mckenzie novels ; 18
Identifiers: LCCN 2020053270 I ISBN 9781250756992 (hardcover) I
    ISBN 9781250757005 (ebook)
Subjects: GSAFD: Mystery fiction.
Classification: LCC PS3558.O8668 W47 2021 I DDC 813/.54—dc23
LC record available at https://lccn.loc.gov/2020053270

Our books may be purchased in bulk for promotional, educational, or business use. Please contact your local bookseller or the Macmillan Corporate and Premium Sales Department at 1-800-221-7945, extension 5442, or by email at MacmillanSpecialMarkets@macmillan.com.

First Edition: 2021

10 9 8 7 6 5 4 3 2 1

FOR
RENÉE MARIE VALOIS

I wish to acknowledge my debt to the late India Cooper, Vienna Crosby, Kayla Janas, Keith Kahla, Jim Mullin, Alison Picard, Alice Pfeifer, Emily Polachek, Sabrina Soares Roberts, and Renée Valois.

WHAT DOESN'T KILL US

JUST SO YOU KNOW

I was shot in the back at close range by a .32-caliber handgun yet did not die, at least not permanently. Dr. Lillian Linder, the emergency medical specialist who saved my life, said it was a miracle. Lilly had patched me up on numerous occasions over the past decade, though, and I knew that she was prone to hyperbole. The cops, of course, were anxious to interview me but Lil had placed me in a coma. Apparently, I had coded twice while she was doing her thing. The second time I suffered cardiac arrest, I was dead for four minutes and ten seconds. To bring me back, Lilly zapped my heart with a defibrillator. That got it pumping again, although erratically. At least, that's what I was told. I wish I could tell you that I saw Jesus while I was gone, but I didn't. I didn't see anything. There was no bright light for me to go to; my mom and dad weren't waiting for me on the other side. I didn't even know that I had died until three days later. Anyway, during those four minutes and ten seconds there was no electrical activity in my brain and no blood circulating. Lilly was concerned that I might suffer brain damage, if I hadn't already (insert your own joke here).

Thus the induced coma. In any case, there was nothing I could have told the cops. I did not see who shot me. I did not know why I was shot. Hell, I was as surprised at being shot as the woman who screamed when the bullet spun my body against hers. Eventually, I would piece the entire story together; my friends related bits and pieces to me while I was recovering. Apparently, I have more friends than you can shake a stick at. Who knew? Their stories began where mine ended, so to speak. They began with the scream . . .

ONE

I had been standing outside the club, looking first right and then left. I saw her when I looked left, a middle-aged woman who was walking toward me in three-inch heels. I found out later that her name was Nancy Moosbrugger. Her hair was brown and her eyes were brown and her body—if I had a body like that I would wear skintight clothes, too. She smiled at me and I smiled at her. I thought she was a working girl, especially after she said, "Hello," with a voice that suggested that all things were possible.

"Good evening," I replied.

She nodded her head and smiled some more and reached past me for the handle of the club's door, moving slowly as if she expected me to stop her.

That's when I felt the hard punch in my back and I tumbled forward. I didn't feel the pain at first, and then I did. I reached for Nancy in a futile attempt to remain upright. She screamed and everything went black.

Someone called 911, I never learned who. Officer Jeremiah Healy arrived five minutes and twenty-seven seconds later, which was an excellent response time. He saw a woman in a skintight dress that was cut low on the top and high on the bottom and splattered with blood. She was sitting on the sidewalk and cradling my head in her lap.

"Someone shot him," Nancy said.

"What?"

"Someone shot him. I heard a shot and he fell against me."

The way Nancy held me in her lap, my back was to the sidewalk, the officer didn't become fully aware of how seriously injured I was until he knelt next to us and the blood pooling beneath me wetted his knee. The bullet that had entered my back and lodged itself in my chest had ruptured at least one major vessel and I was in danger of bleeding to death.

The officer activated the radio microphone attached to his shoulder.

He carefully explained that he was on the scene, that shots had been fired as the 911 caller had reported, and that he found a white male who was badly in need of immediate medical attention. The SPPD was big on what it called "plain speak." For example, Healy was very clear when he said, "Officer requires assistance."

He interviewed Nancy while he waited for it to arrive.

"Who is he?" the officer asked.

"I don't know. I never saw him before."

"Is he a john you picked up?"

"What the hell?"

"It's okay. I'm not judging."

Only Nancy felt as if she was being judged.

"I was walking down the street . . ."

The officer smirked.

"I was walking down the street and I saw him standing in front of the door and I heard the gunshot and he fell against me, and somehow we both ended up on the sidewalk."

"Were you the one who called 911?" Healy asked.

"No."

Her cell phone was in her small handbag. The bag was resting on the other side of the sidewalk where it came to rest after flying out of her hand. Nancy would have had to lay my head on the concrete and crawl over to reach it. The fact that she didn't, that she continued to cradle me in her arms, a complete stranger—well, let's not get emotional. We have a long way to go yet.

Healy asked Nancy if she could identify the man who shot me. It was a leading question, something an experienced investigator would never ask. Good for Nancy, she answered, "I don't know if it was a man or a woman. I didn't see the person." Healy told her that the detectives would want to interview her just the same.

By then the ambulance had arrived. And more cops. And bystanders. Before they reached us, though, Officer Healy had the presence of mind to search me for an ID. He found a wallet in the inside pocket of my black sports jacket and opened it. On one side was my driver's license, conveniently tucked behind a plastic window, which told him that my name was Rushmore McKenzie and I lived across the river in Minneapolis. On the other side, also protected by plastic, was a second ID card that I used primarily to get out of speeding tickets. It proclaimed that I was a proud member of the St. Paul Police Department—retired.

"Oh, shit," Healy said.

Bobby Dunston was playing hoops with his daughter in the driveway of his pre–World War II colonial in the Merriam Park neighborhood of St. Paul. It was the house where Bobby grew up; he bought it from his parents when they retired. It's also where I practically grew up after my mother died when I was in the sixth grade. I didn't have a family except for my father after that and the Dunstons had all but adopted me. It was the reason I never felt like an orphan even after my father passed.

It was approaching eight thirty, yet because of daylight saving time it was still light outside. Bobby was wishing that the damn sun would set already. His daughter was kicking his ass and he wanted to quit while he still possessed a shred of athletic dignity. He suggested, not for the first time, that he was a hockey player, not a basketball player. If he thought his second child would take it easy on him, though, he was mistaken. Katie Dunston had made the Central High School women's varsity basketball team as a freshman and helped lead them to the City Conference finals. She was ferocious. Meanwhile, Katie's older sister, Victoria, was sitting at a picnic table in the backyard and trash-talking him.

The girls bore little resemblance to each other. Victoria had a dark, almost brooding appearance like Bobby's, yet possessed an expressive, outgoing personality that matched her mother's. Meanwhile, Katie was all sunshine and wheat fields like Shelby but possessed the reticent characteristics of her old man. Victoria was the intellectual in the family; she was just finishing up her junior year of high school yet had already amassed enough Advanced Placement credits to qualify as a second-semester college freshman. Katie was the athlete; college scouts were already expressing interest in her. Victoria suggested that was fortunate because the only way Katie was going to get into a decent school was with an athletic scholarship. Katie's response was to quote Princess Leia in *The Empire Strikes Back*—"You stuck-up, half-witted, scruffy-looking nerf herder!"

Eventually, Bobby became frustrated enough with Vic's heckling that he told her if she could do better, she was welcome to try. The girls both oohed and aahed at that. They might not always get along as well as they could, yet it was forever the two of them against the world and the world often included their parents.

Bobby had to admit that he was being a poor loser, only he never felt so old in his life. Or proud. Katie was wearing her practice jersey with a bright red "4" on the back. Number four had been Bobby's number on every jersey in every sport he had ever played.

"One more game," Katie said. "First one to ten."

"I'm coming hard this time," Bobby said.

"You do that."

Before he could check the ball, however, Shelby Dunston came out of the back door and dashed across the lawn to the driveway. She looked panicked, which came as a shock to every member of her family. Shelby never looked panicked.

She halted at the edge of the concrete apron and held out a cell phone.

"Mom?" Victoria said.

"What is it?" Bobby asked.

"McKenzie," Shelby said. "He's been shot."

"Is he dead?"

"Not yet."

Bobby took the cell from Shelby's hand and spoke into it.

"This is Commander Dunston," he said.

"Commander, this is Jean Shipman. I've just been informed that Rushmore McKenzie has just been shot outside a club on Rice Street."

"What the hell was he doing on Rice Street?"

"Who knows."

"How bad is it?"

"Pretty bad, I think."

"Where is he?"

"On his way to Regions if he's not there already."

"The officer who took the call?"

"Jerry Healy. Seven-year man working out of Central. He's accompanying the ambulance to the hospital."

"Tell him to stay there; tell him to wait until I arrive."

"Yes, sir."

"Suspects in custody?"

"No. I don't— Major Crimes just received the call. Probably we wouldn't have it this early except that Healy IDed McKenzie as one of us."

"All right, you take lead."

"Yes, sir."

"Jeannie, I want everybody on this."

"I've sent Mason Gafford to the club; FSU should already be there—"

"Everybody!" Bobby shouted.

"Yes, of course."

"I'm heading to Regions Hospital now. I'll call as soon as I learn anything."

"Yes, sir."

"Do you know if Nina Truhler has been informed?"

"I don't."

"Okay."

Bobby ended the call and stood staring at his wife and wondered what she was thinking. Shelby and I shared a bond that went all the way back to college. The joke was that if I had been the one who spilled his drink on Shelby's dress instead of Bobby, all of our lives would be different. Bobby had never really given it much thought in the twenty-some years that had passed since then. Why would he? After all, he's the guy who won the girl, not me. Yet now it seemed to matter immensely. Was it a joke? Well, of course it was.

Bobby and Shelby moved into each other's arms and held each other as tightly as they ever had.

"I can't believe this is happening," Shelby said.

"McKenzie's always getting into trouble. Remember the last time we got a call like this? Someone tried to blow him up."

"This feels different somehow."

"I'm going to the hospital."

"I'm going with you."

"No."

"Bobby . . ."

"I'll be working."

"Then I'll drive separately. Nina will need a friend."

" 'Kay."

Shelby and Bobby explained the situation to their daughters. I have no idea what they were thinking at that moment, but they must have remembered that I had designated them as my heirs, that they both stood to inherit a couple of million bucks each when I cashed in, mustn't they? Or not. I don't know. I never asked them, not even to be funny.

They remained in the driveway while mom and dad went into the house for their keys and whatnot, opened the garage doors, and walked to their separate vehicles.

"I love you," Shelby said across the roof of her car.

"I love you more," Bobby replied.

The girls didn't say much of anything as they watched their parents drive off. Katie went back to shooting baskets, slowly, methodically, telling herself Just get the ball through the hoop; don't think about anything except getting the ball through the hoop. Victoria soon joined her. Katherine gave her tips. Victoria accepted them. The girls kept shooting until the next-door neighbor told them it was late and the noise and bright garage lights were keeping everyone awake. Katie was tempted to tell the neighbor where he could go, only Vic restrained her. After all, she was the mature sister. Or at least the eldest.

———

Nancy Moosbrugger sat on the passenger side of Detective Mason Gafford's unmarked car parked with a clear view of the club's entrance, her long legs dangling over the edge of the seat toward the street, the hem of her dress hiked up to there. She was trembling like a leaf in a high wind.

"I don't know what's wrong with me," she said. "I was perfectly fine when I was holding that poor man in my lap. I wasn't even bothered by the blood."

Gafford glanced at her legs, at the blood staining her thighs and calves. The EMTs should have given her a towel or something. He wondered if there was one in the trunk. He had never driven that particular unit before so he wasn't sure.

"The cop was more upset than me," Nancy said, "and I hadn't seen anyone shot before."

"Probably he hadn't, either," Gafford said.

"He got real upset when he found out that the man was a police officer."

"Ex–police officer, retired."

"Do you think that's why he was shot, because he was a police officer?"

"I don't know. He often worked as a kind of unlicensed private investigator, so there's that."

"Is that why he was hanging around this part of town? The North End? Rice Street? I mean it's not as bad as the East Side, but still."

"Could be."

"McKenzie? His name was McKenzie, right?"

"Yes."

"Did you know him?"

"We've met."

"He was a nice guy, wasn't he?"

"I thought so."

"I could tell, the way he smiled and said, 'Good evening,' like he meant it. Most men . . ."

Nancy didn't finish the thought. Instead, she glanced down at her hands shaking in her lap as if it was something she had never seen before. Gafford squatted down in front of her. At a distance she could pass for late twenties, but up close she appeared to be in her late thirties, perhaps early forties, especially around the eyes. Gafford rested his hand on top of Nancy's. She slipped one hand on top of his, catching it between both of her hands, and squeezed. Gafford let her even though it hurt.

He glanced around. The officer assigned to crowd control was having a tough time of it; people attempting to enter and exit the club through the front door were treating him with all of the respect given a bouncer brandishing a red velvet rope. Meanwhile, the Forensic Services Unit was carefully inspecting the crime scene under the bright lights that they had taken from the tricked-out van they utilized. If they found anything, they hadn't bothered to inform him.

"Why can't I stop shaking?" Nancy asked.

Gafford decided that he was the one who should be asking the questions. It's what they were paying him for after all.

"Did you see the assailant?" he asked.

Nancy repeated the word, "As-sai-lant," as if she liked the way it rolled off her tongue. "No, I didn't. He must have been standing behind McKenzie."

"He?"

"He. She. I couldn't tell. McKenzie was blocking my view and when he fell I was watching him."

"Did you see anyone else on the sidewalk . . ."

"No."

"While you were walking toward the club?"

"No. Just McKenzie."

"You heard the shot," Gafford said.

"Yes."

"Did the shot come from inside the bar?"

"No. McKenzie was standing sideways to the bar, sideways to the entrance and watching me. The door was closed. I was moving past him to open the door and thinking—the way he smiled and said, 'Good evening,' I thought maybe . . . Then I heard the gunshot."

"Coming from behind him?"

"I guess," Nancy said. "It wasn't loud. Not like in the movies. It didn't go boom, you know? More like crack, crack."

"You heard two shots?"

"No, just the one. Crack."

"What happened next?"

"Then he fell against me. Well, not fell. More like he was shoved. I screamed because—I heard the crack and he fell against me and I knew, just knew that he had been shot. I had never seen anything like this before except in the movies, yet I knew. It seemed so clear to me. He fell and I caught him and kinda lowered him to the ground. I screamed because it seemed like the thing to do. I wasn't afraid. I am now. I can't stop shaking. But I wasn't at the time."

"What happened next?" Gafford repeated.

"A couple of people walked out of the bar and a couple of people walked in. No one bothered to stop and ask what was going on. They must have thought McKenzie was a drunk who passed out or something. It seemed like we were there for a long time although I suppose it was only a couple of minutes before I heard the siren. The cop car siren. All of a sudden the sidewalk was filled with people. One of them called the cop a dirty name. I don't know why. He was just trying to help."

Gafford gave Nancy's hands a shake and stood up.

"You're a good person," he said.

"No, I'm not."

"You are what you do and you did good."

"Should I be honest, Detective Gifford?"

"Gafford."

"Forgive me. Detective Gafford. I'll be honest. I came here tonight to get laid. I would have done McKenzie if he had let me, the way he smiled and said, 'Good evening.' My husband left me for a sweet young thing that worked as an intern in his office and for the past six months I've been sitting around the house feeling sorry for myself, telling myself that I'm old and ugly and no one wants me. Finally, I decided to prove that it wasn't true. Or maybe that it was. That's why I came down here. Alone. To Rice Street. I don't know how I got up the nerve. Then I saw him, McKenzie. I saw him standing outside the club, this good-looking man who smiled and stared at me exactly the way I wanted to be stared at. Now look at me. I look hideous."

"No, you don't," Gafford said.

Nancy's eyes met his.

"My dress is ruined."

"Like I said, I know McKenzie. If he pulls through, I'm going to tell him about you. I bet he buys you a new dress."

"Is he married, do you know?"

"Yes."

"Oh."

"But I'm not."

"Ooh."

Before he left his house in Merriam Park, Bobby made a phone call. It was received by Nina Truhler. She was sitting behind her desk in her office at Rickie's, the jazz club she had named after her daughter Erica, and doing something with her computer. She answered the phone without bothering to check the caller ID.

"Rickie's," she said.

"Nina, it's Bobby."

Something in his voice made her stand up.

"What is it?" she said.

"Hang on to yourself, honey—McKenzie's been shot."

"Shot?"

"Yes. He's . . ."

"Is he dead?"

"No. No, Nina. He's going to be fine."

"Is that a promise?"

"He's at Regions Hospital. I'm heading over right now."

"I'll see you there."

Nina hung up her phone and stared at it for a few beats before forcing herself to move. *Dammit*, Nina's inner voice said. *Four months. We've been married for four lousy months, not even four months, and he does this to me?*

Yet she reserved most of her anger for Bobby.

"You sonuvabitch," she said aloud. "You didn't promise."

Thaddeus Coleman was an entrepreneur. He was currently managing a ticket-scalping operation out of an office in a converted warehouse with a view of Target Field, where the Twins played baseball in downtown Minneapolis. When I first met him, though, back when I was with the SPPD, Coleman was running a small but lucrative stable of girls around Selby and Western, a neighborhood in St. Paul that used to be rich with prostitution until patrons drifted to the next trendy hot spot. Afterward, he dealt drugs around Fuller and Farrington. Sometimes he sold the real thing; sometimes he passed laundry soap and Alka-Seltzer tablets crushed to resemble rock cocaine to the white suburban kids who drove up in Daddy's SUV. I busted Coleman for that—representing and selling a controlled substance, whether it's an actual drug or not, is a felony. Only, the judge threw the case out. I blamed the prosecutor.

While the court might have been lenient with Coleman, though, the Red Dragons not so much. They objected to his activities on what they considered to be their turf, and pumped two rounds into his spine as a way to express their displeasure, thus the wheelchair that he was now sitting in and the nickname he became widely known by—Chopper. I'm the one that scooped him off the sidewalk and got him the medical attention that saved his life. We've been friends ever since, even though six weeks after Chopper wheeled himself out of the hospital in a stolen chair, we discovered the bodies of three Red Dragons under the swings at a park near St. Paul College of Technology. We could never prove who did the deed; although the ME reported that the bullet holes had an upward trajectory as if the Dragons were shot by someone who was sitting down. Still, innocent until proven guilty is what the law says.

Chopper was sitting at his desk, and reviewing the latest computer gadgetry that would help him circumvent the online security systems employed by ticket sellers and allow him to buy bundles of the best seats in the house for whatever concerts and sporting events promised him a hefty ROI. His head came up when he heard my name.

"Go back," he said.

"Huh?"

"Go back, go back."

Herzog was relaxing in a leather lounger and pointing a remote at a flat-screen TV. He had been channel surfing, one of his favorite occupations, landing on one channel before moving to the next and the next, sometimes watching for a few minutes, sometimes only for a second or two, entertaining himself for hours. Chopper had taught himself to block out the distraction, except he had heard someone say, "McKenzie."

"Go back," he said again.

Herzog flicked the channels until he landed on a local TV reporter named Kelly Bressandes who was looking into the lens of a camera as if it were the best friend she ever had. She was wearing a tight sweater so her male audience would know that she had curves. I'd had dealings with her in the past. Believe me, she could be wearing a burlap sack and the world would know that she had curves.

"The third shooting in St. Paul in the past week," she said. "Rushmore McKenzie remains in critical condition in Regions Hospital. Barry?"

The camera moved from Kelly's face to that of her co-anchor, who began talking about a health care initiative that was being argued in the state legislature.

"See if he's on any of the other news programs," Chopper said.

Herzog switched channels. He found a male anchor who seemed put out by the story he was reporting.

"The shooting remains under investigation," he said. "It should be noted that this is not the first time that police have been called to the RT's Basement, located on Rice Street in St. Paul, because of a violent act. Over to you . . ."

Herzog knew what Chopper was thinking.

"Ain't none of our business," he said.

"Shooting remains under investigation means they don't know who did it."

"So?"

"We could find out."

"How we gonna find out?"

"RT's Basement—who we know down there?"

"C'mon, Chop. We don't owe McKenzie nothin'."

"Don't we?"

"It's St. Paul, man. That means fucking Bobby Dunston. He'd like t' put us inside just for the fun of it."

"He's McKenzie's friend."

"He ain't ours, you know what I'm sayin'?"

"Cops always whining about not gettin' no cooperation from the African-American community. We just cooperating is all."

Herzog shook his head and muttered a few obscenities before turning off the flat-screen and climbing out of the chair. He was the largest, hardest man I had ever met in person; you could roller-skate on him. He was also the most dangerous. He had done time for multiple counts of manslaughter, assault, aggravated robbery, and weapons charges, but was working hard to clean up his act. He'd been out on parole for the past four years with one more to go and had been Chopper's right-hand man ever since they released him from the halfway house. He tolerated me—but just barely—because we both liked baseball and jazz and Chopper, and because I had arranged through Nina to get him and his date the table closest to the stage when Cécile McLorin Salvant sang at Rickie's.

"Jus' so you know, I think this is a really bad idea," he said.

TWO

The Surgical Intensive Care Unit was damn near impossible to reach by a visitor using Regions Hospital's overly complicated elevator and corridor system. Except Bobby knew a shortcut. He walked into the ground floor emergency entrance, flashed his badge, and announced that he was a commander in the St. Paul Police Department's Major Crimes Division. Shelby stood by his side as if she had always been there and always would be. They whisked them both up to the third floor in no time.

That's as far as they were allowed to go, however. A woman, who wore a white linen coat but no scrubs, said I was in surgery. Bobby had questions. Instead of answering them, the woman asked how they were related to me. Bobby showed her his badge. That bought him and Shelby visiting privileges but no answers; they were both escorted to a waiting area. Bobby said he wanted to see someone in authority. The woman said she would contact the surgeon in charge when circumstances permitted, turned, and walked away.

"You should have seen his face," Shelby told me later. "Most people are afraid of Bobby, but this woman, she was an admin or something—I don't think she was afraid of God."

Bobby and Shelby settled in a couple of uncomfortable chairs and stared more or less straight ahead. They didn't speak.

"What was there to say?" Bobby told me. "Same story, different room."

I asked them later what they were thinking. Shelby said she was repeating a mantra in her head that she had learned in yoga class in an attempt to remain calm and composed. Bobby said, "I was thinking that you were always doing shit like this, getting in trouble, getting hurt, and I was goddamned tired of it."

While they waited, Officer Jeremiah Healy appeared.

"Where the hell have you been?" Bobby asked him.

Healy raised a paper cup filled with black coffee and gestured toward the door.

"There's a machine down the hall," he said.

"What do you have for me?"

Healy set the coffee down and pulled out a small notebook. Good for you, Bobby thought as Healy started reciting facts— the time he received the call, the time he arrived at the scene, who was present at the scene upon his arrival, how long it took for other officers to arrive, the name of the supervisor who took charge of the scene, and that he had identified the vic by the driver's license in his wallet, which he surrendered to the supervisor who immediately relayed the information to Major Crimes.

"We thought you'd want to know right away," Healy said.

"Yes," Bobby said.

Healy said a plainclothes from the Homicide Unit arrived just as they were loading me into the ambulance, even though the incident was still rated as an aggravated assault, but that he didn't know who it was.

"I accompanied the vic to the hospital in case he woke up and said something, only he didn't," Healy said.

"Okay," Bobby said.

"That's him, isn't it? McKenzie."

"What do you mean, him?'"

"Everyone in the SPPD knows about McKenzie; I heard about him my first week on the job. How he won the lottery, what is it now? Ten years ago?"

"That's one way of looking at it."

"Some say that he sold his badge when he quit the cops to collect the reward on an embezzler he collared off the books. Got fifty cents for every dollar he recovered from the insurance company they say, made millions."

"He didn't sell his badge."

"What do you call it?"

"He took an early retirement to help his father out. Unfortunately, his father passed six months later."

"Yeah, sure."

"You can leave now. I want to see an incident report first thing in the morning."

Healy glanced at his watch to see how much time he had before his ten-hour shift ended.

"Yes, sir," he said.

Detective Jeannie Shipman hated my guts; she especially hated it when I called her Jeannie which I did *because* she hated my guts. She was "young, beautiful; smart as hell"—at least that's how Bobby once described her to me, although I could never see it. She had been Bobby's partner before they made him a lieutenant (all lieutenants were later named commanders, I have no idea what the SPPD was thinking), and remained his cohort of choice on those occasions when he stepped away from his role as a practicing bureaucrat and actually did some investigating. Shelby claimed that we don't get along because we're both jealous of each other's relationship with Bobby, but sometimes she can be overly dramatic.

Shipman traveled to the crime scene because Bobby had said, "Everybody," and she didn't want him to think that my getting shot wasn't worth her undivided attention even though she had way better things to do with her time. The first thing she did was debrief Gafford, who told her that he had been unable to locate a single witness who saw the shooting besides Nancy Moosbrugger. Or at least no witnesses who were willing to discuss the matter with a member of the law enforcement community.

"McKenzie couldn't get shot in Macalester-Groveland," Shipman said. "No, it's gotta be on Rice Street."

"Well, this part of Rice Street, anyway. The rest of the street isn't . . ."

Gafford stopped speaking because of the withering look Shipman gave him, the one that asked, "Are you contradicting me?"

Gafford told Shipman that he had been able to identify the car I drove—a Jeep Cherokee parked up the street. Shipman quickly ordered it towed to the SPPD's impound lot, where I would eventually need to provide proof of ownership, a valid driver's license, proof of insurance, and a credit card to pay all towing and storage fees—no personal checks—in order to recover it. Don't think for a second that the expense and inconvenience it would cause me didn't cross her mind, either.

Shipman dismissed Gafford and made her way toward RT's Basement, making sure to step around the bloodstain. While on her way, she was intercepted by a tech working out of the FSU.

"Hey, sexy," he said.

"Sexy?"

Shipman glanced down at herself almost in self-defense. She was wearing what she nearly always wore on the job, jeans, button-down shirt, and a blazer long enough to conceal the Glock she wore on her hip.

"Everyone knows you're the best-looking woman on the force," the tech said.

"Brian, should I bring you up on harassment charges or just shoot you myself?"

The tech raised a clear six-by-nine-inch polyethylene evidence bag with a white write-on area that had already been filled out for Shipman to see. He was smiling like he had the winning ticket for the Daily Three. Shipman stared at the bag. It looked empty to her.

"What am I looking at?" she asked.

"Spent cartridge," the tech answered.

That's when Shipman saw the half-inch long brass case resting at the bottom of the bag.

"Thirty-two ACP," Brian said. "Which means semiautomatic; a wheel gun wouldn't have tossed it. Which means a pocket gun; the damn thing would fit in the palm of your hand. Which means amateur. I mean think about it. President McKinley was shot twice, once in the abdomen by a .32, only it wasn't that bullet that killed him. It was the gangrene."

"Write it up," Shipman said.

"What? You're not going to give me some love, Jean? You guys from homicide, we solve eighty percent of your cases for you yet you never give us any love."

"Do you know who shot the vic?"

"No, but . . ."

"Write it up, Brian. And don't call me Jean."

RT's Basement promoted itself as a no-frills bar and lounge with live music Wednesday through Saturday, the music leaning toward hip-hop and R&B with a smattering of the blues. Shipman stepped inside the joint which, despite its name, was not located in a basement; she didn't know if it even had a basement. She did see large windows facing the street and plenty of wooden tables, chairs, and booths facing an empty stage with huge speakers mounted on metal stands that were aimed at the tables, chairs, and booths. Most of them were occupied by people who were paying no attention whatsoever to what had been happening just outside the front door or to the flat-screen TVs mounted in the corners broadcasting what looked like post-game interviews with a couple of Los Angeles Lakers basketball players, the Lakers actually a Minneapolis team before it was moved in 1960, thus the name. Some of the people occupying the chairs and tables looked as if they were too young to drive much less drink.

A large black man was standing behind the bar. From his expression, Shipman decided he knew exactly who she was and what she wanted. She walked up to him while pulling a thin leather wallet from her pocket. She opened the wallet and gave the bartender a good look at its contents. Most people were impressed. The bartender glanced at the ID and badge and shook his head.

"Whaddya want?" he asked.

"What's your name?"

He paused as if he didn't want to give it out, finally said, "Richard Thomas."

"Well, Dick . . ."

It was an old cop trick, using a suspect's first name. It removes a suspect's dignity and makes him feel defensive, inferior, and often dependent; it tells a suspect who's in charge. Thomas had been around long enough to know that, though, and he didn't let it bother him. It was the "Dick" that he objected to.

"People call me RT," he said.

Shipman ignored him.

"The man who was shot—" she said.

"Are you guys just about done? I gotta business to run here."

"Oh, are we in your way?"

"Whaddya think?"

"I think maybe I should start checking the IDs of some of your customers, what do you think, Dick?"

The bartender crossed his arms over his chest and waited.

"The man who was shot," Shipman said. "What can you tell me about him?"

"Nothin'."

"Nothing?"

"I hardly noticed him, like I told the other guy, Gifford."

"Gafford."

"My point," RT said, "man comes in for a drink, pays for the drink, drinks the drink, leaves. Why should I pay any attention to him 'less he does somethin' to, you know, attract my attention?"

"Like getting shot?"

"That happened outside. I didn't even know it happened until someone told me and by then you people were here."

"You people?"

"Police blockin' my entrance and shit. I had to let people in and out through the back door in the alley."

"Video cameras?"

RT shook his head.

"You don't have any security cameras in your place?" Shipman asked.

"My customers don't like being spied on by . . ."

"By you people?"

RT shrugged.

"Yeah, I can imagine," Shipman said.

By then the FSU had packed up its equipment and departed. As far as she knew, Shipman was the only police officer left at RT's Basement. She didn't let it bother her, though. She asked more questions of the bartender yet learned nothing. She asked questions of his customers and got more of the same. Finally, she stepped out of the club onto the sidewalk and inhaled deeply the fresh May air, or at least as fresh as it got on Rice Street. The night sky was bright enough that she could make out some of the stars floating overhead despite the light pollution.

Most people would say that fall was the best time to be in Minnesota, yet Shipman had always preferred spring. Fifty degrees in early May always felt warmer to her than fifty degrees in late October. She wasn't thinking about her comfort, though. She was thinking about how little information she had and just how pissed off Commander Dunston was going to be.

Bobby and Shelby were still sitting in their uncomfortable chairs when Nina arrived at the hospital. Normally, there would have been plenty of hugging and gushing, especially between Nina and Shelby. Instead, Nina moved directly to where they were sitting and asked, "How is he?"

Bobby and Shelby both stood.

"We don't know. The woman . . ." He gestured at the admin in the white linen coat sitting behind her desk. "She told us a few minutes ago that McKenzie is still in surgery. There was a lot of bleeding from the bullet that lodged in his chest. It's going to take time."

"How much time?"

"It's been over two hours now," Shelby said.

She reached to take Nina's arm, but Nina pulled it away, spun around, and marched to the desk where the woman dressed in the white coat was seated. Bobby and Shelby followed.

"I'm Rushmore McKenzie's wife and I want to know my husband's condition," she announced.

"Mrs. McKenzie, there are forms—"

"My name is Nina Truhler and you're not answering my question."

"Ms. Truhler, if you care to take a seat—"

"Listen. You know how some people go right off the rails and start screaming and carrying on until you either end up calling security or giving them what they want?" Nina tapped her chest. "I'm exactly that person."

"Just a moment, please."

The woman escaped through the doorway behind her.

"I was counting," Nina told me later. "I was counting slowly to one hundred. The admin returned when I reached eighty-eight."

"What would you have done if you had reached one hundred?"

"Something I'd probably regret later," was all she told me.

The woman in the white coat was followed by Dr. Lillian Linder, who was still wearing her blue surgical gown, the gown stained with blood. Not a lot of blood. Just enough for Shelby to say, "Oh, Jesus."

Lilly smiled and said, "Hi, Nina." Nina wasn't fooled by the smile, however.

"How bad is it?" she asked.

"Serious but stable."

"What does that mean?"

Lilly said it meant that the bullet had been removed; that all the ruptured blood vessels had been repaired, that there had been no damage to the heart, and my vital signs had stabilized. However . . .

"However?" Nina asked.

My blood pressure was higher than it should be, although not so high as to cause Lilly to be overly concerned—so she said—and my pulse rate was hovering around one hundred, which wasn't necessarily cause for alarm, either—so she said. It was her intention to keep me in an induced coma until my vitals returned to normal.

"Coma?"

That's when Lilly explained that I had suffered sudden cardiac arrest twice during surgery. The first time, she zapped me once with a defibrillator. The second time she had to hit my heart three times. There would not have been a fourth attempt. Lilly didn't tell Nina that but she did tell me a couple of days later when she thought I was ready to accept the news without freaking out.

"We induced the coma for a couple of reasons," she said. "The first is so that the body doesn't use any energy in physical movement. This reduces the stress on the heart as much as possible, giving it the best chance of recovery. Right now McKenzie's heart is doing the absolute minimum amount of work, circulating his blood and very little else. That greatly reduces the chance of another SCA."

"What's the prognosis?" Bobby asked, getting to the point.

Lilly ignored the question.

"Another reason for the induced coma," she said, "is that shutting down function gives the brain time to heal itself; time to repair any damaged areas without reducing blood flow to the other parts of the body that are also injured. The brain gets top priority for blood. If it thinks it needs more to fix itself, it'll take more even if that means shutting down the supply to other organs."

"What do you mean, give the brain time to heal itself?" Nina asked.

Dr. Linder told Nina that for four minutes and ten seconds there was a loss of blood to my brain. That my EKG had flatlined. Lilly took a deep breath before adding, "In some cases, when the loss of circulation to the brain is extended, the patient can suffer varying degrees of damage."

"Damage to the brain?" Nina asked.

"Yes."

"When the loss of circulation is extended?"

"Yes."

"Define extended."

"Brain cells can begin to die after five minutes of oxygen loss."

"McKenzie was out for four minutes and ten seconds."

"Yes."

"Fifty seconds shy of five minutes."

"Yes, except there was a slight amount of swelling that occurred when oxygenated blood failed to reach his brain cells."

"But he's going to be all right?"

Lilly answered by smiling confidently—I think she perfected that smile in med school—and wrapping her arms around Nina. Nina spoke into Lilly's shoulder.

"Please," she said. "Tell me he's going to be all right. Lilly? Promise me."

"I think he's going to be fine. I just thought you should know what happened during surgery. You should be aware that there's—that there's a worst-case scenario. I'm your friend. I'm also a doctor. I won't lie to you."

"A lie doesn't sound all that bad right now. How long will you keep McKenzie in the coma?"

"We might bring him out as early as tomorrow. Two, three days at the most. I'll have a better answer for you in the morning."

"In the morning?"

"Nina, we need to stop meeting like this."

It's what Lilly always said when the two women came together over one of my medical emergencies. Usually, the remark would make them both smile but Nina's inner voice was screaming. *She didn't promise. If she's so sure McKenzie will be fine, why won't she promise?*

I have no idea what Lilly was thinking.

Herzog opened the door to RT's Basement and Chopper wheeled himself inside. Herzog never pushed Chopper's wheelchair. He tried it once when he first came to work for him. Chopper didn't like it and told him so in no uncertain terms.

A kind of hush settled over the club as they made their way to the bar. This was not unusual. The sight of happy-go-lucky Chopper in his chair and large and dangerous-seeming Herzog hovering near him often made people stop and go, "Hmm."

The bartender stood waiting for them. He didn't say "Welcome to RT's" or "What'll you have?" or anything friendly like that. He just waited.

"You RT?" Chopper asked, using the nickname Richard Thomas preferred, knowing that was more likely to garner cooperation than insulting the man.

The bartender nodded.

"My friends call me Chopper. This here is Herzog. What are you drinking, Herzy?"

"Got any Booker's?"

"Herzog." RT said the name in a low tone of voice as if he had heard it before and was impressed.

"Huh?" Herzog said.

"Booker's is a little high-end for us," RT said.

"Michter's? Barrell? Maker's Mark? Knob Creek?"

The bartender kept shaking his head.

"Jim Beam?"

RT answered by taking a bottle off the shelf behind him and pouring a couple of fingers into a squat glass. He didn't quote a price.

Herzog sipped the bourbon.

"What can I get you?" RT asked.

"I hear you've had some excitement t'night," Chopper said in reply.

"What of it?"

"Man who was shot named McKenzie."

RT waited for Chopper to finish his thought.

"Man is a friend of ours."

RT glanced at Herzog as if he couldn't believe it. Herzog kept sipping his drink.

"I already talked to the police," RT said.

"I ain't the fuckin' po-lice," Chopper said.

RT looked at Herzog some more.

"Me neither," Herzog said.

"What can you tell us?" Chopper asked.

"Whaddya want to know?" RT asked.

"What was he doing here?"

"Fuck should I know? White man walks into my place wearing an expensive sports jacket, I'm supposed t' ask him questions?"

"You remember him?"

"Yeah, I remember him. Cuz of the jacket. I have my share of white customers, 'cept they don't usually dress as nice. Well, sometimes when I get an act that has crossover appeal. 'Cept it's Tuesday and we don't have music on Tuesdays."

Chopper took a moment to glance around at the tables and booths and at the few customers drinking at the bar with them. There were more white customers than they expected in an African-American joint and a lot of them looked as if they had driven in from the suburbs, men and women both dressed in polo shirts and khakis.

"When did he arrive?" Chopper asked.

"Who?"

"What we talking about, the white man, McKenzie."

"Eight," the bartender said. "Couple minutes before."

"What he do?"

"It's a bar. He ordered a drink. Whaddya think?"

Herzog dropped his empty glass. The sound of it bouncing off the bar was loud enough to make the bartender flinch. After he recovered, he asked if Herzog wanted a refill. Herzog said he did. RT gathered up Herzog's glass, put it away, and pulled out a fresh one. While he poured more Jim Beam, he said "Your friend asked for a Summit Extra Pale Ale."

"Bet you don't pour that, either," Herzog said.

"He settled for a Budweiser."

"Then what?" Chopper asked.

"Then he drank his beer."

"And?"

"I think he was waiting for someone."

"Who?"

"He didn't say."

"How do you know he was waiting for someone?"

"He kept checking his watch. And his phone. Kept glancing at the door."

"But he didn't say who he was waiting for?"

"We're not brothers from another mother, 'kay? It's not like we were having a conversation."

"He went outside," Chopper said.

"Yeah."

"When?"

"I dunno. Eight fifteen? Eight twenty?"

"Why?"

"Why what?"

"Why'd he leave?"

"T' see if his friend was waitin' outside instead of inside? Fuck should I know?"

"Did he settle his tab first?" Chopper asked.

"He paid when I served him. A ten. Told me t' keep the change."

"So he wasn't planning on hanging around when his friend arrived."

"I don't know what he was planning."

"Did you watch him head for the door?"

"No, why would I?" RT asked.

"Did you see who shot him?"

"I didn't see nothin' like I told them cops, first the guy and then the skirt."

"Skirt?" Herzog asked.

"Woman cop," RT said.

"You call women 'skirts'?"

"Gotta be careful what you say these days. Them hashtag MeToo bitches eat you alive."

"Yeah, I can see how callin' 'em skirts be much better."

"What did you see?" Chopper asked.

"Nothin'," RT said. "Ain't no lie. Didn't even know what happened till a customer told me like I said to them cops."

"What can you tell us that you didn't tell them cops?"

The bartender watched Herzog as he swirled what was left of the bourbon in his glass.

"Fuck," he said.

Dr. Linder allowed Nina, Bobby, and Shelby to visit me, if you call standing in a corridor and looking through the sliding glass walls into the recovery room visiting. I was propped at a forty-five-degree angle on a bed. There was a tube in my nose to draw out stomach contents and another in my mouth to help me breathe and a line that was feeding me intravenously and a catheter going to my bladder and cables attached to a monitor where wavy red, green, and blue lines and ever-changing numbers kept track of my vital signs.

"He's looked better," Bobby said.

"The week after I first met him," Nina said, "God, only five days after he tailed that suspect into Rickie's, he ended up in the hospital, this very hospital, with an epidural hematoma. They had to drill two holes in his skull to drain the blood and alleviate the pressure or he would have . . ."

"I remember," Shelby said. "It was after he saved that young woman's life."

"I should've run for the hills then, only I didn't. Now I'm stuck with him."

"It was a lovely ceremony, getting married in the Winter Carnival Ice Palace like that. I still don't know how you managed it."

"McKenzie knew a guy who owed him a favor. McKenzie's preferred form of legal tender, favors. We waited until after the holidays because we didn't want to intrude on anyone's Christmas."

"You wouldn't have intruded."

"You didn't mind the cold, early February in Minnesota? That the ceremony took place at night after the Palace was closed to the public?"

Shelby took hold of Nina's arm and hugged it.

"I didn't mind. No one minded. The Ice Palace. Wow. Bobby and I were married in a church."

"McKenzie and I had been together for over seven years; we lived together for two of them," Nina said. "I thought after we were married everything would stay pretty much the same.

Only it didn't. We became even more . . . I would look at him sometimes and I'd feel a surge of electricity that I hadn't felt before. McKenzie told me that the world seemed brighter to him now. The sun, the moon, stars, colors—they all seemed brighter. Do you believe that?"

Shelby glanced at Bobby who continued to stare at me through the glass wall.

"Yes," she said. "I do."

"Nina," Bobby said. "We need to talk."

"Not now," Shelby said.

"I'm sorry but yes, now."

It was difficult maneuvering Chopper's wheelchair behind RT's desk, the entire office being about the size of a closet, and Herzog wondered why they didn't just turn the computer screen around.

RT tapped a couple of keys, moved his mouse, and tapped a few more.

"This is my primary camera," he said.

The screen displayed an overhead shot of his cash register.

"It ain't about my customers," he said. "It ain't about recordin' no fights an' shit, people doin' business. It ain't about keepin' 'em from doin' what they call dining and dashing, either. Ain't really had much of a problem with any of that. Set up the camera t' keep my employees from rippin' me off, you know? Make sure the cash goes in the till and not someone's pocket. Had problems with that. I had these security cameras installed secret like. I's the only one what knows about 'em."

"You didn't tell the cops?" Chopper asked.

"I ain't no agent of the po-lice. Now this here . . ." RT changed the screen. Apparently, the camera had been mounted on the shelf behind the actual wooden bar. It gave them a wide-angle view of the cash register on one end, the waitress station on the other, and the patrons sitting between them. Over the shoulders of the patrons they could see the club's tables and booths and stage and, in the deep background, the door and the windows with a view of the street.

"Are you recording this?" Chopper asked.

"Yeah. Records for seven days before the overwrite thing kicks in."

"Rewind to when McKenzie was shot."

RT did, but he was slow about it. Herzog came *this*close to shoving him out of the way and doing it himself. Finally, they had a close-up on me sitting at the bar and sipping Bud from a bottle. Eventually, I left it half-finished and made for the door. My figure receded into the background; I was only an inch high at the top of screen. I looked right. I looked left and kept looking left while Nancy Moosbrugger entered the frame. A figure that seemed to be dressed in dark colors came up from behind me. You could only see about half of the figure through the front window; the other half was hidden behind the wall. The figure seemed smaller than me by six to eight inches and wore a hat. Chopper said later that the figure was out of focus, the camera meant only to capture what was happening close to the bar, and he couldn't make out the figure's face or even its race. The figure seemed to raise a hand like it was pointing a finger and I fell. The figure turned and hurried out of the frame.

Chopper, Herzog, and the bartender watched it several times.

"Ain't much to see," RT said.

"Can you burn me a copy of the recording?" Chopper asked. "Just the part from when McKenzie enters the club until after the shooting."

"What you gonna do with it?"

"I don't know yet."

"Gonna give it to the po-lice?"

"Depends on what it'll buy me."

"You know," Herzog said. "The figure in black, my first thought . . ."

"What?"

"The way it moved, the way it lifted the gun, well, its hand, I didn't see no gun . . ."

"What?" Chopper repeated.

"It reminded me of a skirt."

THREE

Nina, Shelby, and Bobby returned to the waiting area where they found the woman in the white linen coat standing there with a clipboard and several sheets of paper for Nina to fill out and sign. Nina took the clipboard and went to the chair where Shelby had been sitting and started writing.

"What was McKenzie working on?" Bobby asked her. "Was he working?"

"He was doing a favor for a friend but he was being vague about it."

"Vague?"

"Usually he's pretty forthcoming about this stuff. Usually he tells me everything."

"Not this time? Why not this time?"

"He said it involved someone I knew personally. He said it was something embarrassing about someone I knew personally and he felt uncomfortable giving me details without permission from the someone."

"What was he doing on Rice Street?" Bobby asked.

"He didn't say."

"What did he say?"

"Last we spoke was late this afternoon. I told him that Maud Hixson, Arne Fogel, and the Wolverines Quintet were in the big room tonight and he told me to save him a seat in the back where we could neck without being seen. I said I would."

"The show started when?"

"Seven P.M."

"He was at RT's Basement at eight."

Nina shrugged.

"He didn't call to tell you he would be late to Rickie's?" Bobby asked.

Nina shrugged some more.

"Goddammit."

"Bobby," Shelby said.

"He must have said something," Bobby said. "He must have given you a clue, a hint about what the favor was, who he was doing it for?"

Nina looked up from the clipboard.

"The way he was being so secretive," she said, "up until a few minutes ago, I thought it was for you."

Dave Deese was watching hockey. Specifically, he was watching the St. Louis Blues at the San Jose Sharks in the NHL Western Conference Playoffs. The Minnesota Wild had already been eliminated. They insist on calling Minnesota the State of Hockey and we are. We have fifty-eight natives playing in the NHL. More than one thousand more have played D1 hockey in the past eight years. Men's and women's teams from Minnesota have won twenty NCAA championships between them and finished second thirteen times. We have sixty thousand high school kids—at least—lacing them up every year. And that's not counting park and rec. Yet our NHL teams haven't won anything ever. Don't get me started . . .

While Dave watched the game, Barbara Deese came through the door carrying a couple of bags printed with the logos of different box stores. Deese didn't ask her what she bought or how much it cost. They didn't have that kind of marriage. Instead, he said, "Have a good time?"

"I did," Barbara said. "I felt a little left out, though. Some of the girls started complaining about how big a jerk their husbands were, only I had nothing to add to the conversation."

Deese thought that was funny and laughed.

"Oh, hey." Barbara put her bags down. "Something I heard on the radio in the car, your friend McKenzie? The guy you play hockey with?"

"What about him?"

"They say he was shot."

"What?"

"I heard on the radio. At least I think it was him. Rushmore McKenzie, right?"

"Yeah, although—no one calls him Rushmore. Are you sure?"

"Pretty sure. It's probably already on the internet; you could check. Didn't he used to be a cop or something?"

Bobby went back down to the emergency room. From there he was directed to a corridor lined with a series of small offices that reminded him of rabbit hutches. He knocked on the door of one that was painted orange and yellow. The young woman sitting at the desk asked, "Can I help you?"

Bobby flashed his badge, identified himself, and said, "A man was brought into the emergency room a few hours ago named Rushmore McKenzie."

"Yes."

"You bagged his belongings."

"Yes."

"Where are they?"

"We have a secure storage area—"

"I want them."

"Sir?"

"His belongings. Get them for me."

"Umm, Officer Dunston—"

"Commander Dunston."

"Commander, we're in a kind of gray area here."

"How so?"

"If Mr. McKenzie had been murdered—"

"He wasn't."

"If he had been murdered we'd turn over his belongings without a fuss. That's because a murder victim doesn't have a reasonable expectation of privacy . . ."

Did some lawyer tell you that? Bobby thought but didn't ask.

"Because Mr. McKenzie wasn't murdered," the young woman said, "then he does have a reasonable expectation of privacy."

"What's your point?"

"I got into trouble over this once before."

Okay, a lawyer did tell you that, Bobby thought.

"What's your point?" he repeated.

She answered as if she was asking a question, "I can't give you his belongings without a subpoena?"

Bobby stared at the woman while thinking that he should take yoga classes, that he should learn how to stay calm, to control his emotions like Shelby.

"McKenzie's wife is upstairs in the SICU," he said.

"Oh?"

"Will you give his belongings to her?"

"That would be much easier."

Herzog aimed his key fob at the black van as they approached and pressed a button. There was a clicking sound and the side door unlocked and slowly rolled open. He pressed another button and a platform slid out of the vehicle and descended until it came to a rest in front of the door. Chopper wheeled himself onto the ramp and locked his chair down so that it wouldn't roll around while more buttons were pushed and the ramp lifted him and his chair up and pulled both back into the van. Herzog closed the door and climbed behind the steering wheel. He turned to look at Chopper.

"Now what?" he asked.

"Now we earn the undying respect, admiration, and gratitude of the St. Paul Police Department."

"I don' wanna ask, but—how we gonna do that?"

"Do you know where Merriam Park is?"

Nina and Shelby were sitting side by side in the SICU's waiting area. Nina was fiddling with her wedding ring. Shelby didn't know if it was because she was nervous or because she was still unused to wearing it.

"You don't need to stay with me," Nina said.

"Yes, I do."

"You've always been kind to me, Shelby. From the moment we met. Treated me like a sister. Yet I've always been jealous of you—from the moment we met—jealous of you while you were being kind to me. I've never had a sister or brother, never had many friends, either, mostly because of my mom—you know all about my mom. Well, maybe not all. And my father who abandoned my mom. I don't blame him for that. I abandoned her myself as soon as I was able. Then I abandoned that abusive creep I married to get away from Mom, God what was I thinking? My ex. There wasn't a lot of stability in my life until—until I took charge of my life; found people I could count on. Then you—I can be jealous of a sister and still love her, can't I? Victoria and Katherine are jealous of each other, they must be. I've heard them fight. Both so smart, so talented, so pretty, so, so, so . . . Jesus, Shelby, I'm gibbering like a, like a—you should just reach over and slap me like they do in the movies."

"Wait," Shelby said. "The gorgeous, successful nightclub owner is jealous of the lowly housewife?"

"Lowly housewife? You're a graphic designer."

"Freelance."

"Who risks her life mapping caves. Who *scuba* dives. Who makes me look like one of Cinderella's stepsisters . . ."

"Says the woman who built a jazz club from scratch while raising a child all by herself . . ."

"Who has such a complete hold on McKenzie's heart," Nina said.

"I don't love McKenzie. I mean I do, but not like that. And he doesn't love me like that."

"I know. I know, I know, I know, but I didn't know, not for the longest time. I thought he was with me because he couldn't be with you; that he proposed to me—three times he proposed to me—because he couldn't marry you. It took me years to figure out that a man could love a woman as much as he loves you and still just be her friend."

"Just be her friend—you say that like it's an insignificant thing. Real friendship like the kind McKenzie and I have, and Bobby, too, is momentous."

"I'm starting to catch on."

"The friendship you and I have . . ."

"Shel—"

"Tell me—if you thought McKenzie was in love with me all these years, why did you stay with him?"

"Because he's the least pretentious man I've ever known and he makes me laugh and he makes me feel safe even though he seems to get beat up every other week. Because I've loved him almost from the moment we met and because in my arrogance I was convinced I could win him away from you even though I didn't need to. What an idiot."

Shelby took Nina's arm, pulled it around her shoulder, and nestled against her.

"For the record," she said, "Vic and Katie are jealous of each other and they fight all the time, but if you mess with one, the other will rip your heart out."

"Sisters."

"Now and forever."

That's when Shelby's cell phone rang.

The young woman gave Nina a bag containing all of my belongings, including my bloodstained clothes, yet only after she proved that she was indeed my wife. Apparently, the young woman had a hard time wrapping her head around the idea that a husband and wife could have different last names, even in this day and age, or that a wife would refer to her husband by his last name. Nina signed yet another document without reading it first, took the bag, and handed it to Bobby. Bobby said he would bring the bag to the FSU.

"What's that?" the young woman asked.

Everyone listened intently.

What that was was Louis Armstrong's unaccompanied

opening credenza to the song "West End Blues," which helped define early jazz. It was also the ringtone of my cell phone. Bobby opened the bag and Nina dug through its contents until she found the cell. Nina swiped right.

"Hello?" she said.

The caller hesitated before saying "I might have the wrong number. I'm looking for McKenzie."

"This is Nina Truhler."

"Oh, hey, Nina. Hi. This is Dave Deese. We met a while ago . . ."

"I remember."

"I'm sorry to call so late, sorry to disturb you, it's just that I heard—I just heard that McKenzie was shot. Is that true?"

"Yes, it is, but he's going to be fine."

"Is he? Oh, okay. Great. God. I'm just . . . wow. That's a relief. You say he's going to be okay?"

"Yes. I'm sorry, Dave, but I have to go."

"Yeah, yeah, I'm sorry to disturb you like I said. It's just— it's just that I'm feeling really guilty about all of this."

"Guilty? Why?"

Deese answered with a question.

"McKenzie was doing me a favor and I'm afraid—is it possible that he might have been shot because of it?"

"Hang on."

Nina held the phone for Bobby to take.

"It's for you," she said.

Barbara Deese was wearing fluffy pink slippers, red pajamas, and a long, thick black robe that she wrapped tight around herself. Bobby said she reminded him of a woolly bear caterpillar. She was sitting on the sofa next to Deese. Deese kept dropping hints—it was late and she had to get up early in the morning; it was going to be a long, boring conversation and he wouldn't blame her if she just went to bed. Only Barbara wasn't going anywhere. How often did a commander of police drop everything to interview her husband? In their home? In the middle of the night?

Bobby was sitting in a wingback chair facing the sofa.

"Tell me about this, DD," he said.

Deese had played hockey with Bobby and me for more than a dozen years and poker nearly once a month for the past five and like old friends we rarely used each other's first names. It was usually last names or nicknames, the nicknames often derogatory in nature because that's the way we rolled.

"The more I think of it, the more I'm convinced that this has nothing to do with me, McKenzie getting shot," Deese said. "I mean it's not like I asked him to steal the plans for the Death Star or anything. He's going to be all right, though?"

"That's what the doctor says," Bobby said.

"Is there any permanent damage? I mean, can he still play hockey?"

"I don't know. C'mon, man."

"I asked McKenzie to do me a favor."

"What favor?" Barbara asked.

"That's what I was going to tell—are you sure you don't want to go to bed? It's awfully late."

"Dave . . ."

"Yeah, Dave," Bobby said. "What favor?"

"It's—it's embarrassing."

"How embarrassing?" Barbara asked.

Deese was staring at his wife when he answered. "I asked him to find out who my father was."

"Your father?"

"Didn't your dad die last year sometime?" Bobby asked.

"Fifteen months ago. He died almost a year to the day after

Mom died. He just didn't seem to care about anything after she passed. I appreciate it that you and McKenzie came to the funeral; I don't know if I told you at the time."

"I don't understand," Barbara said.

"Neither do I," Bobby said.

"You know my sister T," Deese said.

"I don't think so."

"Teeeeeeee," Barbara said, drawing the name out. "Never Theresa. Never Terese. Never Terry or Resa like my friend from college. Always Teeeeeeee."

"C'mon," Deese said.

"She is the loudest, most inappropriate person I know."

"I thought you liked her."

Barbara held her thumb and index finger about an inch part.

"Your sister is terrific in very small doses," Barbara said. "Just ask her ex-husbands."

Deese shook his head at his wife and returned his gaze back to Bobby.

"T had her DNA tested by one of those ancestry websites," he said. "For the longest time she said I should do the same thing, track down all of our long-lost relatives, and I'm like, I have way too many relatives as it is. Finally, I gave in. The ancestry company, whatever, had a half-price sale around Easter; don't ask me what any of this has to do with Easter. So I bought a kit."

"You never told me this," Barbara said.

"I bought a kit. What they do, they send you a vial and you're supposed to spit up to this line—you're not supposed to eat or drink anything, not even water, for a half hour before you spit. You spit in this vial and you pack it up in the return box they send you and then you wait, maybe six weeks or more. I think it was shorter in my case. Still, I kind of forgot about it. Then they sent me an email telling me that my report was ready. They sent it to me the Monday after Mother's Day, do you believe that? I linked on to the website and followed the prompts. It turns out I'm forty percent French. I was always convinced I was like half Scottish; the name Deese having Scottish origins and the things my father told me. Remember I used to joke with McKenzie about being his long-lost cousin? We're not cousins, by the way."

"Uh-huh." Bobby was becoming increasingly impatient, but he was a good investigator. Once he had a suspect talking, he knew it was often best to just let him keep talking until he said something important.

Suspect. Dave Deese was a suspect. Bobby nearly shook the thought from his head, only he didn't want any abrupt movements to distract his friend, our friend, from his soliloquy.

"Turns out I'm not Scottish at all," Deese said. "Not even one percent. Also my Neanderthal markers say that I'm more likely to have straight hair, which I do, and that I am not likely to have red hair, which I don't. All this is important."

"Okay," Bobby said.

"What's important . . ."

Barbara sat straighter on the sofa and leaned closer to Deese.

"What's important—the website asks if you want to link to your relatives. There's a family and friends link. If you say yes, you need to create a profile because they have a policy, the ancestry people. You can't see your relatives without letting them see you. The profile can be anything you want, though. You don't need to give your full name and address or anything like that. You can link on with just your initials, for example. And the amount of ID, age and sex, address—you can control all that, too. What I did, I signed on with my initials. Actually, not my initials. I called myself Dee Dee, what you guys sometimes call me at hockey."

"They call you Dee Dee?" Barbara asked. "But not because of your initials?"

"It's a long story."

"Double D, like some women's breast size?" Barbara fixed her gaze on Bobby. "Men are such jerks."

"DD stands for Dunkin' Donuts," he said.

Barbara didn't believe him.

"Jerks," she repeated.

"Anyway," Deese said. "I clicked on the DNA relative's link. It turns out I have eleven hundred and sixty-four relatives."

"Eleven hundred and sixty-four?" Bobby said.

"Yeah, but eleven hundred and fifty-seven matched less than three percent of my DNA so they're like long, long, long-lost relatives and who cares? But there were seven who were linked much more closely. A first cousin on my mother's side—he and I had an eleven-point-nine percent match. I had two second cousins, also on my mother's side; we had about a six percent match. Except then . . ."

Deese brought his hands to his face and rubbed. At the same time, he began to blink rapidly. Bobby was fluent in body language and knew that Deese was anxious. Bobby leaned forward, indicating that he cared.

"T was on the list," Deese said. "She used her full name T-H-E-R-E-S-A. We were only about a twenty-five percent match."

"What does that mean?" Barbara asked.

"Siblings share around half of their DNA," Deese said. "Half siblings share a quarter."

"What does that mean?" Barbara repeated.

"Do the math!" Deese immediately reached out a hand and rested it on Barbara's shoulder. "I'm sorry. I didn't mean to bark like that. It's just—my sister whose hair is curly, my sister whose hair is red, is my half sister. That's what the DNA results prove."

"She's not your father's daughter?"

"More likely I'm not my father's son."

"Why do you say that?" Bobby asked.

"T is thirty-eight-point-five percent Scottish."

"I don't know what to say," Bobby said.

Barbara did, though.

"Your mother had an affair with someone," she said.

"You believe that shit?" Deese said. "My mother?"

"Do you think your father knew?"

"If he did, he sure as hell kept it secret for how many years? Forty-two?"

"Does T know?"

"My little sister who's always acted as if she was my older sister? I have no idea what T knows."

Barbara seemed surprised.

"You haven't talked to her about this?" she asked.

"No. God no. If I didn't tell you, do you think I'd tell her?"

"Why didn't you tell me?"

"I didn't want you to act differently around her, make her think something was wrong. No, that's not true. I didn't want to have this conversation with you. I didn't want you to know that I wasn't . . ."

"What?"

"I don't know. A Deese, I guess."

"Who gives a shit?"

Both Bobby's and Deese's heads came up as if they were startled by a loud noise. Barbara was like Nina—they almost never cursed and when they did, you best pay close attention.

"Do you honestly think I care what your name is?" Barbara asked. "Do you honestly think I care who your father was or your mother or your sister or your great, great, great, great-grandfather from France? After all these years?"

"Barb—"

"Dammit, David, sometimes you make me so mad."

Husband and wife stared at each other and Bobby thought he should get out of there. He thought that he should let his friends have their moment; he could always come back in the morning. Only he was a cop, after all, and I was lying in a coma in the SICU at Regions Hospital and he wanted to know who shot me.

"McKenzie," he said.

"McKenzie," Deese repeated. "After I found out about all of this, I decided, you know what, screw it. I wasn't going to say anything to anyone. T called and asked if I took the test and I'd say, 'Why would I want to do that?' I could tell, though, that it wasn't all fun and games anymore. She was really bugged. She didn't tell me what she was bugged about, but I knew. Of course, I knew. I knew because she had sent Dee Dee a message the same day that my DNA profile was posted. The website allows DNA relatives to contact each other on the website and T sent Dee Dee a message asking if she—T assumed Dee Dee was a woman. She sent Dee Dee a message asking if she was interested in learning more about the connection between them. Dee Dee replied saying"—Deese closed his eyes and bowed his head. He waited for a few beats before he opened them again—"'Thank you. I have a family.' I just couldn't—I love my family, Bobby. If all of my uncles and aunts and cousins and my sister discovered that I'm not . . ."

"Of course you are," Barbara said. "Whatever else, you're your mother's son."

"It's a little more complicated than that."

"Why is it complicated?"

"I inherited half of my father's business."

"The business where you've been working since you were sixteen; the business that you helped expand; the one that you're running now?"

"Dad didn't leave it to me and T, to David and Theresa. The will said he left equal shares to his children. The will was written a long time ago. I guess he thought he'd have more than just me and T."

"So?" Barbara asked.

"Legally, there might be issues."

"Have you asked anyone? A lawyer?"

"No."

"Why not?"

The shrug he gave told Barbara the answer—he was afraid the answer would go against him.

"McKenzie," Bobby said again.

"McKenzie, yeah," Deese said. "I couldn't make myself call an attorney, but I could call McKenzie."

"Why?"

"After a while, a week, I don't know—I just couldn't shake this, all right? Not knowing who I really was . . ."

"You're David Deese," Barbara said.

"Not knowing who my *real* father was and why he was my real father . . ."

"James Deese was your real father," Barbara said. "The man who raised you."

"You say that, Barb, and it's exactly what I want to hear. I wish my father and mother were available to tell me that. But . . ."

"But what?"

"I wanted to know the truth of my life. It's like those super-hero movies that they keep remaking, Spider-Man, Superman. I wanted to know my origin story."

Deese paused again and in the silence Bobby understood.

"You said that you had seven matches," he told Deese. "Theresa, a first cousin, and two second cousins make four."

"There were three others," Dees said. "One half sibling, a first cousin, and a second cousin on my birth father's side. They all have French ancestry like me; no connection to T at all."

"And . . ."

"And I wanted to find out about them. Find out who they were without them finding out who I was."

"That's when you called McKenzie," Bobby said.

"Yes."

"What did he say?"

"What does McKenzie always say when a friend asks him for a favor?"

"He says, 'Sure.'"

Detective Jean Shipman was working her notes up for a Supplementary Investigation Report, in case one was needed, when the phone rang. It turned out that members of a motorcycle gang had assaulted a bouncer in a club on the East Side called Haven. It was called Haven because all members of all motorcycle gangs were welcome there as long as they didn't wear their colors. The fight allegedly started—cops love the word "allegedly"—because members of one gang who were told they couldn't wear their colors in the bar and be served claimed that they had seen members of a rival gang wearing their colors. Chaos ensued and Shipman thought, Finally, a real crime to investigate.

It was late when Bobby left Deese's house and getting later, which is why he decided to go home instead of back to the hospital. He had left orders to be contacted if my condition changed and since he hadn't heard anything . . . 'Course, he wasn't a relative and the staff at Regions Hospital didn't work for him.

Bobby parked on the street in front of his house directly across from Merriam Park. The front porch light was on and the back porch light was on and the kitchen light was on. Bobby was big on keeping lights burning and insisted his wife and daughters strictly abide by his idiosyncrasy—and don't get me started on his deep affection for locks. The rest of the house was dark, though, and he wondered briefly if Shelby had returned home or was still at the hospital; certainly his daughters were in bed. At least they had better be, he told himself. He stepped out of his car and made his way across the narrow boulevard to the sidewalk.

He saw them before he heard them. Two black men approaching; they were easily identifiable under the streetlamps. His hand went immediately to the Glock holstered at his waist even though one of the black men was in a wheelchair.

"Who are you?" Bobby asked.

Herzog and Chopper glanced at each other, knowing damn well that Bobby knew who they were—I had introduced them.

"You don't remember us, Commander Dunston?" Chopper asked.

"I remember you, Mr. Coleman. Mr. Herzog." Bobby's hand continued to rest on the butt of the nine-millimeter. "What do you want?"

Chopper smiled.

"We can't talk like old friends?" he said.

"Are we friends?"

"We have friends in common."

"That's not the same thing, is it?"

"Fuck, Chopper," Herzog said. "What we doin' here?"

"Good question," Bobby said.

"McKenzie was shot tonight," Chopper said.

"Me and my people are already on it," Bobby told him.

"He's our friend, too. We want to help."

"Leave it to the police."

Herzog didn't speak but he made a mouth noise that suggested he didn't hold the police department in high regard. Bobby didn't appreciate the mouth noise, but he had heard worse.

"Give it to him," Chopper said.

"Fuck 'im," Herzog said.

"Go on."

"Give me what?" Bobby asked.

Herzog reached into his pocket.

Bobby's grip tightened on the butt of his Glock, yet he did not pull it.

Herzog reached out his hand.

There was a flash drive in his palm.

"What is it?" Bobby asked.

"Thumb drive," Herzog said.

"I can see that."

"It's footage taken from a security camera at RT's Basement," Chopper said. "It shows McKenzie getting shot."

"The owner told my people he didn't have a security camera."

"Maybe it was how the question was phrased," Chopper said.

"Or who did the phrasin'," Herzog added.

Bobby took the flash drive from Herzog's hand and slipped it into his own pocket.

"Thank you," he said.

"There are many things we can do that the police can't," Chopper said. "Folks we can talk to."

"I'll keep that in mind."

"Who knows? Next time we talk you might even take your hand off of your piece."

"Like I said, Mr. Coleman, Mr. Herzog—I remember you."

FOUR

Nina was accustomed to late nights: running a jazz joint for the past couple of decades, she rarely went to bed before two A.M. Yet when she did go to bed, she fell asleep quickly and slept soundly. I'd joke, tell her that the zombie apocalypse could break out and she'd still get in a solid eight hours. Only not that night. That night she didn't sleep, she dozed, waking, nodding off, and waking again, usually with a start just a few minutes later, like an unrepentant sinner listening to a sermon in the back of a church. Still, she remained in bed, telling herself that her body needed the rest, even if her brain wasn't getting any.

After a few hours, she rose and began wandering through the darkened condominium, wearing a flowing red silk nightgown and nothing else. Normally, Nina was a gym shorts and T-shirt girl, but the nightgown had always been one of my favorites, so . . .

Our condo had a master bedroom and guest room with en suites, plus a bathroom for visitors. Beyond that, we didn't have rooms so much as areas—dining area, living area, music area where Nina's Steinway stood, office area with a desk and computer, and a kitchen area that was elevated three steps above the rest. The entire north wall was made of tinted floor-to-ceiling glass with a dramatic view of the Mississippi River where it tumbled down St. Anthony Falls. She could barely see the falls at night, though. Only the lights of Minneapolis. They easily reached the seventh floor and illuminated the bookcases on our south wall and the fireplace on the east and all the furniture in between.

Nina stood in the center of the large room and spun slowly; taking in all the familiar shapes, yet found comfort in none of them. She mounted the steps and made her way to the kitchen area. She opened the refrigerator door, looked inside, found nothing that she wanted, and closed the door. She opened and closed cabinets without knowing what she was searching for. Finally, Nina descended the steps and moved toward the north wall. She leaned against it and stared at the lights spreading away from her like stars in galaxies far, far away.

I had not wanted to move to Minneapolis. I was a St. Paul boy, born and raised. You'd think that wouldn't have made much difference, the cities lying directly across the river from each other. Unless you lived here. If you lived here, you'd know that it made a helluva difference which side of the Mississippi you called home. Still, I listened to her arguments while gazing into those astonishing silver-blue eyes of hers and what was it that e. e. cummings wrote? *Love is a place.* My place was with her, wherever that might be. So that was that.

Only that's not what Nina was thinking as she watched the cityscape as it slowly evolved from black night to gray dawn with the rising of the sun. She was thinking how she'd have to move from that place if I died.

"I couldn't live there without you," she told me later. "I'd have to move."

Her words made me feel warm. Loved. Only that wasn't her intention. She meant them as an accusation—see what you almost made me do?

Eventually, she returned to the kitchen area. We had one of those single-cup coffeemakers that used reusable pods that I filled with a variety of coffee blends, mostly from local suppliers like Dunn Brothers, Caribou, and Spyhouse. Only she didn't know which was which. She grabbed a maroon pod at random and shoved it into the machine—it was a light roast called Highlanders Grog from Cameron's Coffee, by the way—and waited. Nina wasn't waiting for the coffee so much as for time to pass.

At exactly seven thirty she tapped an icon on her cell phone. A young woman's sleepy voice answered.

"What?"

"Erica, it's Mom."

Getting a call from her mother was not unexpected. If anything Nina called Erica entirely too much. Really, neither of their lives was so dramatic that daily briefings were required. But at seven thirty in the morning?

Erica was jolted into wakefulness.

"What happened?" she asked.

"It's McKenzie. He's been shot."

"Is he—"

"No. No, no, he's fine. Lilly said he'll be fine."

"Lilly?"

"Lillian Linder. She's a doctor at Regions Hospital. Emergency specialist."

"You know her personally?"

Nina laughed at the question. She didn't know why she thought it was funny, but she did.

"McKenzie," she said, as if that explained everything.

"What happened?" Erica asked.

"He was shot in the back. The bullet lodged in his chest near his heart . . ."

"Oh, God . . ."

"But Lilly, Dr. Linder says he'll be fine. He's not going to die or anything. He's in a coma now—"

"A coma?"

"Induced coma. They're letting his brain heal. His heart, too."

"His brain?"

"It's complicated."

"How complicated?"

"Honey, he's going to be fine. They'll be bringing him out of the coma sometime today. Maybe even right now. I should get dressed and go back over to the hospital."

"I'll see about booking a flight back home . . ."

"No, don't do that."

"I'll use his credit card instead of yours."

"McKenzie gave you a credit card?"

"I wasn't supposed to tell you that."

"All this time while I've been thinking how fiscally responsible you were . . ."

"It was just before I went off to Tulane my freshman year. He gave me the card. He said he was in love with my mother but he wanted us to be friends, too. I asked him if he was trying to buy my affections. He said if they were for sale, sure, why not?"

"That jerk."

"Depends on how you look at it. Mom . . ."

"No, Erica, listen. McKenzie's going to be fine. They'll probably bring him out of the coma before you even get to the New Orleans airport so hold off on buying a plane ticket. Besides, you have finals coming up . . ."

"Next week."

"Hold off. I'll talk to the doctor today and then we'll know what's going on. I'll call you back then."

"Mom . . ."

"It's silly for you to come all the way up here, maybe compromise your studies, just to watch McKenzie walk out of the hospital."

"Will he walk out of the hospital?"

"Yes."

"Do you promise?"

"I promise," Nina said.

Was that so hard? her inner voice asked.

Erica paused before responding.

"Okay, I'll hold off until I hear from you. Mom, who shot him?"

"Who knows?"

Roger Hodapp knocked on the doorframe of the cubbyhole Bobby called an office on the second floor of the James S. Griffin Building and leaned against it, his arms folded, as if he had just dropped by to say hello. He was dressed as befitting a Deputy Chief of the St. Paul Police Department charged with overseeing the Major Crimes Division, which included Family and Sexual Violence, Property Crimes, Homicide and Robbery, Special Investigations, Gangs, Narcotics, and Vice—crisp white shirt and blue tie, matching blue slacks and blue jacket, a gold badge glimmering off his right pocket, bars recognizing his commendations for valor and merit pinned above his left, and a single gold star fixed to each shoulder. The sight caused Bobby to wonder who he was going to have lunch with that day.

"McKenzie," Hodapp said. "Any news on his condition?"

"They put him in an induced coma to rest his heart and

his brain"—Hodapp grinned at the word "brain"—"other than that, the doctor told his wife that he's going to be fine."

"Do we believe the doctor?"

"No reason not to," Bobby said.

"I was the sergeant he called when he pulled the pin to take the price on Teachwell, remember? How long ago was that now? Ten years at least."

"Yes, sir," Bobby said.

"Back when we were both working out of Central."

"I remember."

"Do you remember what I said at the time?"

"You said that you always knew McKenzie was a dumb ass."

"Yet he's been very helpful to us since he put on the cape and became Batman and no matter what I or anyone else thinks about his early retirement—he's one of us."

"Yes, sir."

"This is the sixth shooting in St. Paul this month. Add that to the homicide up in Frogtown last week . . ."

"The suspect has already been arraigned."

"And biker gang activity on the East Side last night. How's the bouncer by the way?"

"Torn cornea. Both he and the bar owner have received threatening phone calls telling them not to cooperate with the police. They are cooperating, though, and so are a surprising number of the bar's patrons. Apparently, starting a fight in the Haven was a serious breach of biker protocol. We've already identified three of the assailants, including the one who waved his piece in the air and threatened to shoot up the place."

"My point being, the damn media has been calling it a crime wave. A columnist writing for the *Pioneer Press* this morning claimed the Saintly City was becoming Satan City."

"Newspapers are declining; anything to build circulation."

"It's just that *we* don't want it to *look* as if you are giving McKenzie's shooting higher priority than all the others. You know what I mean by *we*?"

"Yes, sir."

"'Course, what you do during your spare time . . . I don't need to tell you any of this, though, do I? Not really why I came down here. I came down to tell you—put one of your people on the case. Don't investigate it yourself. It's like what they say about doctors treating family members or lawyers defending their loved ones. Sometimes their judgment gets clouded despite their best intentions. Bobby, I speak from personal experience. Do you understand what I'm saying?"

"I understand."

"Good."

Hodapp pushed himself upright and made to leave.

"Anything you need, you tell me," he said.

"Thank you, Chief."

"For what?"

Riley Brodin-Mulally wore prescription reading glasses even though she was only twenty-eight years old. She claimed that all the computer, tablet, and cell phone screens she had been forced to read off of in the past few years had trashed her eyesight. She had requested that her employees and business associates send her printed reports, but that had proved to be largely impractical although word had spread—if you want to get on the boss's good side . . .

Riley was reading a printed report sent to her by the new director of Muehlenhaus Industries Agriculture Division when Mary Pat Brodin-Mulally walked into the dining room.

"More coffee?" Mary Pat asked.

"Thank you," Riley said.

Mary Pat filled Riley's mug before setting the coffeepot on a warmer mounted near the center of the dining-room table.

"What has you so apprehensive?" she asked.

"What makes you think I'm apprehensive?"

"The way your brow furrows when something bothers you."

"We have far too many cows."

Mary Pat sat across the table and started paging through the morning newspaper that a maid had left there for her to read. The brilliant green emerald set in a white gold band on the ring finger of her left hand gleamed under the chandelier.

"We?" she said.

Riley pointed at Mary Pat, pointed at herself, then waved her hand back and forth a few times, the emerald in her identical ring also catching the light.

"Yes, we," she said. "This report details the current and projected size of our livestock operation excluding dairy and poultry. Our position in cattle and calves is up two percent since last year. It makes sense, of course. Americans today are consuming more beef than ever before, forget all that talk about the environment and the demand for plant-based burgers and steaks."

"In that case, don't we want a lot of cows?"

"The problem—do you really want to hear this?"

"Whatever causes your brow to furrow causes my brow to furrow."

"The problem—we need to go back to 2014. U.S. cattle inventories had reached a six-decade low because of years of record-breaking drought. As a result, beef prices skyrocketed and consumers started switching from hamburgers and steaks to chicken fingers and pork chops. As a result, fewer cows were being slaughtered and fewer cow skins were made available to the leather industry for making hats, coats, gloves, whatever. As a result, leather prices reached an all-time high. Too high. It caused designers to switch from real leather to much cheaper synthetic substitutes. As a result, they became so good at producing synthetic leather products that today most people can't tell the difference. One of the ironies of an interconnected economy—what you eat for lunch actually affecting what your shoes are made of.

"Eventually, the drought subsided and the cattle industry came roaring back. As a result, there is now an overabundance of cow skins on the market. However, the demand for leather hasn't come back in the same way. Companies that switched to artificial leather when the prices were high have no incentive to switch back now that they're low. Even at today's rock-bottom prices, fewer companies are willing to pay for real leather hides."

"As a result . . ." Mary Pat said.

"The U.S. leather industry might all but disappear within a decade."

"Does Muehlenhaus Industries have a presence in the leather industry?"

"Not directly. However, if it disappears, we'll not only be losing one of our revenue streams, the sale of cowhides after we slaughter our beef, we'll be forced to take on the added expense of disposing of all those cowhides. I had hoped that an increasing demand for leather goods from the ever-growing middle class in China might offset our losses, but the on-again, off-again trade war and tariffs have decreased the export of hides to China by over thirty-five percent. As a result, prices for their leather goods are increasing. If there's no end to it, I predict that designers over there will do the same thing as designers over here—find a more predictable alternative. What is causing my brow to furrow, as you say, is that the report doesn't address any of that. I'm going to have to ask our new ag man why it doesn't address any of that."

"Are you telling me that all this about the leather industry, that's off the top of your head?"

"It's not like I think about it every day."

Mary Pat smiled as she continued to page through the newspaper.

Riley removed her glasses, turned the report upside down, and pushed it away.

"I'm boring you," she said.

"No. Well, yes. That's not why I'm smiling, though. I was just thinking—The Muehlenhaus Girl. Remember when they called you that?"

"They still do."

"They thought your grandfather was insane when he put you in charge of the family's sprawling business empire . . ."

"They still do," Riley repeated.

"They didn't know what your grandfather knew, what I know, what everyone who does business with you learns sooner or later—you're kind of a genius."

"Hardly." But now Riley was also smiling. "Come to Minneapolis with me."

"To do what? Watch you move pieces around a chess board?"

"At least meet me for dinner. We'll stay over at the apartment tonight; catch a play at the Guthrie."

"What's on stage?"

"Who cares as long as we get some us time."

"I can't," Mary Pat said. "As much as I'm tempted—we're in the process of opening the patio, the deck; giving customers access to our docks. The weather has improved so much that boat traffic on Lake Minnetonka is really starting to ramp up. Casa del Lago does nearly seventy percent of its business between May and October, you know that."

"I'll buy your restaurant. I'll give you a million dollars. Then all you'll have to do is hang out with me."

"One million is a little low."

"Five million."

Mary Pat pointed an index finger at Riley.

"Write up a purchase agreement," she said.

"Seriously?"

"No."

"Two years we've been married and you're already tired of me."

"Oh, God, no."

"I was joking . . ."

"Look at this."

Mary Pat left her chair and circled the table, folding the newspaper as she went. She sat in front of Riley, who was quickly donning her reading glasses.

"What am I looking at?" she asked.

"It's McKenzie. He's been shot."

Dr. Lillian Linder entered the waiting area outside the SICU and walked to where Nina was sitting. She was dressed in fresh scrubs, her clean hair pulled back in a ponytail, her eyes bright and rested, and Nina thought, What a bitch.

"Have you been here all night?" Lilly asked.

"No."

At the same time, Nina's inner voice said, *I went home because there was nothing I could do. But you? Why weren't you here all night? You're McKenzie's friend. You're my friend. You said so yourself.* She knew she was being unreasonable. Still . . .

"You're dressed in the same clothes," Lilly said.

Nina looked down at herself, wondering how that happened.

"Did you get any sleep at all?" Lilly asked.

"More than enough."

"Where's your friend?"

"Shelby's taking care of her girls."

"Nina, go home and take care of yourself. McKenzie's not going anywhere."

"You said you were going to bring him out of his coma today."

Lilly sat next to Nina and patted her hand.

"No, I said we might bring him out today," she said. "People don't always respond the same way to the procedure. Most of the time we'll put a patient into an induced coma for twenty-four to thirty-six hours. Sometimes it'll take a little longer than that. We might wait three days to see how the cardiac arrest affected the brain. In McKenzie's case, he's always been a contrary SOB. I'd like to wait until at least tomorrow morning before making a decision."

"Tomorrow morning? Why?"

"McKenzie's brain is healing," Lilly said. "The swelling is down. Just not down as much as we'd like to see."

"You said he was going to be all right."

"He will be, but we need to give him time. The man was shot. The bullet lodged very near his heart; there was a lot of damage. Nina, it seems like a long time to us, but he's been here for less than twelve hours."

"You said . . ."

"I simply want to give it another day or two, give McKenzie's heart and his brain more time to reboot, more time to rest. My greatest fear is another SCA."

"Sudden cardiac arrest," Nina said.

"If it happens again—even if we're able to bring him back, it won't do his heart or his brain any good."

"I understand."

Lilly patted Nina's hand some more.

"He's going to be fine," she said.

"Do you promise?"

"Go home. Get some sleep. If there's any change, I'll call you."

Nina gathered her belongings and stood. So did Lilly. Nina pulled the strap of her bag over her shoulder.

"I trust you, Dr. Linder," she said.

Except what Lilly heard was, "I'm holding you responsible."

"Thank you," she said just the same.

"Can I see him before I go?" Nina asked.

"Of course."

A few moments later, the two women were standing outside my room, the sliding glass wall between us.

"He looks so pale," Nina said.

Lilly gestured at the monitor above my head.

"Pulse, respiration, all within acceptable parameters," she said.

"Acceptable," Nina repeated.

"The EEG, electroencephalography, that's the blue lines on the monitor. It records electrical patterns in the brain. The waves you see, that's good. That's a good sign."

"When McKenzie's in a coma like this, can he dream?"

"Oh, yeah."

Okay, I'm going to tell you about my dreams now. Is there anything more boring? It's like a guy coming up to you and saying, "I'm going to tell you a fantastic story about something that never happened and doesn't have a point." Why would you listen to that if you weren't being paid? In any case, I promise that this has nothing to do with the narrative. It's what Elmore Leonard called "Hooptedoodle." Feel free to skip ahead.

What happened is that after I was shot, I slipped into a

kind of netherworld where I couldn't differentiate between what was real and what was not. There was plenty that was real, too; plenty of times when I was aware of what was happening around me—the bright lights, noises from machines and people, nurses speaking in hushed tones like they were afraid of waking me, Dr. Lillian Linder. I knew her going back to when I was with the SPPD. She was very smart and I liked very smart women. 'Course, I had always been ambitious. I remembered calling to her, only she didn't hear me. Instead, Lilly boarded the Green Line, the train that ran between downtown St. Paul and downtown Minneapolis, and I never saw her again.

She was replaced by a man in a white coat who looked a lot like Gert Fröbe, the actor who played Goldfinger in the James Bond movie. He was keeping me prisoner; chained to a metal table. There was a laser above the table and Gert would turn it on so he could slice me in half and I'd say, "Do you expect me to talk?" and Gert would say, "No, Mr. McKenzie. I expect you to die." Over and over and over and over and over again. And I'd scream at him—"Fuck you, Gert!"—over and over and over and over and over again. Which is a sign of insanity, isn't it? Doing the same thing over and over and expecting a different result. Except, in my case, I didn't die. Which was the outcome I was hoping for, so . . .

I was told later that the brain is always grasping for narrative, for understanding, even in a mostly unconscious state. In my long, rambling dream the narrative was my many attempts to escape, to get off that damn table. Sometimes I'd free myself and walk into Target Field and watch the Twins play baseball and never lose or find myself in a jazz club—never Rickie's; it was always a huge club and I was always alone and Ella would be singing to me, or Louis, or Coltrane playing sax, or Hampton on vibes, or sometimes it was Nina sitting at her Steinway, the piano I bought her, playing soft and low and singing, "Summertime and the living is easy . . ." Sometimes I'd free myself and turn the laser on Gert and his henchmen, but that was never particularly satisfying and I'd see myself standing in the corner watching me attacking Gert and muttering, "C'mon, man. You can do better." Mostly, though, I'd be lying on the metal table staring up at the laser and thinking, "Nah, uh-uh, not this time, bitch."

I just thought you ought to know.

FIVE

Bobby paced in front of the conference-room table where Jean Shipman and Mason Gafford were sitting. Both of the detectives thought he looked tired yet neither was foolish enough to mention it.

Bobby carefully set a flash drive in front of Shipman.

"What's this?" she asked.

"Video of McKenzie being shot taken from the security cameras at RT's Basement."

Bobby didn't ask Shipman why she didn't get the video herself, yet she heard the question just the same.

"The club owner said he didn't have security cameras," Shipman said.

"A witness lying to the police, imagine that."

"I should have been more—"

"Thorough?" Bobby asked.

"Yes. Sorry."

"The suspect could be a woman but it's hard to be sure; the video is very poor quality. After we're done here, take the drive to FSU. See if the image can be enhanced. If not, we'll go back to the source material, see if that'll make a difference."

"What about the thing at the Haven last night? I was going to—"

"I passed it off to Eddie Hilger and Sarah Frisco."

"But I caught it."

"You also caught the shooting of McKenzie, didn't you?"

Shipman couldn't believe this was happening. Being forced to give up the chase of three armed members of a biker gang because of me? Bobby couldn't possibly be this unfair.

"Commander Dunston," she said.

Bobby stared at her for a few beats. Believe me; the stare was much worse than a lecture.

"Yes, Detective?" he asked.

"Nothing. I'll get the flash drive over to FSU."

Bobby stared some more. Finally, he said "What do we know? We know that McKenzie was doing a favor for a friend named Dave Deese."

He explained what the favor was, adding that Deese had given me the username and password for Deese's ancestry account, information that he also shared with Bobby. Gafford took notes; Shipman did not.

"Whether or not this has anything to do with McKenzie getting shot remains to be seen," Bobby said. "Seems as good a place to start as any, though."

"Can't we just wait for McKenzie to come out of the coma?" Shipman asked.

Bobby ignored the question.

"We also know that McKenzie made a date to meet Nina Truhler at seven P.M. at Rickie's," he said. "He made the date at four fifty-seven P.M. according to this phone log. He received and made several phone calls after that, but no texts. We have phone numbers but no names."

"We know this because . . ."

Bobby set my cell phone in front of Shipman.

"The security functions have been disabled so we have complete access," he said. "Take this to FSU, too. Put names to the phone calls before and after Nina's."

"Yes, sir."

"McKenzie arrived at RT's Basement at eight P.M." Gafford was perusing his notes while he spoke. "Apparently he was there to meet someone if the club owner can be believed. So who arranged the meeting?"

"What we need to find out." Bobby rubbed his tired face with both hands. "Where is McKenzie's vehicle?"

"Impound lot," Shipman said.

"Please tell me he was driving the Mustang."

"No. That piece of crap Jeep Cherokee."

"Dammit."

"What difference does it make?" Gafford asked.

"The Mustang has GPS," Bobby said. "The Cherokee, I'm not even sure if it has power windows. McKenzie bought it a decade before he came into his money and he's been nursing it along ever since."

"That part of town—I could see why he'd drive the Cherokee instead of the Mustang. Doesn't mean he wasn't driving the Mustang prior to that, though. We can still trace his movements prior to that."

"If he was driving the Mustang," Shipman said.

Nina was in the parking ramp at Regions Hospital, her heels echoing across the concrete as she approached her Lexus. Her cell phone alerted her. She didn't feel like talking to anyone, yet swiped right when she saw that Bobby was calling.

"What is it?" she asked.

Bobby was taken aback by Nina's brusque manner; he actually used those words when he told me about the conversation later—taken aback. His first question was about me. Nina repeated what Dr. Linder had told her.

"I'm trying real hard not to scream until I'm inside my car," she said.

Bobby's second question was about the Ford Mustang GT that Nina had given to me for my birthday two years ago.

"It's in the shop," Nina said.

"For how long?"

"Two, three days."

"Why?"

"His check engine light went on so he took it to his guy. Turns out he had a bad oxygen sensor. McKenzie said it wasn't necessarily a big deal except that his guy was so backed up he said that it would take a while before he got to it. McKenzie left the Mustang and told his guy to take his time and just let him know when it was ready."

"In the meantime, he drove his Jeep Cherokee," Bobby said.

"The damn thing is older than your kids. It's older than my kid and she's twenty-one."

"You'd think with his money . . ."

Bobby thought I was personally making it just as hard as I could to catch the person who shot me, but didn't say so out loud.

"Anything else?" Nina speaking in that brusque tone again.

Bobby asked about gaining access to my computer.

"I know McKenzie keeps notes," he said.

"I'm not going home," Nina told him. "I'm so angry right now I might start throwing stuff off the balcony. I'm going to the club. I'll call security and tell them to let you in, though. Okay?"

"Me or one of my people; depends on how the day shakes out."

"Your way of saying that you're not dropping everything to find the person who shot your best friend?"

"I have other responsibilities. Crimes don't happen one at a time. McKenzie would understand."

"I know, I know. It's just . . . It reminds me of that old Skeeter Davis song. *I wake up in the morning and I wonder why everything's the same as it was.*"

"About his computer, does it have a password?"

"Same as his cell phone."

"Given what McKenzie does in his spare time, you'd think he'd be a little bit more security conscious."

"You would, wouldn't you?"

Schroeder Private Investigations was a cop shop. Every field operative who worked there had been an investigator for one law enforcement agency or another—local police, sheriff's department, state cops, even the FBI. They all acted like it, too, answering calls in white shirtsleeves and shoulder holsters, sitting behind gray metal desks with cigarettes dangling out of their mouths, their sports jackets hanging over the backs of the chairs they sat in, both men and women. SPI also employed a platoon of computer geeks that ran skip traces, conducted background checks, hunted identity thieves, vetted jurors, uncovered hidden assets, and conducted cyber investigations without ever leaving the comfort of their workstations. They were the ones dressed like they were either doing yard work or about to walk the red carpet at the Golden Globes, take your pick.

Riley Brodin-Mulally walked into the office, made her way

to the reception desk, and tapped the top of the desk to get the attention of the receptionist. The receptionist was named Gloria. She said, "How may I help you?"

"I wish to see Greg Schroeder," Riley answered.

Gloria looked at her computer screen.

"Do you have an appointment?" she asked.

"No."

"I'm afraid Mr. Schroeder is unavailable. I'm sure one of our other operatives would be happy . . ."

"Tell him that Riley Muehlenhaus is waiting. Tell him that I won't be waiting long."

Gloria recognized the name. Instead of picking up a phone she smiled slightly, asked Riley to take a seat, and went to Schroeder's office in person. A moment later she returned, asked Riley to follow her, and led her through the maze of desks and cubicles where the operatives sat, not one looking up to catch Riley's eye.

Schroeder was waiting for Riley in a corner office with a splendid view of U.S. Bank Stadium in downtown Minneapolis. His tie was neatly knotted and pushed all the way up to his throat and he was wearing his suit coat, something he seldom did when meeting clients for the first time. Greg Schroeder was a trench coat detective; at least he tried hard to maintain the image. He actually wore a gray trench coat over his rumpled suit when the weather permitted. He drank his coffee black and his whiskey neat and liked to sneer while he ran his thumb across his chin like Humphrey Bogart did in his tough-guy movies. Yet now he looked and behaved like a banker.

"Ms. Muehlenhaus," he said and extended his hand.

Riley shook it as Gloria closed the office door, disappearing behind it.

"Actually, it's Brodin-Mulally now," Riley said. "I only use the name Muehlenhaus when I wish to make an impression."

"Of course. How is your grandfather?"

"Thriving."

"Excellent."

Schroeder gestured toward a couple of chairs arranged around a glass table in the corner. Riley took one and he took the other.

"It's been a while since we've last spoken," Riley said.

"If I recall, we did not part on the best of terms."

"That's because you were working for my grandfather against my personal interests."

Schroeder raised his hand slightly and let it fall again as if it was a subject not worth discussing.

"You are aware that I am now president of Muehlenhaus Industries," Riley said. "My grandfather retains the title of CEO but serves only as a figurehead."

"I heard."

"You performed many tasks for him that I did not approve of at the time. That I don't think others would approve of if they knew."

"If I did, I can't recall what they were."

"You don't need to prove your discretion to me, Mr. Schroeder. I'm aware. In fact, I am relying on it."

"Oh?"

"I wish to hire you."

"Then know, Ms. Brodin-Mulally, you don't come here. Not ever." Schroeder reached into his jacket pocket and produced a business card. He slid the card across the table at her. "If you wish to contact me, use any of these cell phone numbers or email addresses. If it's important that we meet in person, that will be arranged at a secure location. But you don't come here and I don't go to your office."

"Is this a service that you provide to all of your clients?"

"Precious few, if you must know."

Riley took the card and placed it into her small bag.

"Thank you," she said.

"What can I do for you?"

"It might be a very small favor or it might be very big. I don't know yet. It's one of the things I need you to find out."

"All right."

"Are you aware that Rushmore McKenzie was shot last night?"

"No, I wasn't. How is—"

"If I am not mistaken, you know Mr. McKenzie well."

"Yes."

"He's in a coma in Regions Hospital in St. Paul. Beyond that I've heard nothing. It's entirely possible, Mr. Schroeder, that the police have already identified his assailant and are taking the necessary steps to see that justice is served. If so, please inform me. That's the small favor. If, however, this does not prove to be the case, if the police are somehow unable to bring Mr. McKenzie's assailant before the courts, well, that's where the big favor comes in."

"I understand."

"Do you?"

"Some words do not need to be spoken. Some words should not be spoken."

Riley stared at the private investigator for a long time after that; it was like she was trying to see inside his head.

"Mr. Schroeder," she said. "McKenzie saved both my honor and my life at the risk of his own. I assure you when I speak those words I am not attempting to be fanciful."

"I didn't think you were."

Riley stood.

Schroeder stood.

She offered him her hand and he shook it.

"Thank you for your time, Mr. Schroeder," Riley said.

"My best to your grandfather," Schroeder replied.

Detective Shipman parked her car on a downtown Minneapolis side street and, ignoring the meter, marched into the lobby of the building where my condominium was located. She did not want to be there. She didn't want to squander valuable St. Paul Police Department resources—meaning herself—on finding out who shot an obnoxious, self-important, unlicensed kibitzer—meaning me—when there was a perfectly good gang-related assault to investigate. If that wasn't enough, Major Crimes had received a call just after Bobby had finished speaking to Nina Truhler. An armed robbery, no less. But did Shipman get that case? Hell, no. Leave it to Bobby and Mason Gafford to catch whoever shot up a fast-food restaurant while she wasted precious time trying to find out who put a bullet in me, when who gave a shit really? She was convinced the only reason she was there was because Bobby was still annoyed about the surveillance tape screwup. She decided she needed to have a conversation with Dick over at RT's Basement about that the first chance she got.

Shipman pulled her badge from her pocket when she reached the security desk and held it up for the guards to see.

"Detective Jean Shipman, St. Paul Police Department," she announced.

The first thing they noticed was that there wasn't a uniform from the Minneapolis Police Department accompanying her. The uniform would have been a formality, of course. The cops in St. Paul and Minneapolis might labor in separate jurisdictions, yet they're more than willing to help each other out; happy to search for a suspect or a car, check out an address, gather intel, and report back to the other agency. Only that didn't mean a detective was welcome to cross the river and flash her badge anytime she damn well pleased. Protocol dictated that she first notify the Minneapolis Police Department and, if the case was hot, arrange for one of its officers to accompany her. The fact that Shipman hadn't made the guards wonder how seriously she was taking my case.

I should point out that the two security guards were friends of mine. Their names were Smith and Jones and they were dressed in the identical dark blue suits, crisp white shirts, and dark blue ties of their profession; I could never tell them apart without reading their name tags. They had made it clear when Nina and I moved in a few years ago that they had checked me out—acting under building management's orders, of course; it was SOP for all new tenants—and they knew who I was and what I did. They had also made it clear that they were ready, willing, and able to assist me should ever the need arise.

"The job can get so boring," they told me.

So, on occasion, I'd seek their help in exchange for items I'd find lying around the building, like a case of Irish whiskey and Minnesota Twins tickets that I would turn in to the lost and found because security personnel weren't allowed to accept gratuities from the tenants.

Smith picked up a clipboard and thrust it at Shipman.

"Sign in, please," he said.

"Are you kidding me?"

"We have rules."

"Someone should have called to tell you that I was coming."

"Ms. Truhler called. Sign in, please."

Shipman yanked the clipboard out of Smith's hand and started filling in the sheet that was attached to it. That's when she had an idea.

"Did McKenzie have any visitors between five and, say, eight P.M. last night?" she asked.

Smith and Jones glanced at each other.

"We have rules concerning the privacy of our tenants," Jones said.

"C'mon guys," Shipman said. "Do I have to call Nina?" She used my wife's first name as if they were friends. They're not. "Do I need to get a subpoena? Someone shot the man. Help me find out who."

Smith and Jones glanced at each other some more.

"A woman arrived yesterday, I want to say about six P.M," Smith said.

"We didn't log her in because she didn't stay," Jones added. "Instead, she gave us an envelope that she said she wanted delivered to McKenzie. She said to deliver it forthwith."

"Forthwith?" Shipman asked.

"Word she used," Smith said.

"What did you do?"

"Called McKenzie and said there was a message waiting for him," Jones said.

"And?"

"And he came down and picked it up," Smith said.

"What did it say?"

"We don't read other people's mail," Jones said.

"McKenzie—what did he do?"

"He opened the envelope and read the message," Smith said.

"What did he say?"

" 'Huh.' "

"What did he say?"

" 'Huh.' "

"Are you deaf all of a sudden? What did McKenzie say?"

"That's what he said."

" 'Huh'?"

"Exactly."

"Wait, what?"

"He opened the envelope, removed the sheet of paper inside, unfolded it, read the message, and said, 'Huh.' How many times do I have to say it, Detective?"

Shipman didn't like how Smith made her title sound like an insult, yet let it slide.

"What happened next?"

"McKenzie refolded the message, put it back into the envelope, put the envelope in his pocket, wished us both a good evening, and returned to his condo. Ten minutes later, he left."

"He left?" Shipman repeated.

"We saw him on our monitors locking his condo and taking the elevator to the parking garage," Jones said. "A few minutes later he drove out of the lot."

In his old Jeep Cherokee without GPS, Shipman thought. Where the hell were you, McKenzie, she wondered, during the two hours between leaving here and arriving at RT's Basement in time to get shot? She shook the question from her head. First things first.

"I need you to do something for me," she said.

The way Smith and Jones glanced at each other yet again somehow reminded Shipman of Shakespeare's *Richard III—I am not in the giving vein today.*

"You have security cameras," Shipman said. "Could you pull up the footage of the woman who came into the building last night? It could help us identify the person who shot McKenzie."

"We'll need to contact our supervisors, but I doubt that there will be a problem," Smith said. "It'll take a few minutes, though."

"In the meantime, could you take me up to McKenzie's condominium?"

"Come this way," Jones said.

Jones led Shipman to the elevator, to the seventh floor, and to my door. Along the way, she contacted the Forensics Services Unit, which had taken possession of my bloodstained clothes from Bobby. Most of its members were working either the Haven assault case or the shooting at the fast-food joint, however Brian, the tech who found the spent cartridge at RT's Basement, the one who wanted love from Shipman, had been left behind to answer the phones.

"Brian, I need you to do something for me," Shipman said.

"What do I get out of it?"

"My undying gratitude."

"How 'bout lunch?"

"How 'bout I don't break your face the next time I see you?"

"Goodness gracious, how long have you been this cranky?"

"Since I was fourteen and discovered men. What I need is for you to pull McKenzie's clothes and check his pockets for a note."

"We haven't gone through his clothes yet. We didn't think McKenzie's shooting was a higher priority than what FSU already had on its plate."

"Tell me about it," Shipman said.

"We haven't had a chance to look at the video on the flash drive or examine the cell phone, either."

"Don't tell Commander Dunston that."

"Bobby doesn't scare us none," the tech said.

"Then you're a member of a very small minority. The note, Brian."

"All right, hang on." Brian returned a few minutes later. "Nothing."

"Nothing?"

"I have a receipt signed by Commander Dunston saying that McKenzie's cell phone and wallet had been logged into evidence. All that's left is some cash and keys."

"There's no note in an envelope?"

"No, there's not."

"Huh."

If it was possible to pace in a wheelchair, then Chopper was pacing. He had nearly a dozen computer stations in his office yet only four of them were occupied, each by an African-American geek. All of Chopper's employees were African-American. He said he'd become an equal opportunity employer when the white business community became equal opportunity employers.

Chopper wheeled himself from one geek to the next, glancing over their shoulders at the screens in front of them. Three were selling tickets and one was buying. He stopped behind the buyer, Chopper's chief computer geek.

That was Chopper's term, not mine. I preferred computer nerd. The geek-in-chief was wearing a T-shirt with a pic of Commander Geordi La Forge, the character played by LeVar Burton in the *Star Trek: The Next Generation* TV series. The shirt looked like the geek had been wearing it since he was three years old.

"Well?" Chopper asked.

"It's working," he said.

"It is?"

"We're able to bypass all the CAPTCHAs and the re-CAPTCHAs pretty easily; I'm not having any problems buying bundles of seats."

Chopper's eyes lit up. Like most ticket scalpers, he had been hampered by availability. He would have associates sitting at every terminal to grab concert and sports tickets when they became available online. Or he would hire guys to stand in line at the on-site ticket booths. Or he would tap insiders who had access to the events.

But most ticket sellers had strict rules about how many seats a person could reserve at a time, usually four, and sophisticated security systems in place to prevent cheating. Not only that, it was illegal. While there was no federal law against ticket scalping, many states had their own restrictions. There was also the Better Online Ticket Sales Act of 2016 which made it unlawful nationwide to use bots to vacuum up tickets at a rapid rate. Which Chopper claimed was un-American because it prevented him from amassing enough product—that's how he viewed tickets, as product—to make an honest living.

Chopper's new software, however, purchased just the day before by a white boy who seemed very nervous, as if this was the first time he had stepped out of line, was allowing his bots to circumvent the ticket sellers' bots so he could now buy an unlimited number of the best seats in the house, wherever that house might be, which he could then resell for whatever his customers were willing to pay.

"Fans dictate the market price," Chopper once told me. "If people refuse to pay the prices I charge, I have to lower my prices, right? It's called capitalism, the backbone of America."

"Software was worth the price then," is what he told the geek.

"For the time being," the geek said. "It's just another advance in artificial intelligence that someone will probably counter next week."

"Till then, buy my man, buy. Bieber, Bruno, Elton John, Lizzo, John Legend, Snoop Dogg, Taylor Swift, Monster Jam, vroom, vuhroom . . ."

"We've got the list."

"Buy, baby, buy. Vroom."

While they were buying, Herzog walked into the office.

"Yo, Herzy," Chopper said. "Where you been, man?"

Herzog gestured with his head for Chopper to join him next to Chopper's desk where the geeks wouldn't hear them talking.

"Know a man named Jamal Brown?" Herzog asked.

"No. Should I?"

"Jamal used to run wit' the Red Dragons."

"Fuckin' dead and gone, them Dragons."

"Not all of 'em. Jamal, he's been thrivin' since the gang went under. Dealin' opioids."

"I'm outta that life. You are too, ain't ya?"

"That's not the point."

"What's the point?"

"Where Jamal's been gettin' his supply."

"Do we care?"

"If you don't wanna know."

Herzog turned and started walking away.

"Wait," Chopper said.

Herzog turned back. He was grinning.

"What?" Chopper asked.

"RT's Basement."

"The fuck you say."

"Word is Jamal's been getting' his opioids outta the back room."

"I didn't know the place had a back room."

"Lotta shit RT didn't tell us. We asked so politely, too."

"We should ask again, maybe not so polite this time."

"What I was thinking," Herzog said. "See if he's gotta camera pointin' at the back room."

"Be fucking dumb if he did, recordin' the commission of a crime."

"Anything 'bout RT tells you he ain't dumb?"

"First thing, though, I think we should talk t' Jamal. Can you arrange that?"

"Hard or soft."

"Soft," Chopper said. "I don' care what Jamal does for a livin'."

"'Kay."

"RT dealin' outta the back door of his place, think the police know about that?"

"Some might be takin' the price to look another way. Bet I know one cop who ain't, though."

"We'll have a conversation with Commander Dunston once we know what we're gonna say. You surprise me, though, Herzy. Steppin' up to find out 'bout McKenzie after actin' like you didn't care."

"I know how much you like the man."

SIX

Shipman had been inside my condominium twice before. The first time was to interrogate me about a truck belonging to a friend of mine that exploded, sending a sliver of shrapnel through my shoulder. The second time was after a man was shot to death in St. Paul. Since he had lived in my building, she naturally assumed I was somehow involved. 'Course, at the time, so did I. In neither case did she have the opportunity to get a good look at the place. Now she had all the time in the world.

After hanging her coat and bag on the rack near the door, Shipman went to the refrigerator, surveyed its contents, and retrieved a bottle of Summit EPA—who does that? After opening it, she started exploring. I wouldn't have been surprised to learn that she sat on all of our chairs and sofas one at a time to see if any of them were just right. I did learn that she stopped at the north wall and gazed through the tinted glass at the mighty Mississippi. That's because she asked me later how much the view cost. I told her about a half million bucks when we bought the place; much more now. She said it was nice, but not that nice.

Next, she sat at Nina's Steinway and played a few tunes—

seriously, who does that?! She told me she figured the baby grand must have retailed for $60,000. Around there, I said. She said she had an old Yamaha upright that she bought used for six-fifty that sounded just as good. I was detecting a trend.

Eventually, Shipman perused our library. She said she was impressed by both the variety and number of titles we owned. She asked if we had read them all. Between Nina and me we had read about eighty-five percent, I told her. She said she didn't know I could read. I said I didn't actually read the books, just looked at the pictures. She said she was a big reader, too, but that she got most of her books from the public library. Well, okay then.

Shipman was half a beer down by the time she arrived at my desk. The first thing she did was riffle through the stack of papers, mostly bills, on the top of the desk and then searched the drawers. She was looking for the note in the envelope I had been given and didn't find it. Next she checked the wastebasket at the desk. When that proved fruitless, she examined the contents of the wastebaskets in the kitchen, the master bedroom, and the bathrooms. Still nothing. She wondered if I might have left it in the Jeep Cherokee and made a note to herself to check.

Afterward, Shipman sat behind my desk again and fired up the computer, using my code to gain access—KILLEBREW3. While Bobby wore the number four when he played sports, I had always worn three because that was the number worn by Hall of Fame slugger Harmon Killebrew, whom I met at TwinsFest when I was just a kid. I remember him as being very cool and very kind.

It didn't take Shipman long to find what she was searching for. I had a folder labeled FAVORS on the desktop. She clicked on it and found a bunch more folders. She clicked on the one tagged DEESE. There was only one document in the folder, also tagged DEESE. She opened it and found my notes.

I kept notes on all my "cases" pretty much the same way I had when I was with the SPPD, utilizing the "Just the facts, ma'am" approach that I had been taught when I studied criminology at the U way back when, although I sometimes recorded my impressions about the people I met and the places I visited as well. What you need to remember, I didn't write my notes with the idea that Shipman or someone else might read them. I kept them only for myself; I knew what it meant when I wrote "CakeWalk late afternoon," even if no one else did. From my notes, Shipman was able to more or less figure out what I had been up to; who I spoke to and why. Only it required a certain amount of translation and interpretation. (And some say she's a substandard investigator.) I won't ask you to work that hard. Instead, I'll just tell you.

This is what happened.

MONDAY, MAY 18

Northfield, Minnesota, was a college town. It was home to both Carleton College, founded in 1866 by descendants from the English Puritans, and St. Olaf College, which was started by a group of Norwegian-American immigrants in 1874. It was best known, though, for being the home of Malt-O-Meal and the place where the Jesse James–Cole Younger outlaw gang was decimated during an attempted bank robbery in 1876, an event reenacted every September during the Defeat of Jesse James Days. In fact, if you visit the Northfield Historical Society on Division Street, you'll come away believing those were the only two things of any significance that ever occurred in Northfield.

The Historical Society was housed in the actual building where the First National Bank had been located, the target of the James–Younger gang. I visited it while I killed time waiting for my meeting with Dave Deese's second cousin on his father's side.

I had met Deese in his office Monday morning. He told me about his DNA discovery and that he wanted me to find out who his father was. I offered an argument about why this wasn't necessarily a good idea only he wasn't having any of it.

"I need to know," is what he told me.

I explained that there were things that you can't unlearn.

"I get it," Deese said. "Believe me, I get it. The DNA people, they tell you right off the top that by surrendering a bit of saliva, you'll also be surrendering a bit of privacy, yours or someone else's. They tell you that you might learn something that could make you uncomfortable, only I didn't pay any attention. It never occurred to me that I wasn't . . ." Deese paused long enough to shake his head. "Now that I know the truth I want to know *all* of the truth. Here's the thing, though—that doesn't mean anyone else needs to know the truth. I have a sister, kids, aunts, uncles, nieces, nephews, cousins—they don't need to know the truth. I mean, this affects all of them, doesn't it? In one way or another? Do they really need to know that they have no biological connection to people they believe are blood relatives?"

"I can see how that might make for an awkward Thanksgiving dinner conversation," I said.

"How would you feel if you found out that your father wasn't really your father?"

"It would shake me to my core."

"Then you'd know how I feel."

"On the other hand, there wasn't a day in my life when he didn't make me feel loved."

"My father was the same way. My father . . . jeezuz, McKenzie."

"Tell me what you know about your mother."

"She was an angel come to earth."

Not always, my inner voice said.

"What was her name?" I asked aloud.

"Anna."

"Maiden name?"

"Chastain. It means chestnut trees, something like that."

"Middle name?"

"Theresa."

"Did she meet your father right out of school?"

"No, she was what? Twenty-five when she met"—Deese hesitated before finishing—"Dad."

"What did she do?"

"She was a secretary."

"For who?"

"I don't know."

"Your aunts and uncles—you could reach out to them."

"And ask them what?"

"About your mother when you were born. Where was she working? Was she a member of a club? What did she do? Where did she go? Did she have a special friend?"

"What reason would I give for asking those questions?"

"What about your sister? Maybe she has some insights."

"What part of keeping this private don't you get?"

"I don't know if you can keep it private, Dave, I'm just saying."

"I can try."

"All right, all right. What exactly do you want me to do?"

"Never mind Mom. Reach out to these people, my second family."

"Why can't you do that?"

"Because I don't want them reaching out to me."

"You don't want one family intruding on the other."

"I don't want strangers with DNA evidence stating that we're related wanting to become part of my family because it isn't just my family, you know? I can't make a decision that affects everybody without asking permission."

"You're not going to ask permission, are you?"

"Hell no."

"Okay."

"What I'm asking—it's a big favor."

"Okay."

"I'm asking that you contact these people pretending to be me. Not me, but . . ."

"Dee Dee."

"Yes. I want you to tell them that you're Dee Dee."

At the time I thought, What could it hurt?

Deese had given me his member ID and password so I was able to access his account from my own computer. Most of Deese's eleven hundred and sixty-four long-lost relatives included their full name, sex, birth year, and city, state, and country in their profiles. Some even uploaded their photographs. His half sibling did not, listing only his name and location—Charles K., Orono, MN. It made me go "Hmm." Still, how hard could this be, I thought. Given the prevalence of social and business media sites like Facebook and LinkedIn it shouldn't be too difficult to locate a Charles K. in Orono, should it? Yeah, maybe I didn't believe it, either.

The DNA site also reported that Deese had a first cousin who shared 13.1 percent of his DNA who listed himself as Marshall from Minneapolis. I didn't know if that was a first name or a last name, yet it didn't matter, I told myself. The fact that he existed indicated that Charles K.'s father must have had a sibling, who helped produce a cousin for Charles to play with.

Finally, there was a second cousin with 6.11 percent of Deese's DNA named Elliot, who revealed nothing in his profile including his location. Again, it could have been a first name or a last. Either way, I figured Elliot was the child of Marshall or of God knows how many other King relatives who were not listed on the DNA site.

Before attempting a computer search, however, I messaged each of Dee Dee's relatives:

> My name is McKenzie. I live in Minneapolis. I apologize for imposing on you, but apparently we are related. I would like to learn how. I promise that I am asking for nothing from you except enlightenment. We can communicate on this website or in any other way that you are comfortable with. Thank you for your courtesy.

I made a sandwich. Elliot had sent a reply by the time I returned to the computer.

> Oh. My. God. You popped up on my feed a week ago but I was afraid of contacting you. I mean, you're obviously related to me but you're not, you know? Is McKenzie your first or last name?

It occurred to me then that if Elliot or any of the other relatives were smart, they could easily research me the way I intended to research them. That was part of the favor, though, wasn't it?

> McKenzie is my last name, what everyone calls me including my wife. What about Elliot?

> My first name. Everyone I've seen out here is related to me. I mean I know who they are. You're a secret.

> Yes, for forty-four years.

Are you forty-four?

I am. I'm as old as the dirt in your backyard.

LOL. You're actually a year younger than my dad, although older than my aunts and uncles.

I wrote—*Who are your aunts and uncles?*—and hit send. I knew immediately that it was a mistake. I was pushing too hard too fast. Probably Elliot thought so as well. It took a few long moments before he replied.

When I decided to take the DNA test my father told me to be careful what I revealed about myself to strangers.

That's very good advice. I probably would have told you the same thing myself.

Do you have children?

I flashed on Erica, Victoria, and Katie yet typed *No* just the same.

I was an only child. My mother died when I was twelve and my father, the man I thought was my father, passed about ten years ago. I didn't have any other family that I knew of. When I did the DNA test, I thought I would only find sixth or seventh cousins. Imagine my surprise.

I waited a few more long moments before Elliot replied.

I can't imagine. I have no idea what you must be going through.

I admit I've had my ups and downs at first. Now I just want information.

Would you like to meet?

Yes, but you should check with your father first. I'm sure he'd have a few words to say about meeting strangers.

Yes, he would. You should have heard the lecture he and Mom gave me before I went to college freshman year. I didn't know they had such a low opinion of men.

I'm confused. You're not a man?

LOL. I get that a lot because of my name. My friends mostly call me Ellie.

Well, Ellie, I would very much like to meet you. But I want you to feel safe; I want you to feel comfortable. You pick the location and bring as many friends and relatives as you want.

Now you really do sound like my dad.

Which is what brought me to Northfield, about a forty-five-minute drive south of Minneapolis if you obeyed the prevailing traffic laws.

MONDAY, MAY 18 (LATE AFTERNOON)

I ate a pretty good burrito in Kahlo Restaurante Mexicano while I waited for Elliot, although that's not where we had arranged to meet. Instead, she asked me to find her at CakeWalk, where we could get a decent cup of coffee along with custom cakes and desserts, located directly across Division Street from where I was sitting. I was watching the front door because I wanted to see Elliot when she arrived; I wanted to see who her friends were. Mostly, though, I wanted to see if she drove there from Carleton College, where she was majoring in English with a minor in creative writing. A license plate number could be very helpful, I told myself.

Elliot appeared a good ten minutes before I was scheduled to arrive, which I thought was intentional. She did not drive. Instead, she had walked the half mile from the dorms at Carleton. She had four friends with her, three guys and one woman. I identified her by the way she seemed to be giving instructions to the others. The three guys were big enough that they could give me a hard time if they knew how to handle themselves, which I doubted. The woman was petite, with bright blond hair cut short. Elliot had long auburn hair that she wore in a ponytail.

All five of them went inside the CakeWalk. I took my time finishing the burrito and a bottle of Mexican Coca-Cola, which was sweetened with cane sugar instead of that high-fructose corn syrup crap you get in the United States, policed my table, and stepped across the street. I arrived at CakeWalk two minutes before the appointed hour. One of the guys and the woman I had assumed was Elliot were sitting together on a black leather sofa in front of a coffee table. The other two guys were sharing a small table against the wall. The petite blonde was sitting between them at an undersized pink picnic table beneath a sign that read I NEVER MET A PROBLEM A CUPCAKE COULDN'T FIX.

It was the blonde who stood when I entered.

"Mr. McKenzie?" she asked.

"Ms. Elliot?" I said.

She stepped toward me as I approached. She seemed to be debating whether she should hug me or not. I solved the dilemma by offering my hand.

"Thank you for seeing me, Elliot," I said.

"You're welcome, cousin. Should I call you cousin?"

"McKenzie is fine."

We sat at the table and stared at each other for a few beats. She had one of those round faces that made it easy to imagine what she had looked like as a baby—dimples, big bright eyes, easy smile. She was cute. She'd be cute when she was sixty.

I gestured toward the glass cases at the far end of the café loaded with desserts. Two employees were standing guard behind them.

"May I buy you coffee?" I asked. "A cupcake?"

"Thank you," Elliot said. She gave me her order and I stood. "What about your friends?" My wave carried over the three men and the second woman. "What can I get you guys? Know what—just order what you want. I got this."

They glanced at one another as if they were surprised while I made my way to the glass cases. I bought a café mocha and a cupcake called a Sassy Cass with a raspberry on top for Elliot—kids, I thought—and a black coffee for myself. I left my credit card with the waitress and motioned at the others. They were already lining up to order. The young woman with the ponytail said, "Thank you. You're very kind."

"Not at all."

"How did you know we were together?"

"Experience."

"You're an interesting man."

Did she think you were interesting in the way that you might think someone you just met at a party was interesting, my inner voice asked, *or did she Google you?* Take my word—

search for McKenzie Minneapolis and you'll find all kinds of weird stuff.

While the CakeWalk staff made the mocha, I took the cupcake and black coffee back to the pink picnic table and set them down. Elliot smiled at me.

"I hope you don't mind that I brought my friends," she said.

"Truthfully, it would have broken my heart to learn that a woman who was related to me would be dumb enough to meet a stranger alone."

Elliot scooped the raspberry out of the frosting of her cupcake with her index finger. "Cousins," she said, and ate the raspberry.

We chatted mostly about Carleton College. Elliot liked it there. It was a good school, she said, and small. "Intimate, you know?" It was far enough from her home in St. Paul that she could get away from her nosy family, yet close enough that she could reach out whenever she needed help.

While we chatted, two of the guys returned to their stations. The third said, "Ellie."

She didn't move.

"Elliot," he barked.

Elliot's head came up as if she was surprised to hear her name spoken aloud.

"Your café mocha." The man gave her a white cardboard coffee cup with a brown cardboard sleeve.

"Thank you," she said.

Meanwhile, the other young woman had settled back into the leather sofa. She was behind me, yet I was aware that she was leaning toward the picnic table, trying to hear every word we spoke while pretending not to. I nearly asked her to join us but decided against it. Why ruin her fun?

"About your family," I said.

"I'm not sure what to tell you," Elliot said. "I texted my father after we chatted online, but I couldn't get ahold of him."

"Instead of texting, did you think to actually call him?"

Elliot had a quizzical expression on her face, as if I had suddenly switched from English to a foreign language.

"I'd be happy to speak to your father," I said. "I'll give you my number. You can have him call me. It might be better that way. Secrets have been kept from me for forty-four years. No doubt they have been kept from much of your family for the same length of time. You don't necessarily want to be the one to reveal them. It's liable to cause a lot of tension. I know I'm tense."

Elliot tilted her head just enough to look past me without seeming like it. I realized that she was taking cues from the young woman behind me.

"Your profile on the website—Dee Dee?" she asked.

"Name of a girl I used to date when I was about your age."

"Why Dee Dee? Why not use your real name?"

"I guess I wanted to find out who I was related to before they found out they were related to me."

"Is that because you're a millionaire?"

"That and other reasons. I didn't know I was going to learn what I learned."

"You found Jelly's gold. You saved that super rich woman's life—Riley Muehlenhaus."

I shrugged at the references.

"You did your homework," I said. "Good for you."

"You help people."

"When I can."

Elliot glanced around me again.

"You could be helpful to us," she said.

"In what way?"

"Things in my family are going kerflooey."

"'Kerflooey'?"

"It's a real word. An adjective. It means awry or kaput. It dates back to 1918."

"You really are an English major. That doesn't answer my question, though."

I heard a voice behind me. "McKenzie." I turned to face the young woman sitting there. "What's your blood type?"

I didn't know Dave Deese's blood type. Why would I? So I gave her mine without hesitating so she'd know I was telling the truth.

"A-negative," I said. "Why?"

She didn't answer, but her eyes grew wide with surprise.

"That's rare," she said. "Only one in sixteen people have A-neg blood."

"So I've been told. Why?"

"Just . . . thinking. I don't know how DNA works."

"I'm not sure it has anything to do with blood type." I spun back to the woman who called herself Elliot. "What's your blood type?"

"O-positive. Does that mean we're not compatible?"

"Like I said, I don't think blood type enters into it—DNA, I mean."

Elliot glanced around me again.

"I need to get back to campus," she said.

She stood up.

I stood up.

The three guys and the young woman stood up, too.

"I need to speak to my father," Elliot said. "I hope you understand."

"I do understand." I fished a business card from my pocket printed with only my name and cell number and gave it to her. "I'd appreciate it if you gave him this."

"I will."

"Don't believe everything you read about me online, either. Most of the stories have been greatly exaggerated."

Elliot smiled brightly.

"Thank you for coming down here to see me," she said.

"It was my great pleasure. I hope to see you again."

All five of the students made their way to the exit. I called to them as they were passing through the door.

"Elliot."

Only instead of the petite blonde, it was the young woman with the auburn ponytail who turned her head.

"I like clever girls," I told her.

My notes didn't end there, of course. Only Shipman was getting a little antsy hanging around my place alone. She transferred my notes to a thumb drive and turned off the computer. Give her props—when she finished the beer, she at least had the courtesy to rinse out the bottle and drop it in the recyclable bin. Either that or she was hiding the evidence.

She left the condominium and took the elevator to the ground floor. Smith and Jones were waiting for her at the security desk. They told Shipman that they had been granted permission by their employers to share their security camera footage without demanding subpoenas and such. They motioned her behind the desk and gave her a chair in front of one of their computer screens.

"By the way," Smith said. Or was it Jones? "I remembered the woman's name. We didn't write it down because, like I said, we didn't check her in. I remember asking—here."

He manipulated the computer keyboard and an image of a woman appeared. She entered the building and approached the desk, an envelope in her hand. She extended her hand and Jones took the envelope. She turned and made to leave, but paused.

When she paused Smith or Jones tapped a key and image on the computer screen froze.

"I asked her what her name was," he said. "There was no name on the envelope so I asked her what name I should give McKenzie. And she paused. You can see her pausing as if she didn't know if she should answer or not and then she did."

Smith or Jones started the video again and Shipman could see the woman pause, utter a word, and walk away.

He halted the video again.

"Elliot. I asked her who I should say delivered the envelope and she said 'Elliot.'"

Shipman felt a thrill of excitement run through her body, yet beat it down. She was convinced that Smith and Jones had just solved her case for her, only she didn't want them to know it. As it was, Shipman stared at the image of the woman, once again frozen on the screen. She saw blond hair and a round face. She didn't see bright eyes, an easy smile, or dimples. She didn't see cute, either. The more she stared the more she saw a face that seemed beaten down. 'Course, that could have been caused by the quality of the video, she told herself. Or not.

Shipman leaned back in her chair.

"It's never this easy," she said.

SEVEN

Bobby Dunston and Mason Gafford knew two things almost immediately when they arrived on the scene. The first was that it wasn't an armed robbery, after all. The second was that it was sure to become a "fucktard" story, one that cops would tell for years to come whenever the topic of how completely nuts people can be came up in conversation, which was frequently. Bobby didn't care much for the term itself; he thought it was derogatory. 'Course, cop slang often was. It referred to someone who was not mentally challenged, yet acted as if they were. Case in point—actually, there were a couple of people to point fingers at.

Start with the young woman who had yet to go to bed and sleep off the hard partying she had engaged in the evening before. She had gone to the fast-food joint while still wearing her short, sequin dress and demanded a sausage, egg, and cheese sandwich with decaf coffee and a hash brown patty on the side. If her dress hadn't been enough to demand the attention of the administrative coordinator working out of the St. Paul school district, her high-pitched voice was. He admired her from a distance because she was both stacked and old enough not to be a student—apparently the school district had rules.

Unfortunately, the kid working behind the counter said he was unable to serve the young woman a sausage, egg, and cheese sandwich with decaf coffee and a hash brown patty on the side because the restaurant stopped serving its breakfast menu at ten thirty A.M. sharp and it was now ten thirty-seven. The woman didn't care. She wanted a goddamned sausage, egg, and cheese sandwich with decaf coffee and a hash brown patty on the side and she wanted it now. She told the kid to stop being "anal-retentive," was the word she used. After all, it was only seven minutes past the deadline and she was wearing a short, sequin dress that showed off her chest, so c'mon.

The kid didn't comment on the short, sequin dress or her chest, but did say that he was sorry; the ten thirty shut-off time could not be ignored, the instructions coming down from corporate itself. Could he interest her in a burger or a crispy chicken sandwich, instead? The woman would accept no substitutes, however. To prove it, she pulled a small handgun from her bag, waved it at the kid, and said she would have a sausage, egg, and cheese sandwich with decaf coffee and a hash brown patty on the side "by any means necessary."

The administrative coordinator had been watching the exchange between the counter kid and the young woman from his booth with increasing amusement. He had made up his mind to intervene on the woman's behalf; it would give him the opportunity to get to know her better, so to speak. When she pulled her gun, though, he pulled his, a Kimber Micro 9 Stainless Raptor—the man had a Permit to Carry a Pistol issued by the Ramsey County Sheriff's Department. He testified later that he had been waiting for a moment like this for years. He shot at the woman; emptied his gun, in fact; six rounds in the mag and one in the throat. He missed her completely, although he did graze the shoulder of the kid behind the counter and blast apart a lot of the equipment, including a coffee machine that began leaking everywhere.

The woman took exception to being used for target practice and turned on the coordinator.

"What is wrong with you?" she wanted to know.

"You have a gun," he reminded her.

She pointed it at him and squeezed the trigger.

A steady stream of water hit him right between the eyes.

She laughed.

He whacked her in the face as hard as he could with the butt of the handgun, knocking her down.

That's when the police officer arrived.

He saw the woman writhing on the floor, blood pouring from her nose and upper lip.

He saw the kid holding his arm, blood seeping between his fingers.

He saw the smashed and leaking coffee machine behind the kid.

He saw the man waving his Kimber nine-millimeter handgun and screaming, "It's all her fault!"

The officer drew his Taser and hit him with 50,000 volts.

By the time Bobby and Gafford had arrived, the counter kid was being treated by an EMT for what the kid clearly thought was a life-threatening wound but the EMT diagnosed as superficial.

"If it were up to me, I would have given her a sausage, egg, and cheese sandwich with decaf coffee and a hash brown patty on the side," the kid said. "But corporate . . . They're going to be so upset."

Both the man and woman had been taken into custody and were being held in the backs of separate patrol cars. During questioning, they were both adamant that they had done nothing wrong, the man in particular. He kept insisting that he had "acted within my God-given Second Amendment rights" and that "the St. Paul Police Department would pay for its racist behavior" because the officer who tased him looked like he had Hispanic origins. As for the woman, apparently her twenty-three years on the planet had prepared her for days like this.

"Life is so unfair," she said. "But what are you gonna do?"

Bobby knew the sergeant who was supervising the scene; he had worked with him many times. The sergeant was shaking his head sadly at the entire situation.

"What a bunch of fucktards," he said.

"Shh," Bobby hissed. "Not so loud."

"Hey. What's this I hear about McKenzie? He took a round in the back? Is he gonna be all right?"

"Last I heard."

"I remember working with McKenzie out of the Phalen Village Storefront in the Eastern District back when—God, we were both kids. We used to call him 'Mac' back then. He hated that."

"Still does."

"Do we know who shot him?"

"Not yet."

"Reason I bring it up—maybe you should know something. Maybe you already do."

"Know what?"

"There's a PI"—the sergeant quoted the air—"making inquiries about the shoot. Claims to be a friend of Mac's."

"Is that right?"

"What I heard."

"Did you hear a name?"

"Something Schroeder works out of an office in Minneapolis."

Nina Truhler moved through her club like a set of Newton balls, the desk toy that has five steel balls hanging from thin wires on a wooden or metal frame, also called a Newton's cradle. When a ball on one end of the cradle is pulled away and then dropped, it hits the other balls, sending energy through the middle three and flinging the ball on the opposite end of the row into the air. That ball then swings back to strike the other balls again, starting the chain reaction in reverse that will eventually throw the first ball into the air, and so on and so forth, demonstrating the principle of the conservation of energy and momentum and making an obnoxious clickety-clack sound that never seems to end. At least that's the way Jenness Crawford, Nina's manager, explained it to me later.

"It was like Nina was afraid to stop moving and take a deep breath," Jenness said. "She wasn't her usual pleasant self, either. Normally, she's like the nicest boss on the planet. She gives orders as if they're suggestions. 'I was thinking this would be a good idea,' she'd say or 'You know what I'd like to see?' and we'd all jump to it. Only when you were in the coma, it was like 'Hey, dummy.' Well, not dummy. She never actually said that or anything like that. It was just the tone of her voice, you know?"

Actually, I didn't know and I never asked Nina about it because once I had recovered enough that Nina felt comfortable raising her voice at me, we had plenty of other subjects to deal with, mostly regarding what she deemed to be my reckless and ultimately selfish behavior, even though none of what happened was actually my fault.

Among the many things that knocked her emotions out of whack were the phone calls. The shooting was mentioned in the papers and on the radio and TV and that aroused the curiosity of a lot of friends and acquaintances. Most of the people that called Nina for an update were men, including the guys I played puck with. There were also a lot of women, though, including Perrin Stewart, who was executive director of the City of Lakes Art Museum. And Erin Peterson-Gotz, who presided over Salsa Girl Salsa. And Vanessa Szerto, who owned the Szerto Corporation. And Maryanne Altavilla, who was the chief investigator in Midwest Farmers Insurance Company's Special Investigations Unit. And Genevieve Bonalay who became my lawyer after I helped her get a client off on a murder charge.

"So many women," she told me. She wasn't particularly upset about it, though, because she had met most of them at one time or another and understood our relationships were, as a man once said, strictly business. Unfortunately, one name did cause her to stop and say, "What?" Penelope Glass, a songwriter I knew before Nina and I had officially committed to each other.

"Did you sleep with her?" Nina asked.

"She was the wife of an FBI agent," I said.

"That doesn't answer my question."

"No, of course not."

"Was she pretty?"

"She had blue eyes. Not as blue as yours . . ."

"She was very concerned about your health."

"I hadn't seen her in seven years," I said.

"Then why would she be so concerned?"

"I saved her once from some New York mob guys."

"Saving women seems to be a common occurrence with you."

"The only woman who ever saved me was you."

"I think that's a non sequitur, but I like the sound of it."

It was while Nina was bouncing off the club's furniture that Greg Schroeder entered Rickie's. He moved to the downstairs bar, sat on a stool, and ordered a Jameson, neat. The bartender set the straight whiskey in front of him.

"Ms. Truhler."

Schroeder spoke soft and low in a voice that demanded action, something he had perfected while watching black-and-white Robert Mitchum movies. The bartender hesitated only for a moment before taking the hint and going off to find the boss.

Nina was not happy to see Schroeder. I don't think she had anything against the man. The worst thing she had ever said about him was, "He's all right." Yet seeing him sitting in her place caused her already high level of frustration to edge upward a few notches.

"Am I in danger?" Nina wanted to know.

The question and the blunt way she asked it caused Schroeder to flinch.

"No," he said. "I don't think so."

"Every time I've seen you here it was because McKenzie hired you to protect me from some hooligans that he had unnerved."

"Hooligans?"

"You know what I mean."

"No, Nina. You're not in any danger that I'm aware of. I'll be happy to post a few guys around if it'll make you comfortable, though."

"It would not."

"It'd be no trouble. No trouble at all."

"What are you doing here, Greg?"

"I like Rickie's. I like the food, the music . . ."

"Don't banter with me. I'm not in the mood."

"I want to help find out who shot McKenzie."

"Bobby Dunston is already working on it."

"How far has he gotten?"

"He hasn't said."

"If he tells you anything, I want you to feel free to call me. Maybe I can help."

"Who are you working for?"

"If all you do is watch crime shows on TV, you'd think that the police and private investigators don't get along. That's not necessarily true. Most PIs used to be cops or worked in some other branch of law enforcement; that's where they received their training and the six thousand hours of experience required before they can get a license. I used to be a cop in Minneapolis, myself. Twenty years. So, there's a kind of loose camaraderie between the groups. I have a lot of friends who carry badges and vice versa. We help each other out all the time."

"Stop changing the subject, Greg," Nina said. "Who are you working for?"

"I'm not at liberty to say."

"Then I'll ask you to leave."

"Nina . . ."

"It's not me and it's not McKenzie and it sure as hell isn't Bobby Dunston, so . . . There's the door."

"Nina."

"Do I need to raise my voice? I ask because I've been wanting to scream at someone all day."

"I don't suppose my client would mind me telling you. I know you're friends."

"Who?"

"Riley Muehlenhaus."

Nina shook her head as if she was surprised, yet just barely.

"Riley doesn't call herself that," she said. "Her father's name is Brodin; her name, too. Brodin-Mulally since she's been married. Muehlenhaus is Riley's grandfather's name. She doesn't care for it."

"No, but she'll use it if it'll help her get what she wants."

"What does she want?"

"She wants to know who shot McKenzie."

"She can't wait for the police to do their job like the rest of us?"

Schroeder made a production out of lifting his glass off the bar and taking a sip. Nina watched him do it.

"You're kidding," she said.

Schroeder didn't smile or grin or make any facial expression at all as he slowly set the glass back on the bar.

Nina muttered under her breath.

"Riley, what are you doing?"

"She owes him a favor," Schroeder said. "For saving her life."

Another one, Nina thought, but didn't say.

"Not that big of a favor," she said aloud.

Schroeder merely shrugged.

"There's nothing I can give you," Nina said. "McKenzie's computer and his notes, his phone—I turned all of that over to Bobby."

"He was doing a favor for someone, wasn't he?"

"A guy McKenzie played hockey with named Dave Deese."

"What favor?"

"It was personal. Something to do with Dave's DNA and the people he's related to. I don't have any details. I didn't even know that much until last night."

"Where does Deese live?"

"St. Paul. He has a business. Deese, Inc. That's all I know."

"That's all I need."

"Greg, tell Riley not to do this."

"Do what?"

"You know what."

"Honestly, Nina, I have no idea what you're talking about."

Shipman was troubled by the video of the blonde. She watched it three more times after she returned to her desk in the Griffin

Building and it still didn't make sense to her. She wrote notes to herself on a yellow legal pad.

Was the message meant to lure McKenzie to RT's Basement?
Envelope was not signed.
Was the note signed?
How else would McKenzie know who sent it?

Shipman grabbed her landline and called the security desk at my building. Jones answered, although she didn't know that at the time. Like me, she had a hard time telling the guards apart.

"When McKenzie came down to get the message, did he ask who left it for him?" Shipman asked.

"Huh?"

"Let's not start that again."

"Yes, Detective," Jones said. "He did."

"What did you tell him?"

"Just a sec."

Jones must have covered the mouth of the phone because Shipman couldn't hear what was being said. After a few moments, Jones started speaking again.

"After McKenzie read the note he asked, 'Who sent it? Did you get a name?' And we said we did. We said it was delivered by a small woman with short blond hair who said her name was Elliot. Like we told you."

"Thank you."

Shipman went back to her notes, crossing out the last two and rewrote them.

The note was not signed. If it had been signed, McKenzie would not have asked security who sent it.

Security told McKenzie small woman with blond hair delivered note.

The blonde said her name was Elliot, but that was an afterthought. She hadn't intended to leave her name.

(113)

Is it possible sender was smart enough to know that cell phone or landline or email could be captured and traced; yet not sophisticated enough to use a burner phone?

Is it possible she was too dim-witted to realize that whoever delivered the message would be filmed by condo security cameras? That guards would ask for a name?

Shipman understood, of course, that it could have happened exactly that way. She knew what Bobby knew and I knew and the vast majority of people working in law enforcement knew; that most criminals were pretty dumb. That's why they were criminals. Yet this didn't seem dumb to her. It seemed deliberate, like the blonde was meant to be seen by the cameras.

Something else nagged at her.

If the note was unsigned, how could the sender be sure McKenzie knew who sent it without leaving a name?

Was McKenzie expecting a note?

Shipman crossed out the last line. She told herself that if I had been expecting a message telling me where to meet someone at eight P.M., I wouldn't have made a date with Nina Truhler for seven P.M. Shipman continued writing.

If sender had wanted to remain anonymous, why give her name when asked? Did she panic and simply say the first thing that came to her mind?

Shipman circled the last sentence several times and picked up her phone. She called the SPPD impound lot located just south of Holman Field, the airport along the Mississippi River that served downtown St. Paul, and told the man who answered what she needed. He said he'd call right back.

Shipman set her notes aside, slid the flash drive into her computer, and resumed translating and interpreting my notes.

What happened next.

MONDAY, MAY 18 (EVENING)

Normally, it would have taken me thirty-five minutes to drive home from Northfield—I have a get-out-of-speeding-tickets-free card after all. Only by the time I reached it, the Twin Cities was in full-blown rush-hour mode so it took me nearly double that time. Along the way I thought about Elliot. Was she really the young woman with the ponytail as I suspected or was I merely being overly suspicious? I've been accused of that before. Still, I felt something wasn't quite right. Blonde or brunette, Elliot seemed more interested in what I could do for her family than what she could do for me. That's why I decided not to give her the benefit of the doubt and wait for someone to call.

Instead, the moment I returned to my condominium I sat down at my computer and Googled "Elliot Carleton College." I was given a whopping twenty-seven results. After eliminating all of the last names, I was left with six first names.

I went to Carleton's website and clicked on the "directory" link, but it refused to grant me access to student information unless I had an account with the school. It did, however, reveal names of its faculty and staff—Elliot Kohn was an administrative assistant and Elliot Prall was an instructor of both German and Russian languages.

I continued surfing and discovered that Elliot Moua had received a "Congratulations" on Facebook from the Carleton College Mathematics and Statistics Department for his paper "Graphical Inference with Convolutional Neural Networks," which received an honorable mention in the Undergraduate Statistics Research Competition sponsored by the American Statistical Association and the Consortium for the Advancement of Undergraduate Statistics. Good for him.

Elliot James had a LinkedIn page, even though he wouldn't graduate for another two years, that he used to help promote his summer job tutoring college athletes in computer science and mathematics.

Elliot Robey, also a woman, was named Female Athlete of the Week in the Minnesota Intercollegiate Athletic Conference for winning six first-place titles—four individual and two relays—at the Rochester Invitational Swimming Meet in December. The photo of her holding up all of her medals revealed a tall woman with short black hair and a glittering smile.

That left Elliot Sohm.

The first thing that came up—Elliot Sohm wins the Samuel Strauss Prize for Humorous Writing for her short story "The Hippopotamus in the Room" from the English Department at Carleton College, Northfield, Minnesota. The second—Elliot Sohm on Pinterest. The third—Elliot Sohm on Instagram.

Instagram revealed instantly that Elliot was, in fact, the cute blonde with a round face, wide eyes, ready smile, and dimples that I had met at CakeWalk. But among her 182 posts was a pic of the young woman with auburn hair worn in a ponytail who was sitting behind us. In the pic she was eating the most flamboyant cupcake I had ever seen. I clicked on the image and was given a column of copy to read under the heading "Exploring Our Back-Up Careers." Among the posts: "Making cupcakes and thrifting and real talks with my favorite cousin Emma King. #Emma&EllieForever."

In the back of my mind I heard my inner voice shouting, *Aha.*

I switched my search parameters to "Emma King Carleton College." The first thing that popped up was an article that appeared in the *St. Paul Pioneer Press* three years earlier. The piece listed the names and photos of all of the students who had finished in the top one percent of their high school graduating classes that year. Under St. Paul Academy it read:

Name: Emma King
Parents: Jenna King
College: Carleton College, Northfield, MN
Quote: "I have been through some terrible things in my life, some of which actually happened."—Mark Twain

This is where I would normally have performed a victory dance; imagine just about anyone who scores a touchdown in the NFL these days. Except, as often happens to me, the answer I found led me to yet another question that made me go "Hmm." For example, I couldn't help but notice that there was only one name listed under parents—Jenna King. That meant that Jenna did not list her husband's name. This is supposing, of course, that Jenna had a husband when Emma was born and that his name was King and there was no reason to assume that other than current social norms. Which raised the question—who was Emma's father? Was Charles K. her father? Did the *K* stand for King? Why wasn't he listed? Is this what Elliot meant by things in her family going kerflooey?

I searched for "Jenna King Orono Minnesota" and got one—count 'em, one—hit, an administrative assistant working for Medtronic, a medical device company based in Minneapolis. Unfortunately, she couldn't have been Emma's mother unless she gave birth at the age of nine. Still, I saved the contact.

I kept looking and discovered 178 additional Jenna and Jennifer Kings in Minnesota. I tried to narrow the search by adding the name Emma, but that only made it worse.

No one said this would be easy, my inner voice told me.

I kept at it, finding nothing that identified a Jenna King

living in Orono who was the mother of a young woman named Emma. There was an article that piqued my interest, though, that appeared in the *Minneapolis / St. Paul Business Journal* under the title "40 Under 40—the most influential young people in business in Minnesota today."

Among the forty were sixteen women and among those was—

Jenna King, 31, president of Social King, Inc., the fast-growing start-up that helps companies large and small actively manage their social media presence across multiple sites. Headquartered in St. Paul, she launched her firm with only $10,000 in funding loaned to her by her brother Porter. King admits to being an overachiever. She double-majored and double-minored in business subjects at Carleton College in Northfield, Minn. She has attended executive management training at the Aspen Institute, the Menninger Foundation, and the Stanford School of Business Executive Leadership Program. When not working, she makes personal time for her daughter and the violin. King summed up her business style thus: "Never stay still. Always keep moving forward. Patience is a virtue and one that I am sorely lacking."

What made me stop and stare were five separate lines. The first—*headquartered in St. Paul.* Emma attended high school in St. Paul. The second—*She double-majored and double-minored in business subjects at Carleton College in Northfield, Minn.* Was it possible that her daughter attended Mom's alma mater? The third—*she makes personal time for her daughter and the violin.* But not husband. Four—*Jenna King, 31.* The article was published six years ago, which would make Jennifer thirty-seven years old today. Emma was twenty. Which meant Jenna was only sixteen or seventeen when Emma was born.

That would explain why there was no husband mentioned. Emma was the result of a teenage pregnancy. Which would also explain the name. King is Jenna's name; that's what she gave Emma instead of a father. Which would make Jenna an impressive woman, I told myself, excelling in school, starting a business, and raising a child while barely more than a child herself.

If, my inner voice reminded me, *this particular Jenna King was Emma's mother.*

There were just too many coincidences to blow off. Unfortunately, the article had been published half a dozen years ago and did not include a photograph. I kept searching and found only one other related story, and that was three brief paragraphs appearing in the business section of the Minneapolis *Star Tribune* announcing that a large technology firm located in Seattle had bought St. Paul–based Social King, Inc. for $12,621,000, a very specific number, I thought, wondering how they came up with it. That was two years ago. Since then, nothing. No more newspaper or magazine articles. No Facebook, LinkedIn, Instagram, Pinterest, Twitter, Tumblr, Tinder, Reddit, Snapchat; no Skype. I had the presence of mind to access the website of the Minnesota Judicial Branch which allowed me to search through most of the court records in the State of Minnesota Court Information System. No Jenna King in Orono or St. Paul had ever received so much as a parking ticket, or was involved in a civil, family, and probate case, or had a judgment filed against her.

Again, I stopped and went "Hmm . . ."

For a woman of her age and background to be nearly erased from the internet required effort.

Which brought me to the fifth line in the profile that fired my imagination—"her brother Porter."

"Porter King," I said aloud.

I Googled the name. Unlike his sister, Porter was everywhere.

Mostly, though, his name popped up in his capacity as director of marketing for KTech, Inc., a Golden Valley tech company that provided "practical artificial intelligence" to the business world. The company's website claimed KTech "unifies problem solving, learning, and memory capacity" with its reasoning engines and humanlike memory systems.

Okay, this is where I became distracted. Instead of sticking with the problem at hand, I started reading about the company. Basically, KTech's mission in life was to eliminate the biggest drawback of using artificial intelligence—for all of its advantages, AI simply cannot emulate the creativity and reasoning ability of the human brain. An example that was used, someone says "I dropped a lead weight on top of a glass table and it shattered." The human brain would know immediately that it was the glass that shattered and not the lead weight because we understand the world we live in and how things work. AI would not. It only knows what it's taught and who's going to teach an AI that lead is harder than glass? Another example: "I'll be done in a second." Because we also understand how language is used, most people would know that in this case "a second" meant "very soon"; that it wasn't supposed to indicate a precise measurement of time. An AI unit would take the phrase literally.

KTech, though, promised its clients to provide AI and automation software that would overcome this confusion. It even promised the automotive industry that it would not only teach driverless vehicles the rules of the road, but the unwritten rules as well, such as staying in the right-hand lane on the freeway when driving at the posted speed limit.

I didn't know if I believed them or not, but somebody surely must have because KTech was valued at $8.1 billion according to *Twin Cities Business*. Or not. Which brought me back to Porter King.

According to *TCB*:

KTech lost 5.2 percent of its stock price on the second day of volatile trading as investors reacted to the unexpected absence of Charles King, the company's founder and CEO, at the company's annual meeting Tuesday.

KTech directors and executive staff scrambled Thursday to put concerned investors and clients at ease.

"The man has a bad case of the flu," said King's brother Porter King, Director of Marketing. "He'll be fine in a few days. We know people were disappointed that he was unable to attend the annual meeting. They would have been more disappointed, though, if they had caught his virus."

It was Porter King who had grabbed the mic at the meeting held Tuesday in the ballroom of the Marquette Hotel in downtown Minneapolis and at once beamed gung-ho optimism and bullishness for the company's future. Yet his buoyant attitude and Paul Bunyon–like plaid shirt and jeans weren't enough to calm the anxious crowd.

"People hear flu and they immediately think coronavirus," said Martin Brandon, 42, a banker working in South St. Paul. "Charles King is more than just the CEO," said Steve Zibell, 77, a retired lawyer from Shoreview. "He *is* KTech. I don't know if this company has a plan to move forward without him or even if it could."

"Wow," I said aloud. Charles K. of Orono was Charles King, often referred to as King Charles by detractors and supporters alike. "He couldn't possibly be Dave Deese's half brother, could he?" I continued surfing and discovered that Charles King was a helluva businessman and not the least bit media-shy:

CHARLES KING ANNOUNCES PLAN TO SYNC OUR
BRAINS WITH ARTIFICIAL INTELLIGENCE

CHARLES KING WARNS THAT ADVANCED AI WILL
SOON MANIPULATE SOCIAL MEDIA

KING CHARLES'S SPAT WITH THE SEC IS OVER BUT
NOT FORGOTTEN

THE BILLIONAIRE WHOSE COMPANY MAKES
ARTIFICIAL INTELLIGENCE SYSTEMS FOR VEHICLES
AND ROCKETS BLASTS WHAT HE CALLS "DUMB
TECHNOLOGY"

CHARLES KING'S TWEETS MATTER. JUST ASK THE SEC

KTECH'S MARKETING STRATEGY PROVES IT'S TIME
FOR CEOS TO GET SOCIAL

KTECH IPO GENERATES OVER $6.3 BILLION FOR AI
SOFTWARE COMPANY

CHARLES KING BUYS AI START-UP, CLAIMS
"ARTIFICIAL INTELLIGENCE ISN'T THE FUTURE, IT'S
HERE ALREADY"

CHARLES KING SELLS REALMONEY TO ONLINE
RETAIL GIANT

REALMONEY, CHARLES KING'S ONLINE PAYMENT
SYSTEM, APPROACHES PAYPAL NUMBERS

MINNEAPOLIS INVESTMENT BANKER LAUNCHES
MONEY TRANSFER SERVICE

King's origin story was well documented. He graduated summa cum laude from the University of Minnesota with a degree in economics and went to work as an investment banker for one of the country's more recognized financial institutions. He left the bank, evidently on good terms, because it gave him a loan to help establish RealMoney, a company that supported online money transfers and served as an electronic alternative to credit cards, checks, and money orders. RealMoney soon became big enough to cause PayPal to look over its shoulder if not challenge it outright. He then sold the company for the proverbial undisclosed amount of cash and bought Palmer, Inc., which he quickly renamed and turned into a leading player in the field of artificial intelligence.

Only not everything was sunshine, lollipops, and rainbows in King's world. A week ago he missed a court-ordered meeting with members of the U.S. Securities and Exchange Commission. Last fall, King had sent out a barrage of tweets that implied that he was actively pursuing funding to take KTech private. He later said that he was merely venting his frustration with the company's board of directors. The subsequent swings in KTech's stock price, however, caused the SEC to object, claiming the tweets were false and misleading, that they transmitted inaccurate "material" information to KTech shareholders, and that King's conduct was reckless. King settled the dispute by promising that in the future he would receive preapproval for any social posts about KTech from a committee that he would set up. Except, King never set up a committee and continued to fire off tweets. The SEC asked a judge to hold King in contempt. The judge scheduled a hearing to consider both sides of the argument. King didn't show up and didn't explain his absence. Add that to the fact that he was a no-show for his company's annual meeting, and you have a business community wondering out loud if this was simply the flamboyant King being King or if it was symptomatic of a more serious problem.

Meanwhile, I now had certain knowledge that Charles was Dave Deese's half sibling, along with Porter and Jenna King. I was sure Dave would be happy to hear it. Would the King family be happy to hear from him, though? Deese had done all right for himself. Only these guys were Silicon Valley millionaires, even if they didn't actually live in Silicon Valley. Plus, they had a media presence. Lord knows what TMZ and the other gossipmongers would have to say if they heard about this. It was no wonder Elliot Sohm and Emma King were cautious about what they told me when we met.

'Course, I had yet to uncover a single reference to King's parents; not a word identifying the King patriarch—Charles's, Porter's, Jenna's, and apparently Dave's father—and that, after all, was the favor I was asked to perform.

The obvious move would be to look up the birth records of Charles, Porter, and Jenna King. In Minnesota, anyone can get a noncertified copy of a public birth record of anyone else. It'll cost you all of thirteen bucks. Except, to acquire the record—in person or by mail—I would need to provide answers to the specific questions found on a noncertified birth record application such as the first, middle, and last name of the child, the child's date of birth, city of birth, and county of birth—this assuming that the child was actually born in Minnesota—plus the first, middle, and last name of the child's parents including their last names before the marriage. In other words, to get the information that a birth certificate would give me, I needed to have the information that the birth certificate would give me.

I decided to make a phone call instead.

———

"What do you want?" H. B. Sutton asked instead of saying hello.

"A very good evening to you, too, H," I said.

"It's past business hours."

Her voice was cold and hard and utterly humorless and hearing it always made me want to turn up the thermostat; this despite the fact that H. B. was actually a very pleasant woman and usually good company—once you got to know her. Or, rather, once she got to know you well enough to crack open a door in the wall she built around herself. I blamed her flower children parents for the wall. After knowing her for about three years, she reluctantly confided to me what the H. B. stood for.

"Heavenly-love Bambi," she said.

"Lord Almighty."

"Try growing up with a name like that, especially while wearing the peasant blouses and skirts my parents dressed me in, the flat sandals. Try going to high school or college; try getting a job."

"Do you even speak to your parents?"

"Only during the summer solstice."

Which partially explained why H. B. lived on a houseboat moored to a pier on the Mississippi River next to Harriet Island in St. Paul; why she worked alone as a personal financial advisor out of the houseboat.

I asked her once why she didn't go to court and have her name changed.

"Would I be the same person if I had been named Elizabeth or Joan?" she asked.

"You certainly would have had to endure a lot less teasing; a lot less discrimination in school and the workplace."

"Says the man whose parents named him after Mount Rushmore."

"Hey, I was conceived in a motor lodge while they were taking a vacation in the Badlands," I told her. "And it could have been worse. It could have been Deadwood."

H. B. laughed at that, one of the few times I had heard her laugh. From that moment to this, we've been pals.

"Sorry for calling so late," I told her. "I lost all track of time."

"S'okay. What do you need?"

"Information."

"About your investments?" H. B. asked. "You do read those quarterly statements I send you, right?"

"Just the bottom of the first page where it tells me that despite buying expensive condominiums and cars and pianos and such for the past ten years, I'm currently worth three times as much money as I started with. How is that even possible?"

"Because I'm very good at my job?"

"The rich get richer . . ."

"McKenzie, you called?"

I could picture the frown on her face. I knew that Elliot Sohm, with her dimples, big bright eyes, and easy smile would be cute when she was sixty because H. B., with her dimples, big bright eyes, and somewhat reluctant smile was cute at sixty. She was all of five two and one hundred and ten pounds dripping wet, not that I've ever seen her dripping wet.

"What do you know about Charles King?" I asked.

"Very charismatic, very smart. He knows crap about artificial intelligence technology but he sure knows how to hire people who do. Why? Are you concerned about his sudden disappearance, too?"

"Should I be?"

"You do have about five percent in his company."

"I own five percent of an eight-point-one-billion-dollar tech firm?"

"No, McKenzie. You have about five percent of your net worth invested in an eight-point-one-billion-dollar tech firm."

"Oh. That's different. Wait a minute. I thought you were a big proponent of index funds."

"Why do I bother? McKenzie, eighty-some percent of your account is in index funds; the rest is in active investing. I don't have the exact figures in front of me. Read the damn statements. God, McKenzie."

"About King. Not showing up for his company's annual meeting and the hearing with the SEC last week, is that really a big thing?"

"King Charles is a lot like Elon Musk, Jeff Bezos, Mark Zuckerberg, Jack Dorsey, and Steve Jobs and Bill Gates before them. They're not only the CEOs of their companies; they're the face of their companies. When something happens that puts them in the news and they're always in the news—the day Jack Dorsey announced that he was moving to Africa, Square lost nearly five percent of its stock price. Twitter, that he helped build before Square, it lost money, too. So yeah, King being out of sight for the past few days has had a negative impact on KTech's stock price. McKenzie . . . ?"

"H.?"

"Are you involved in this somehow?"

"No."

"Does this have something to do with one of your adventures, one of those favors that you do?"

"No, no, no. King's name came up while I was looking into something else, is all."

"Cuz, knowing what's going on with King Charles, that's the kind of insider information that could make someone very, very wealthy."

"Seriously?"

"Seriously."

"Well, if I learn anything, H., I'll let you know."

"Please," she said.

"Before I go—what do you know about Jenna King?"

"Used to own Social King, a social media firm—apparently the Kings name everything after themselves. Social King did all right for a while. I stayed away from it, though."

"Why?"

"I heard that Charles was calling the shots for his sister. I wasn't sure how true that was, but it was enough for me to keep my distance. I'm not a big fan of absentee landlords."

"The company was eventually sold."

"Yes, it was. Which was another thing, knowing a company is being built just so it could be sold to the highest bidder—it makes me question its valuations and projections."

"I'm not entirely sure what you're talking about but I'm rich because of you so . . ."

"It's nice to be appreciated, McKenzie."

"Whatever happened to Jenna King, do you know?"

"I only know the rumors which, by the way, I always listen to but rarely act upon."

"What rumors?"

"That she had personal issues."

"Such as?"

"Drugs."

"Drugs?"

"Haven't you heard, McKenzie? We're suffering through an opioid epidemic."

Detective Jean Shipman's phone rang. She tore herself away from my notes to answer the call. It was the man from the impound lot. He told her that he had searched my Jeep Cherokee and didn't find any notes in unaddressed envelopes or otherwise. Shipman thanked him and noted the fact on her yellow legal pad.

She wrote down a second note as well and circled it several times.

Opioids?

EIGHT

Nina loved music almost as much as I did. Actually, she probably loved it more but hey, it's not a competition.

She was sitting in her office, leaning back in her chair with eyes closed and listening to Mary Louise Knutson, a Minnesota pianist that she had hired many times in the past. Knutson was playing "I've Grown Accustomed to Her Face" soft and low on her *Call Me When You Get There* CD and Nina was thinking that I had been right all those times I had told her that she should go back to playing piano professionally.

Nina had played relentlessly when she was a kid; it had helped her cope with a lousy childhood. She had made money at it when she was in college, too, and during those first difficult years when she was establishing her club. Except she had stopped playing somewhere along the line. When I asked her why, she simply shrugged and said she had fallen out of the habit. I've often encouraged her to get back into it and from time to time she would vow to return to performing, especially after I gave her the Steinway. Only she had never followed through. I don't think it was fear of performing. After all, she had done it before. I think it was because she had met so many great pianists over the years that she felt inadequate. She had convinced herself that she could not possibly play as well as Knutson, or Butch Thompson, the great ragtime and stride jazz pianist that she had also hired, or Peter Schimke or Laura Caviani or Chris Lomheim.

Mostly she played at home, with me lying beneath the Steinway, my head propped on a huge throw pillow with the logo of the Minnesota Twins. She'd riff on Dave Brubeck and Bill Evans or pound out Jay McShann's "My Chile" or Otis Spann's "Spann's Stomp" and say, "What do you think?" and I'd tell her that I knew of a jazz joint where she could play happy hour gigs or put together a group and play the main stage. "I have connections," I'd say. Sometimes she would crawl under the piano with me.

That's what she was thinking of when the knock came on her door, of me and her cuddling beneath her baby grand.

"What is it?" she asked.

"Man to see you," her bartender said.

"Okay."

Nina said okay, but she really wasn't, she told me later. She was tired and frustrated and angry and she was astonished at how much energy it took to be pleasant when she was tired and frustrated and angry. She was sure that the man who came to see her was another one of my friends who was anxious about my health, though, and she was determined to appear optimistic even if that wasn't how she felt.

She stepped into the downstairs bar. The bartender gestured at a large man sitting alone at a table in the center of the room. He was dressed in a blue blazer, white shirt with blue tie, and gray slacks that reminded Nina of a uniform. She had not met the man before but that was true of most of my friends, including half the guys I've played hockey with over the past twenty years.

Nina forced a smile onto her pretty face and approached the table.

"Good afternoon," she said. "I'm Nina Truhler."

He gave her a nod and a sneer as if she was a counter clerk who had finally given him the takeout he had ordered after a long wait. He pointed at the chair across from him.

Nina nearly went off yet she managed to smother the explosion, telling herself that there must be a very good reason why this man that she didn't know, who had asked to speak to her, was being rude to her in her own place while her husband was in a coma in the hospital.

Nina eased into the chair.

"It's terrible what happened to McKenzie," the man said, although his tone of voice suggested that it wasn't terrible at all.

"Yes, it is," Nina said.

"Maybe now he'll learn his lesson."

"Lesson?"

"Not to fuck around in someone else's business."

"Who are you?"

"He was warned and now you're being warned—keep your big mouth shut."

Nina smiled. At least she told me that she smiled; I have a hard time believing it myself.

"Warned about what?" she asked. "Be specific."

"Don't make the same mistake he did, or you're going to end up just like him. Do you understand, bitch?"

What happened next happened so fast that Nina told me later that she didn't even think about it. "Just boom," she said.

The boom was her curling her right hand into a tight fist and punching the man in the mouth just as hard as she could.

The blow spun the man out of his chair. He rose to his feet with his hand covering his lower face. Nina told me she could see blood.

"Are you crazy?" he said.

Nina was also on her feet and holding her arm.

She had felt the shock of the blow surge through her fingers, through her wrist, and into her elbow. She was convinced that she had hurt herself more than she had hurt the man.

"Who are you?" she shouted.

The man backed away.

"You come into my place and threaten me? Who are you?"

The man spun and moved quickly toward the door.

"You're nuts, lady," he said.

Nina gave chase even as she tried to shake the pain from her arm.

"Who are you?" she repeated. "Why are you threatening me?"

The man made it to the door and pulled it shut behind him. Nina yanked on the handle and felt a lightning strike of pain ripple through her arm.

She stepped back and shook it some more.

Through the window she could see the man running toward the street. A car stopped for him. She couldn't identify the make or model; she didn't know cars, she told Bobby later. Besides, all cars looked the same these days, she said. She also said she had been unable to read the license plate as the car sped away.

She spun to face the bar. Her staff and all of her early afternoon customers were staring at her with expressions ranging from amusement to terror. Nina wanted to say something but didn't know what.

"I know you would have had some smartass remark to make," she told me. "It's one of my life's great disappointments I couldn't think of a thing."

Instead, she went to her office and called Bobby.

Dave Deese was startled when his office phone rang. Usually his secretary screened his calls; for one to get through unannounced meant the caller was among the small handful of people who had his private number.

"Hello, this is David," he spoke into the receiver.

A female's voice said, "Hello, Dee Dee."

A surge of adrenaline nearly knocked him out of his chair.

"Who is this?" he asked.

"Who do you think?"

Deese rose to his feet even though his legs wobbled beneath him.

"I don't know," he said.

"Jeezus, David. It's T."

"T?"

"Your sister T, goddammit."

"What do you want?"

"What do I—I want to talk. Come over."

"To your office?"

"To the house. Tonight. I'll make something for dinner. David, it's time we had a private conversation."

"About what?"

"What the fuck do you think? What we should have been talking about two goddamn weeks ago—Dee Dee."

Deese said he'd be there. T hung up the phone and Deese thought, She would never have spoken like that in front of our father.

Shipman was jealous. Eddie Hilger and Sarah Frisco, the detectives that Bobby had given the biker case to, burst noisily into the large office that housed all of the detectives working

Homicide and Robbery in Major Crimes. They were so very pleased with themselves. It turned out that while Shipman was wasting her time reviewing my notes, they were busy scooping up one of the bikers who had assaulted the bouncer at Haven. The detectives discovered him on the stoop in front of his house, wearing his gang colors. He had been waiting for the police with two handguns and a blackjack in his pocket. The detectives couldn't help but notice the guns and suggested that the biker move away from them very carefully. He said he had a permit to carry his guns. Sarah said, "Funny, so do I." They stared at each other for a few beats like gunfighters waiting for the other to make the first move. The biker must have decided he didn't like his chances against Sarah, especially with Eddie and a couple of uniforms backing her up, because he rose slowly to his feet, leaving both guns on the stoop; his empty hands in the air.

"For a moment there, I thought things might go sideways," Sarah said.

Shipman repeated the words under her breath in that catty tone of hers—"For a moment there, I thought things might go sideways"—and looked away. She and Sarah were the only women working as detectives in Major Crimes. You'd think that alone would create a sense of camaraderie between the two, only it didn't. Maybe it was because Shipman's desk was toward the back of the room closest to Bobby's office while Sarah's was nearest the door, but what do I know?

After the biker was taken into custody, he was tag-teamed by both Sarah and Eddie, yet refused to identify the other men involved in the fight at Haven and eventually refused to answer their questions without a lawyer present. Once he was taken to the Ramsey County Adult Detention Center, though, he demanded to make a phone call. He called his ex-wife. Even though a taped message told him that his call was being recorded and could be used against him in court, he told his ex-wife to call his lawyer. "The cops arrested me because they know I beat on that fuck bouncer at Haven last night and then threatened to shoot up the place and I need all the help I can get," he said.

"Guy confesses on the telephone," Eddie said. "What a fucktard."

Shipman ground her teeth together—at least I picture her grinding her teeth—and told herself, it's not even one thirty P.M. and they've already closed their case. Dammit.

"You think that's dumb," Gafford said. He had been sitting at his own desk near Shipman. "The boss and I caught a shooting at a fast-food joint this A.M. Talk about comedy."

He related the entire story, speculating at the end that the young woman who started it all would probably get a suspended dis con while the "Second Amendment guy" might take a fall for as many as seven years for felony assault with a deadly weapon.

"If he had kept his cool—misdemeanor assault and he ends up paying a fine at the most," Gafford said.

"He didn't want to keep his cool," Sarah said. "He wanted to shoot someone in the worst way and so he did."

"*I love mankind . . . It's people I can't stand,*" Eddie said. "Charles M. Schulz wrote that. You know. The *Peanuts* guy."

"I'm sorry," Shipman said. "Am I the only one around here with work to do?"

That generated the response from her colleagues that you might expect including Sarah's imitation of an angry cat, her hand curled like a claw and her mouth making a hissing sound.

"Bitch," Shipman muttered quietly to herself.

She turned her attention back to my notes.

What happened to me next.

The first thing I had written that morning was **DO SOMETHING NICE FOR NINA** in all caps and bold type. That was because the woman proved once again that she trusted me implicitly, even though I had involved her in God knows how much nonsense over the years. You need to love a woman like that.

It was about ten A.M. Since Nina rarely went to bed before two it was actually early for her. She saw me sitting at the computer while she prepared to leave for Rickie's and asked what I was working on. I told her I was doing a favor for a friend, which didn't surprise her at all. I also told her I was unable to reveal the extent of the favor or the name of the friend without permission for fear of embarrassing him, which didn't seem to surprise her, either. Instead, she asked if I would see her later. I said I wasn't sure. She said to give her a call.

She embraced and kissed me good-bye as she headed for the door. Unlike the usual quick hug and peck on the lips or cheek that I usually received, Nina kissed me as if she wanted to be talked into staying home. So, I tried to talk her into staying. "You work way too hard," I said.

She smiled and laughed and said she enjoyed managing her club almost as much as I enjoyed doing favors for friends, at least during business hours. After closing time was a different matter, though. Nina gave me that look, you know the one I mean, and said, "You will make time for me?"

"Nothing shall keep me away," I said.

Jean Shipman wrote on her yellow legal pad: "What kept you away? You are such an idiot, McKenzie."

I hadn't received a phone call from Elliot Sohm's father or anyone else for that matter and I was wondering if I would. I checked Dave Deese's DNA website for messages and found two. The first was from Marshall of Minneapolis:

> I appreciate the courtesy you showed my daughter yesterday. However, I have discussed the matter with several of my relatives and it was decided that, while we wish you well, we don't believe it will be helpful to pursue this relationship. You must realize, this revelation does not affect just you and I and Elliot, but a great many other family members as well who will be devastated by the knowledge that you bring us. Thank you for understanding the gravity of our position. Good luck.

The second message I received came from Elliot:

> It was so much fun meeting you yesterday. You might not have noticed—I hope you didn't notice—but I spent a lot of time studying your face to see if we had the same eyes, the same nose, the same chin. I think smile? It's so cool to have an uncle that looks like he plays sports—please tell me that you play sports. I play soccer and softball. No one else in my family does anything except for my cousin Emma who does everything. I hope to meet with you again soon.

Elliot's message came a half hour after the one sent by Marshall from Minneapolis, which meant that either she wasn't aware of her family's decision concerning me—Dave Deese, actually—or she was rebelling against their wishes. I felt a little guilty about that. All I was looking for was a little information that I would hand off to Deese to do with as he pleased. I certainly didn't mean to cause a rift between her and her family.

Before I replied to either father or daughter, I decided to do a little more research. This time I surfed the net for Marshall Sohm. The first thing I learned was that Sohm was a German name originating in the high country, wherever the hell that was. It's not like I looked it up on a map.

The second thing was an article that appeared in the *Spooner Advocate*, a newspaper published in northwestern Wisconsin:

Marshall Sohm, Sr. of Shell Lake, Wisconsin, will celebrate his 75th birthday at an open house from 2 to 4 P.M. Oct. 25 at the Shell Lake Arts Center.

Cards may be sent to 802 First Street, Shell Lake, WI, 54871.

His children are Marshall, Jr. and Krystal Sohm of St. Paul, MN, Jerome and Tonya Sohm of Ogden, Iowa, and Cynthia and Rob Johnson of Madison, WI. He has seven grandchildren and one great-grandchild.

Marshall was born on Oct. 25, 1941. He married Mary Ann on Sept. 8, 1972. Marshall served in the U. S. Navy, became a farmer, and raised cattle, hogs, and sheep. He was a 4-H leader, a Ham radio operator, and volunteer firefighter. He is currently retired but still raises sheep and continues to donate blood. He has donated almost 27 gallons over the years.

My inner voice screamed at the computer—*Mary Ann who? Is she a King? Is she still alive? Is Marshall, Sr. still alive? He was seventy-five when the article was printed. That was eight years ago.*

I went to the website of the *Spooner Advocate*. It had a section devoted solely to obituaries. I searched for Marshall

Sohm, Sr. and found the same photograph that appeared with his birthday announcement and the following:

Marshall Sohm, Sr., 78, died on Monday, April 23. He was born on October 25, 1941, in St. Paul, MN. He served in the U. S. Navy for 20 years. After retiring from the service, he studied agriculture at the University of Minnesota. He bought his own farm in Washburn County, raising cattle, hogs, and sheep. In retirement, he joined the Shell Lake Fire Department and was active in 4-H. He was welcomed to heaven by wife Mary Ann, parents Paul and Colleen Sohm, brother Peter and sister Roberta. Marshall will be missed by all who knew him, especially his children, Marshall, Jr. (Krystal), Jerome (Tonya) and Cynthia (Rob); grandchildren Steven, Linda, Martin, Elliot, Robert, Olivia, and Debra; great-grandchild Claire. A memorial service will be held at Northern Wisconsin Veterans Memorial Cemetery. Memorials are preferred to Shell Lake Fire Department.

"Oh for God's sake," I said aloud. "Aren't you supposed to list the wife's maiden name in obituaries?"

I quickly searched for Mary Ann King and came up empty. "Dammit."

I leaned back in my chair and rubbed my eyes.

Why is this so hard? my inner voice wanted to know. *It shouldn't be this hard. It's not like we're searching for the Lost Ark of the Covenant.*

I surfed some more for the name Marshall Sohm, this time adding "Junior" to the parameters. There was more about Elliot online than there was about her father, but then he didn't have a Facebook, Instagram, Snapchat, or Pinterest account. I did find a small piece that appeared in the *St. Paul Pioneer Press* business section last fall:

St. Paul–based AgEc, Inc., a global provider of food safety technologies and services for agriculture firms, announced that Marshall Sohm, Jr. has been promoted to executive vice president.

"Looks like you didn't stray too far from the old man's farm in Shell Lake, Wisconsin," I told Marshall from St. Paul, even though he wasn't there to hear me.

So now what, I asked myself.

When in doubt, my inner voice said, *agitate.*

I went back to Deese's DNA website and sent two messages. The first was addressed to Elliot.

Baseball and hockey. In fact, I still play hockey despite my advanced years. Unfortunately, I suck at both. I hope to see you again, too.

The second message was sent to Marshall.

Mr. Sohm, as I stated in my earlier message, I want nothing from you or the rest of the King family including recognition. I certainly don't mean to add to the problems that Charles, Porter, and Jenna seem to be experiencing these days. Hell, I actually own stock in KTech. I am asking only for answers to a few simple personal questions. I wish merely to know where I came from. I was very sorry to learn that your mother had passed. If Mary Ann were still alive, I might have been able to ask her; apparently she was my aunt. I was saddened to hear about your father Marshall, Sr. as well. He seemed like a very good man. Growing up on a farm in Wisconsin must have been quite an adventure for you and something that I simply cannot relate to.

I purposely included Marshall's name and information about him and the Kings so he would know that I already knew more than he wanted to tell me. I had hoped that would convince Marshall to answer my questions and send me on my way. I miscalculated. Twenty minutes later he replied with this message:

Don't fuck with us!

To which I replied:

Do you kiss your daughter with that mouth?

Detective Shipman shook her head as she added even more notes to her yellow legal pad. "You just can't help yourself, can you, McKenzie," she said to herself. "What a fucktard."

NINE

The police sergeant sitting behind the bulletproof partition at the entrance to the James S. Griffin Building worked a lever that opened a metal drawer.

"Identification please," he said.

The State of Minnesota requires that licensed private investigators carry an identification card with them at all times that clearly states the license holder's name, company logo if any, address, and the PI's photograph and physical description. Greg Schroeder had that, of course, plus the word PRIVATE printed across the top and INVESTIGATOR printed across the bottom, both in block letters reversed out of black. That was on one side of his wallet. On the other side was a gold coplike badge with Private Detective embossed across it. The Private Detective and Protective Agent Services Board doesn't require a badge. In fact, I think it frowns on it. Schroeder, however, liked to carry one for dramatic effect.

Schroeder slid his wallet into a metal drawer. The drawer was retracted so that it could be accessed on the other side of the glass. The sergeant opened the wallet, perused the contents carefully, put it back into the drawer, and returned it to Schroeder. He didn't seem impressed.

Afterward, he made two phone calls before passing the detective up to the second floor where Major Crimes was located. Schroeder stepped off the elevator and was confronted by a large desk that effectively blocked his path. The woman sitting behind it smiled brightly as he approached.

"Mr. Schroeder?" she asked.

"Yes."

"Identification, please."

He showed it to her.

"Just a moment, please."

Schroeder nodded as she left her post and disappeared behind a secured door on his right. There was another on his left. The elevator had closed behind him, of course, leaving Schroeder with the impression that he was sealed inside a bandit trap. He wasn't going anywhere. After several moments, the door on his right opened and both the woman and Bobby Dunston stepped out. The woman went behind her desk. Bobby moved directly to where Schroeder was standing. Schroeder immediately offered his hand.

"Commander," he said.

"Mr. Schroeder."

Bobby had thought long and hard before he made the call. Greg Schroeder was correct when he told Nina that the police and private investigators often worked together. Not side by side, of course. More like a PI might go to the cops and ask for information on a case the cops weren't actively working; maybe even something in their cold files. In return, the PI would be ready, willing, and able to assist the police should ever the need arrive. In fact, he had better be. If word got out that a PI wasn't playing nice, he might as well set up practice in North Dakota for all the help he was going to get in the Cities. Bobby finally called Schroeder Private Investigations to see if he was willing to play nice. He identified himself and asked to speak to Greg. Gloria, the receptionist, said that Mr. Schroeder wasn't in, would Bobby care to leave a message. Bobby said that he was sure that Gloria could contact him.

"Do so immediately," he said. "Tell him to call me at the Griffin Building. Tell him I'll be waiting."

He waited exactly six minutes before Schroeder returned his call and arranged a meeting.

Bobby shook Schroeder's hand and, without speaking, ushered him through the doorway and down a corridor until they reached the large room where the investigators working in the Homicide and Robbery Unit were located. Bobby led Schroeder into the room and past several desks toward his cramped office. Detective Shipman stood as they approached.

"Boss," she said.

"In a moment," Bobby said.

He gestured for Schroeder to enter his office. After he did, Bobby closed the door behind them.

"Have a seat, Greg." Bobby circled his desk while Schroeder took the chair directly in front of it. "I'm going to call you Greg because I know we're going to be friends."

"We are?"

"You're working the McKenzie shooting, yes?"

"Yes."

"Who are you working for?"

"Myself."

"Don't lie to me again."

Schroeder lifted his hand and let it fall.

"What I'm trying to decide is if we're both on the same side, Greg," Bobby said. "You're off to a bad start."

"McKenzie is a friend of mine. We've worked together in

the past. He even hired me a couple of times to keep watch on his lady love."

"You say 'worked together.' I remember him telling me a story about a case you were both involved in concerning Riley Muehlenhaus, 'cept you were hired by the grandfather, Walter, and he had been working for Riley. How did that play out, by the way?"

"She's alive and for the record, she doesn't use the name Muehlenhaus. It's Riley Brodin-Mulally now."

"Nina Truhler told me the same thing," Bobby said.

"When?"

"About an hour ago."

"Ah. Well, if you already knew who I was working for why did you ask?"

"It was a test to see how forthcoming you were going to be."

"I'll tell you everything I can as long as it doesn't compromise my client," Schroeder said.

"Fair enough. Go 'head."

"McKenzie's friend, Dave Deese?"

"My friend, too."

"He's clean."

"I kinda knew that."

"I didn't," Schroeder said.

"What else?"

"I've only been working the case for a couple of hours."

"You will tell me if you learn anything that I don't already know, though, right?"

"Quid pro quo; isn't that how it works? I give you something and you give me something in return?"

"I can play that game," Bobby said. "About an hour ago a man entered Rickie's and threatened Nina Truhler with bodily harm if she and McKenzie didn't learn to keep their big mouths shut. She responded by punching him in his big mouth."

"Is she okay?"

"Shaken, but not stirred."

"Should I tell you a secret, Commander? I've always liked her."

"Me, too."

"She's way too good for McKenzie."

"We at least agree on one thing."

"I offered her protection," Schroeder said. "She turned it down."

"Offer again."

"No, I think I'll do what McKenzie had me do the last time. Send guys to keep an eye out and not tell her. Can she identify the man who threatened her?"

"No."

"What is it she and McKenzie are supposed to keep quiet about?"

"She doesn't know," Bobby said. "I told her next time she should gather more intel before she hits the guy."

"McKenzie was shot because of something he knew. That's apparent now. It would be nice if he woke up and told us what it was."

"From your lips to God's ear."

"Anything else, Commander?"

"That covers it for now."

"For now?"

"It's possible that I might reach out to you again. It depends on how the situation evolves. McKenzie might wake up in five minutes and tell us everything."

"Or he might not, in which case . . ."

"Don't be unpleasant," Bobby said.

"You'll want to get a jump on this. What is it they say about the first forty-eight hours?"

"I have a detective tracing his movements for the past few days."

"The pretty little thing who stood up when we passed her desk?"

"Oh, please, go out there and call her that, but only after I've had time to get some popcorn so I can enjoy the show."

Schroeder started laughing, I don't know why.

"Greg, if you learn anything you had better tell me and to hell with the quo," Bobby said.

"Yes, Commander."

"Don't mess with me. Please. Not over this. Absolutely not over this."

"We're good," Schroeder said.

The two men rose and shook hands. Bobby went to the door and opened it. He stood in his doorway and watched Schroeder leave. Once Schroeder had exited the large room he glanced at Shipman and gave her a come-hither gesture.

"Boss," she said when she reached his side.

Before she could say anything more, however, Sarah Frisco slammed down her phone, stood up from her desk and waved a sheet of notepaper in the air like it was the winning Powerball ticket.

"We have a shooting on the Green Line," she said. "Uniforms have stopped the train at Dale and University. Two victims, condition unknown. Suspect in the wind."

"You and Eddie," Bobby said. "No, everybody."

"Boss," Shipman repeated.

"Not you. You're already working a case. Tell me something interesting when I get back."

Shipman watched her fellow investigators head for the door, all the while telling herself that Bobby was being unfair. She not only should be investigating the shooting, she should be lead.

"This is all McKenzie's fault," she shouted across the empty room.

Shipman returned to my notes.

What happened next was this.

I stared at the message I had sent to Marshall Sohm on my computer screen, thinking that wasn't the smartest thing I had ever done. Honestly, all I wanted was a name. Something King. That's it. Why was the family being so secretive about it? Were they afraid that once I—once Dave Deese—proved paternity I would sue for an inheritance?

Paternity.

Maternity.

"McKenzie, you're an idiot." I didn't need my inner voice to tell me that. I said it out loud.

I returned to the website of the *Spooner Advocate* and clicked on the obituary link. Only this time instead of typing King, I typed Mary Ann Sohm. Bingo.

Mary Ann Sohm, 62, of Shell Lake, Wisconsin, died Tuesday, September 11, in the arms of her beloved husband Marshall, Sr. and surrounded by her family at the Shell Lake Health Care Center following a courageous battle with cancer. She was born in Minneapolis, Minnesota, on June 14, 1948, to Porter and Emma (Schullo) King. She was married in St. Paul, Minnesota, on September 8, 1972 to Marshall Sohm, Sr. They moved to Shell Lake in 1984 where they farmed for years. Mary Ann will be dearly missed by all who knew her as a hardworking, loving, and dedicated wife and mother. She is survived by her children Marshall, Jr. (Krystal), Jerome (Tonya) and Cynthia (Rob); grandchildren Steven, Linda, Elliot, Martin, Robert, Olivia, and Debra. Mary Ann was preceded in death by her parents and her brother, Gerald. Visitation will be from 4 to 7 P.M. on Thursday, Sept. 13, at the Skinner Funeral Home in Shell Lake with a prayer service at 6:30 P.M., and for one hour before the funeral on Friday at St. Joseph's Catholic Church, Shell Lake, with Father John Piza officiating. Burial will be at Northern Wisconsin Veterans Memorial Cemetery.

What made me smile was the line *Mary Ann was preceded in death by her parents and her brother, Gerald.*

I immediately typed Gerald King into a search engine and discover that, damn, there were a lot of Gerald Kings in the world. I narrowed the search to Minnesota and then to Minneapolis. I searched everywhere that I could and discovered nothing that linked a single Gerald to the other Kings or to Mary Ann. One item that appeared in the *Bayfield County Journal* in May 2000 caught my eye, though:

CAR OF MISSING MINNEAPOLIS MAN DISCOVERED IN
BUFFALO BAY MARINA PARKING LOT IN RED CLIFF

It was because of the headline and the 120-word story that followed that I eventually wrote four lines in my notes:

Chief Neville—Bayfield

LT Rask

IRS requires six-year limit on keeping record for closed business; sixteen years ago; can't prove Anna worked there

Dave isn't going to like this

———

Only, I didn't provide further details. Shipman scrolled my notes up and down and couldn't find an explanation for what I had written. She actually yelled at her computer screen. "What? You write precise details for one thing but not the other?"

The reason I didn't write expansive notes—and again, you need to remember I was writing them for myself and not for someone like Shipman to read—was because I was hungry. I was also a little bored. A computer is an astonishing tool. Certainly it's a more efficient and reliable source of intel than going to courthouses and searching records or visiting the morgues of daily and weekly newspapers and looking up old stories on microfiche. Only I had been staring at my own PC for most of the morning and my neck and shoulders ached and my head throbbed and my leg twitched from inactivity. So I wrote what I wrote. I knew exactly what my notes meant and if Shipman didn't, well she could just follow my footsteps. I mean, do your job, woman!

Which she did.

A quick computer search told Detective Shipman that "Chief Neville—Bayfield" referred to Chief Jeremy Neville who supervised the tiny police department in the city of Bayfield, a thriving tourist town located on the south shore of Lake Superior in Wisconsin. She called the number she found. The woman who answered directed her call to the chief. Shipman identified herself and explained why she was calling.

"Is McKenzie going to be all right?" the chief asked.

"I don't know. The last I heard he was still in a coma."

"I'm sorry to hear that. I like McKenzie. He did me a favor when he was up here a couple years ago. It doesn't surprise me that he got himself shot, though. We hadn't had a serious crime up here in decades. He arrived and the bullets started flying everywhere. It was very disconcerting."

"My information, he called you Tuesday," Shipman said.

"Yes, about a twenty-year-old cold. It wasn't even ours."

"Can you tell me . . ."

"Yeah, yeah, yeah. Twenty years ago, twenty-one actually, the department received a call—I wasn't here back then. I was working in Houghton, Michigan. According to the records that I accessed for McKenzie, the department received a call that a car had been abandoned in a marina parking lot for over three weeks. The marina is located in Red Cliff, an unincorporated town seven miles north of us. We provided service to Red Cliff back then. Now, you need to remember that it was a marina. A vehicle sitting in the lot for a long period of time wasn't unusual. People would often park their cars, jump on their boats, and sail off onto Lake Superior for a couple of weeks at a time. Except it was getting late in the season and most people were starting to take their boats out of the water for storage.

"We received the call and sent an officer to check on the car and discovered that a BOLO had been issued for it by the Minneapolis Police Department. The car belonged to a businessman named Gerald King who had gone missing three weeks earlier. We alerted the MPD and they sent up a team to impound the car and tow it back to the Cities. All we did was secure the vehicle until they arrived.

"Later, we were asked by the MPD to accompany an investigator who canvassed the marina; interviewed the people who worked there or who had boats in the marina; some who actually lived on their boats during the summer. He flashed King's photograph to everyone we could find, although there weren't that many. Like I said, it was toward the end of the season and most of the regulars were gone. He flashed the photo and asked if anyone could remember speaking to King, seeing King. No one did. At least no one admitted it. And that was that. That's all I could find in the supplementals. That's all I could tell McKenzie."

"You said that an investigator from the MPD did the canvassing," Shipman said. "Who? Do you have a name?"

"Ah, it's right here. A sergeant named Clayton Rask."

Shipman was a little afraid of Lieutenant Rask. Truth be told, I was a little afraid of him myself. She sat across from LT in his office in Room 108, which was actually a suite of offices that served the Minneapolis Police Department's assault, robbery, narcotics, forgery/fraud, sex crimes, and homicide units, among others, located in the Minneapolis City Hall–Hennepin County Courthouse. Rask had been running the Homicide Unit for as long as I could remember. He didn't move up and he didn't move sideways. Instead, he devoted his entire law enforcement career to catching killers. He was very good at it.

"McKenzie," he said. "There have been times when I wanted to shoot him myself. Once, though, he did me a favor. I can't tell you what the favor was. It's—sensitive. That favor buys him a lot of slack with me, though. Don't think he doesn't know it, either."

"I understand, LT."

If you had a relationship with him, you didn't call him Lieutenant or Rask and certainly not Clayton. You called him LT.

Rask glanced at his watch. He was always glancing at his watch.

"What can I do for you, Detective?" he asked.

"You spoke to McKenzie Tuesday."

"I did."

"Can you tell me what you spoke about—if it's not sensitive?"

"It was about a missing persons case. Actually, I believe it was murder, although it was never designated as such."

"Murder?"

"Gerald King was a businessman. Owned a finance company here in Minneapolis. One day, poof, he was gone. He was last seen leaving his office at five thirty P.M on a Wednesday in September in the year 2000. We did not get the call from his family. His wife had died four years earlier. His family, his immediate family, consisted at the time of a son named Porter, age twenty-one, and a son named Charles, age nineteen. They were both attending Northwestern University at the time. There was a daughter, age sixteen, named Jenna who was a sophomore at Minnehaha Academy. She and her father lived in the house alone. No, the call came from business associates who were alarmed that he hadn't shown up at his office, blowing off several important meetings without explanation."

"Odd," Shipman said. "Usually, it's the family who makes the call."

"Within twenty-four to thirty-six hours of the subject going missing, too," Rask said. "The children, however, claimed that it was not unusual for their father to stay away from home for days at a time. The middle child, Charles, accused the father of being an abusive, absentee father who slept around. He was very angry."

"Was he?"

"Yes. The sister didn't seem particularly happy, either. She confirmed what her brother had said."

"What about the other son, Porter?"

"He didn't say much of anything. Both Charles and Porter were in Chicago when Gerald disappeared. Well, Evanston. I didn't discover that until later when I delved deeper into the case. At the time, I thought Gerald King had simply gone out for a pack of cigarettes and kept on going. A rich, middle-aged widower who became disenchanted with his life and simply walked away from it. It's always been easy for Americans to go somewhere else and start over. That's what our ancestors did. That's why America exists today. You're too young to remember the director of the Minneapolis City Council. She packed her bags, arranged for an attorney to pay off her debts, and, poof, she was gone. Nobody knew where she went. Everybody had a theory—she had embezzled money and was on the run or she had taken up with a secret lover or had been abducted or had been murdered. Turned out she had gone to San Francisco to become a different person. That's what I was thinking about when I caught Gerald King's case. There was no sign of foul play, as they say. No evidence of a crime."

"What changed your mind?" Simpson asked.

"The car."

"King's car that was found in the parking lot of a marina on Lake Superior? Wouldn't that have fit your initial theory? Park the car, jump on a boat, and sail to God knows where. Sail off to Canada."

"Except we impounded the car and went over it. We found hair samples and a single drop of dried blood in the backseat that belonged to King."

"So? It was King's car."

"What do you drive?" Rask asked.

"A Ford Prius."

"Nice car."

"Thanks."

"Does it have a backseat?"

"Of course."

"Ever sit there?"

Shipman found herself thinking about it.

"No," she said.

"How long have you owned the car?"

"Four years."

Rask spread his hands in a do-you-get-it gesture.

"That's not evidence of murder, of course, but it was enough for me to expand the investigation," he said. "Starting with the kids. I couldn't place Charles and Porter in Chicago the night of the disappearance, but I could early the next morning. It's an awfully long drive from there to here and then back again. There was no evidence that Jenna had ever left the house after she came home from school. We checked the phones and found that she had made one call to her aunt Mary Ann Sohm in Shell Lake, Wisconsin, that had lasted about five minutes. We interviewed both parties separately and they agreed—Jenna had called because she was worried when her father failed to come home from work. Her aunt told her not to worry, that he would turn up; he always did.

"Next we interviewed the people who worked for him. At first we got the usual answers, especially from the men—he was a nice guy, a demanding but fair boss, and so on and so forth. The more we pressed though—it turned out that he was a lying sonuvabitch who had been abusing his female employees for years, especially the young, single, and vulnerable women; blackmailing them, forcing them to exchange sexual favors for their jobs."

"How many?"

Rask held up four fingers.

"That's the number that would talk to us on the record," he said. "Who knows how many more were keeping quiet because of fear or embarrassment or I don't know what. Who knows how many more had been abused who were no longer working there?"

Shipman thought—Anna Theresa Chastain? Was she one of them? Is this what McKenzie meant when he wrote "Dave isn't going to like this"?

"No one said anything?" she asked aloud.

"This was long before the hashtag MeToo Movement, Detective. Back in those days, women were rarely believed when they accused a man who wasn't a stranger of sexual assault, rarely taken seriously unless there was plenty of physical evidence, like strangulation marks on their throats. Even then it was always their fault because of the way they were dressed or because they had a drink in a bar or because—ah. You know the story. Us." Rask tapped his chest. "Law enforcement. We had a lot to do with that, too, God forgive us. It wasn't just us though. It was the politicians, the entertainment industry, the porn industry; it was—when King first started preying on his female employees back in the seventies, people like Phyllis Schlafly were working to kill the Equal Rights Amendment, saying things like 'sexual harassment on the job is not a problem for virtuous women.'"

"I don't care about the circumstances," Shipman said. "The women should have done something."

"Not everyone gets to carry a gun, Detective. In any case, I believe that someone did do something. A woman. Or perhaps her husband or boyfriend, father, brother, cousin. I think Gerald King was executed by one of his vics or someone close to one of his vics and his body was disposed of, probably in Lake Superior."

"Why Superior, though? There are ten thousand lakes in Minnesota."

"McKenzie asked the same question, only he said there were 11,842 lakes in Minnesota."

"Leave it to him to know the exact number. Still, why not one of the 11,842 lakes? Or dump his body in the Mississippi River? Or the Minnesota? Or the St. Croix? Or bury him in one of our—what is it—fifty-nine state forests? Why drive two hundred and thirty-five miles to Red Cliff, Wisconsin? And why Red Cliff? Superior is a big fricking lake. You could toss his body anywhere."

"I don't know," Rask said. "If I did, I would have closed King's case twenty years ago. That's what I told McKenzie. I also told him that I didn't particularly care one way or the other. Not then and not now. I know I'm supposed to care. Care deeply. You can't choose the victim; one of the first things they teach you at the academy. The law works for everybody or it doesn't work for anybody. But of all the murders I caught and haven't solved—I promise I don't lose sleep over this one."

"What about the King kids? What did they do when Daddy didn't come home?"

"Nothing. Here in Minnesota, a missing person is considered alive and well. It's only after the person is missing for a continuous period of four years that he will be presumed dead and probate can begin. So, for four years the King children continued to live as if their father was still alive; as if he'd walk back in through the front door at any moment. Porter and Charles moved back to the Cities; both enrolled at the University of Minnesota. They lived in their house in Linden Hills with their sister Jenna, went to school, paid the bills— they had access to the old man's accounts and apparently they found a man to run Gerald's business as if Gerald was on vacation, paying the kids their fair share of the profits as they went along. After four years, a judge declared Gerald dead and they finally collected their inheritance, sold the business, and moved on from there."

"From what I've read, they seemed to have done pretty well for themselves," Shipman said.

"Except now Charles King is missing."

Victoria Dunston was lying on her bed and reading a textbook when she heard a knock on her bedroom door. The door opened and her sister stepped inside without waiting for a reply.

"Hey," she said.

"Hey."

Katherine crawled onto the double bed and sprawled alongside Victoria.

"I'm hungry," she said.

"Then eat."

"I better wait for dinner. You know Mom."

Victoria did know her mother and knew that she had never once objected when her daughters grabbed an apple or banana or a handful of grapes when they came home from school. Cookies and chocolate bars, however, were a different matter. She glanced at her watch. It was a good two hours before dinnertime.

"Where is Mom, anyway?" Victoria asked.

"In the kitchen cleaning."

"Again?"

"She just finished talking to Nina. There's no change in McKenzie's condition."

Victoria sighed dramatically as if that was not the news she had wanted to hear.

"Did Dad find out who shot him yet?" she asked.

"Dad never talks about his work, you know that."

"This goes a little above and beyond his usual cases, wouldn't you think?"

"That's what I told him this morning."

"What did he say?"

"What does Dad always say?"

"Let me guess—'We'll see'?"

"Man of a thousand words, that's him."

Victoria lifted her arm and her younger sister curled up

against her, resting her head against her shoulder. Victoria lowered her arm and pulled her closer.

"How are you doing?" she asked.

"About the same as you," Katherine said.

"That well, huh?"

"What are you studying?"

"Biology."

"Let me see."

Victoria gave her a good look at the page she was reading.

"Looks like gibberish to me," Katherine said.

"You need to study more. Seriously."

"You need to get out of the house and play some ball. Seriously. Hang out with friends and talk about something besides what college has the best ROI."

"I'll start doing the one if you do the other."

"Deal."

"I have a cache of snack bars hidden away in my desk drawer. Help yourself."

"I'm good. Thanks for offering."

"Katie?"

"Vic?"

"Never mind."

"Me, too, sister. Me, too."

TEN

The office that housed the Homicide and Robbery Unit of the Major Crimes Division was empty when Shipman returned to the Griffin Building. She sat behind her desk and waited for the phone to ring, wishing for a felony; hell, she'd even settle for a gross misdemeanor—anything that would get her out and about instead of squandering her time trying to discover who shot me. Only the phone didn't ring, so she went back to my notes.

What I did next.

After hearing what Chief Neville and Lieutenant Rask had to say, I decided to give Marshall Sohm another try.

Mr. Sohm, I apologize for my hissy fit. It was uncalled for. But you must understand how important this has become to me. I repeat that I want nothing from you or your daughter. Nor will I impose myself on your cousins and my half siblings Charles,

Porter, and Jenna King. I wish merely to learn only about their father Gerald (and apparently my father, too). I need to know about his relationship with Anna Theresa Chastain, a secretary who might have worked for him forty-four years ago. I keep thinking that a twenty-minute conversation is all that I require from you or one of the Kings or even from some as yet unidentified source with knowledge of the situation. We don't even need to have it in person. Please help me out. I am not going to let this go.

I waited and waited, yet Marshall did not respond. If he had really been my cousin, I would have been very disappointed in him. I might have even crossed him off my Christmas card mailing list. If I had a Christmas card mailing list.

I asked myself who else I could contact. There was Elliot Sohm and Emma King, of course, but I decided that they should be my absolute last resort. I even typed a note next to their names—"When all else fails."

Beyond the girls, there were the Kings themselves. Somehow I didn't think King Charles would make himself available to talk to a man claiming to be his long-lost brother, especially while the SEC was looking for him. Porter was a possibility, yet given all the controversy swirling around his family and KTech, he would certainly view me with suspicion. That left Jenna and the question—how do I find her?

Carleton College would know where she lived, I told myself. Only I couldn't think of a gag that would convince them to give up her address or phone number and again, I didn't want to involve Emma. It just seemed so tawdry.

What's a step up from tawdry? my inner voice asked.

Mendacious, I told myself.

I searched my notes for a phone number and called it. A

woman with a perky voice said "KTech Marketing Department. How may I direct your call?"

"Porter King," I said.

"I'm sorry, Mr. King is unavailable. May someone else assist you?"

"I hope so. My name is McKenzie. I'm calling on behalf of the *Minneapolis / St. Paul Business Journal.*"

"Mr. King will be answering questions concerning the absence of Charles King . . ."

"Miss?"

"At two thirty P.M. in our auditorium . . ."

"Miss, please."

"For members of the press and interested shareholders."

"Miss, I'm not calling about that."

"No?"

"No, although if you have some insider information . . ."

"I do not."

"I'm sure my employers will appreciate it."

"What is it that you want, Mr. McKenzie?"

"I'm a freelance writer. The *Journal* hired me to work up a where-are-they-now piece about some of the businesspeople who have appeared in our annual Forty-Under-Forty series over the years. Are you familiar . . ."

"I am."

"Six years ago, Ms. Jenna King appeared in the *Journal*. She was president of Social King, Incorporated, at the time. Since then, of course, Ms. King sold Social King to a firm in Seattle . . ."

"Yes."

"And we lost track of her. The phones numbers we have for her office are no longer valid, of course, and neither are the numbers for the home phone where she lived in St. Paul with her daughter Emma."

"Yes."

That yes confirms that Jenna and Emma are mother and daughter, my inner voice told me, in case I had any doubt.

"We certainly want to include her in the piece; especially since she is still under forty," I said aloud. "I was hoping that Porter King, Jenna's brother, could supply me with a phone number or email address or even a land address so that we might contact Ms. King and arrange an interview. Or perhaps I might even impose on you. I would be happy to supply you with my own number and email address and if you could forward them to Jenna, she'd be welcomed to contact me at her convenience. Is that possible?"

Perky Voice paused before she answered, "I'll have to check."

"I appreciate this very much. My number is . . ."

"I have your number on my computer."

"Of course."

"I will contact you as soon as I can."

"Thank you again."

"Good-bye, Mr. McKenzie."

"Good-bye."

After I hung up I thought, This should work. Only it didn't. I waited and waited some more. I had a late lunch and waited again. Perky Voice didn't call back. 'Course, she might have been too busy to reach out to Porter, so I decided to call her again and give her a nudge. Before I could even say hello and identify myself, Perky Voice, speaking in a very non-perky manner, said "Who do you think you are? More to the point, sir, who do you think *we* are that we would reveal personal information to any liar who calls us on the phone?"

"Miss . . ."

"You are not a freelance writer, Mr. McKenzie. Nor are you employed by the *Minneapolis / St. Paul Business Journal.* As far as we are concerned, you are nothing more than a criminal engaged in a fraudulent activity. Do not call this number again. Have a nice day."

I was laughing as she hung up the phone. Have a nice day; even while telling me off she had to be polite. Minnesota Nice. Oh, well. At the same time I laughed at myself because of my own carelessness. What I should have done was taken a name off an article that had appeared in the *Minneapolis / St. Paul Business Journal* and used that.

If you're going to lie, you need to commit to it all the way, my inner voice said.

Words of wisdom, I told myself.

Now what?

It was becoming increasingly obvious that I had exhausted pretty much all of the options available to me by personal computer and phone. I would need to leave the comfort of my condominium if I was to learn anything more about Dave Deese's second family. But where would I go? What would I do? March down to KTech or AgEc and demand that Porter King or Marshall Sohm receive me? After the security guards escorted me off the premises, then what? Stage a sit-in?

I glanced at my all-purpose watch, the one that monitors my heart rate, counts the steps I walk, the calories I burn, the minutes I sleep, and only incidentally tells the time. One forty-four P.M. I reminded myself that Perky Voice said that Porter King would be answering questions concerning the absence of Charles King at two thirty P.M. in the company's auditorium for members of the press and interested shareholders.

You're a shareholder, my inner voice reminded me. *Aren't you?*

"Now what?" H. B. Sutton asked.

"Your telephone manner leaves much to be desired, you know that, H?" I said.

"I have caller ID. I know who's on the line."

"So, it's just me?"

"What do you want, McKenzie?"

"There's a shareholders' meeting being held at the KTech building this afternoon. I'm thinking of going."

"Good for you," H. B. said. "I'd be interested in hearing what the powers that be have to say myself. Will you tell me?"

"Sure, but I'll probably need a pass or something to get in, right?"

"Haven't you ever been to a shareholders' meeting before?"

"No."

"Please tell me you at least vote your proxies."

"Umm . . ."

"God help me," H. B. said. "All right, all right, no problem. What you need to do—I'm sure they'll have people sitting at tables outside the venue. Just walk up to one of them and tell them who you are. You'll probably need an ID. They'll search their lists, find your name, and give you a pass."

"Can I use your name?"

"No. Why would you even ask that?"

"I'm afraid they might not let me in."

"Why not? McKenzie, what have you done?"

"It's possible that I might have annoyed the King family."

"How did you do that? Don't tell me. The thing is, the King family doesn't actually own KTech. The shareholders do. 'Course, they are the majority shareholders . . . Anyway, all shareholders have the right to attend the meetings. Berkshire Hathaway, the company owned by Warren Buffett? You don't even need to own a share to get into their meetings. All you need is a pass and passes—shareholders who possess at least one share of Class A and Class B stocks can request as many as four meeting passes. A lot of them will then turn around and put the passes up for auction on eBay and other places. That's how you get forty thousand people from around the planet traveling to Omaha, Nebraska, every May to hear Buffett speak. The event has become known as Woodstock for capitalists, I'm not exaggerating."

"Have you ever gone?"

"Oh, yeah. Sitting in the shadow of the Oracle of Omaha— so very, very cool."

"And people say that you don't know how to have fun."

One of the things about H. B. Sutton, you can actually hear her smirk over the phone.

"McKenzie," she said, "in many cases, especially with limited liability companies, the bylaws can stipulate that attendance to meetings depends on holding a minimum number of shares. In KTech's case—hang on . . ."

I hung on.

"Still there?" H. B. didn't give me time to answer before she started reading. "The right to attend a general shareholders' meeting shall accrue to the holders of at least three hundred shares, provided that such shares are registered in their name in the corresponding book-entry registry five days in advance of the date on which the general shareholders' meeting is to be held and provided also that they present evidence thereof with the appropriate attendance card or share certificate issued by any of the entities participating in the institution that manages such book-entry registry, or directly by the company itself, or in any other manner permitted under law."

"Wow," I said.

"That's in the KTech bylaws. My point—you have eighteen hundred shares. Legally, they can't turn you away."

"How much is that worth, by the way? My shares?"

"At the current price, which has gone up by the way, ah . . ."

"I thought the stock was going down because of the uncertainty surrounding Charles King," I said. "Why would it be going up all of a sudden?"

"Because someone is buying it? Here it is—$155.74 a share. Do the math—just a sec—that's two hundred and eighty thousand, three hundred thirty-eight dollars, and forty cents.

"That's a lot of money."

"About four-point-seven percent of your portfolio. Read the goddamn statements."

"I will, I will, from now on, I promise."

"Let me know what they say about King Charles, the sooner the better."

The meeting was held at the KTech Tower, a ten-story building located just off I-394 near the Ridgedale Shopping Mall. Over four million people lived in the greater Twin Cities area and apparently a large percentage of them seemed to be at the event. I was surprised by the crowd. After all, the meeting had been scheduled during midafternoon, making it as inconvenient as possible for shareholders who had full-time jobs to attend.

The marketing staff of KTech made it clear from the moment I walked through the door that this would not be a typical shareholders' meeting where directors would be elected, financial records would be reviewed, business practices would be debated, and corporate policy would be evaluated. Instead, it was labeled as "an informal get-together." They even set up several bars that served free wine and beer and directed a waitstaff to move among the shareholders with trays loaded down with an enticing selection of desserts. The caramel and Chinese five-spice snickerdoodle and hazelnut chocolate mousse were both amazing. Okay, I had two desserts. I owned eighteen hundred shares, so . . .

Informal or not, the place vibrated with anxious energy. Standing in the reception area outside the auditorium with my fellow shareholders and members of the media, waiting for the doors to open, reminded me of attending the world premiere of a play with Nina and wondering what kind of show we were in for.

I have to admit, the meeting was nothing like I had expected. More about that later. First, I need to speak to some people . . .

Shipman thought there should be another page of notes, only there wasn't. She scrolled up and down the document looking for something, anything that she might have missed and found, "Nothing. What again? You've got to be kidding me."

She scrolled some more.

"Is that it, McKenzie?" Shipman asked even though I wasn't there to answer. "Is that's all you've got? You are so lazy."

The detective slumped in her chair and stared at the screen of her computer. She studied my last line scrupulously.

"You need to speak to what people?" Shipman said aloud. "Did you speak to them and just didn't have enough time to transcribe your conversations into your notes before you were shot? Is that what happened?"

Shipman reached for her phone and punched the numbers that connected her with the Forensic Services Unit. Most of its members were covering the shooting on the Green Line. She ended up speaking to the same tech that she had spoken to earlier that day; the one who enjoyed flirting with her.

"Brian, the numbers on McKenzie's cell phone, I need to know the names of the people he spoke to," Shipman said.

"Yeah, about that, Detective . . ."

Shipman glanced at her watch and did the math.

"You've had almost six and a half hours since I gave you the phone," she said.

"Oh, wow. Six and a half hours. That's a long time."

"Brian, I know you're busy. So am I. Hell, we're always busy. I need those names."

"All right, I'll squeeze it in. Speaking of squeezing . . ."

"Don't go there, Brian."

"What a dirty mind you have. I was going to ask about lunch. Again."

"Tell you what—if those numbers give me what I need to close this lousy case, I'll let you take me to lunch."

"Actually, I was hoping you would take me to lunch."

"Brian, I would like to see the names first thing in the morning, if not sooner."

"I'll do my best, Detective."

"Thank you, Brian."

Chopper studied the young African-American man sitting on the edge of his seat, both hands on top of the square table in front of him as if he was preparing to leap up and dash out of the bar at the least provocation. Herzog sat close beside him to make sure he didn't.

"You seem nervous," Chopper said.

"Herzog says you want to talk to me, how am I supposed to feel?"

"I'm not tryin' t' fuck with you, Jamal."

"You fucked the Red Dragons, killed most of 'em."

"Did I?"

"You maybe didn't pull the trigger, but you pointed the gun, fuckin' machine guns, two of 'em."

Chopper found himself rubbing his face at the memory. The massacre Jamal was referring to was the result of a brief but bloody war between two rival gangs fighting over the heroin and OxyContin trade in Minnesota and he had nothing to do with it, although he might have nudged it along a bit and later celebrated the outcome. He would have corrected the young man's assumption but reasoned long ago that possessing a reputation for terrible revenge might have its advantages down the road.

"You a Dragon?" Chopper asked.

"Not anymore."

"You're still dealin' Oxy."

"Man's gotta make a livin'."

Truth was Chopper looked more like a drug dealer than Jamal Brown. So did Herzog. Hell, so did I. For one thing, despite Jamal's slender frame, he had the appearance of good health, like someone who included plenty of fruits and vegetables in his diet; who was accustomed to running and not just to catch a bus. For another, he dressed like a lawyer working for the ACLU, pleated dress slacks, starched shirt, suit jacket, black-rimmed glasses. But then Jamal catered to a mostly white, upper-middle-class clientele, the soccer moms living in Edina and the investment bankers in Golden Valley, and he needed to look presentable.

For a couple of decades, pharmaceutical companies had been bribing and otherwise convincing doctors and health clinics to overprescribe what they claimed were "nonaddictive pain medicines" but what were really the exact opposite. Perfectly legal drugs like Vicodin, OxyContin, Percocet, and others hooked over two million Americans on opioids; one hundred and thirty of them overdosed and died every day. A member of the Centers for Disease Control claimed that Big Pharma had addicted an entire generation.

After about a half million deaths, the government finally

caught on and began monitoring the behavior of doctors and health clinics that prescribed opioids; regulations and insurance policies were established. As a result, the prescription market began to contract. Many in the white community were suddenly cut off from their supply—the vast majority of opioid addicts were white for the simple reason that they had greater access to traditional health care—and they had to seek their fix elsewhere.

Enter Jamal, who was happy to meet their growing needs at a cost of about five dollars for a single Vicodin that usually went for a buck twenty-five or fifteen dollars for a fifteen mg tablet of OxyContin with a retail price of six-fifty. 'Course no one ever bought just one pill. Usually it was in lots of one hundred or more.

While these prices were certainly steeper than they—or their insurance companies—had paid when they received their pharmaceuticals legally from the medical clinic or the corner pharmacy, Jamal's customers were content knowing that they weren't stooping so low as to buy fentanyl or, shudder, heroin, the opioids of choice in the poorer quarters, from some back-alley drug dealer working the North Side of Minneapolis. Oh, no. They were acquiring perfectly legal prescription drugs purchased from a polite, young, well-dressed African-American who would drop them off at their homes or offices or the coffee-house near the mall when it was convenient and then tell them all to have a nice day.

"What you care if I'm slinging?" Jamal asked.

"I don't," Chopper said. "Was a time I'd probably be workin' the trade with you. I just want some information and then I'm outta your life."

"What kind of information?"

"I heard you've been buyin' your shit at RT's Basement off of Rice Street."

"No."

"No?"

"Nah, uh-uh. That's just where I pick it up. Used to be I'd get it in the mail. FedEx, man. UPS. Now, my supplier, I don't know if he thinks RT's is safer or more convenient."

"So, what do you do?" Chopper asked. "Knock on the back door, give a man your money, he gives you your product and you walk away?"

"That's exactly what I do."

"What man?"

"Who's ever workin' the door. I don't ask no questions, ask no names. If the order is correct, and it always is, that's all I care about."

"Who's your supplier?"

Jamal refused to answer.

"Who's your supplier?" Chopper repeated.

"You gonna put a gun to my head, convince me you'll squeeze the trigger if I don't tell you?"

"That can be arranged," Herzog said.

Jamal stared at him as if he could picture the scenario unfolding.

"Fuck, man," he said. "C'mon."

"Is it RT?" Chopper asked.

"No. Like I said, his place is just the drop."

"Does your supplier hang there?"

"The fuck I know? Lookit, I don't know where the Oxy comes from. I met a man while back, he hooks me up. Probably he's a middleman just like me. Haven't even seen him in months. I call him on a burner, place my order, he lists a price, and I do what I say I do—knock on the door, pay the price, and get my goods. Simple."

"RT's Basement," Chopper said. "Is it just the distribution

center or do the users hang out there? Maybe there's someone sellin' shit table to table."

That would explain the unexpected number of white customers frequenting an African-American bar, he thought.

"Couldn't say," Jamal answered. "I've never been inside, not even for a taste. I don't linger, man. I get my supply, I get out. It's a job, not a life. 'Kay? This is not my long-term career goal, dealin'. Once I'm outta college and clear of my student loans, I'm goin' basic."

"Yeah," Chopper said "I reached the same conclusion you did only I got there late. Way late." He rolled his chair back and forth a couple of inches to emphasize his point. "It's hard to give up ballin'."

"Not me, man. I'm gonna be fuckin' Bill Gates."

"How you gonna do that?" Herzog asked.

"Stock market, man."

"Gates be rich because he built something that never existed before."

"No. Bill Gates be rich because he owned stock in the company that built something that ain't never existed before."

"His company."

"My point, it's the stock that matters."

"You looking for another Microsoft to buy into?"

"Not the only way it works. Another way you go to a broker and borrow shares of a company. You sell the shares. You wait for the stock to go down. You buy back the shares at the lower price. Then you return the shares to the brokerage firm you borrowed them from, pay your interest, and pocket the difference."

"Selling shorts," Chopper said. "Dangerous when the stock don't do what you want."

"Huge rewards when it does."

"How would you manage that, a black man in America not even got a college degree yet?" Herzog asked.

"I'm makin' connections."

That caused Chopper to raise an eyebrow.

"The investment bankers you sell to?" he asked.

"And others. Them rich soccer moms, sometimes they need more than their prescriptions filled, you know."

"I know."

"Not just a good fucking, either. Sometimes, they're looking for a friend."

"You that friend?" Herzog said.

"I'm a businessman. I'll be whatever my customers need. Whatever gets me where I want to go."

"I predict that you'll go far, Jamal," Chopper said.

Jamal was excused, but only after Chopper admonished him to keep their conversation private.

"I promise," Jamal said before leaving in a hurry.

"You believe what he say?" Herzog asked.

"Yes, I do."

"So, whaddya think?"

"I think a white man in a nice jacket walks into a black man's bar where Oxy's on the menu, the clientele thinking he's there to fuck with 'em, anything can happen."

"Could've gone down that way, 'cept it don't explain what McKenzie was doing there in the first place. Can't see 'im chasin' the opioid trade. Just not somethin' he'd do."

"You know, McKenzie. One thing always leads to another."

"What we gonna do?"

Chopper looked at his watch.

"What say we run down to On's Kitchen on University and get some Thai and then later see what's happenin' over to RTs Basement?"

Deese rapped on his sister's front door and opened it at the same time, something that was not uncommon in the Deese family. He called her name, "T," stepped into the foyer, and shut the door behind him. T was standing in the living room. She was dressed for her job as a marketing analyst for a cosmetics firm located in Blaine—black jacket, black skirt, black hose, black pumps, and red shirt—and Deese decided, my sister is a pretty woman, something he hadn't really thought about until that moment, go figure.

"You're early," T said.

Deese shrugged in reply.

T pressed her closed fists against her hips.

"Well, David, what do you have to say for yourself?" she asked.

Deese's mouth was so dry that he couldn't speak even if he had wanted to. He told me later that all he could think of at the time was the T never called him David unless she was pissed off.

"David?"

He shook his head, instead.

"Oh, what the hell?" T said.

T marched across the living room into the foyer. She brought her hands up and Deese braced himself for the blow he was sure would follow. Instead, T wrapped her arms around him and hugged him so tightly that he nearly lost his breath.

"You are such a jerk," she said. "You have always been a jerk, even when we were kids, but I love you so fucking much, anyway."

Deese did something then that he hadn't done even when his mother died. He wept.

One man was killed and another was critically injured, although he was expected to survive, in the shooting on the Green Line. According to witnesses, a man boarded the train and made his way toward a back bench where he sat with another man who clearly knew him. They spoke for a few moments, and then the first man pulled out a gun and shot his friend in the face. Next, he got up and made his way to the door. A second man was standing there. The first man shot him in the head—he's the victim who was expected to survive, according to Dr. Lillian Linder at Regions Hospital. The train stopped at the next designated station, the door opened, the first man disembarked, and walked away. Detectives Sarah Frisco and Eddie Hilger were currently working with Metro Transit to identify the suspect from a surveillance video taken on the train. Mason Gafford was attempting to identify the murder victim and trace his movements. At least, that's what Commander Dunston told Shipman when he returned to the Griffin Building.

"Bobby, I resent this." Shipman was standing in front of his desk in his cramped office. "I really do."

"Exactly what do you resent, Jean?" Bobby asked.

"This, this—being made to go after McKenzie's assailant when there are so many other things I could be doing."

"Other things that you believe are more important?"

"The shooting on the Green Line; I should be on that. I should have been the lead on that biker thing."

"Because?"

"I'm the best investigator you have."

"Are you?"

"Well, yes."

Remember I told you about Bobby's stare? He unleashed its full fury at his detective; enough anyway that Shipman found herself taking a few steps backward.

"Listen to me—very carefully—because I don't want to have to repeat myself." Bobby staggered his voice, something I've only seen him do when he was very, very angry. "There is nothing—absolutely nothing—happening in this office— that is more important—than this—than finding McKenzie's shooter—nothing. I've known McKenzie since he was five years old. Since kindergarten. We went to the same schools together. We played on the same teams together. We cried together when his mother died. We cried together when his father died. He is my best friend. More than that. He is my brother. He is my wife's brother. He was best man at my wedding. I was best man at his. My daughters are his heirs. Deputy Chief Hodapp said I shouldn't—investigate—this crime—myself. He said that I might allow my emotions—to cloud—my judgment. He said it would be better if I let one of my people take lead. He was right. Given that, you tell me, Jean, who should I have given this case to? Who should I send—to find—my friend's shooter? Who would you send?"

"I'm sorry," Shipman said.

"You didn't answer—my question. Who—should—I— send?"

"Your best investigator."

"Do you want off this case, Jean?"

"No, sir, I do not."

"Do you have anything else to tell me?"

"I'm developing leads."

"I'm very pleased to hear that."

Shipman moved toward the door, thought better of it, and turned back.

"Commander," she said. "Bobby."

"Yes, Jean?"

"About one of those leads, I suppose now would be as good a time to go as any. Try to beat the worst of the rush-hour traffic."

"Go where?"

"Northfield."

ELEVEN

Shipman's first thought was that the GPS got it wrong. Instead of leading to the City of Northfield Police Department, it had somehow directed her instead to an elementary school that looked as if it had been built yesterday. The walls were a mixture of brown, tan, and red decorative bricks and it had more windows than you'd think the law would allow. She might have driven past it except for the U.S. and Minnesota State flags flying near the entrance and the parking lot on the side that contained a single black-and-white Ford sedan with a push bar attached to the front bumper, a light bar mounted on the roof, and the words "Northfield Police" printed in capital letters on the side.

She parked her unmarked car and made her way to the front door which was mostly glass and Shipman wondered if anybody working in law enforcement down there had ever worried about their safety. There was a large rubber mat in front of the door with the words "Northfield Police" printed inside a blue outline that resembled a badge. Shipman refused to wipe her feet on the badge, instead tiptoeing around the mat until she reached the door and opened it.

Inside the foyer she encountered a lot of forms and pamphlets stacked on shelves fixed to the wall as well as a box where citizens were encouraged to dispose of their unneeded prescription medications, illegal drugs, and drug paraphernalia, no questions asked. Shipman was tempted to look inside to see if the program had worked even a little bit but decided against it for fear that it would only confirm her already rampant cynicism.

She opened the glass door that led inside the building and found an information window, only there was no one sitting behind it. Nor was there any noise that she could hear suggesting that people actually worked there.

"Hello," she said in a loud voice.

"Hello," a voice answered.

A door opened and an officer stepped into the corridor. He was wearing a black uniform that made his gold badge seem that much brighter. There was a five-pointed star in the center of the badge and a full-color image of the Minnesota State flag in the center of the star.

"Sorry there was no one here to greet you," he said. "The building is usually closed this time of day. I kept the door open for you. Detective Shipman?"

"Yes."

Shipman dove into the pocket of her blazer for her ID and gave him a look at it. The officer didn't seem to care if she had one or not. Instead, he smiled at her as if she were his long-lost cousin from Nova Scotia.

"I'm Kyle Cordova," he said.

He offered his hand and Shipman shook it. She noted that he didn't try to overpower her with his grip like most of the men she met while on duty. She also noted that he was two inches taller than she was and at least a decade younger.

"Thank you for agreeing to meet with me, Officer," Shipman said.

"The pleasure is entirely mine, I assure you. Please, call me Kyle. We're all friends here, aren't we? The thin blue line and all that?"

The officer kept smiling at Shipman as if he actually meant it and Shipman wondered if it was a small-town thing, a male officer acting so graciously toward a female officer—although twenty thousand people lived in Northfield and it was only forty minutes from the Cities. Could he actually be a nice guy?

"Call me Jean," she said.

It was an unusual gesture on Shipman's part, telling a man, any man, to use her first name and for a moment she wondered why she had done it.

"I must say, you're not what I expected," Cordova said.

"What did you expect?"

"Someone older."

"Sorry to disappoint."

"Did I say I was disappointed?"

He smiled some more and Shipman thought, Okay not a small-town thing. It's universal. Boy meets girl.

"Here's the deal," Cordova said. "Your Commander Dunston called my chief of police, who called the deputy chief, who called my sergeant, who called me, probably because my name is at the bottom of the roster. We have twenty-three officers in the NPD including four investigators and an evidence technician. I'm the newest hire. I was told that you wanted to interview a student over at Carleton. I was told to escort you there and assist you in any way you require, being how the Northfield Police Department is always happy to help our colleagues from other jurisdictions."

"I'm sorry you got the duty," Shipman said.

"Not at all. I'm happy to do it, especially now that I've seen you."

"Excuse me?"

"You're gorgeous."

"You're way out of line, Officer," Shipman said. "That is a highly inappropriate and unprofessional thing to say to me."

"Yet true, nonetheless. Should we be off then?" Cordova held his arm out as if he was escorting her to the prom. "And it's Kyle, remember?"

Shipman hesitated for a moment before hooking her arm around the officer's.

"Kyle," she said. "I can see that you and I are going to get along just fine."

Carleton College was only two-point-three miles from the Northfield police station. Apparently everything in town was only two-point-three miles from the police station including Officer Cordova's favorite bar where he said he would be delighted to buy Shipman a drink before she headed back to St. Paul.

"Technically, I'm off duty," he said.

"Once I've finished this interview, I will be, too."

"Perhaps we could start our own joint task force."

Shipman liked that Cordova was flirting with her. She had always received her fair share of attention from men *before* they knew what she did for a living, but not so much afterward. Being a cop, Cordova understood at least some of what she experienced day to day, which she considered a good thing. On the other hand, none of her previous relationships with police officers had worked out and that, plus the forty-five miles and ten years that separated them, made a relationship problematic at best. Still . . .

Concentrate, she told herself. Stay focused.

While she might have been resentful before, Shipman was now desperate to solve my case. She wanted to please Bobby. While driving down to Northfield she imagined how impressed or at least grateful he would be. It would also allow her to one-up her colleagues in Major Crimes—who's the best investigator; the one Bobby trusted the most? Not to mention, it would give her something to lord over me until the day one of us died. She wasn't going to let some young cop screw that up for her, she didn't care how damn cute he might be.

Seven minutes after they started, Cordova parked his patrol car illegally and led Shipman to a building called the Hoppin House, which was an actual house complete with porch and fireplace. That's where the Carleton College campus security force was located.

Cordova knocked on the front door and opened it as if he had been expected, and held the door open for Shipman to pass through. As she did, a large man dressed in a white uniform shirt with a patch on his right shoulder and a microphone attached to his left circled a cluttered desk and approached her with his hand outstretched.

"Chad Volkert," he said.

"Detective Jean Shipman, St. Paul PD."

She reached into her pocket, yet Volkert didn't seem to care if she had an ID any more than Cordova had.

"How may I help you?" he asked.

Cordova answered for her—"She's here to interview a student." When he saw the look in Shipman's eyes, however, he folded his hands over his belt buckle and stood at attention.

"I apologize," he said. "I overstepped."

Shipman hadn't heard a lot of apologies coming from men, either, and quickly accepted his.

"It's okay, Kyle." She used his first name to prove there were no hard feelings. To Volkert, she said "I would like to speak to a student, an English major named Elliot Sohm. S-O-H-M. Female. Age twenty. But understand, gentlemen. The young lady is not wanted for anything. There will be no arrests. I wish merely to question her concerning a matter that occurred recently in St. Paul of which she may—or may not—have personal knowledge. So, let's not embarrass the kid in front of her classmates, okay? I don't want to summon her. I don't want her escorted across campus by one of your white shirts."

"That's considerate of you," Volkert said.

Considerate hell, Shipman told herself. I want the kid to think I'm on her side until I'm not on her side.

Out loud, she said "Tell me, Mr. Volkert, how I can interview Elliot Sohm without the entire student body knowing about it?"

Volkert went to his computer and typed for about fifteen seconds, used his mouse, and typed some more. When he finished, he said, "Ms. Sohm is being housed in Burton Hall." He glanced at his watch. "Most students are probably still at dinner. They could be eating at any one of three locations, Burton Dining Hall, East Dining Hall, and Sayles Hill Café, but Sayles has a grab-and-go menu after lunch. Think fancy takeout. That leaves Burton and East. Burton is closest. We could find her there, walk up and say 'Hi' like we're old friends."

"We?" Shipman said. "The three of us would look like a posse."

Volkert gave it a few moments thought.

"Students are used to seeing security wandering through the residences, academic buildings, the Bald Spot, everywhere on campus," he said. "We want them to be used to seeing us. It would not cause concern for any of them to see me doing a walk-through in the dining halls. You're not in uniform. If you were to enter a few minutes behind me, I doubt anyone would even notice."

"Thank you."

"Do you know Ms. Sohm?"

"From a distance. We've never met."

Volkert gestured at his computer. There was pic on the screen of a pretty girl with short blond hair, round face, bright eyes, easy smile, and dimples. Shipman studied it for a moment.

"Okay," she said.

She and Volkert spun toward Officer Cordova.

"Should I wait here?" he asked.

"You are my ride," Shipman said.

Theresa Deese had made fettuccine alfredo with grilled chicken that everyone in her family said was as good as if not better than what they could find at Olive Garden. She never told them that the recipe actually came from the restaurant; she found it online.

She picked at the meal, though, while Deese dug in as if he hadn't eaten in three days. You might have thought it would be the other way around.

"I can't imagine what you're going through," T said.

"My first thought was that this was a huge mistake," Deese said. "I thought that they must have mixed up my results with someone else's. Once I was convinced that they were accurate . . . It felt as though the foundation on which I had built my life had been pulled out from under me, you know? I was wobbling for a while. At the same time, I was afraid to tell anyone. Not you. Not even Barb. It took a while to regain my balance. Regain my balance—like I have. I haven't. Not really.

At least I'm not angry anymore. I became so angry that I had been lied to by the people I love the most and then I became sad and then—I had taken it for granted my whole life that when I looked into the mirror I was seeing not just myself but my whole family. Now I look and I wonder where did that other half come from?"

"It doesn't change anything with me, you know that don't you?" T said. "You're my brother and I love you whether you're a half, three-quarters, one-quarter, an eighth . . ."

"Thank you, T. You'll never know how much that means to me."

"You're not going to start crying again, are you?"

"No."

"All right then."

"About the business; about our inheritance . . ." Deese said.

"In Minnesota, an individual has a full year to challenge a will or make a claim on an estate after a person dies," T said. "A judge might waive the statute of limitations in the case of fraud, only there wasn't any fraud, was there? We both believed what we believed . . ."

"You looked all this up?"

"Of course I did. Didn't you?"

"No."

"Dad would be so fucking disappointed in you. I mean, that was careless, David."

"If you want to contest Dad's will . . ."

"I'm not going to contest the will, you jerk. I just wanted to know how things worked in case papers needed to be signed or something. Besides, I really like what you're doing with the business. You're making me a helluva lot more money than I'm getting in alimony, so . . ."

"T . . ."

"What?"

"I love you."

"Oh, shut up."

Only now it was T's eyes that welled with tears.

"What are you going to do about this, anyway?" she asked.

"Nothing. I mean, what—I'm going to announce to the family that our mother cheated on our father? That she was . . . This is our mother we're talking about. The kindest, most considerate, most loving, most, most . . ."

"She was a woman like any other woman. Sometimes mistakes are made."

"Don't tell me that I'm a mistake."

"That's not what I meant."

"I know, I know. But, T, what am I going to do? Call her out two years after she died? How is that going to make anything better?"

"Most of the family would be very angry if you did."

"You think?"

"I won't, though. I promise I'm good with whatever you decide."

"Right now I'm thinking that we keep it a deep, dark secret. Just you, me, and Barbara."

"Until someone else in the family decides to play DNA detective."

"Cross that bridge when we get to it, I guess. Honestly, T, I wish I had never opened that box, Pandora's box. I blame you."

T snorted as she laughed.

"Yeah," she said. "I thought it would be fun. Important, even, the idea of being able to trace our family tree. The DNA company tells you that you may learn unexpected things about yourself and your family and that you can't unlearn them, except it's all in the small print. They should have warnings like they do on packs of cigarettes—the surgeon general has determined that DNA research can screw up your life."

"There's no such thing as privacy anymore," Deese said. "No such thing as keeping secrets. Everything is available to everyone who knows how to look. In twenty years, fifteen, hell, in ten years privacy won't even be a word that we use anymore. It'll become archaic, like dirigible and man-at-arms and political courage."

"I wonder why Mom did what she did? Was she swept off her feet by some handsome gallant—how's that for an archaic word? Was she angry at Dad? Was she drunk? Did someone take advantage of her? That's a possibility, I guess. David, have you given much thought to your—I was going to say father. Birth father, I guess. Who he was, what he did; if he's still alive?"

"I have. I'd like to know. I'm not sure if I'd do anything with the information once I have it, though. I haven't decided if I want to reach out to him or his family. I asked a friend to look into it for me, a kind of freelance detective I play hockey with. I don't know if he's learned anything yet. Turns out someone shot him last night."

"You're kidding."

"I don't know if it had anything to do with me or not. There's a cop at the St. Paul police station, someone else I play hockey with. I might've mentioned him. Bobby Dunston?"

T shook her head.

"He said he'd let me know once they have it all figured out. The thing with McKenzie, though; he's always involved in something."

They found Elliot Sohm at East Hall, which as the name suggested was located on the eastern side of the campus on the ground floor of the Language and Dining Center; its upper floors hosting the majority of the language courses offered at

Carleton. They had arrived just in time. Burton Hall, with its more formal dining-room vibe, continued serving meals until eight P.M. However, East Hall, which looked and sounded like a cafeteria, stopped serving at seven P.M. and most of the students had already departed when Volkert and Shipman arrived.

Shipman recognized Elliot immediately, only not from the video. She recognized her from the image on Volkert's computer screen. The young woman was seated at a square table facing a floor-to-ceiling window near the beverage station with a fellow student. The student was shoving books into a backpack. Elliot was playing with her cell phone. Volkert found a perch near the entrance where he could see but not hear the conversation. Shipman approached the table.

"Elliot," she said.

The woman looked up from her phone, a startled expression on her young face.

No, absolutely not the woman captured on the security cameras at McKenzie's condo, Shipman told herself.

"May I sit down?" she asked.

Shipman pulled out a chair and sat before either of the students could respond.

"I'd like to ask you a few questions if it's not inconvenient," she said.

The two women glanced at each other and back at Shipman.

"Who are you?" the fellow student asked.

Shipman studied her only for a moment. The long auburn hair worn in a ponytail gave her away.

"My name is Jean Shipman." She reached into her pocket and produced the thin wallet that carried her badge and ID. "I'm a homicide detective with the St. Paul Police Department."

Elliot gasped at the word "homicide" which was exactly why Shipman had used it. She slid the wallet across the table toward the young woman.

"I'm also a friend of McKenzie's," she said. "You both know McKenzie, don't you?"

Elliot opened the wallet cautiously. Unlike Officer Cordova and the security guard, she seemed intensely interested in what she found inside. She stared at it for a moment and pushed the wallet over to her friend. Her friend studied the contents and closed the wallet.

"What do you want?" she asked.

"I'd like to speak to Elliot privately," Shipman answered.

"No." Elliot seized her friend's hand and squeezed tight. "I don't want her to leave."

"I'm not going anywhere." The friend glared at Shipman defiantly. "I'm staying."

"That's fine." Shipman deliberately gave her voice a conspiratorial tone. "Elliot, where were you last night at . . ."

"Wait." The friend had lowered her voice, too, and leaned in. After all, they were three women sharing secrets. "Wait a minute. Elliot doesn't need to answer any questions without a lawyer present. She doesn't have to answer any questions at all."

"Don't be so melodramatic, Emma," Shipman said. "You are Emma King, aren't you?"

The two friends glanced at each other some more.

"Emma and Ellie forever, am I right? Listen . . ." Shipman sought Elliot's eyes and held on to them. "I could have had the Northfield Police Department drag you out of class, shove you into the back of a patrol car, and drive you to the St. Paul Police Department where I would have interviewed you beneath a single lightbulb inside a bare room about the size of a closet. Or after I arrived here, I could have had one of the campus security guards escort you across the campus to Hoppin House. I didn't do that because I didn't want to embarrass you in front of your classmates. I just want to ask a few questions and then I'll be on my way."

Shipman shifted her gaze to Emma.

"The fact that you're talking about hiring lawyers before you even know what those questions are makes me wonder," she said.

"We're sorry." Elliot averted her eyes like a nun listening to a smutty story. "It's just that we've never been questioned by the police before. It's kinda scary."

"I get that a lot."

Shipman didn't admit that it was one of her favorite things, frightening the unsuspecting.

"You said you were a friend of McKenzie's?" Emma asked.

"Yes. The man you met two days ago at CakeWalk."

"You know about that?"

"Was it supposed to be a secret?"

"No. Not a secret. Just . . ."

"Private?"

"Yes."

"What is this about?" Elliot asked.

"You don't know?" Shipman said.

Elliot glanced at her friend again and slowly shook her head.

"Where were you at eight thirty last night?"

"Here." Emma was too quick to respond, Shipman thought. "We were right here."

"In this exact spot?"

"Well, no, but . . ."

"Burton Hall," Elliot said. "We were in our dorm room."

"Doing what?"

"Studying," Emma said.

"Eating," Elliot said.

"That's right. I had a teriyaki turkey burger with grilled pineapple and onions."

"I had eggplant parmesan with mushroom risotto. We bought it at Sayles Hill Café."

Shipman told herself that the food had changed since she went to college.

"When did you buy your meals?" she asked aloud.

"I don't know," Emma said. "It was late. Eight?"

"Did you pay cash?"

"No," Elliot said. "We have what they call a OneCard. It's like a debit card except that it also allows you to enter buildings and stuff. You put the money for your meal plan on the card and then when you go to eat you order what you want and swipe the card."

"There should be a record of what you bought and when you bought it then," Shipman said.

"So you can check." Emma seemed relieved that there was a way to verify her alibi. "That would prove that we were here, right?"

"It would prove that someone used your card. Never mind that. Where were you at six P.M.?"

"Last night? Here," Elliot said. "In Burton. Studying. We have midterms this week."

"I'm going to ask you that question again, later," Shipman said. "But first—you're wondering what this was about. Someone shot McKenzie in the back at approximately eight thirty P.M. last night outside of a club in St. Paul called RT's Basement."

Elliot was looking at Emma when she said, "Oh my God."

"What happened?" Emma asked. "Is McKenzie all right?"

"He's in a coma at Regions Hospital," Shipman said.

"He didn't die?"

"I'm told that he'll recover."

"Thank God."

"Why thank God?"

Emma hesitated before saying, "He seemed like a nice man."

"Emma," Elliot said.

Emma rested a hand on her hand.

"It'll be all right," she said.

"Will it?" Shipman asked.

"You said McKenzie will recover."

"What if he doesn't? Besides, there's still the small matter of who shot him in the first place. There's the matter of who lured him to RT's Basement so he could be shot. Have you been to RT's?"

"I've never heard of it," Emma said.

Shipman turned her eyes on Elliot who merely shook her head.

"What does that have to do with us?" Emma asked.

"With you, I don't know. With her . . ." Shipman gestured at Elliot.

The young woman began to tremble and Shipman was surprised that she actually felt sorry for her. She didn't know why. She never felt sorry for suspects, especially rich college kids. It had taken Shipman years to pay off her student loans.

"Where were you at six P.M. last night?" Shipman repeated.

Elliot shook her head some more only this time the movement was so slight that you might not have noticed unless you were watching closely.

"What does that mean?" Shipman asked. "You don't know or you refuse to answer?"

Elliot shook her head again.

"See, McKenzie received a message at six P.M. It was delivered to the security desk in the building where McKenzie lived. A few minutes later, McKenzie left the building. A couple of hours after that, McKenzie was shot."

Elliot kept shaking her head, only now Shipman was sure that it was just part of her overall trembling.

"The reason I'm here is that I have witnesses who claim that the message was delivered by a pretty blonde who said her name was Elliot."

Elliot covered her mouth with both hands and turned toward her friend. Emma gave her nothing, though.

Again, Shipman felt a pang of guilt. She had lied to the young women, or at least hadn't told them the entire truth; that the video would seem to prove Elliot's innocence. She had wanted to see how they responded, though. To be honest, I might have done the same thing.

"Tell me about this, Elliot," Shipman said.

"I can't," Elliot said.

"Convince me that you had nothing to do with my friend getting shot."

My friend, Shipman thought. Where did that come from?

"I can't," Elliot repeated.

"Leave her alone," Emma said.

"Ladies, think about this," Shipman said. "Think about how much trouble you're in, Elliot." Shipman gestured at Emma. "You, too, if you're covering for her."

Neither of them had anything to say.

"You have the opportunity to do yourself some good. I'd wish you'd take it."

They didn't have anything to say to that, either.

"Elliot," Shipman said. "Elliot, look at me. Sometime tomorrow I'm going to take my witness statements to a judge. The next time you see me, I'll have an arrest warrant in my pocket. I won't be asking you questions; I won't be asking to hear your side of the story. Instead, I'll be telling you that you have the right to remain silent and that anything you say can and will be held against you in a court of law. I'll wind a pair of stainless steel handcuffs around your wrists and lock you in the back of a patrol car and transport you to St. Paul where I will turn you over to the county attorney for prosecution."

Elliot began to weep. Emma pulled her close enough so that she could rest her head on Emma's chest.

"Stop it," she said.

"I can't even imagine what might happen to a pretty little thing like you in prison."

"You bitch," Emma said.

"You have no idea," Shipman said. "Elliot." Shipman softened her voice. "I'm pretty sure that you didn't shoot McKenzie. I'm pretty sure you were in your dorm room eating your eggplant whatever when the shooting took place just like your cousin says. I'll check to make sure, yet for now I believe it. I also believe that you're not the one who delivered the message that lured him into an ambush. I believe someone used your name."

Elliot's and Emma's heads snapped toward her as if they were both surprised by Shipman's admission.

"But, Elliot, Emma, I think you both know who did shoot McKenzie. At least you know who delivered the message that set him up. You know who is now setting you up."

Elliot and Emma continued to hold each other, yet said nothing.

"I've seen this so many times," Shipman said. "Women, especially young women, who are so desperate to protect someone they love, usually some guy, that they end up taking the fall for a crime they didn't even commit. Most aren't even aware that they're being used until it's too late. Don't be like that. Don't sacrifice yourselves out of loyalty to someone who doesn't deserve it. I'm begging you. Don't throw your lives away. Elliot?"

The young women gave her nothing.

"Have it your way," Shipman said.

She stood up. The young women watched her do it as if they were afraid of what she might do next. Shipman swept her wallet off the table and put it back into her pocket. From her pocket she withdrew two business cards and set one on the table in front of Elliot and then Emma.

"In case you come to your senses before it's too late," she said.

Shipman spun around and moved toward the exit. Volkert rose to intercept her and they both walked out of the Language Center and made their way back toward the Hoppin House. They didn't speak until they reached the house. Volkert held the door open for her.

"How did it go?" he asked.

"Could have been better," Shipman said.

TWELVE

Jenness Crawford stepped up to the high table in the back of the club where Nina was sitting on an equally high stool, careful not to block her view of the stage. Nina glanced at her briefly before returning her gaze to the Southside Aces, a traditional New Orleans jazz band that was just about to make the jump on "Just a Closer Walk with Thee" from its slow and lovely start to its fast and hot finish.

"You have that look on your face," she said.

"What look?" Jenness asked.

"The one that says, 'Nina, you're not going to like this.'"

"Remember that guy you punched?"

"Vividly."

The palm and knuckles of her hand and lower wrist were wrapped in an Ace bandage. Nina caressed them almost unconsciously. The physician at the urgent care clinic who examined her X-rays said her hand and wrist would be fine in a day or two but because of the way they ached she didn't believe him.

"I think he's back," Jenness said.

"Are you sure?"

"No, but there's a guy sitting at the bar who was watching carefully as you climbed the stairs to the performance hall and who keeps glancing at the staircase as if he's waiting for you to climb back down. Should I call the police? Your friend Commander Dunston?"

"Yes. No. Wait."

Nina took a deep breath and tilted her head to look up at the ceiling with the exhale. She tried to remember a time when her life wasn't rocked by chaos. There must have been a year, a month, a week, only she couldn't think of one even before she had met me.

"I'd say that this has been the worst day of my life except it's not," Nina said. "There are stories I could tell you about my childhood that would bring bitter tears to your eyes. My ups and downs with McKenzie"—she chuckled at the words—"since mostly they've been way up, I shouldn't whine so much. All right, let's take a look."

She and Jenness moved to the staircase, careful not to disturb their customers. They descended the stairs side by side until they reached the crowded lounge that made up Rickie's ground floor.

"He's sitting over there," Jenness said.

"I see him."

He was not the man who had threatened Nina earlier, although he looked a lot like him, tall, and wearing slacks, shirt, and blazer that reminded her of a uniform, except—no tie. He was sitting at the corner of the bar and nursing a tap beer.

Nina waved her manager away and walked close enough past the man to brush his shoulder. He didn't so much as glance at her. She moved to the business side of the bar, this time passing directly in front of him. Again, he acted as if he hadn't noticed. To Nina, this was a dead giveaway. She had explained it to me once at a black-tie gala about a year after we started seeing each other.

"At the risk of sounding even more conceited than I am, I expect to be watched," she told me. "Are you telling me you don't ogle pretty girls when they walk by? Don't lie, McKenzie. I've seen you do it. I've even seen you do it when you were out with me."

"I didn't think women noticed," I said.

"Of course we notice. You guys are so obvious. Besides, a woman—we can feel it. It's almost instinctual. We don't have to look around for it. We just know."

The fact that the man sitting at the bar hadn't even glanced at her told Nina that Jenness had been correct about him. He was there for her. The question that nagged her—was he a friend or foe? Her instincts said foe, except when she told Bobby about the man who had threatened her earlier that day, he said, "I'll take care of it," and now she wondered. Did he take care of it?

Nina found Jenness and told her what she wanted. Afterward, she poured a tap beer into a tall glass, moved to the corner of the bar, and set the glass in front of the man who sat there.

"I didn't order this," he said.

Nina leaned in close. If you didn't know any better, you'd think she was making a pass at him.

"See the woman standing over there?" Nina gestured at Jenness. "She has a cell phone in her hand. If I so much as glance at her she'll call the police."

"What?"

"You're either a guy who's having a very bad day just like me in which case I'll be so embarrassed I'll probably give you a lifetime pass to the music upstairs. Or you're here to make my day even worse. Or, let's hope, you're here to make my day better. Which is it?"

He rotated the glass in front of him one quarter turn at a time.

"How did you make me?" he asked.

"I walk by and a guy doesn't so much as glance my way, it makes me nervous. Makes me think I'm losing my youthful good looks."

The man chuckled.

"I find that hard to believe," he said.

"You haven't answered my question."

"Schroeder is going to be so pissed off at me."

Nina exhaled. Up until then she wasn't even aware that she had been holding her breath.

"Show me," she said.

The man reached into his pocket.

Nina raised her hand.

The man pulled out a wallet and opened it. On one side was an ID card identifying him as a detective working for Schroeder Private Investigations and on the other was a gaudy gold badge.

Nina lowered her hand.

"Schroeder could have told me," she said.

"He said that you wouldn't want us here."

"Normally, I wouldn't. You said us?"

"I have two partners."

"Where?"

The detective pointed out a couple sitting at a table.

"I hadn't noticed," she said.

"So I'm the only one who screwed up?"

"Enjoy your beer. You and your partners enjoy whatever you want, on the house."

"Thank you."

"I'll be leaving soon to go to the hospital. Regions Hospital. Okay?"

"Okay."

Nina squeezed the detective's hand as if they were old friends.

"If you're concerned about getting into trouble with your boss, we can pretend that I don't know that you're here."

"I'd appreciate it."

"But I'm glad that you're here."

Herzog held the door open while Chopper wheeled himself inside RT's Basement. The hip-hop artists working the stage had just finished their set and there was a lot of commotion in the club, some patrons heading for the restrooms and others for the door and still others lining up at the bar. A square table in the center of the room opened up and Chopper rolled himself toward it while its previous occupants flowed around him. Herzog pulled one of the now empty chairs out of the way and Chopper slid into the vacant spot. Herzog sat next to him and pushed the glasses and bottles left by the previous tenants to the far side of the table.

"Place is bustling," he said.

"More white customers than you'd expect, don't ya think?"

"Does look integrated. Wonder how many of 'em be customers of Jamal."

A young black woman arrived at the table as if she had been waiting for them and began loading her tray with the used bottles and glasses.

"What you drinking?" she asked.

"What do you have on tap?" Chopper asked.

The woman closed her eyes and listed eight brands from memory in alphabetic order.

"Bud's fine," Chopper said.

The woman pointed at Herzog.

"Jim Beam neat," he said.

"You're Herzog, aren't you," the woman said.

"Could be."

"If he's Chopper then you need to be Herzog. RT, he's the owner . . ."

"We've met."

"He said to tell him if you came in."

"Was he expecting us?" Chopper said.

"I dunno. I guess. Be right back."

Herzog's eyes followed the woman to the waitress station where she had to line up behind two other waitresses before she could place their order. RT wasn't behind the bar; a tall, thin African-American poured the beer and Jim Beam. He placed the drinks on the woman's tray where she had abandoned it before stepping through the door that Herzog knew led to RT's office. She emerged a moment later, retrieved the tray, and brought it back to the square table where she served the drinks.

"What did he say?" Herzog asked.

"What?"

"When you told RT that we were here."

"He said he'd be right out."

"Good."

The woman left the table to work the rest of the bar. Chopper sipped his beer.

"How can you drink that shit?" Herzog asked him.

"Did you hear the woman say Lift Bridge or Surly or Bent Paddle or any other decent craft beer when she recited her list?"

"No, but . . ."

RT appeared at the table, interrupting his thought.

"Knew you'd be back," he said.

"We have more questions," Chopper said.

"Yeah, Jamal told me."

"Mr. Brown, he broke his promise."

RT took a seat.

"He owes me a lot more than he owes you," he said. "'Sides, Jamal mighta broke his promise, but he didn't lie. Everything he said to you was the truth. I gotta nice side hustle here lettin' certain parties rent my back space goin' to waste anyway, so you now know why I don't want no po-lice fuckin' around. Don't want you fuckin' around, either. I know you. Everyone in the Cities know you, 'specially after what happened to the Dragons last year, so I'm willin' to step back some. Comes a time, though, when a man's gotta protect his own, know what I'm sayin'?"

"You're sayin' we should forget that our friend is lying in the hospital with a bullet in his back," Herzog said.

"I's sorry 'bout your friend. But one thing ain't got nothin' to do with the other."

"Somebody lured McKenzie here to shoot him," Chopper said.

"Look 'round. Plenty of white folk might have a grudge against your friend. Or maybe an Oxy junkie got spooked seeing a white man in an expensive sports jacket looking out of place, thinking he's po-lice. Don't mean it's got anything to do what's going on in my back room."

"We don't know that," Herzog said.

"What more you want me to do? You got the video. You know everything I know."

"Do you have cameras in your back room?" Chopper asked.

"Your friend wasn't shot in the back room and no I don't, fuck, man."

"We could ask questions of your clientele; go table to table."

"If it was just me I wouldn't give a shit. Ask away. But . . ."

"But?"

"Some of 'em ain't my customers so much as my . . ."

"Partner's?"

"He ain't my partner. His business ain't my business. Tenant, let's say. Lodger. Look. What if I put you and my tenant together? Don't know what that would get you, but maybe you can figure it out without disrupting business."

"Business being the main thing," Herzog said.

"Isn't it always?"

"All right, see what you can do," Chopper said. "Long as you set the meeting someplace we can get a decent beer."

Shipman agreed to have a drink with Kyle Cordova because she thought she needed one. They were both seated in the back of a basement pub called the Contented Cow as far away from the stage as they could get even though Shipman liked the acoustic music the Jugsluggers played. Cordova had slipped a windbreaker over his uniform, yet it didn't provide much camouflage. The bar's other patrons still glanced cautiously at them.

He was sipping tap beer; Shipman was drinking vodka. Cordova was flirting hard but she was too deep in thought for him to get much traction out of it.

"Tough case?" he asked.

"I can't discuss it."

"I understand. It must be fun, though."

"Fun?"

"You get to work a lot of stuff in the Cities that we just don't get down here in Northfield. I think the last murder we had was when Jesse James rode into town."

"Yeah, lots of fun. Those girls—they're protecting someone. Take them up to St. Paul for some intense Q and A; I'd probably scare it out of them. Unless they lawyer up. Their family has major connections. No, it's better to leave them down here. Right now they're freaking out. Probably making phone calls.

Demanding explanations. What is it that people say—this ain't my first rodeo? Well, it's their first and they're scared to death. Especially Elliot. So, I'll sit back for a while and wait to see which way they jump. They have my number. If they call, great. If someone else calls, that might even be better. In any case, I can always scoop them up later." Shipman chuckled. "But like I said, I can't discuss it."

Cordova smiled at her. Shipman liked the smile. She liked the way he lightly brushed one finger over the knuckles of her left hand.

"No rings," he said.

"That's very observant of you."

"Perhaps I should be a detective."

"Let's see if you qualify. College degree?"

"Magna cum laude," Cordova said.

"Police academy?"

"Top of my class."

"Excellent physical and mental health; good stamina?"

Cordova curled his arms like a professional wrestler and kissed both biceps.

"Well then it's just a matter of gaining work experience, building a resume; scoring high on a few exams," Shipman said.

"That's where I could use some help. If only I had a mentor to guide me."

"Why do so many women do so many things that aren't necessarily in their best interests?"

"You're asking me?"

"No. I already know the answer. Kyle, I'm in a mood."

"What does that mean?"

"I want you to take me back to the NPD so I can retrieve my car."

Cordova's smile went away.

"Then I want you to lead me to your place."

And the smile returned.

"Try not to talk too much," Shipman said.

The staff at the SICU in Regions Hospital seemed more concerned about the health and well-being of a man who was shot in the head on the Green Line than they were with me, which Nina found irritating. After all, she reasoned, I was there first.

She still wasn't allowed to enter the room where they were keeping me in the coma. Instead, she leaned her forehead against the glass wall and watched the multicolored numbers and wavy lines on the monitor above me. After a few moments, she felt a hand on her shoulder. The hand made her flinch and spin around abruptly.

"Sorry," Dr. Lillian Linder said.

"Good evening," Nina said.

"Closer to good morning."

Nina glanced at her watch.

"Is it?" she asked.

"Have you been here long?"

"Just a few minutes."

Lilly noticed Nina's swollen knuckles and the Ace bandage wrapped around her hand and wrist.

"What happened?" she asked.

"I hit something hard."

"I know that waiting is difficult, frustrating, especially when you're waiting for news about someone you care desperately about . . ."

"Lilly, I didn't punch a wall or do anything stupid like that because I was upset. I hit a man in the face when he called me a bitch."

"That's different then."

"You think so?"

"There are a lot of men I want to hit in the face, too. Nina, McKenzie's going to be fine. The swelling's down; his vitals are strong."

"Strong enough to bring him out of the coma?"

"Maybe tomorrow."

"Maybe?"

"It's only been one day since he was shot."

"Seems longer."

"Give it time," Lilly said. "Time is our friend. That isn't always true in medicine, yet it is in this case."

"You say that . . ."

"It's true."

"I believe you. It's just . . . You'd think I'd be used to this sort of thing by now."

"If McKenzie was my husband, I'd kill him."

Nina didn't know why she thought that was funny, yet she laughed just the same.

"The thing about the hours I keep," the doctor said, "I know where all the best late-night coffeehouses are. Have a cup with me?"

"No, Lilly, thank you, but I—I've been angry all day. Snapping at people. Snapping at my employees, at the friends who call to find out how McKenzie is doing; snapping at my daughter just a couple of hours ago even while I was trying to convince her that everything was going to be just fine; snapping at people who are trying to protect me, Jesus. Snapping at you this morning. Probably snapping at you again if we go out together. I'm afraid if I stop snapping I'll cry and that's not allowed."

"Why is it not allowed?"

"A deal I made with McKenzie a long time ago, a promise. I'm not allowed to cry because of him, because of something that he says or does, because of anything that might happen to him. Become angry, furious—that's acceptable. But not cry, not even tears of joy, although I've never cried tears of joy. Have you?"

"Once in a while, not often."

"Anyway, I made a promise and I always keep my promises. I guess that's the same reason why you won't promise me that McKenzie is going to walk out of here all in one piece, his brain undamaged. You say he will, except you won't promise because it's a promise you might not be able to keep."

Nina turned toward the figure lying on the bed on the other side of the glass wall. Lilly took her arm and spun her back around.

"Nina," she said. "Nina, look at me."

"What?" Nina snapped.

"I promise," Lilly said.

Nina fell into the doctor's arms and wept for all she was worth.

THIRTEEN

Detective Jean Shipman yawned. Brian, the tech from FSU, saw her do it.

"Long night?" he asked.

"It had its moments."

Shipman didn't return to the Cities until about six A.M. She showered off all remnants of Kyle Cordova, took a thirty-minute power nap, dressed in jeans, shirt, Glock, and blazer, ate a bagel with blueberry cream cheese, grabbed a Starbucks, and was sitting at her desk by eight. She sipped what was left of her coffee and studied Brian. He was younger than she was, although not nearly as young as Cordova, and smart. Shipman liked smart. Only she had been in an office romance once before and while it had been fun if not downright exciting, it had affected her work and she vowed never to allow that to happen again. Besides, she reasoned, if she wanted unencumbered and uncommitted sex, she now knew exactly where to find it.

"What?" Brian said.

"What?" Shipman repeated.

"You're staring."

"I'm just wondering what you're doing here."

Brian held up a sheet of paper.

"I put names to the telephone numbers on McKenzie's cell," he said. "As you requested."

"They have this wonderful new invention you might have heard of. It's called email."

"Yes, but then I wouldn't have been able to see your beautiful smiling face."

"As my father would say, you're cruisin' for a bruisin', Brian."

"Would you put me in handcuffs, first?"

Shipman made a gimme gesture with the fingers of her hand. Brian handed over the sheet of paper.

"I did send you an email," he said. "There's nothing like a hard copy, though, don't you think?"

"Thank you."

Brian moved around Shipman's desk so he could hover over her shoulder. There were four names on the list. Shipman recognized two of them. The others meant nothing to her. She decided to take them in order, thinking that one call might have led to another.

"Now, about that lunch." Brian spoke quietly. His soft breath tickled Shipman's neck.

Shipman's desk chair was on wheels. She pushed it back, putting space between the two of them.

"Do I need to give you a very long list of reasons why you and I are not going to happen?" she asked.

"That's today. What about tomorrow?"

"Tomorrow the list will be longer."

"*Audentes fortuna juvat.*"

"Excuse me?"

"Fortune favors the bold. I'll see you around, Detective."

Shipman watched the tech move toward the door and felt compelled to call out to him.

"Hey, Brian." He turned to look back at her, only Shipman couldn't think of what she wanted to say. "Never mind."

Brian smiled as if that was exactly what he had wanted to hear.

According to FSU, I had spoken to Justus Reinfeld on the phone for all of six minutes late in the afternoon of the day I was shot. Yet what piqued Shipman's immediate interest wasn't that his name appeared first on the list. It was the fact that I didn't call him. He had called me.

Shipman did some quick research on Reinfeld, which was a lot more than I had done. She discovered that he was what my old man would have described as a wheeler-dealer. One website labeled him an American investor and philanthropist. Another said Reinfeld was a hedge fund manager, entrepreneur, and company advisor. They both agreed that he was the proprietor of All Uppercase Investments, a venture capital fund with $3.8 billion in assets under management that specialized in investing in early-stage technology companies such as Twitter, Lyft, Netflix, Instagram, Kickstarter, and KTech. Prior to founding All Uppercase, Reinfeld had worked on mergers and acquisitions for a multinational investment bank with offices on Wall Street.

Shipman punched his number into her phone. It was answered after the fifth ring.

"Who is this?" a male voice asked.

"Mr. Reinfeld? My name is Detective Jean Shipman. I'm with the St. Paul Police Department."

"Goddammit."

"Excuse me?"

The phone went silent. At first Shipman thought Reinfeld

had hung up on her. A few moments later, however, a female voice repeated the question "Who is this?"

"Like I said, I'm Detective Jean Shipman of the St. Paul Police Department."

"How dare you call Mr. Reinfeld's private number?"

"If I might be allowed to speak with Mr. Reinfeld . . ."

"Concerning what matter?"

"I could explain that his private number was on the cell phone of a man who was shot Tuesday evening just minutes after Mr. Reinfeld called him."

"What does this have to do with Mr. Reinfeld?"

"Good question," Shipman said. "If we could arrange a time for me to speak with—"

"Absolutely not."

"It would save a lot of time and trouble."

"Mr. Reinfeld is under no legal obligation to answer your questions. However, if you wish to submit your questions in writing I will ask him if he cares to respond. Under no circumstances, however, will you be allowed to subject him to a police interrogation."

"You are?"

The voice identified herself as an attorney in the employ of AUI—that's how she identified the company.

"One of many," she said.

"We are not accusing Mr. Reinfeld of anything . . ." Shipman said.

"I should hope not."

"We merely wish to learn if he can help us investigate—"

"As I said, you may forward your questions via email."

"I understand your desire to protect Mr. Reinfeld's reputation . . ." Shipman said.

"What does that mean?"

"According to my research, he's scheduled to receive a plaque at the Ordway Center Saturday evening commemorating his many philanthropic endeavors."

"How dare you?"

"You keep asking that," Shipman said. "I'm just trying to do my job."

"By making scurrilous accusations?"

"I'm not accusing him of anything."

"You'd be happy to drag Justus Reinfeld into a police station in front of every TV camera crew and newspaper vulture that you can find, though, wouldn't you? You'd love that? Get your face on television."

"I'd be happy to speak to him under the most private conditions he'd care to arrange with you and your whole army of attorneys holding his hand."

"Outrageous."

"What I find outrageous is that neither you nor Mr. Reinfeld has bothered to ask who was shot or what condition he's in. It makes me think that you already know."

This time Shipman was sure—they hung up on her.

"Dammit," she said.

"What?"

Shipman looked up to find Bobby Dunston hovering above her desk.

"Hey, boss," she said.

"What?"

"I hit a snag. One of the people who had spoken to McKenzie on his cell just before he was shot refuses to talk to us."

"Who?"

"Justus Reinfeld."

"Where have I heard that name before?"

Shipman explained.

"He refuses to submit to an interview?" Bobby said.

"That's what his lawyers say."

"Which is his right."

"Also what his lawyers say."

Bobby thought about it for a moment.

"Perhaps we can get him to change his mind," he said. "Why don't you come into my office? You can give me a full briefing on what you have so far and then we'll make a few calls."

Nina's long, therapeutic cry and the midnight coffee she had with Dr. Linder afterward seemed to have done her good. At least, she slept comfortably all the way through what was left of the night, rousing only when her cell rang. Unfortunately, the ringtone jolted her wide awake as if it heralded the worst possible news. Her heart was beating wildly as she fumbled for the phone; the caller ID said Shelby. That didn't make her feel any better.

"What is it?" she said.

"Nina? It's Shelby. I didn't wake you, did I?"

"No, no, I was—I was startled. Sorry if I was rude . . ."

"You weren't rude."

"What is it?"

"I'm calling—do you want company? At the hospital, I mean? I know that they're planning to bring McKenzie out of his coma this morning."

"No."

"If you would rather be alone . . ."

"No, I wouldn't rather be alone. Shel, that's not what I meant. I meant—I'm still half asleep, honey . . ."

"I did wake you up. I'm so sorry."

"Hang on a sec."

Nina tossed the covers back and swung her legs off the bed. The mere act of standing seemed to bring her completely back into the real world. She left the bedroom and moved into the kitchen area, her final destination being the coffeemaker. Nina spoke as she walked.

"I spent some time with Lilly last night," she said. "She gave me a kind of tutorial on how all of this works. She said if your critically ill loved one is a straightforward admission to intensive care following elective or planned surgery or a soft admission because of some minor emergency, then your critically ill loved one should come off the respirator and out of the induced coma within twelve to seventy-two hours."

"Your critically ill loved one?" Shelby repeated.

"Sometimes Lilly speaks as if we're all sixth graders who have been held back a year."

"I've noticed that about doctors."

"I like her though."

"What else did she say?" Shelby asked.

"She said if your critically ill loved one . . ."

"Stop saying that."

"McKenzie was a more complicated admission, more unstable partly because of the damage caused by the bullet and partly because he suffered cardiac arrest during surgery. In his case, Lilly said they might keep him in a coma upwards from seventy-two hours. Possibly even a week."

"Why didn't she tell us that in the first place?"

"Because she didn't know. She still doesn't. At least not for sure."

"What does she know?"

"She was very positive, Shel. Very encouraging. She said she'd make a decision sometime this afternoon. She said she'd call this afternoon."

"All right."

"Something else."

"What?"

"She said waking up a coma patient isn't like turning on a bedroom light in the morning and telling your kid it's time to get ready for school. She said it's more like a process."

"Believe me, getting the girls ready for school is a process."

"She said McKenzie will wake up gradually once they start eliminating the drugs from his system and even when he does he'll probably be disoriented and confused."

"Why should he be different from the rest of us? What are you going to do, Nina?"

"Go to Rickie's and wait for Lilly to call. What else can I do?"

"Let me buy you lunch."

"Why don't you come to the club and I'll buy *you* lunch. That way I can introduce you to my bodyguards."

"You have bodyguards? Why?"

"Some guy came into Rickie's yesterday and threatened me."

"Wait. What? Does Bobby know this?"

"I told him and I assume he told Greg Schroeder because not long after that his guys started following me around."

"Who's Greg Schroeder?"

"A private investigator that owes McKenzie a favor."

Unlike KTech, All Uppercase Investments didn't have its own building. Instead, it occupied three of the forty-two floors of the Campbell Mithun Tower in downtown Minneapolis, named after an advertising and marketing firm that doesn't even exist anymore. Greg Schroeder took the elevator to the first of the three floors; it wouldn't stop on the next two. The doors opened to reveal an opulent reception area with comfortable furnishings and huge windows that looked out on buildings nearly as tall as the tower. In the center of the reception area was a high mahogany desk with the letters AUI artfully carved into it. Behind the desk stood two women, one brunette and one blonde, who looked as if they both could be runway models. Schroeder made his way to the desk. He noticed that there were no chairs behind it and Schroeder imagined the models strutting about all day on three-inch heels like the girls you see caressing cars at the auto show.

The women spoke first.

"Good morning," they said in unison.

"Good morning."

"How can we help you?" asked the blonde.

"I'd like to see Mr. Reinfeld," Schroeder said.

"Mr. Reinfeld doesn't accept visitors without an appointment," said the brunette. "Is there someone else who might be able to help you?"

"How do you know that I don't have an appointment?"

"He would have told us who to expect and when."

"He coordinates that closely with you?"

"We are given that privilege," the blonde said.

"During business hours," the brunette added.

"I haven't even told you my name," Schroeder said.

"Mr. Reinfeld would have told us your name . . ." the brunette said.

"If you had an appointment," the blonde said.

"Nonetheless, I'm sure he would agree to see me if you would be kind enough to inform him that I'm here."

"So many people say that who are soon briskly escorted by security out of the building. Some kicking and screaming."

"I'll take my chances."

The brunette smiled almost gleefully as if she was looking forward to watching the scenario unfold.

"What is your name?" she asked.

"Riley Muehlenhaus."

Schroeder had been standing near the windows and gazing more or less at U.S. Bank Stadium. He had attempted to locate his own office but failed because it was too close to the ground. The ding of a bell caused him to spin around. Turned out there was a second elevator that Schroeder hadn't realized was there until a wall slid open. A fiftyish-year-old man wearing Nikes, blue jeans, a white shirt with button-down collar, and a goatee that made him look like a villain in a superhero comic book stepped out. He looked around, saw nothing that interested him, and moved quickly toward the reception desk.

"Mr. Reinfeld," the brunette said.

"Where is she?" he asked.

The two models glanced at each other.

"She?" the blonde asked.

"Riley Muehlenhaus."

They both gestured at Schroeder who was making his way toward the desk.

"He's not Riley goddamn Muehlenhaus," the man said. "Didn't you at least check his ID?"

The brunette grabbed a phone, hit a button, and spoke loudly.

"Security," she said.

"Mr. Reinfeld," Schroeder said.

Reinfeld averted his gaze as if Schroeder was a particularly gruesome accident he didn't want to witness and headed back toward the hidden elevator.

Schroeder pulled his cell from his pocket, tapped a couple of links, and held it up for everyone to see and hear. The screen was filled with the image of a young woman with brown hair and a face liberally sprinkled with freckles. She was smiling when she spoke.

"Justus, I just want you to know how grateful I am that you've agreed to help my friends . . ."

Reinfeld stopped and stared.

"I am aware, of course, of the unfortunate dealings you've had with my family in the past. My grandfather was not kind to you . . ."

Two well-dressed security guards stepped off the public elevator. Another two appeared from around the corner. They both looked to the brunette for instructions. She pointed at Schroeder.

"So for you to make an effort to help the authorities—and me—discover who shot my dear friend McKenzie, that is an act of kindness and generosity that I simply cannot help but acknowledge . . ."

Reinfeld held up his hand like a traffic cop; stalling the four guards in their tracks.

"You must know how important McKenzie is to me. He literally saved my life and I would do anything for him in return . . ."

Reinfeld waved at the guards; dismissing them. They vacated the reception area without a word even as Reinfeld moved slowly forward until he was standing directly in front of Schroeder and staring at the image on the phone.

"I will be in attendance at the Ordway Saturday evening in St. Paul when you accept your award. I hope to express my gratitude to you in person. Again, Justus, thank you."

Schroeder tapped a few more icons and slipped the cell back into his pocket.

"McKenzie really did save Riley's life," he said. "Her grandfather tried to keep the story out of the papers, away from the media, because of his disdain for publicity. But then you know Mr. Muehlenhaus personally, don't you? You know the power he wields. Still, the story got out anyway, how Riley was kid-

(220)

napped and what McKenzie did to save her. You should know that Riley has been searching for ways to reward him ever since. Only McKenzie keeps blowing her off, saying that her smile and her thank-you are more than sufficient. Riley is determined, though. Were you invited to her wedding?"

"No one was invited to her wedding," Reinfeld said. "It was a very private affair."

"McKenzie was there. You've met McKenzie, if I'm not mistaken."

Reinfeld glanced over his shoulder at the models manning the reception desk. Both were pretending to be interested in something else.

"Dammit," he said.

Emma King had been unable to sleep, tossing and turning most of the night. Now she was having difficulty concentrating in class, something that rarely happened to her. She had been a terrific student her entire academic life, better than her mother even and her mother, Emma's uncles had often assured her, was the smartest person either of them had ever met. 'Course, that was then. Now . . .

Now, Emma wasn't sure where to turn. It was clear that her family could no longer be trusted. At least not about this. And Elliot, sweet, caring Elliot, the kindest person she knew, had been paralyzed by her kindness, unable to make a decision.

"We should just wait and see what happens," Elliot had said over breakfast.

Which wasn't necessarily bad advice, Emma decided. "The two most powerful warriors are patience and time," she remembered Leo Tolstoy writing in *War and Peace.*

On the other hand, Benjamin Franklin said, "You may delay, but time will not," and for the past few weeks Emma had felt as if she had been living in the top half of an hourglass; the sand slowly disappearing beneath her feet. There couldn't be more than a couple weeks of it left.

Instead of listening to the lecture, she fingered the business card that Detective Jean Shipman had given to her the evening before. Only she didn't trust the police officer, either. Shipman, Emma decided, was only interested in finding someone to lock up and that wouldn't solve her problem.

It was only after the lecture had concluded and her fellow students were filing out of the classroom that Emma decided to visit her uncle.

Schroeder was shocked at how dark Reinfeld's office was. There was an entire wall of floor-to-ceiling windows with what must have been a spectacular view of the city, except the drapes had been tightly drawn. The only lights in the large room came from a small lamp with a green shade sitting on a table near the door and three flat-screen computer monitors arranged in a semicircle on a mahogany desk shaped like a half-moon. One of the screens was devoted to the constantly updated stock prices listed on the Dow, S&P 500, Russell 2000, NASDAQ, and Euronext.

Reinfeld stood in the middle of the office and glanced around as if he wasn't sure what he was doing there. He glared at Schroeder.

"Who are you?" he asked.

Schroeder recited his name and occupation. He produced his credentials as if to prove he was telling the truth, only Reinfeld ignored them. He made his way to the large windows and opened the drapes just far enough to allow a narrow shaft of bright sunlight to divide the room in half. Reinfeld stood on one side; Schroeder on the other.

"Are you working for the police?" Reinfeld asked.

"I'm working for Ms. Muehlenhaus."

"I heard that Riley doesn't like that name; that she insists on being called Brodin-Mulally, her married name," Reinfeld said.

"She's trying to project a kinder, more caring image than her grandfather had. I wouldn't trust it, though."

"Did she tell you what her grandfather did to me?"

"No."

Reinfeld stepped into the shaft of sunshine and gazed out the window. For a moment, Schroeder thought he was going to tell him the story, only he didn't. Instead, he backed out of the light and spun to face Schroeder.

"What I tell you can't go any farther than this office," he said.

"I can't promise that."

"What can you promise?"

"Very little."

"I get that you'll report to Riley . . ."

"Yes."

"Tell her everything I say."

"Word for word."

"What about the police?" Reinfeld asked.

Schroeder lifted his hand the way he does and let it fall.

"I don't work for the police," he said.

Reinfeld nodded as if he was satisfied with the answer.

"I didn't do anything wrong," he said.

"No one says that you did."

"What exactly do you want?"

"McKenzie," Schroeder said.

"McKenzie is a . . ."

"Yes?"

"McKenzie is a friend of Riley Muehlenhaus. I didn't know that at the time."

"What do you know?"

Reinfeld told him:

He had seen it before, the bridled excitement of shareholders about to attend a meeting where they would be told how much money they were going to make—or lose. It had always reminded him of gamblers waiting for the ball to drop into the roulette wheel or the dice to stop rolling on a craps table. Normally, Reinfeld would have disregarded the meeting and what was said there. He had attended more than his share in the past and had even conducted a few himself. He knew marketing when he saw it. Except this was different. The disappearance of Charles King had disrupted his plans. He didn't know if he should accelerate them, put them on hold, discard them altogether, or dump his KTech stock and run like hell. Reinfeld had been hoping that the shareholders' meeting would help him decide.

While the other shareholders congregated near the entrances to the auditorium, anxious to get a seat near the front, Reinfeld stood off, content to remain in the back, hopefully unnoticed. While they were comparatively well-dressed, he looked as if he were preparing to clean his basement. While they seemed both surprised and delighted by the delicacies distributed by the waiters and waitresses on behalf of KTech's marketing department, he sipped what he considered to be a mediocre white wine with quiet disdain. The contrast was intentional and carefully cultivated; it gave Reinfeld a sense not so much of superiority as personal pride. He wasn't like the other shareholders after all, he told himself. He had built a multibillion-dollar investment fund. What had they done?

Except for his black sports jacket, one man who caught Reinfeld's eye seemed to have purposely dressed down almost as much as he had. Reinfeld watched him devour first a caramel and Chinese five-spice snickerdoodle and then follow it with a hazelnut chocolate mousse. He didn't have a napkin, however, and since he was holding a craft beer with his other hand, he appeared confused as to how to wipe his fingers. Reinfeld offered his paper napkin.

"Thank you," the man said. He used the napkin to wipe his mouth and clean his fingers before depositing it in a wastebasket.

"Did you enjoy the desserts?" Reinfeld asked.

"Yes, I did, and since I'm pretty sure that our dividends are paying for them, I'm thinking of hijacking the bakery truck and taking it to my house. Want in?"

Reinfeld thought that was awfully funny and nearly laughed. Instead, he stifled a smile and offered his hand.

"Justus Reinfeld."

He spoke as if he had fully expected his fellow shareholder to recognize his name. The fact that he displayed no reaction whatsoever suggested to Reinfeld that the man knew exactly who he was and was pretending not to.

"I'm McKenzie," the shareholder said. "So, you come here often?"

Reinfeld thought that was funny, too, yet again refrained from laughing.

"No," he said. "Like everyone else I'm here to see if Charles King rises miraculously from the dead like Lazarus."

"If he does, I'd sure like to chat with him."

"You and me both, brother. How many shares do you own?"

"I have about four-point-seven percent in KTech, give or take."

Like a high-stakes poker player, Reinfeld had taught himself to keep his tells in check; to not give too much of himself away, only McKenzie's answer had tripped all of the alarm bells in his head. He took a long pull of his cheap wine to hide his emotions even while telling himself that this man might actually be a brother.

"So, you've been losing money, too, since King Charles disappeared," Reinfeld said.

"Haven't you heard?" McKenzie said. "KTech's stock price has been going up. Seems someone has been acquiring shares during these troubling times. I wonder why."

Reinfeld again turned to his wineglass for support, only it was empty. He glanced around for another tray loaded with drinks, saw a waitress, waved her over, and switched his empty glass for a full one while his mind raced. Reinfeld had all but convinced himself that this McKenzie knew exactly who he was and what he was contemplating.

He took a sip of the wine.

"I own exactly four-point-seven percent of KTech stock myself," Reinfeld said.

He took another sip.

"What a coincidence," McKenzie said.

"I know three other shareholders who also control just under five percent."

"No kidding? Maybe we should start a club."

"He's parking," H. B. Sutton said.

"I don't know what that means," Detective Jean Shipman replied.

H. B.'s number had been second on the list of those captured by my cell phone the afternoon that I was shot. After briefing Bobby—he wasn't sure he approved of how Shipman handled Elliot Sohm and Emma King, by the way. He said he might have been inclined to bring Elliot in, meaning he would have questioned her in the confines of the SPPD. He thought that the surroundings alone would have impressed on her the seriousness of the situation and might have even persuaded her to be more cooperative.

"Or it could have convinced Elliot to demand her free phone call and dial D-A-D-D-Y," Shipman said. "Certainly that's what her BFF Emma would have told her to do, assuming she didn't call the cavalry herself. Who knows what that might have led to, the Kings and all that money?"

"You might be right. We'll see."

While she was pleased that Bobby was pleased with her progress, Shipman was shocked when he called Greg Schroeder and asked him if he could suggest a way to brace Justus Reinfeld. Shipman had never seen or heard of Bobby reaching out to a PI before. Schroeder said he had an idea only he couldn't share it without permission from his client. Bobby said to get back to them with whatever he learned. Schroeder said he would.

After the conversation was concluded, Bobby asked Shipman what her next move would be. She said she was going to contact H. B. Sutton, which is what brought her to H. B.'s houseboat on the Mississippi River.

Shipman had never been on a houseboat before and she felt uncomfortable, although she couldn't explain why.

"I call it the earthquake effect," H. B. said. "The idea that the deck is constantly moving beneath our feet. Some people find it very disconcerting."

"I've been on boats before and it hasn't bothered me."

"You've been on boats for only a few hours at a time, if that, usually with the sun and sky and water and the shoreline to orient you. Have you ever been inside a boat, sitting at a kitchen table and drinking coffee while unseen waves lap against the hull and make the boat bob just so?"

"I haven't."

"It takes some getting used to."

"How do you live here in the winter?"

"That's probably the most asked question I get," H. B. said. "I heat the boat with space heaters."

"Yes, but . . ."

"I have electricity."

"I get that, but . . ."

"The boat is extremely well insulated, trust me on that. I have three electric heaters including a mini-fireplace that keeps the inside nice and toasty, plus an electric blanket in case of emergencies. Also, the boat has pretty great circulation and plenty of dry heat to prevent all my stuff from getting damp and growing mold. In some boats, the temperature difference between the inside and the outside can cause condensation to form everywhere. My neighbor, because of all the damp and mold in his boat, one day he discovered that all of the suits in his closet were wrinkled from condensation on just the one side facing the hull.

"The outside—my boat is protected by bubblers, what we call these little underwater fountains that circulate the water to prevent ice from forming against the hull. That's why I don't get stuck in the ice all winter; why ice doesn't crush my hull. The worst thing, the water is shut down on the docks because the pipes would freeze. So, I have to use long hoses from pumps on land to fill my water tanks, which is a major pain and makes for very short showers. That, along with shoveling snow off the deck, is my biggest gripe. It's a small price to pay, though."

"Your home is very beautiful," Shipman said.

"Thank you."

"It just seems so isolated."

"That's why I like it."

"What does McKenzie say about it?"

"Like most people, he thinks it's a great place to visit; he just wouldn't want to live here."

"About McKenzie . . ."

That's when Shipman asked H. B. if she could remember what we talked about during the phone call I had made to her.

"McKenzie wanted to know about a hedge fund manager he met named Justus Reinfeld who owns All Uppercase Investments."

"What about him?" Shipman asked.

"He's parking."

"I don't know what that means."

"It means—according to McKenzie, Reinfeld said that he and at least three other parties each held just under five percent of KTech stock. I can think of only one reason to do that. Reinfeld is trying to steal KTech from the King family. My theory, Detective Shipman . . ."

"Call me Jean."

"Jean. Thank you. Jean, parking is a time-honored method that corporate raiders use when they wish to take over a company. In 1968, Congress passed what is known as the Williams Act. Along with the Securities Exchange Act of 1934, it demands that investors who own more than five percent of a company's stock tell the SEC how many shares they own, the source of the funds used to purchase the shares, and the reason for the acquisition. 'Course, when you give the SEC this information, you're also telling the company, and for obvious reasons raiders rarely want the company to know what they're up to. So, what some of them do, maybe most, I don't know, is hide their position in the company by transferring their shares to other parties, no one holding as much as five percent. That way neither the SEC nor the management of the company will know the true extent of their stock ownership. Then, when they're ready to make their move, they'll have the parties transfer the stock back to them, usually for a small profit, and boom. As I said, this is called parking and it's illegal."

"If it's illegal, why would Reinfeld tell McKenzie his plans?"

"He didn't tell McKenzie his plans. That's just me figuring it out. He told McKenzie that he and the three others each owned just under five percent of the stock because McKenzie told him that he had four-point-seven percent of the stock and Reinfeld thought that meant McKenzie was on his side."

"Wait. McKenzie owns four-point-seven percent of KTech stock?" Shipman asked.

"Oh hell no. Four-point-seven percent of McKenzie's net worth is in KTech. It's inappropriate for me to tell you that, privacy rules and all, but I don't think he would mind."

"Thank you, Lord. McKenzie rich is a pain in the ass. Superrich he would be insufferable."

"Actually, I've always found him to be a pretty nice guy and I don't know that many nice guys."

H. B. delivered the compliment as if she were challenging Shipman to contradict her. Instead, Shipman said, "It's complicated," and let it go at that.

"For argument's sake," she said, "let's assume that Reinfeld thought McKenzie owned four-point-seven percent of the stock and tried to enlist him in his scheme only to discover later that McKenzie didn't own four-point-seven percent of the stock . . ."

"I'd think he'd be very upset, wouldn't you, believing that he had revealed valuable insider information to some sort of corporate spy? At best, McKenzie could use the information to enrich himself. At worst, he could take it to the King family. Or the SEC. In any case, Reinfeld and his plans would be compromised."

"Not if McKenzie was dead."

"Yeah, well, there's more," H. B. said.

"More?"

"McKenzie told me that he told Reinfeld that even if they—meaning Reinfeld and McKenzie—vacuumed up all of the outstanding shares in the company, the King family would still be the majority stockholders and could squash any plans they might have. Reinfeld told McKenzie, not if one of the Kings was willing to flip."

"Flip?"

"Vote with Reinfeld and the other minority stockholders."

"Against their own people?"

"It's been done before."

"Oh, this just keeps getting better and better."

FOURTEEN

"What happened next?" Greg Schroeder asked.

Reinfeld began to pace slowly, his hands behind his back, careful not to cross the shaft of light to Schroeder's side of the office.

"We chatted about this and that," he said. "Mostly about the King family. McKenzie said that he thought the Kings were very secretive. I told him I couldn't agree or disagree. I had never met any of the Kings."

Schroeder couldn't see Reinfeld's eyes. He didn't know if they were darting back and forth or if he was blinking rapidly or if Reinfeld had closed his eyes for more than a second or two before answering. Yet the way he kept looking upward to his left as if he was accessing his imagination instead of his memory, Schroeder was convinced that he was lying. Or at least holding something back.

"It was about then that the doors to the auditorium finally opened and we followed the rest of the shareholders inside," Reinfeld said.

Reinfeld and McKenzie secured seats in the second to last row near the door, sitting side by side. The auditorium was well lit, although the stage was dark. After a few minutes, the auditorium lights dimmed and the stage lights came up just enough for the audience to see a podium off to the side and a huge screen in the back. The shareholders hushed themselves without being told to. A lone man wearing boots, jeans, and a plaid shirt stepped onto the stage and crossed over to the podium. Applause followed him, yet it seemed to be generated mostly from KTech's marketing people.

"Good afternoon," he said. "I'm Porter King, executive vice president responsible for marketing at KTech."

There was more applause, but he raised his hand to silence it.

"I appreciate that," he said. "Only none of you came here today to listen to me."

He turned and gazed at the giant screen which suddenly lit up to reveal a younger man also dressed in plaid. His face was clean-shaven and his blond hair neatly coiffed, yet his eyes had the dull sheen of a man who hadn't slept for three days. The smile on his haggard face, however, was dazzling.

"Hello, Charles," Porter said.

Loud, sustained applause followed; half of the shareholders were on their collective feet. Charles King seemed to drink it in like a man dying of thirst who suddenly stumbled upon an oasis.

After a few minutes, Porter raised his hand again to quiet the crowd.

"So what do you have to say for yourself, Charles?" he asked.

"I look like hell," Charles said. "I feel like hell. But I'm getting better."

The crowd erupted as if he had just told each shareholder that they were getting a free car and the keys were beneath their seats. Porter let it go a bit longer this time before he signaled for silence.

"As you know, Charles, there has been some speculation as to your health," he said.

"Let's put that to rest, shall we, Porter? My health sucks and has sucked for the past couple of weeks. At first, I thought it was the cupcakes my niece and her roommate had baked for me. I have since been assured by the world's finest medical minds that what I have is a particularly virulent case of the flu. The real flu, not coronavirus. I was tested. I do not have COVID-19. What I do have is a fever that becomes the chills and then the fever beats me up again. My throat is sore, my nose is runny, my muscles ache, my head throbs, and I'm exhausted, mostly from running to the bathroom every twenty minutes. Which isn't that big a deal when you think about it. I've been reliably informed that about eight percent of the population gets the flu every year. It was just my turn. The problem is that we live in a particularly media-conscious world, both social and otherwise. Whenever anything unexpected happens, the conspiracy theorists at TMZ and *The New York Times* go nuts. If you believe what you read on Twitter, I died a week ago. Or was it yesterday? 'Course, I'm just as much to blame for this as anyone. The SEC was right. I tweet way too much."

There was some snickering at that.

"Honestly," Charles said. "If I had known the state of my health was going to cause so much concern, I would have shown up at the annual meeting last week and infected you all."

Charles leaned toward the camera and coughed twice.

"Sometimes I wish I had," he said. "I hate suffering alone."

"I, for one, am glad you didn't," Porter said.

"I'm sorry for causing you all so much concern. On the other hand, having so many people freaking out because I can't keep my lunch down is kind of cool. It makes me feel important."

"You are important," Porter said.

"Not that important. Let's address the elephant that wandered into the room when my temperature reached a hundred and one degrees, shall we? KTech isn't just me, although it's my face you see whenever you turn on Bloomberg or CNBC. We have a lot of outstanding operating managers working for this great company; you heard from a couple of them last week during my absence. People who are one hundred percent prepared to assume responsibility for KTech's future in case of our departure, either by natural causes or the SEC."

There was a smattering of laughter that followed Charles's joke, although not much.

"It would be irresponsible to our company, to our employees and business partners, and to all of you who have invested your hard-earned money in KTech not to have plans in place to replace our leadership. A plan of succession, if you will. I call it the AYFKM plan, as in Are You Fucking Kidding Me? Excuse my language."

The way the audience laughed and applauded, apparently they had.

"Now understand, I don't expect this plan to kick in until—how old is Warren Buffett? Ninety? How old is Charles Munger? Ninety-six? So, please, while I appreciate the outpouring of concern, we got this."

The audience erupted again. When Porter managed to get it settled down, he said "We'll let you go now, Charles. Drink plenty of fluids."

"Wait," Charles said. "Don't you want to hear about our plans to educate driverless cars?"

More laughter and applause followed before Charles launched into an exploration of artificial intelligence and the way people actually drive which, according to him, only occasionally reflected existing traffic laws . . .

"Then what?" Schroeder asked.

"McKenzie leaned toward me and asked 'What do you think?'" Reinfeld said. "I told him that I thought it was a very good performance, worthy of a hustler of Charles King's caliber, but I wouldn't trust him as far as I could throw KTech Tower."

"Why not?"

Reinfeld looked up to his left again before answering.

"Just a hunch," he said.

"What happened next?" Schroeder asked.

"Something odd took place."

"Odd?"

"McKenzie kept leaning toward me as if he wanted to ask something else . . ."

They had moved so smoothly and so quietly that neither Reinfeld nor McKenzie realized they were there until they sat down: two very large, very well-dressed men. One sat next to McKenzie and gazed at the image of Charles King on the giant monitor as if it were the only thing that held his interest. The other found a seat directly behind McKenzie. He leaned forward and rested a heavy hand on McKenzie's shoulder.

"Good afternoon," he said.

Reinfeld could tell that McKenzie was agitated yet was trying hard not to show it.

"Good afternoon," he said. "It took you long enough."

The large man next to McKenzie turned his head as if he had just been insulted.

"What?" he said.

"I had thought you guys would have gathered me up when I signed in to get my meeting pass," McKenzie said.

"We had other concerns."

"I'm sure that's it."

The man sitting behind him gripped McKenzie's shoulder enough to make him wince.

"Our employers wish to meet with you," he said.

"That's why I came."

"Please, don't make a scene. We wouldn't want to disrupt the meeting."

"Of course not. After all, I own stock in the company."

"Eighteen hundred shares, we know."

"What?" Reinfeld spoke loud enough to be heard several rows away. "Eighteen hundred shares? I thought . . ." He ceased speaking when he noticed that people were looking at him.

"Mr. Reinfeld, please," the large man said.

"Have you met Justus Reinfeld?" McKenzie said.

The man tightened his grip on McKenzie's shoulder.

"You told me you owned four-point-seven percent of KTech stock," Reinfeld said.

"I said that four-point-seven percent of my net worth is in KTech stock."

"That is not what you said."

"Maybe not those exact words . . ."

"Why is that important?" Greg Schroeder asked.

"It's not," Reinfeld replied. "Just some confusion . . ."

The two large men must have sent a private signal to each other because they both stood in unison.

"Mr. McKenzie," one of them said.

McKenzie rose reluctantly.

"See you around, Justus." He spoke loudly enough for people to turn and gaze at him. It was as if McKenzie wanted them to see him being escorted from the auditorium by two security guards . . .

"Are you sure they were security?" Schroeder asked.

"Who else?" Reinfeld said.

"Where did they take him?"

"I have no idea."

"Did you see McKenzie again?"

"No."

"You did contact him, however."

"Did I?"

"The police found your private number on McKenzie's cell."

"Oh, that's right," Reinfeld said. "I called him. I called to ask what happened after he was led away."

"What did McKenzie say?"

"He said that he couldn't speak right then, that he had something important that he needed to do, and that he would get back to me later."

"That's it?"

"Yes."

"He was lying," Schroeder said. He was sitting in his car in a parking lot across the street from the Ruth's Chris Steak House in downtown Minneapolis and speaking to Commander Dunston on his cell phone; Detective Shipman listening in. "According to your FSU, the call lasted six minutes. It wouldn't have taken McKenzie that long to say he'd call right back."

"I agree," Bobby said.

"Considering H. B. Sutton's theory of what Reinfeld is up to," Shipman said, "I can't believe he would call McKenzie just to ask him what happened with the security guards."

"More likely he wanted to know McKenzie's exact intentions," Schroeder said.

"Or buy him off," Shipman said.

"Or threaten him with bodily harm if he doesn't keep his big mouth shut," Bobby said. "Like someone did with Nina Truhler."

"So now what?" Schroeder asked.

"I'd love to question him myself, but a man like that would lawyer up in a heartbeat."

"I agree."

"Let me think about it," Bobby said.

"What should I do next?" Schroeder asked.

"I'm open to suggestions."

"Why don't I run out to KTech and see if anyone in security will answer my questions; find out where they took McKenzie and why."

"You might need some leverage. I'm going to reach out to a friend of mine to see if he'll help supply it."

"Does he owe you a favor?"

"No, but he owes McKenzie."

Shipman laughed.

"Who doesn't owe McKenzie a favor?" she asked.

Neither Bobby nor Schroeder answered.

"What are your plans, Detective?" Bobby asked.

"More phone numbers," Shipman said.

"Good."

Everyone said good-bye and hung up and Shipman muttered so no one but her could hear, "When this is over you are so going to owe me, McKenzie."

Chopper liked his geek-in-chief's blue T-shirt printed with the words:

YOU MATTER
UNLESS YOU MULTIPLY YOURSELF
BY THE SPEED OF LIGHT SQUARED
. . . THEN YOU ENERGY

He didn't say anything, though, for fear that he would be subjected to a lecture about Einstein's theory of relativity or how African-American nerds are marginalized in geek culture—he had heard them both before. Instead, he rolled his chair back and forth behind the geek's computer terminal.

"That didn't take long," the geek said.

"What?"

"The ticket site; they've already countered the software we installed yesterday."

"What does that mean?"

"Their bots are battling our bots for supremacy. Their bots are winning."

"What does that mean?" Chopper repeated.

"It means we're no longer able to circumvent their security measures. We're no longer able to buy bundles of seats. We're back down to a maximum of four."

"What about the other ticket sites?"

"They're still open for business."

"Then buy."

"I know. Vuhroom, vuhroom . . ."

"Have you ever been to Monster Jam?" Chopper asked.

"Giant trucks making lots of noise, isn't it?"

"I don't get it, either."

The geek went back to buying, Chopper returned to his desk, and Herzog entered the office. Chopper looked at his watch.

"Tryin' to run a business, here," he said. "Kinda hard when your employees come and go as they please."

"I wanted to check on a few things."

"What things?"

"Talked to RT. He said his tenant be happy to sit down with you."

"Happy?"

"What the man said."

"Where?"

"Como Pavilion," Herzog said.

"In St. Paul? That's crazy."

"Just repeating what was said."

Chopper leaned back in his chair.

"Am I the only one who thinks this is fucked?" he asked.

"Oh, it is. Totally. That's why I was checking it out."

"What do you think?"

"If you still want to go through with it . . ."

"I do."

"Against my advice . . ."

"It's a public place; plenty of people about."

"So?"

"So, maybe he's as afraid of us fucking with him as we are of him fucking with us."

"Whatever, man. There are some tables set way in the back of the pavilion overlooking the lake. Time comes, we're gonna get there early so we can pick the one we sit at."

There were plenty of places to park when Schroeder reached KTech Tower. He selected a slot with a sign that read Visitor

Parking Only and waited. Apparently, he waited long enough that the guards monitoring him on their security camera became anxious. Two of them exited the building and approached Schroeder's vehicle, one on each side. Schroeder watched them in his rear- and side-view mirrors, two very large, very well-dressed men and he immediately thought of the two guards that, according to Justus Reinfeld, had escorted McKenzie from the auditorium. He waited until one of them used his knuckle on the driver's side window.

Schroeder powered down the window.

"Can I help you?" he asked.

"I'd like to see some identification," the guard asked.

"Who are you?"

The guard sighed dramatically.

"I work the security desk for KTech Tower," he said.

"Proprietary or contract?" Schroeder asked, enjoying the moment.

"Excuse me?" the guard said.

"Do you work for the owners of the building or do you work for a private security firm that has a contract to secure the building?"

"What difference does it make?"

"My experience, private security firms are more professional, more likely to adhere to the rules set down by the board of Private Detective and Protective Agent Services. Guys working for the building have been known to bend the rules to please the owners of the building. Do you guys ever bend the rules to please your employers?"

"Let me see some ID."

Schroeder decided the guard was about to lose his temper, so he handed him his wallet. The guard took one look and tossed it over the roof of the car to his partner.

"Fuckin' shamus," he said.

"Most people don't use that word anymore," Schroeder said, "unless they watch a lot of old movies on TCM."

The second guard tossed the wallet back. The first guard pretended to accidently drop it on the asphalt and then accidently step on it.

"Oh, sorry," he said.

He ground the wallet under his heel some more before picking it off the ground and tossing it inside the vehicle.

"Don't worry about it," Schroeder said. "I have plenty more."

"What do you want?" the guard asked.

"Is that an existential question?"

"Why are you here, asshole?"

"I'm waiting for a friend. When my friend arrives, I'll step inside and all will be revealed."

The guard took a step backward and grabbed at Schroeder's door handle.

"Step out of the vehicle," he said.

The door didn't open. Schroeder had locked it when he saw the two guards approaching.

"No, no, it'll be safer if I stay right here," he said. "If I step out of the car you might provoke a confrontation that would result in me kicking your ass all over the parking lot. You wouldn't want your friends to see that."

The guard took another step backward and Schroeder realized that he had pushed his luck as far as it would go, especially when the guard unbuttoned his coat and swept it back to reveal his piece. Schroeder was convinced the guard would have reached for it, too, except at that moment another vehicle entered the lot and maneuvered to a stop just a couple of parking slots away. The two guards and Schroeder watched as the driver slid out of the car and approached them.

"Can I help you, sir?" The second guard's words were polite but his tone not so much.

The driver pulled a wallet of his own from his suit pocket, opened it, and held it near his face as if he wanted to convince the crowd that it matched the picture on his identification.

"Special Agent Brian Wilson, Federal Bureau of Investigation," he said.

Schroeder opened his car door. The guard was startled by the sound and glared at him.

"The friend I was telling you about," Schroeder said.

"Fuck," the guard said.

"Now that's a word that nearly everyone uses."

I never did learn her name, the admin who manned—womanned?—the reception desk in the Surgical Intensive Care Unit at Regions Hospital, the one that Shelby said wasn't afraid of God much less Bobby Dunston. I picture her, though, looking a little like a feisty librarian, wearing her white linen coat, and sitting behind her desk. I picture her looking over the lenses of her reading glasses at the man who appeared in front of her.

He was a big man, but that didn't impress the admin, and he wore a blue blazer, white shirt with blue tie, and gray slacks, which didn't impress her either.

"I'd like to see a patient named McKenzie," he said.

"Mr. McKenzie is not accepting visitors," the admin answered.

"I need to speak to him."

"What is your relationship to the patient?"

"Excuse me?"

"Are you a relative?"

"A relative? Yes. We're cousins."

"What is your name?"

"Look, lady, all I want is five minutes with the man."

"Mr. McKenzie is not receiving visitors."

"If he's asleep I can come back . . ."

"He won't be receiving visitors then, either."

"What exactly is wrong with him?"

"We do not release patient information except to immediate family."

"I'm his cousin."

"Then you should contact his wife."

"Nina Truhler." The man spoke as if he had just won a trivia contest. "See, I know McKenzie's wife."

"I'm sure she knows you, too," a voice said.

Both the man and the admin turned to find Dr. Lillian Linder approaching the desk. She gestured at the bruise and slight swelling at the side of the man's mouth.

"Is that where Nina punched you?" Lilly asked.

The admin scooped up the handset of her telephone and punched a button on the base.

"Security to SICU," she said.

The man's head pivoted from Lilly to the admin and back to Lilly again. He turned and made for the exit. Once he departed, the admin hung up the phone.

"I haven't had this much fun since the virus," she said. "How about you?"

I love Harry, the nickname bestowed on Special Agent Brian Wilson because of his uncanny resemblance to the character actor Harry Dean Stanton. Harry didn't particularly care for the nickname; okay, I'm the one who gave it to him. Only it was better than some of the other things he had been called by friends and colleagues alike, the worst being Surfer Girl when he was at Quantico, because he shared the same name as the man who co-founded the Beach Boys. Also Kokomo. "Hey,

Kokomo." He hated that, too. We became pals about eight years ago when I helped the FBI and ATF bust a gun-running operation out of Lakeville, Minnesota, mostly by accident. It's a long story.

Harry waved his credentials at the security guards standing with their mouths hanging open in the parking lot of KTech Tower.

"Two days ago, a man named Rushmore McKenzie was escorted from a shareholders' meeting held in the auditorium of this building." That was pretty much Harry's style, no chitchat; getting directly to the point. "Would you two gentlemen happen to know anything about that?"

The guards glanced at each other. It was the first guard who spoke.

"No license holder shall divulge to anyone other than the employer, or as the employer may direct, except as required by law, any information acquired during—"

Harry raised his hand like he was stopping traffic.

"I'll take that as a yes," he said.

The guard pointed at Greg Schroeder.

"He's the one who brought up the board of Private Detective and Protective Agent Services," he said.

"You Schroeder?" Harry asked.

Schroeder nodded.

"Let's see some ID," Harry said.

That caused Schroeder to crawl inside his vehicle to retrieve the wallet the first guard had tossed there. He handed it to Harry who couldn't help but notice the scuff marks and dirt on the outside and the dented badge and creased plastic identification card on the inside.

Schroeder gestured at the guard.

"He stepped on it," he said.

"It was an accident," the guard said.

"What are you guys, eleven?" Harry tossed the wallet back to Schroeder and pointed his jaw at the guard. "Let's go talk to your employer."

"Wait," the guard said.

Only Harry didn't wait. He marched directly to the entrance of the Tower, Schroeder and the two guards following behind. He stepped inside the building and moved in a straight line to the desk, where two security guards in matching suits were sitting. Harry flashed his own ID again; I think he enjoyed doing that as much as Shipman did.

"Special Agent Brian Wilson, Federal Bureau of Investigation," he said. "I'd like to speak to the supervisor."

One of the two guards stood and offered his hand.

"Travis Toft," he said. "I'm the watch commander."

Harry liked hearing that, watch commander. It was a police term. It meant Toft was an ex-cop; a professional.

"Two days ago, a man named Rushmore McKenzie was escorted from a shareholders' meeting held in the auditorium of this building," Harry repeated.

"Yes."

"Why?"

"He violated the golden rule," Toft said.

"He who has the gold makes the rules?"

"That's the one."

"Could you be more specific?"

"It was a private meeting, held only for shareholders and invited guests. Our employer believed that Mr. McKenzie was there under false pretenses. We were asked to remove him and hold him until his identity and intentions could be verified."

"Hold him?"

"We have a—a private reception area in back."

Toft threw a thumb over his shoulder in case Harry wanted to know where "in back" was located.

"That was a little harsh, don't you think?" Harry said. "Some might even consider your actions akin to false imprisonment."

"Mr. McKenzie had called our marketing department earlier that morning claiming to be a journalist employed by the *Minneapolis / St. Paul Business Journal.* That was a lie. We have the call on tape, by the way."

"How long did you hold him?"

"A half hour. After the shareholders' meeting, Mr. King came down and spoke to him."

"Charles King?"

"Porter King," Toft said. "Charles was not on the premises Tuesday afternoon."

"What did they speak about?"

"I don't know. We were asked to leave the room while Mr. King and McKenzie spoke privately."

"Afterward?"

"They emerged from the room, shook hands, and went their separate ways."

"They shook hands?"

"Whatever their differences, they seemed to have been resolved."

"I would like to speak to Mr. King," Harry said.

"He is not on the premises."

"Since you guys seem to enjoy quoting regulations"—Harry thrust his jaw at the first guard—"Section 1001 of Title Eighteen of the United States Code, prohibits you from knowingly and willfully making false or fraudulent statements, or concealing information, in any matter within the jurisdiction of the federal government of the United States. It's the reason why Martha Stewart went to jail."

Toft folded his arms across the front of his suit jacket and grinned.

"Really, Special Agent Wilson," he said. "You felt the need

to pull that card out of the deck? Up until now I thought we were friends."

Harry grinned back.

"That was cheap, I apologize," he said. "However, it's important that I speak with Mr. King."

"You could try his home."

FIFTEEN

Bobby didn't want to have lunch with Shelby, much less with Nina, much less with the two of them together for the simple reason that he knew they were going to ask a lot of questions that he didn't have the answers to. Still, he explained as much as he could, including why he wasn't actually working the investigation himself.

"I'm afraid I might become so angry or frustrated that I'll screw it up," he said. "Take Justus Reinfeld. There's a certain subtlety involved in questioning a suspect . . ."

"Reinfeld is a suspect?" Nina asked.

"Of course he is. A lot of suspects love to talk to the police, too, because they think they can convince us that they're not suspects. Thank the Lord for that because, seriously, it makes our job so much easier. Apparently Reinfeld is a smart man, though. If he saw me coming he'd lawyer up in a heartbeat and I would never get to question him. Ever. I don't know how I'd react to that, all things considered. Probably badly. As it is, the only reason Reinfeld agreed to speak to Greg Schroeder in the first place is because he was afraid of Riley Muehlenhaus. Now that he's had time to think about it . . . I don't know."

Normally, Bobby never spoke of his work outside the office. Not to anyone, much less family and friends, except from time to time to tell a few "fucktard" stories. Partly it was because he didn't want to inadvertently compromise an investigation. Mostly, though, it was because he felt it wasn't something he should do; one of the reasons he didn't have many friends in the news media.

As it was, he felt uncomfortable as he nibbled at his shaved ham and poached pear sandwich, something new to Rickie's lunch menu. He had even argued with Nina over paying for it. Finally, she told him that if he felt that guilty about being comped, Bobby should do what I always did—leave a tip for the waitstaff big enough to pay for the meal, because he wasn't going to ever see a bill.

It was because he felt uncomfortable, Bobby told me later, that he didn't notice the man-and-woman surveillance team studying their table until he was nearly half-finished with his sandwich.

He lowered his voice to a conspiratorial drawl.

"Man and woman sitting at a table off your left shoulder," he said.

"Oh, my bodyguards." Nina spun in her chair and spoke to them across the restaurant. "How are you guys doing?"

The woman raised her wineglass in a salute. The man smiled and said, "Best job I've ever had."

"If you need anything just let me know."

"Thank you," the woman said.

"Tell us when you're ready to go back to the hospital," the man said.

"Not for a while yet," Nina said.

Nina turned to face Bobby again.

"Ron and Celeste," she said. "They're very nice. I think they're sweet on each other. Greg Schroeder sent them."

Bobby nodded as if he knew all along.

"There's another sitting at the bar," Nina said. "Steve."

"I missed him."

"I did, too, at first."

"I'm glad they're here."

"Me, too."

"Especially after what happened at the hospital," Bobby said.

"What happened at the hospital?"

Bobby related the contents of a phone conversation he shared with Dr. Lillian Linder just a few minutes before he went to meet Nina and Shelby.

"They're still after McKenzie," Nina said. "Whoever they are."

"Yes," Bobby said.

"Why?"

"He's vulnerable," Shelby said.

They were the first words she had spoken in some time and they nearly startled her companions.

"What did you say?" Nina asked.

"Reinfeld. He's vulnerable."

"What does that mean?" Bobby asked.

"You said Reinfeld only spoke to Schroeder because he was afraid of Riley Muehlenhaus. That has to be nagging at him right now. He lost his nerve because of a freckle-faced young woman . . ."

"I like Riley's freckles," Nina said.

"That has to be driving an alpha male like him up the wall. He'll want to do something about it. He'll want to do something"—Shelby quoted the air above her head—"manly.

Something to prove that he's still a real man, a man's man; a man that women want."

"Like sending someone to threaten Nina?" Bobby asked. "Sending someone to threaten McKenzie some more?"

"If Reinfeld met the right woman right now, at this minute. A catch. A prize." Shelby quoted the air again. "A trophy that other men would covet, he'd spill his guts."

Bobby had to give it a few moments' thought before he realized what Shelby was suggesting.

"Hell no," he said.

"I know the perfect girl, too."

"Absolutely not."

Lake Minnetonka was a "lake" in the same way that van Gogh's *The Starry Night* was a "painting." The word didn't quite do it justice. For one thing, Lake Minnetonka—or "Big Water" if you speak Dakota—was less a lake than a sprawling maze of interconnected bays, inlets, channels, peninsulas, and islands with a water surface that covered twenty-three square miles and a shoreline that stretched for one hundred and fifty miles. It would take a couple of hours to drive around it and when you did, you'd be passing through some of the most prosperous zip codes in Minnesota. To own a home on the actual lake—what's the old joke? If you have to ask you can't afford it? I know I personally couldn't afford it and there are people like Jean Shipman who insist I'm a member of the one percent.

The address in Orono that Harry had been given was located on the north shore of a bay called West Arm. An enormous house surrounded by an immense emerald lawn that sloped gently to the lake. Given the size of the house, the unattached four-car garage, the elaborate gazebo, the two-hundred-foot-long shoreline braced with a wall of enormous stones, the wide, wooden dock, its planks covered with water-resistant polyurethane, and the huge boat that was moored to the dock, Harry expected to be greeted by a maid or butler when he knocked on the front door. Instead, it was opened by a middle-aged man wearing a Minnesota Twins sweatshirt.

"Yes?" he said.

"Mr. King?"

"I'm Porter King."

Harry flashed his credentials.

"Special Agent Brian Wilson, FBI," he said.

"I've been expecting you," Porter said.

Harry nodded at the admission.

"Your security people are very good at their jobs," he said. "Very professional."

"I'm glad to hear it." Porter looked over Harry's shoulder toward the person standing directly behind him. "You are?"

"My name is Greg Schroeder. I'm a private investigator."

"Yes, of course. Riley's man. Come in, both of you."

They stepped past Porter into the foyer of the house. From there Harry could gaze into other rooms and admire the exquisite furnishings and artworks they contained. His first thought was to wipe his feet. The gesture didn't go unnoticed by Porter.

"I know," he said. "The place is like a museum. Sometimes I find myself walking around throw rugs and hesitating to sit on chairs for fear a guard will toss me out."

Porter started moving through the house. Harry and Schroeder followed behind.

"You don't live here?" Harry said.

"I live in Linden Hills in Minneapolis. I live in the house we all grew up in, which is a pretty nice house in a pretty nice neighborhood, but this . . ." He spread his arms wide as if he was having a hard time taking it all in. "This is spectacular, don't you think? Charles lives here. Charles loves spectacular. Gentlemen, can I get you anything?"

Porter had led them into a room with plenty of shelves that held plenty of books; Harry didn't know if it was a library or a study or if there was a difference.

"Nothing for me," he said.

"I'm good," Schroeder said.

"Gentlemen, you're not going to make me drink alone, are you?" Porter drifted to one of the shelves and nudged the spine of a book. "Watch this."

A large section of the bookcase slid one foot forward and silently glided off to the side. The small bar that it revealed rolled slowly out into the room. Porter chuckled as he watched.

"It never gets old," he said.

There was a small refrigerator built into the base of the bar. Porter bent down, opened it, and retrieved a dark brown long-neck bottle with simple gold lettering. He held it up for Harry and Schroeder to see.

"Westvleteren Twelve, I hope I'm pronouncing that correctly," Porter said. "Brewed in Belgium. Some say it's the best beer in the world."

"Since you've already gone to so much trouble," Schroeder said.

"Don't tell anyone," Harry said. "I'm supposed to be on duty."

Porter popped the tops off two bottles and handed them out. He kept a third for himself. The three men sat in comfortable chairs that had already been arranged so that they faced each other as if the space was often used for informal gatherings. After Harry and Schroeder had a chance to sample the beer, Porter asked them what they thought. Both said they thought it was terrific.

"It's a little a bit fruity for me," Porter said. "Charles loves it, though. So, guys, our people say you want to talk about Mc-Kenzie."

"Excuse me, Mr. King—" Schroeder began.

"Porter, please. You say Mr. King and I automatically turn around to see if my brother is standing there."

"Porter, you're aware that I'm employed by Riley Brodin-Mulally?" Schroeder asked.

"Riley called us earlier this morning. Darling girl. Smart as hell. Fierce. She reminds me of my niece, Emma."

"Why would she do that? Call you, I mean?"

"Apparently, you had informed her this morning that our mutual friend Justus Reinfeld was engaged in less than scrupulous stock manipulation. She felt compelled to pass the information on to us."

"You and Riley are friends?"

"I wouldn't go so far as to claim that. More like acquaintances with a common interest—we both dislike Reinfeld intensely. We were grateful for the call, of course. However, we were already aware of his machinations."

"McKenzie," Harry said.

"Interesting man."

"He does have his moments."

"We believe that McKenzie revealed to us what little intelligence he possessed in an effort to prove that he was a friend and not a foe, but again, we knew about Reinfeld's somewhat nefarious activities long before our little get-together."

"Get-together?" Harry asked. "You make it sound friendly. In actuality, you had McKenzie taken into custody, escorted from the shareholders' meeting, and locked in a cell—isn't that so?"

"Locked? Hardly. McKenzie was always free to leave at any time. He stayed because he wanted to talk to us. Truthfully, we wanted to talk to him. He had made quite a nuisance of himself in an attempt to ingratiate himself with our family; even met with my niece and her cousin near their school. Because of the lies he told—calling himself Dee Dee, claiming to be a reporter working for a local business magazine among others—we had assumed at first that he was in league with Reinfeld. That's what my sister Jenna and our cousin Marshall claimed anyway. Seeing the two of them together at the shareholders' meeting seemed to support that theory. Finally, we decided enough was enough. Let's find out what the man wants. I must admit that McKenzie surprised us. Believe me when I tell you that we are not a family that is easily surprised."

"How did he surprise you?" Harry asked.

"He claimed that DNA evidence gathered by an ancestry site suggested that he was our brother, half brother."

"Is that possible?" Schroeder asked.

"Oh, yes. Our father . . . We won't discuss him today. But yes, it is conceivable—do you like that word, conceivable? It's conceivable that McKenzie is our brother."

"That must have been upsetting news," Harry said.

"Not at all." Porter took a long sip of his ale. "When Mc-Kenzie first approached us, approached Marshall and his daughter Elliot, we viewed him with suspicion. Granted, our judgment was colored by both his lies and Reinfeld's activities. Still, the reason that Charles submitted his own DNA to the ancestry site—actually, gentlemen, we are now drifting into an area that is, if you'll excuse me, none of your business."

"Oh, c'mon, Porter."

The three spun in their chairs toward the doorway to the study. A man stood there, his arm supported by a woman. He was tall with blond hair—only about four percent of the male population in America had blond hair; something Harry had learned in the course of his employment. The man looked old and tired.

"The news is going to get out sooner or later," he said. "We can't keep it a secret forever."

"Gentlemen," Porter said. "This is my younger brother, Charles, and my even younger sister, Jenna."

Both Harry and Schroeder stood; Porter did not. Jenna helped Charles to an empty chair facing all the other chairs. Charles didn't offer to shake hands with the men and they didn't offer to shake hands with him.

"Don't worry," Charles said. "I'm not contagious. I don't have the virus or anything like it. I have a liver disease. Primary sclerosing cholangitis to be precise."

Jenna helped Charles sit and stepped away from the chair. She looked as worn out as Charles did. Though much smaller than her brother, she also had blond hair—about four percent of American women are natural blonds, the remaining forty percent have blond hair because that's the way they want it. Hers was cut short.

"I'm sorry to hear that you're ill," Schroeder said.

"Thank you," Charles said. "I see you found the Westvleteren."

Schroeder told me later that Charles King reminded him of a character in a Raymond Chandler novel, *The Big Sleep*, Schroeder's favorite. Because of one ailment or another, General Sternwood couldn't drink, so he took pleasure in watching Philip Marlowe drink. "Nice state of affairs when a man has to indulge his vices by proxy," Sternwood said in the book. "It's pretty pathetic when the only pleasure I get these days is watching other people drink my booze, but there you are," Charles said in his library. "I have a case of scotch that I bought in Edinburgh over the winter. You guys should take a few bottles when you leave."

"Then what will we use to toast your recovery?" Porter asked.

"Good point. Never mind."

"Mr. King . . ." Schroeder said.

"Charles."

"Charles, we're told that you're aware that Justus Reinfeld is making a move on KTech . . ."

"You might say we've encouraged it."

"Encouraged it?"

"We understood that once Charles stopped coming into the office, once he stopped appearing in public, shareholders would become anxious and start unloading their stock," Porter said. "The price would decline."

"So we scattered a few bread crumbs for Reinfeld to find," Charles said. "Gave him the impression that KTech was a prime target for a takeover, which is untrue by the way. He started buying. Other shareholders saw him do it so they started buying, too. Right now our stock price is the highest it's ever been."

"It's not hard to profit from the herd mentality when it comes to the financial markets," Porter said. "Especially if you're driving the herd."

"Who's been dropping the bread crumbs?" Harry asked. "Not you two?"

"Jenna." Both Charles and Porter turned and smiled on their sister. "It was her idea. She's always been smarter than her big brothers despite her troubled past."

"Which is in the past." Charles spoke as if he was daring her to contradict him.

"Which is in the past," Jenna repeated instead.

"Tell me, though, Special Agent Wilson," Charles said. "Do you think that's why McKenzie was shot, because he discovered Reinfeld was trying to game us?"

"We're looking into it," Harry said.

"That would be"—Charles paused as if he was searching for the perfect word—"ironic."

"Excuse me, sir," Schroeder said. "What'll happen to KTech if things don't work out the way you plan?"

"Who gives a shit, really? Like the man said, you can't take it with you."

"I don't understand."

"I'm dying," Charles said. "I have two and a half, three weeks tops. Unless I receive a liver transplant. Most of my family and closest friends, people we trust, have been tested to determine if they're compatible. Unfortunately, they're not."

"Is there a donor list?" Schroeder said.

"There is. I'm in the bottom third."

"Couldn't you . . ."

"There are some things that money simply can't buy."

"Go public. Advertise . . ."

"That would destroy my company."

"A small price to pay," Schroeder said.

"You think so? In any case we have time, not much, but a little time before we need to make that decision."

"McKenzie," Harry said.

"McKenzie was a potential donor," Porter said. "He and Charles even have the same blood type. Once he was made aware of the situation, he seemed keen to help us. That's the part that caught us by surprise. He hesitated before making a full commitment, however. My impression was that he wanted to make a phone call first. Perhaps he wished to discuss the matter with his wife."

"Porter called almost immediately to tell me about it," Charles said. "When you reach my position, any good news no matter how iffy—what did Emily Dickinson write? *'Hope' is the thing with feathers that perches in the soul . . .*"

"Then McKenzie was shot," Porter said.

Jenna turned and silently left the room. Porter called to her. "Jenna?"

"I need to go home to St. Paul, take care of some things," she said. "I'll be back later."

Her brothers watched her go.

"I worry about her," Charles said.

The third of the four phone numbers on the FSU's list confounded Detective Shipman, but like I said, she was a substandard investigator and prone to confusion. Okay, maybe she wasn't as bad as all that. Bobby liked her and his judgment was usually pretty sound. I say 'usually' because I remember this one time when he decided it was a good idea to go down the slides at the Longfellow Elementary School while standing up. It's the reason I have a chip in my front tooth. Anyway, the phone number confused Shipman. Instead of calling it, she decided to visit the owner, the Transplant Care Department of M Health Fairview Clinics and Surgery Center in Minneapolis, the *M* standing for the University of Minnesota.

According to the website, University of Minnesota Health had one of the oldest and most successful transplant programs in the world. It could boast of more than fifty years of experience in the clinical care of more than 12,000 heart, lung, kidney, liver, pancreas, islet, and intestine transplant recipients as well as 4,600-plus living organ donors. It was also consistently ranked as a top provider by national and local publications. Which is why Shipman was disappointed when she walked into suite 300 on the third floor of the building located on the east bank of the university campus. She had expected something grand. Instead, she told me that it reminded her of the waiting room of her dentist's office.

She approached the woman sitting at the reception desk and flashed her credentials.

"Yes, Detective?" The receptionist spoke without fluster or

surprise as if being confronted by a plainclothes police officer happened to her at least twice a week.

"You received a phone call early Tuesday evening . . ."

"Yes."

"From a man named Rushmore McKenzie."

"Yes."

"Whom did he speak to?"

The receptionist stared as if Shipman had spoken in a foreign language that she now needed to translate. After a few moments' pause, she turned in her chair and spoke to no one in particular.

"Who was on the phones Tuesday night?"

A voice answered her.

"Lisa."

The receptionist spun back to face Shipman.

"Lisa Kohl might be able to help you. She's not in. Won't be until . . ." The receptionist glanced at the clock on the wall. "Not until after lunch, anyway."

"You don't keep a log?" Shipman said.

"Of everyone who calls and when they call? Why would we do that?"

Because it would make my life so much easier, Shipman thought but didn't say.

"Lisa might remember this Rushmore McKenzie," the receptionist said. "I can't help you."

A woman had appeared behind the reception desk during the conversation. She was reading from a clipboard but her head had come up at the sound of my name.

"What about Rushmore McKenzie?" she said.

"Do you know him?" Shipman asked.

"I wouldn't say I know him. I spoke with him Tuesday. I remember because of the name. Rushmore."

"Did he tell you where it came from?" Shipman asked. "His name?"

"No."

"Lucky you."

Shipman flashed her credentials again and asked if she could speak to her.

"Sure," she said, another woman who wasn't intimidated by Shipman's badge. "I'm Sara Barsness."

"May I ask what you do here?" Shipman said.

"I'm a transplant coordinator."

Shipman sat across from Barsness in her small office.

"Why did McKenzie call you?" she asked.

"He didn't call me specifically. He called the department and his call was transferred to me."

"What did he want?"

"He wanted information about liver transplants."

"For himself?"

"Could have been for himself," Barsness said. "Or a family member. Friend. He kept using masculine pronouns, he, his, so I concluded that he was speaking about a man, other than that . . ."

"He didn't give a name?"

"No."

"You didn't ask?"

"No."

"What did you tell him?"

"General information."

"Such as?" Shipman asked.

"Such as nationally, nearly 17,000 individuals wait for liver transplantation each year, while only 6,700 deceased-donor organs, those coming from brain-dead donors, become available and many of them are rejected, meaning that the survival rate is not—it's not what we would like. I told him that a positive outcome is much more likely to be achieved for transplants involving live donors, but convincing someone to donate a portion of their own liver to someone they don't know is daunting at best. The vast majority of live donors are family members or extremely close friends. Strangers donating to strangers is extremely rare, only about two hundred a year."

"What did he say to that?"

"He asked what it took to become a live donor and I told him that matching livers with recipients is based on age, blood type, organ size, and other factors."

Shipman flashed on one of my notes—the one where Emma King asked about my blood type.

"What about A-negative blood?" she asked.

"Patients with type A blood can receive a liver transplant from someone else with type A blood or from someone who has type O, the universal donor. However, a donor who has type A blood can only donate to someone else with type A or type AB blood. The rhesus, the Rh factor in blood, positive or negative, is not relevant."

"Is it better that a family member donates as opposed to a friend or stranger?"

"McKenzie asked the same question. It's better but not by a great deal. It does help with tissue matching. Other than that—we're also concerned that the donor's body mass index is thirty-two or less, that his liver, kidneys, and thyroid are healthy, that he hasn't been exposed to transmittable viruses such as hepatitis, HIV, and COVID-19. Also, we want the donor and recipient to be close in age and roughly the same size physically. What I'm saying is that a lot of different issues can influence the patient's outcome."

"What else?" Shipman asked.

"He asked how long it took. I told McKenzie that typically, a liver donor spends approximately seven days in the hospital, and will have an additional six to eight weeks of recovery time. After all, we are taking a piece of his liver and giving it to someone else; it'll take time for the donor's liver to regenerate, to return to normal size. I also told him that there were risks involved, such as the possibility of infection, blood clots, pneumonia, and bile leakage. Only he wasn't interested in any of that. He wanted to know how much time before the procedure could take place. I told him that usually the process takes from four to six weeks including consultations with an independent living donor advocate and psychiatrist, although in rare emergency situations, it could be completed in as little as forty-eight hours."

"What did McKenzie say to that?"

"He said, 'Good to know.'"

"What else?"

"That was it. That was the extent of our conversation."

"You didn't ask for a name? You didn't demand to know who he was calling about?"

"We don't push, Detective," Barsness said. "We guide. We explain."

Harry and Schroeder had driven separately, yet their cars were parked close enough in Charles King's driveway that they could walk to them together.

"I like the King boys," Harry said. "You wouldn't think that anyone that rich would be that unpretentious. More to the point, I believe them."

"So do I."

"Too bad about the scotch, though. Can you imagine?"

"Jenna King seemed upset when her brother started talking about his illness; the way she left the room," Schroeder said.

"Do you blame her?"

"McKenzie said that Reinfeld said that one of the Kings might vote his way in a takeover attempt. Do you think he meant Jenna?"

"Could be. Could also be a bit of tradecraft; Jenna pretending to be on Reinfeld's side when in actuality she's setting him up for her brothers."

"I'd like to interview her."

"She lives in St. Paul," Harry said. "It shouldn't be hard to get an address."

"You're going to stay on the case?"

"I play poker with McKenzie once a month. What do you think he'll say if I blew him off to go back to work?"

"I hear you," Schroeder said.

"Except that I have to go back to work. There are a few things that I need to take care of first."

"What things?"

"Government things." Harry glanced at his watch. "How 'bout we meet in a couple of hours."

"Where?"

SIXTEEN

Club Versailles took up a large chunk of a peninsula more or less in the center of Lake Minnetonka, about five miles from the King estate by land. It appeared as if the builders had insisted that it closely resemble Sun King Louis XIV's palace, only more luxurious. I had been there twice. Both times I expected to see a troop of Musketeers patrolling the grounds.

The club had private docks, a golf course, numerous tennis courts, two swimming pools, sauna, steam room, whirlpool, 2,400-square-foot fitness facility, formal dining room, and a grand ballroom. Only it was the bar that interested Shelby most because that's where Justus Reinfeld's model/receptionists said he would be. He was sitting alone at the far end and sipping what looked to her like straight whiskey and munching from a bowl of trail mix—trail mix! At Club Versailles. Swear to God.

Shelby was too smart to walk right up to him, though. Instead, she mounted a tall, walnut stool with a leather cushion and a high back that she was convinced cost more than her entire dining-room set. She swiveled to face the bartender, her skirt riding dangerously up her thighs.

Her dress was black, contrasting nicely with her strawberry hair, low-cut, inexplicably tight, and ended a half dozen inches above her knees when she was standing straight. It had originally belonged to Nina. Shelby had borrowed it three years ago because she said she was on a mission and claimed there was nothing in her own closet that would do. "I'm the mother of two teenage daughters," she complained at the time. Later she said that the dress had been so well received that she didn't want to give it back. I didn't know what that meant and I didn't ask. Nina, on the other hand, said, "Keep it, honey. I have more if you need them."

The dress was only slightly inappropriate for Club Versailles at that time of day. The bar was about half-filled. A third of the patrons were dressed for golf or tennis; another third looked as if they had ducked out of the office early. The final group, well, they looked as if they were on a mission, too.

The bartender leaned in and Shelby ordered a martini. Give her credit, she didn't say "vodka" and she didn't say "shaken not stirred." Also give her credit; she stared straight ahead until the martini was served. It was only after she took a sip of the drink that she tilted her head just so to look at Reinfeld and found that he was staring at her. She smiled, yet said nothing.

"I like your outfit," Reinfeld said.

"This old thing?"

"I appreciate a woman who dresses for cocktail hour."

"You never know what a cocktail hour might lead to."

Reinfeld gestured at the empty stool closest to Shelby.

"May I?" he asked.

"Be my guest."

Reinfeld moved himself and his drink, but not the trail mix, down the bar and cozied up next to her.

"I'm Justus Reinfeld," he said.

"Justus Reinfeld the investor?" Shelby smiled like she was meeting her favorite celebrity.

"You heard of me?"

"I read the business section."

"You are?"

"Shelby Mullin," she said, which was only partially a lie; Mullin being her maiden name.

"I like the name, Shelby. Is it yours or did you make it up?"

"Excuse me?"

"Shelby, I can't help but notice that you have an indentation at the base of your third finger left hand where your wedding ring would be if you were wearing your wedding ring."

Give her credit some more, she didn't panic. Instead, Shelby raised her hand, examined it front and back, and said "That's odd. I wonder what could have caused it."

Except the game was up.

"Who do you work for?" Reinfeld asked.

"Work for?"

"Did you really think I was stupid enough to fall for something as antiquated as the badger game?"

"I don't understand."

"Who do you work for?" Reinfeld repeated. "The King family?"

"I don't know the Kings."

"That asshole McKenzie?"

"McKenzie?"

"Or are you just a freelance whore trolling for victims?"

"Mr. Reinfeld!"

"Whatever you are, you're not a member of the club, are you? You're not the guest of a member."

Reinfeld waved the bartender over and spoke into his ear. The bartender went quickly to the manager. A few moments later, two security guards were escorting Shelby off the premises, each holding an arm.

"Let me go." Shelby attempted to wrench her arms free, but they were held firm.

As the guards were pulling Shelby out the door, a second woman entered the bar. The two women were careful not to let their eyes meet.

The second woman paused, navigated past a thrashing Shelby and the guards, and moved around the bar to near where Reinfeld was standing. Unlike Shelby, she was dressed for success in a tailored blazer, matching high-waisted pencil skirt, and a white embroidered top. 'Course, it never mattered what she wore. Even clothed in a green plastic garbage bag she would still have been the most beautiful woman in the room.

"What was that about?" she asked. "You know what? I don't care."

The woman continued to the bar and mounted a stool between where Shelby and Reinfeld had originally sat. Reinfeld watched her closely as she pulled her cell phone from her bag and set both on top of the bar. She tapped a couple of icons on the cell and spoke loud enough for Reinfeld to hear.

"This is Heavenly," she said. "I'm at Club Versailles. Where are you?"

She tapped a couple more icons and leaned back. The bartender approached.

"Vieux Carré," Heavenly said.

"Vieux Carré?" the bartender repeated.

"Rye whiskey, Cognac, sweet vermouth, Bénédictine liqueur . . ." Heavenly held up her hand. "How about an old-fashioned?"

"Coming right up."

The bartender retreated.

Reinfeld moved forward. His glass of whiskey was close

enough to where Heavenly was seated that speaking to her as he reached for it would not have seemed like an overt violation of her space.

"Excuse me," he said.

"Hmm."

"Vieux Carré, a difficult drink to make."

Heavenly continued to stare at her cell.

"I hadn't noticed," she said.

The bartender returned with her old-fashioned and a tab. Heavenly signed it, using Riley Brodin-Mulally's account number. 'Course, Reinfeld didn't know that.

"Are you a member of the club?" he asked.

"I'm not a joiner. However, my"—she deliberately hesitated as if she didn't know which word to use—"friend is."

"Boyfriend?"

"You're being a little personal, aren't you?"

"I'm just trying to find out who I have to kill."

"Oh my, what a clever line." Heavenly lifted her glass. "Impress me some more, will you?

Reinfeld mounted a stool one removed from hers and set down his own glass.

"I apologize," he said. "I can't recall ever meeting a woman as attractive as you before and for a moment my brain turned to mush. Please forgive me."

Heavenly wagged a finger at him.

"That was much better," she said.

"I'm Justus Reinfeld."

"Heavenly Petryk."

"That's a lovely name and very appropriate, if I might add."

Heavenly grinned and shook her head.

"Two steps forward, one step back," she said. "Maybe you should quit while you're ahead."

"I didn't know I was ahead. Ms. Petryk, you must admit that Heavenly is an unusual name."

"I was christened after a character in a play called *Sweet Bird of Youth*. My mother was very much a cultural maven; very interested in classical music, the ballet, theater. She adored Tennessee Williams. I'm only grateful that she didn't name me Blanche."

"Blanche DuBois from *A Streetcar Named Desire*."

"Did you see the play?"

"No, but I saw the movie."

Heavenly laughed as if that was the funniest thing she had ever heard.

"An honest man." She tapped Reinfeld's hand. "Another step forward. Excuse me."

Heavenly gathered up her cell phone and bag, slipped off the stool, and made her way toward the restrooms. Reinfeld watched her go. As soon as she was out of sight, he waved the bartender over and told him what he wanted. Next, he went to his own smartphone and Googled Heavenly's name.

'Course, that's exactly what Heavenly had expected him to do; the reason she had spent an hour uploading business profiles for him to find.

She gave him seven minutes to do it.

When she returned to her stool and set down her cell and bag, the bartender placed a squat glass filled with dark liquor and a lemon peel on a coaster in front of her.

"What's this?" she asked.

"Vieux Carré," the bartender said.

"I asked him to make you one," Reinfeld said. "He had to look up the recipe."

"I did," the bartended admitted.

Heavenly took a sip.

"Nicely done, sir," she said. "Thank you." She turned toward Reinfeld. "Thank you both."

"You're welcome," Reinfeld said. "I was named after my grandfather, by the way. On my mother's side."

Heavenly raised her glass to him and took another sip. Afterward, she picked up her cell phone, tapped a couple of icons, and set it upside down on the bar in front of her. Reinfeld took that as a good sign.

"So, what do you do, Justus?" Heavenly asked.

"I'm chairman and CEO of All Uppercase Investments. We're a venture capital firm that provides early stage funding for technology firms."

"Such as?"

"Twitter, Lyft, Netflix, Instagram, Kickstarter, Zoom . . ."

"No kidding?"

"We have about $3.5 billion in assets under management."

"At the risk of sounding mercenary, that's a very big step forward."

"What do you do?" Reinfeld asked as if he didn't already know.

"I'm an economist. I do analysis for an investment bank, researching potential opportunities mostly in agriculture and energy."

"Oh? What should I invest in?"

"Solar. You smirked, don't pretend you didn't. But consider— fifteen years ago, coal cost between seven and fourteen cents per kilowatt hour depending on where you lived, natural gas was priced between seven and ten cents, wind four and nine cents, and nuclear came in at fifteen cents. At the same time, solar power cost more than a dollar per kilowatt hour and everyone laughed. I would have, too. Today, this morning to be precise, fossil fuels were priced at between five and seventeen cents, wind was six cents, and solar—solar was four cents per kilo-watt hour. You don't need to fight the environmentalists in court every single day to produce it or build pipelines to ship it, either."

"Solar is cheaper than coal?" Reinfeld asked.

"Coal is dead. They just haven't buried it yet. For one thing, you can't go just by its kilowatt price. There's an additional three-point-four cents in adverse health impacts according to the National Academies of Science and another two-point-two cents in climate change–related damages."

"I'm impressed."

"You're not going to say something insulting like I'm too pretty to be this smart or I'm too smart to be this pretty?"

"I would never say that."

"Because I've heard it before. Consider it a deal breaker."

"I'm still trying to make up for my first dumb line."

"So far so good."

"Should I be honest?"

"Better now than later."

"I researched your name while you went to the restroom. You have a very impressive curriculum vitae."

Heavenly made a dramatic sigh and took another sip of her Vieux Carré.

"I should be insulted, but I'm not," she said. "I suppose a man in your position needs to be careful."

"Didn't you Google me?"

"No, I spent most of my time trying to find out why my date stood me up."

"At the risk of taking another step backward, anyone who stands you up is a damn fool."

"I'm glad somebody thinks so."

"May I buy you another Vieux Carré?" Reinfeld asked.

Heavenly paused before answering as if to carefully con-sider her words.

"Time and experience has taught me to maintain a low risk profile," she said.

"Meaning?"

Heavenly held up her still half-full glass.

"I'll just keep sipping this one for now," she said. "Safer."

Reinfeld smiled as if he admired her caution.

"I tend to be more high risk," he said. "More opportunistic."

"You can afford to be," Heavenly said. "So tell me, Justus Reinfeld, who was named after his grandfather, what should I invest in?"

Reinfeld paused for a moment like a Texas Hold'em player before he goes all in.

"KTech Industries," he said.

"I'm not familiar."

"Based here in the Cities, specializes in artificial intelligence designs . . ."

Heavenly snapped her fingers.

"What's-his-name, umm . . . King Charles."

"Charles King, yes."

"That's really not my field, but they're up-and-coming, aren't they?"

"Very much so. You say solar power is the future. Believe me, AI is a few steps in front of it."

"How much are you putting into KTech?"

Reinfeld grinned.

"What?" Heavenly asked.

"Can you keep a secret?"

"You'd be surprised."

"I'm going to buy it."

"I didn't know it was for sale."

"It's not."

Heavenly grinned back at him.

"You're a pirate," she said.

"I like that, thank you. It sounds so much more appealing than corporate raider. People hear that term and they think of Michael Douglas in the movie *Wall Street*."

"Who claimed greed was good."

"I'd much rather be Errol Flynn in *Captain Blood*."

"Wouldn't we all, but, Justus"—Heavenly leaned close and lowered her voice as if she was now part of a grand conspiracy—"isn't that dangerous? A hostile takeover? Charles King is the face of KTech in the same way that Steve Jobs was the face of Apple. After the board fired him in '85 the company nearly tanked. Twelve years later, they had to bring him back in order to save it."

"Yes, but how has it done in the decade since Jobs passed?" Reinfeld asked. "Pretty good, I'd say, since it's one of the ten most profitable companies in the world. I believe KTech could do exceptionally well even without Charles; I'm betting on it. It might be a moot point, anyway. Rumor has it that he's very ill."

"How do you know?"

"Let's just say a little birdie told me and let it go at that. When word gets out about Charles, I'll probably be hailed as a white knight by the other shareholders."

"You'll make sure word gets out, too, won't you?"

"After I take over the company."

"What's keeping you then?" Heavenly made a production out of glancing at her jeweled wristwatch. "The markets won't close for another six minutes."

"There have been a couple of glitches. For one, word about what I was attempting got out prematurely." Reinfeld tapped his chest. "My fault. I was careless. Fortunately, that seems to have been taken care of."

"How?"

"The man who guessed my plans was shot. He's in a coma."

Heavenly backed away, an expression on her face that could be interpreted as a mixture of both surprise and delight.

"You had a man"—Heavenly lowered her voice and leaned in again—"you had a man shot? Oh, now you *are* Captain Blood."

"Except, I didn't do it," Reinfeld said.

"Don't think that's a step backward. You had a man shot. Wow."

"I honestly didn't do it, Heavenly. I called him; I threatened him. I'm not proud of that. Later, I sent a man to discuss the issue with him and his wife; threaten them again or buy them off was my intention. Only I didn't shoot him. I didn't have him shot."

"Are you sure?"

"Of course, I'm sure. I thought about it. I mean, that was the first thing that came to mind, killing the asshole. But no, no, no—what kind of a man do you think I am?"

"I think you're like most of the men I've known," Heavenly said. "You meet a pretty girl and—what was it you said? Your brain turns to mush?"

She spun back to the bar and turned her cell phone right side up. She leaned forward and spoke into it.

"Do you need anything more?" Heavenly asked.

"No, that'll do," a male voice replied. "I'm satisfied."

"All right. See you in a minute."

"What?" Reinfeld was speaking loudly enough that the bartender and half the patrons in the joint turned toward him. "What the hell?"

Heavenly slipped off the stool and gathered up her cell and handbag.

"For the record," she said, "if you had been responsible for hurting my friend, I would have obliterated you. You and your business. I would have made it my mission in life."

"Who are you?" Reinfeld wanted to know.

Heavenly drained the Vieux Carré and held the glass up for the bartender to see.

"Needs work," she said.

Bobby Dunston was sitting in his car in the parking lot of Club Versailles, Shelby at his side. They both slid out of the vehicle when Heavenly approached. She tossed the cell phone. Bobby caught it.

"I know now that Reinfeld had nothing to do with McKenzie's shooting," he said. "Saves me some time and effort. Thank you."

"You're welcome," she answered.

Shelby was less subdued. She hugged Heavenly who hugged her back.

"You look fantastic in that dress, by the way," Heavenly said.

"It actually belongs to Nina."

"Give her my love."

"Give it to her yourself."

"I need to go now. I'll call in a few days after McKenzie's up and around. I presume he'll be up and around."

"You don't need to go anywhere," Shelby said. "You're just being your usual aloof self."

"No, I do. I need to catch a plane for Edinburgh."

"What's in Edinburgh?" Bobby asked.

"A brooch that once belonged to the Queen of Scots that's now on display in Holyrood Palace at the bottom of the Royal Mile. Rumor has it that it's about to go missing."

"Heavenly . . ."

"I'm not a thief, Commander Dunston."

"Yet you have no qualms about acting as a go-between for thieves."

"An acquaintance of McKenzie once accused me of being a mercenary bitch who profited off the misfortune of insurance companies. Do you have a problem with that?"

Bobby didn't answer.

"At least stay for dinner," Shelby said. "Nina and I have told the girls stories. They'd love to meet you."

"You're very kind, but I really do need to go."

"Ms. Petryk," Bobby said. "Justus Reinfeld looked you up on the internet and then you spoke convincingly about the energy industry . . ."

"The key to a successful grift is backstory, Commander. You should know that."

"Perhaps one day you'll tell me yours."

"If I haven't told McKenzie, what makes you think I'd tell you?"

Heavenly pivoted and started walking away. Bobby called to her. She turned her head, yet didn't even slow down.

"Be good," he said.

SEVENTEEN

Como Park in St. Paul was one of my favorite places. It sprawled out over 384 acres and included a large zoo where you could see all manner of creatures large, small, wet, dry, and in flight for free. The Marjorie McNeely Conservatory was the most spectacular public garden between Philadelphia and San Francisco (in my opinion) and everybody had their wedding pictures taken there. There was an amusement park complete with a hundred-year-old carousel, an eighteen-hole golf course, public pool, athletic fields (where Bobby and I played softball back in the day), historic sculptures, picnic shelters, a seventy-acre lake surrounded by hiking trails and plenty of foliage, and the open-air Lakeside Pavilion.

The pavilion had a roof but no walls and had been built on a slight incline overlooking Lake Como. It was large enough for several hundred people to sit on benches facing the stage where music, amateur theatricals, and dance recitals were performed. A couple of the benches were filled with retirees even though there were no performances scheduled. A few of the metal and wooden tables scattered along the back railing and on both sides of the benches were also occupied by people eating early dinners and by mothers, grandmothers, and a few grandfathers engaged in supervising children who had just been released from school.

Chopper noticed them all as he wheeled his chair up a ramp into the pavilion.

"I don't like this," he said. "Too many people."

"Or not enough," Herzog said. "We could cancel."

"We here now . . ."

Herzog directed Chopper to a table nestled against the back railing more or less in the center of the pavilion. Chopper was ready to settle himself at the head of the table, his back to the stage, only Herzog cleared space for him on the side so that he could park against the railing, the stage on his right and the lake on his left.

"Better view," Herzog said.

He was right about that. The rear of the pavilion was a good story and a half above glistening Lake Como and Chopper found himself resting his chin against his hand and staring wistfully at the piers jutting out into the lake and the pedal boats, kayaks, paddleboards, and canoes people were using to navigate it. Herzog left him to it, excusing himself and crossing the pavilion to the entrance of the Spring Café, the name of the restaurant that was attached to the pavilion and located directly behind the stage. He returned with a couple of IPAs and two menus.

Chopper spoke as he sat across from him.

"When I was a kid, during the winter, they used to clean the snow off a big part of the lake so you could skate," Chopper said. "Right over there. Speed skaters used it before they built the oval in Roseville. There was a shed next to the pier where you could rent skates. We'd come down here on Saturday after-noons and skate for hours and hours, drink hot chocolate with marshmallows . . ."

"You can skate?" Herzog asked.

"Used to."

This is where most people would say something; say I'm sorry, recognizing that Chopper wouldn't happily skate away a Saturday afternoon again, ever. That's not something you said to him, though. He didn't take sympathy kindly, especially when your compassion reminded him that there was some-thing he was no longer able to do. Herzog knew this, of course and studied his menu without speaking. Eventually, Chopper did the same.

"I am not eating here," Chopper said. "I don't care what this tenant of RT's has to say 'bout it."

"I don't know. The Cubano looks good."

Chopper tossed the menu on the table.

"It's picnic food, man," he said.

"Look where we at."

"Don't mean we gotta eat slop."

Herzog let the conversation drop. He knew that it wasn't the menu that his friend was upset about.

Chopper glanced around himself some more, paying partic-ular attention to the children who were using the pavilion as a playground. A few of them dashed to the railing not far from where he sat, looked down at the lake, giggled, and ran back to their mother. Chopper didn't know what was so funny, yet he giggled, too. Herzog caught him out of the corner of his eye and wondered briefly if Chopper was physically able to have children. He didn't think now would be a good time to ask, though. He didn't think there would ever be a good time to ask.

"Where is this prick, anyway?" Chopper said.

"We early."

"You got this, right? If he comes at us I don't wanna be sittin' here with my dick in my hand."

Herzog continued to read the menu.

"They have one of them plant-based hamburgers supposed to taste like a real burger," he said. "Ever eat one of those?"

"Fuck no."

"I might give it a try. Comes with avocado."

"They here."

Herzog didn't even turn his head to watch the two groups of men approaching.

"I see 'em," he said.

He pretended to study the menu some more as the group coming from the south entrance of the pavilion, two black men and one white, separated and scattered themselves among the table and benches, effectively blocking any retreat in that direction. The other group came in from the north entrance. It was led by a tall, good-looking white man with the hale and hearty appearance of someone who spent the first hour of every day in the gym followed by a breakfast of oatmeal with berries and nuts. Jamal Brown walked a step to his right and two steps behind him; a salt-and-pepper team brought up the rear. Halfway before they reached the table, the group stopped and the white man glanced about as if he were surveying a building site.

"You got this?" Chopper asked again.

"Uh-huh."

"I see seven of them."

"I can count."

"Maybe he brought so many cuz he's afraid we're gonna bushwhack him."

"He should be." Herzog glanced up from the menu and found Chopper's eyes. "That's an interesting word—'bushwhack.' Where'd that come from, you know?"

"I look like an etymologist to you?"

"Etymologist?"

"Person who studies the origin of words. You know that."

"Would I speak the way I do if I be well versed in the science of linguistics?"

"This banter shit, this is your way of sayin' not to worry, isn't it?"

"Fuck, Chop, I always worry when I hang with you. Never know what's gonna happen."

The white man waved his hand, a commander to his troops, and the two men trailing behind him separated and found seats with an unobstructed view of the table where Chopper and Herzog sat. The white man and Jamal approached cautiously. Chopper smiled brightly as if he didn't have a care in the world.

"Hey, Jamal," he said. "Who's your friend?"

The white man spoke with the irritation of someone who had expected to be addressed before anyone else.

"I'm Dr. Hammel," he said.

"Doctor your first name?" Chopper asked.

"Dr. Hammel, this is Chopper," Jamal said. "And Herzog."

Chopper extended his hand. Hammel raised his own the way fake TV Indians do when they say "How."

"Germs," he said. "Nothing personal."

Chopper glanced at Herzog who was still studying his menu.

"We got germs," he said.

"Everybody got germs."

"Gentlemen, should we get to it?" Hammel asked.

"You nervous, Doc-tor?" Chopper said. "I thought we were gonna have a quiet conversation and here you bring an army."

"We're aware of your reputation."

"Some of it might even be earned," Herzog said.

Chopper gestured at the chair at the head of the table. Jamal pulled it out like a servant might and Hammel sat in it so that his back was to the stage and his front toward the lake. After a quick glance around himself, Jamal grabbed an empty chair from the nearest table and positioned it so that he was one step over and one step behind the doctor. Herzog smiled slightly, dropped his menu on the table, and gazed out at Lake Como as if he was already bored.

"Tucker," Hammel said.

"Hmm?"

"My first name is Tucker. Dr. Tucker Hammel."

Chopper set a hand on top of the menu and eased it toward the doctor.

"Since we be friends now, what'll ya have?" Chopper asked. "On me."

Hammel pushed the menu away.

"No, thank you," he said. "We didn't come here to eat."

"You don't know how happy that makes me."

"You've been interfering in my business. I want it to stop."

"Not interfering. Just askin' questions. Ain't that right, Jamal?"

Jamal glanced at Hammel as if he was seeking permission to speak, but none came so he shrugged and said nothing.

"Doc-tor Hammel," Chopper said. "You a medical doctor?"

"I have that privilege."

"Not surprised a doctor be dealin' opioids," Chopper said. "After all, it was you medical people what started the epidemic in the first place. Only wouldn't it be much safer to sell outta your office instead of on the street?"

"Safer, but not as lucrative. New government regulations have significantly curtailed the health care industry's ability to meet the growing needs of our customers."

"Don't you mean patients?"

"Patients," Hammel said. "Of course. Because of the restrictions recently placed upon the medical community, many patients have been forced to rely on more unconventional sources to satisfy their requirements, at a much higher price I might add. You could say that I am merely providing market equilibrium."

"Supply and demand, the essence of microeconomics," Chopper said.

"You understand our business model . . ."

"Fuck you say, man? Don't pretend you're a humanitarian. You dealin' shit to people who can't say no cuz of genetics or psychology or social factors or fuck all in order to turn a profit just like a million other people who've come before you, just like I used to do."

"You sold drugs? When?"

"Before I knew better. So let's stop talkin' shit, 'kay, like you providing a public service."

"It's a victimless crime."

"Whatever lets you sleep at night, Doc-tor. I don't give a shit 'bout that, anyway. What I want to know—"

"What I want to know—"

"Don't interrupt me, Doc-tor."

"Who do you think you're speaking to? Do you honestly believe I'm frightened by you and your thug? Look around." He held his arms wide as if he was embracing the entire park and not just his men. "I came here as a favor to RT. Not to be threatened by a, by a . . ."

Chopper leaned back in his chair and waited for the word that would make further negotiations impossible.

"By a petty criminal," Hammel said instead.

"What are you?" Chopper said.

"Chop," Herzog said. "Man's gotta medical degree. Show some respect."

"My mistake." The way he smiled, you'd think that Chopper was suddenly humbled. "Doc-tor Hammel, I apologize if my manner offends you. I assure you I have no interest in your business. I merely seek your assistance in learning the identity of the individual who shot my friend."

"Why should I help you?"

"Call it professional courtesy."

"I require more than that if I'm to compromise one of my—patients."

"So you do know the person's name."

"Why is this so important? Why would you care if a white man was shot?"

"Let's just say I owe him and let it go at that."

"If I do this thing for you, then you will owe me."

"Within reason," Chopper said.

"No. You will do what I tell you to do when I tell you to do it." Jamal visibly winced at Hammel's words and looked away. Chopper smiled just so.

"That's unacceptable," he said.

"Then we have nothing further to discuss," Hammel said.

"There's my reputation that you seemed to be concerned about."

"That doesn't frighten me. I could have you killed like that." Hammel snapped his fingers. "Given your reputation, do you think the police would care? Do you think they'd even bother searching for your killer? They'll write it off as just another drive-by shooting. Just another street crime."

Chopper spun toward Herzog, his eyes wide and his hands spread as if he was asking him if he was going to do something about this. Herzog sighed dramatically.

"Can't we all just get along?" he said.

"I would be doing you both a favor having you killed," Hammel said. "Punks like you, your time has passed."

Jamal winced again.

Herzog planted his elbow on the table and raised his arm and spread his five fingers apart.

Two red dots centered on Dr. Hammel's shirt just over his heart.

A third dot appeared on Jamal's shirt.

The dots were emanating from three different laser sights attached to three different high-powered rifles held by three different sharpshooters hidden in the foliage along the far shore of Lake Como, the reason that Herzog had chosen that exact table for the meeting.

"Please," Jamal said. "I'm just trying to pay my tuition."

"What is this?" Hammel waved at the dots with his hand as if he expected to brush them away. "What are you doing?"

"Like I said, some of our reputation is deserved," Herzog said. "Don't make any sudden movements and you'll be fine."

"You'll never leave this place alive," Hammel said.

"First you die, then him." Herzog gestured at Jamal. "After that, do you really care what happens to us?"

"This is insane."

"It's unnecessary, is what it is," Chopper said. "You could have answered my questions very easily, but oh no. You had to prove that you're the toughest gangster on the street. I think my friend is right. Somethin' about you doctors—is it medical school that teaches you be such arrogant assholes? You have this omnipotent power over people who are ill or injured so you . . ."

"Chopper." Herzog gestured with his head. "My hand is getting tired."

"Yeah, yeah. You. Doc-tor. Who shot my friend? And don't think you can give me any name and then send your people to come for me later. You give me the wrong name and I promise I'll be coming for you."

"You can't shoot me," Hammel said. "The police . . ."

"The po-lice will check into your background, discover that you're dealin' Oxy and write you off as just another casualty in the drug wars. 'Cept since you're a doctor, you won't be considered a victim. You'll be a dealer. Bet your family'll love hearing that said out loud at your funeral."

Hammel sighed his compliance.

Herzog lowered his hand and the red dots disappeared. Jamal started to rise slowly.

Herzog barked at him.

"You know better than that," he said.

Jamal reclaimed his seat.

"RT's Basement is only one of my distribution centers, my St. Paul location," Hammel said. "I have three others and usually I don't go anywhere near them."

"This is important because . . ." Chopper said.

"I'm merely attempting to explain that it was unusual for me to come into contact with one of my patients outside the office. I recognized her—I had treated her at the clinic in Orono; that's how I knew who she was. Severe sprain. She twisted her ankle while jogging. I prescribed a thirty-thirty, thirty-milligram tablets of OxyContin to be taken three times a day for thirty days."

"A thirty-day supply of opioids for a sprained ankle? Let me guess—by the end of the month she was hooked." Chopper nodded as if he was impressed. "Expand your customer base; the goal of any retail business, am I right?"

"I didn't actually see her pull the trigger," Hammel said. "I merely saw her running around the corner of the club after the shot was fired. I didn't even see a gun."

"I still haven't heard a name," Chopper said.

Hammel turned in his chair to face Jamal as if seeking support. Jamal didn't want to answer.

"She's one of my best customers," he said.

"We talked about this, remember?" Hammel said.

"Who?" Chopper asked.

"Name Jenna King."

Hammel nodded his head to lend confirmation.

"Lives on Lake Minnetonka," Jamal said.

Instead of her usual ponytail, Emma King was wearing her auburn hair down around her shoulders when she walked into the waiting room outside the Surgical Intensive Care Unit at Regions Hospital. The room was empty except for the two women facing each other near the window. One was wearing blue hospital scrubs, so Emma assumed she was a doctor. The other had short black hair and the most amazing silver-blue eyes she had ever seen. They were speaking as if they were both trying to hide how annoyed they were with each other.

Emma gave them a wide berth and moved to the desk. There was no one sitting behind the desk, so she decided to wait. While she was waiting she listened to the conversation between the two women. The way they were speaking to each other, Emma couldn't really help but listen.

"All this takes time," said the doctor.

"How much time?"

"It depends on the individual. You need to remember that powerful anesthetics were used to induce the coma. We can't just turn them off. Instead, we'll gradually reduce the drugs while carefully monitoring brain activity and other vital signs. Your critically ill loved one should be able to come off the respirator as the anesthetics are minimized . . ."

"Critically ill loved one? Swear to god, Lilly—it's not what you say that makes me want to throw you out a window, but how you say it."

"What?"

"He isn't my critically ill loved one. He has a name. McKenzie. His name is McKenzie."

That caused Emma to snap to attention.

"You're right, Nina. I'm sorry. Sometimes I slip into doctor lecture mode. What I'm trying to say is that waking up is a gradual process; it won't happen straight away. After the drugs have been removed from his system, McKenzie should slowly but surely wake up. Once he does, though—the man was shot. McKenzie isn't going to get up and walk out of the hospital and take you dancing . . ."

"As if he ever does."

"His body will need time to heal, too, not just his heart and brain."

"Excuse me," Emma said.

Lilly spun toward her. "What?" She saw the young woman take a step backward, an expression of alarm on her face. She raised a hand and lowered her voice. "I'm sorry. What can I do for you?"

Emma hesitated a moment before she answered.

"I apologize for eavesdropping but you said—you mentioned McKenzie," she said. "A man named McKenzie. Could you tell me—is he going to be okay?"

"Do you know McKenzie?" Nina asked.

"Yes. Well, kinda. We met only once. I'm pretty sure he's my uncle, though."

That caused the two women to glance at each other.

"Who are you?" Nina asked.

"My name is Emma King."

Nina burned through her emotions like a highway flare, starting with anger seasoned with a pinch of hate and eventually settling on curiosity. She knew from what little she had been able to drag out of Bobby Dunston that the King family was involved with the shooting. She told herself that if she remained calm, if she supported my lie, she might just find out how.

"I'm Nina Truhler." She offered her hand; Emma shook it reluctantly. "If McKenzie's your uncle that makes me your aunt."

"My aunt? Oh, God, I am so sorry."

"What are you sorry about, Emma?"

"About what happened. About—I heard you." She was talking to Dr. Linder now. "You said it would take a long time for him to heal."

"Yes."

"He's going to be all right, though?"

"Barring unforeseen complications."

"That's a relief. I'm happy about that, but it means he can't help."

"Help what?" Nina asked.

"My uncle. My other uncle."

"Why don't we sit over here and talk?"

Nina gestured Emma toward a chair in the center of the waiting area. Dr. Linder glanced at her watch.

"I need to go," she said.

"When will you begin?" Nina asked.

"Begin weaning McKenzie off the anesthetics? When the anesthesiologist arrives."

Nina made a production of looking at her own watch.

"Yes, I know," Lilly said.

A moment later, she was gone. Nina sat next to Emma. She told me later that it took her a few moments to compose herself; for her to turn her thoughts away from me and to the young woman sitting by her side. She rested her hands on the arms of the chair, closed her eyes, and practiced one of the deep-breathing exercises that Shelby had taught her. Slowly she opened her eyes.

"Are you okay?" Emma asked.

"I'm trying to be. You said McKenzie is your uncle?"

"You're married to McKenzie?"

"Yes."

"But you call him by his last name?"

"He doesn't like his first name."

"I didn't know that."

"One day I'm sure he'll tell you the story, Emma."

"I am so, so sorry."

"You keep saying that. Emma, why are you sorry?"

"I might have caused all this. I mean—I can't really believe it. It would mean my family—but that doesn't make sense to me. My uncle . . ."

"Tell me about your uncle," Nina said.

"I met McKenzie last Monday . . ."

"Not that one."

"Charles. Charles King. He owns KTech, a company that works with artificial intelligence. He's famous. Some people call him King Charles like he's some kind of royal despot or something only he's not. He might be the kindest person I've ever known. He's always been kind to me."

"What about him?"

"He has primary sclerosing cholangitis. That's a liver disease. If he doesn't receive a liver transplant soon, he'll die. I took some tests to see if I was compatible. It was the least I could do after all the things he's done for me, only I wasn't a match because of my blood type. Elliot, she's my best friend. She's also my cousin. Second cousin. She took the tests, too. She wasn't compatible, either. Her size. Most of my family took tests. My other uncle, Porter. Elliot's father, Marshall. No luck. My mother couldn't donate because—just because. Then we met McKenzie and we thought—Elliot and I thought—maybe he could help. He's family after all. At least that's what the DNA results prove. So we drove back to the Cities. We went to Elliot's house. Her father was there, Marshall. After we started telling him what we thought, he called my mom and she came over and it was just us and the two of them. I don't know why they didn't call Charles or Porter. It doesn't make sense."

"What doesn't make sense, Emma?"

"They seemed angry. I mean angry at us, me and Elliot. We told them about McKenzie and Marshall started lecturing us about involving complete strangers in family matters. I told him that McKenzie wasn't a stranger, that he was family, and that we had met him and he seemed like a nice man. Is he a nice man?"

"Yes."

"It didn't matter. Not to Marshall or Mom. They said that McKenzie—he could open up a can of worms that could really hurt the family and I'm like 'Can of worms? What the fuck does that mean?' I'm sorry."

"That's okay," Nina said. "It's not like I haven't heard the word before."

"It just didn't make any sense to me. I kept asking, 'What can of worms?' They wouldn't tell me. All I got—my mom said, 'It happened before you were born.' I'm like 'What happened?' She wouldn't tell me. Only I wouldn't give it up—McKenzie, I mean. Elliot and me, we said that we hadn't actually involved him in anything. We didn't tell McKenzie about Uncle Charles. My mom said, 'Don't. Don't tell him.' I said, 'Shouldn't we let Uncle Charles make the decision?' After all—and this is important, at least I thought it was important. He's the one who put his DNA up on an ancestry website in the first place in case something like this might happen.

"Marshall said, 'You're right, you're right,' like he agreed with me. He said that it was Charles's decision and that he would tell him everything I had told him and Mom. That's where we left it. Elliot and I had to get back to Carleton before quiet time. Only nothing happened. We didn't hear anything from anybody. Not Tuesday. Not Wednesday. Then Wednesday night, last night, this policewoman showed up at school, a detective, and she told us that McKenzie had been shot and she blamed Elliot and then she said she was kidding, that she knew Elliot didn't do it and I'm like, What is wrong with you, lady?"

"The detective, was her name Jean Shipman?" Nina asked.

"Yes. Do you know her? Is she always this mean?"

"I couldn't say. McKenzie doesn't like her, though."

"I don't either, but I started wondering about something she told us. Something unbelievable. She said that a woman delivered a message to McKenzie, delivered it to his building, and that the message might have been what lured him to the place in St. Paul where he was shot."

"RT's Basement on Rice Street?"

"Yes. She said, Detective Shipman said, that the woman who delivered the message had short blond hair and told the security guards that her name was Elliot. Only it wasn't Elliot. She was in Northfield with me when all of this happened. We can prove it, too. Only that's not what's unbelievable. What's unbelievable—I can't believe I'm saying this or even thinking it."

"What's unbelievable?" Nina asked.

"My mother has short blond hair."

"Your mother?"

"Jenna King."

Nina took Emma's hand in hers and spoke to her as if she were her daughter.

"Emma, honey, I need you to talk to someone for me," she said. "A policeman."

"A policeman? I . . . I . . . I . . . I can't do that. It's family."

"McKenzie is your family, too," Nina said.

She told me later that she had felt sympathy for Emma, for the position she was placing her in, but at no time did she consider telling the girl the truth—that I wasn't her uncle. I told her that I would have done the same thing; that she was starting to think like me. Nina said that was a lousy thing to say and I should apologize. Anyway . . .

"My mom," Emma said. "We're talking about my mom."

Nina gave the young woman's hand a reassuring squeeze.

"You don't really believe that your mother shot McKenzie, do you?" she asked.

"I don't know. Some of the things she's done lately because, because . . ."

Emma closed her eyes as if she was recalling some of the things and opened them slowly.

"No," she said. "I don't believe it. Something's going on . . ."

"Will you talk to my friend?" Nina asked.

"The policeman?"

"Yes."

"Not Shipman."

"No. No, no. His name is Bobby. He's McKenzie's best friend."

"Will I have to go to the police station?"

"I think we can avoid that."

The way they had left it with Dr. Tucker Hammel—"What you got here is an adverse patient outcome," Chopper told him. "My advice, forget this one and move on to the next patient. Your practice is still intact, 'kay? I won't have any more reason to mess with you unless you have reason to mess with me. 'Kay?"

Hammel didn't respond one way or another.

A few minutes later, Herzog was driving the van south on Lexington Avenue toward I-94.

"We gonna deal with Jenna King ourselves or are we gonna pass her name to the po-lice?" he asked.

Chopper didn't reply.

"Kinda quiet back there, partner," Herzog said.

"Hmm? What?"

"Just askin', are we going to call Bobby Dunston or take care of Jenna King our own way?"

Chopper still didn't answer.

"Somethin' on your mind, Chop?"

They were crossing University Avenue; a White Castle restaurant was located on the corner.

"Pull in here," Chopper said.

"What?"

"Pull in, pull in."

Herzog swung the van into the parking lot, found an empty slot and stopped.

"You won't eat a plant-based burger but you're happy to load up on sliders?" he asked. "Talk about extremes."

"I need to think."

"'Bout what?"

"The doc-tor—he wants us to kill Jenna King."

"Whaddaya mean?"

"He wants us to do his dirty work for him."

"Chop . . ."

"He wanted us to have that name, Jenna King. He played the part like we was forcing it outta him, but ask yourself—if he didn't want us to have the name, why would he have agreed to a meeting in the first place, at least one that we walk away from? Somethin' else. This woman, Jenna King, who lives on Lake Minnetonka—you know what we're talking about when we say a person lives on Lake Minnetonka?"

"Money."

"Lots of it, too. So tell me—what's a white woman from way out on the rich side of Minneapolis doing on Rice Street? A woman like that, it would be dangerous for her to go down to RT's."

"She was looking to get her prescription filled," Herzog said. "She heard from somebody who heard from somebody that RT's Basement was the place to go t' get her Oxy, you know how it works."

"Except that she already had Jamal doing home deliveries for her. One of his best customers, he said. So why would she go to RT's?"

Herzog let that sink in for a few beats.

"She went there to see McKenzie," he said.

"Why RT's, though? If she arranged the meet, she would've picked a spot closer to home. People live on Lake Minnetonka; they don't even cross the river to go to the state fair, man."

"McKenzie picked the spot. You know how he likes his tunes."

"He's too upscale for a second-rate dive like that. 'Sides, RT's doesn't have music on Tuesday nights. What I'm thinking, maybe Jenna King doesn't have anything to do with McKenzie. Maybe she's a loose end of some sort that the doc-tor wants to snip and he decided to get us to do the snipping."

"Or Jamal's behind it."

"Could be Jamal, only he didn't want to give her up."

"He acted like he didn't want to give 'er up," Herzog said.

"When we met the first time, Jamal said he didn't even know McKenzie was shot until someone told him."

"Unless he was lying. I thought so at the time, remember. Got no reason to change my mind."

"What we should do, we should find out more about this Jenna King before we do something maybe we regret," Chopper said.

"How you want t' go about it? Anybody we could call?"

Chopper gave the question a full-throated chuckle before answering.

"Usually," he said, "I'd call McKenzie."

EIGHTEEN

The final phone number on the list that had been given to her by the FSU belonged to Marshall Sohm, Jr., only he refused to meet Detective Jean Shipman at AgEc, Inc. or anywhere near the building where he worked in downtown St. Paul. He didn't want to talk to her at all, didn't even want to say "Hello," and probably wouldn't have—apparently he understood his rights as well as Justus Reinfeld—except that his daughter had told him about her interview with Shipman.

"You're the one who accused Elliot of being involved in the shooting," he said. He was angry when he said it.

"Here's your chance to explain to me all the reasons why I'm wrong."

Still, Marshall might have blown off the detective anyway except that when he started to hem and haw Shipman said, "A message was delivered to McKenzie by a woman with short blond hair who claimed her name was Elliot. Immediately afterward McKenzie received a phone call from this number, your number, the number we're using now. Five minutes later, he left his building. The next time anyone saw him, Mc-

Kenzie was lying on a sidewalk with a bullet in his back. You may refuse to cooperate with the police. That's your right. I'm sure the Ramsey County prosecutor will understand. I'm sure a subpoena won't be issued that would force you to testify in front of a grand jury. After all, McKenzie was a retired police officer and we never take care of our own."

Marshall agreed to meet with Shipman at his home in Woodbury.

Unlike RT's, Rickie's actually had a basement and in it Nina had recently built a lounge complete with bar and small stage that she called—wait for it—the Lounge. She promoted it as an intimate hideaway perfect for private parties and small wedding receptions and she did quite well with it even though Erica and many of her employees insisted that it was haunted. Which is another long story I'll tell you one of these days.

The Lounge was closed in the late afternoon; there was only Nina, Emma, and Bobby sitting at a square table away from prying eyes, away from the happy hour music and noise found upstairs. Despite the bar, no one was drinking, at least not alcohol. Nina had given Emma a tall glass filled with ice water that the young woman sipped from more to have something to do with her hands than because of thirst.

Like Nina, Bobby spoke to Emma as if he was comforting one of his daughters.

"How much time does Charles have, do you know?" he asked.

"It can't be much more than a couple of weeks." Emma's eyes welled up with tears when she spoke about her uncle, yet she refused to let them fall. "That's why it doesn't make sense to me what my mom and Marshall are doing."

"Do your mother and your uncle get along?"

"Oh, God, are you kidding? They're like . . ." Emma wiped

her tears away and smiled. "I was going to say they're like brother and sister only they're so much closer than that. Their father abandoned them when they were still young. My mom— Mom was sixteen and pregnant with me at the time. Instead of falling apart, though, they united. I don't know how else to say it. My uncles were at Northwestern and they both transferred to the University of Minnesota to be near Mom and they've been taking care of each other ever since. My uncles made sure Mom didn't drop out of school; made her go to college and she just excelled, you know? They motivated themselves to do well, too. To do fantastically. Meanwhile, the three of them raised me. I have no idea who my father was; Mom never told me; never told anyone as far as I know. That's okay because I have two fathers and they're both so damn"—Emma paused if she was searching for the perfect word and came up with— "fatherly. What doesn't kill us makes us stronger, something you hear people say. Personally, I think Friedrich Nietzsche was full of crap. But the three of them are so strong, especially together. I think that's why no one has married, yet."

"Why would your mother want to arrange a meeting with McKenzie?" Bobby asked.

"I'm not sure that she did, I don't care what that detective said. My mom doesn't look anything like Elliot. You would never see them standing side by side and say, oh, they must be related, although—although she does have short blond hair and she is roughly the same size."

"And she knows Elliot's name," Bobby said.

"She knows Elliot's name." Emma took a sip of water. "It doesn't make sense."

"Honey?" Nina rested her hand on Emma's. "I know this is very hard for you."

Emma nodded.

"You love your mother," Nina said.

"Of course."

"You told me before that your mother was unable to take the tests to see if she was a compatible transplant donor . . ."

"Yes."

"You also told me that you were anxious because—what did you say—because of some of the things that she's done lately? Could you tell us about that?"

The tears returned as Emma took yet another sip of water.

"Mom hasn't had an easy life," she said.

"No, she hasn't," Bobby said, resting his hand on hers, proving that he was on Emma's side.

"She got involved—involved with drugs some years ago after she had her social media business humming. I think she became bored, met some people, I don't know. She kicked the habit, though. My uncles saw to that. They got her help. They gave her support. So did I. Now I think, I think she might be using again. There's this man she's been seeing. He's black and he's way younger than she is, only a year or so older than me, in fact. I don't care about that. God. What I care about—she seems kind of dependent on him and that's, that's just not like her."

"What's his name?" Bobby asked.

"I don't know. We've never been introduced. I've only seen him at a distance, which is something else that's crazy."

"Where is your mother?"

"I haven't spoken to her today. She's either at the lake or at home. My uncle Charles has this palace on Lake Minnetonka and my mom and Uncle Porter spend most of their time there; they even have their own bedroom suites, like a hotel. But they also have their own homes. Porter has a place in Linden Hills in Minneapolis and Mom has a house on Summit Hill here in St. Paul. It's only a couple miles from where we are right now, actually. It's where I grew up. Mom thought it would be better for me growing up there than in Charles's palace on the lake. So we lived in St. Paul, just the two of us, all the time I was in school. A small house. Charles calls it 'the little cottage' although its way bigger than that. I told Mom that she's not allowed to sell it; that if she doesn't want it anymore she has to give it to me. It's not like she needs the money. She became rich when she sold her business. All of the Kings are rich. Well, not all. I don't even get an allowance. Mom pays my tuition and room and board, so poor, poor pitiful me, but I have to work a part-time job in Northfield for spending money. My family thinks it builds character."

"Is it possible that your mother is at home now?" Bobby asked.

"I don't know. I could call her."

"No, but if you would be kind enough to give me the address . . ."

"So you can ambush her like Detective Shipman did with me and Elliot?"

"You said yourself that your uncle doesn't have much time."

"I'm going with you."

"No, I don't think that's a good idea."

"Please."

"There are questions I need to ask your mother that she might not answer if you're in the same room with us."

Emma stared as if she was trying to imagine what those questions might be.

"You mean about family secrets?" she asked. "About—about that can of worms?"

"Yes."

"I'm not a child anymore."

"You're her child; that's how she'll look at it."

"Do you have kids?" Emma asked.

"Two girls; both just a couple of years younger than you."

"Do you keep secrets from them?"

"Yes."

"Let me guess—for their own good."

"No, for mine."

Emma found a spot on the wall to stare at for a few moments. While she did, Bobby heard her mutter a single word—"Mom." Afterward, Emma glanced at Nina as if she was seeking her advice.

"Don't look at me," Nina said. "I need to go back to the hospital and check on McKenzie."

"Will you call me?" Emma asked. "Will you tell me how he's doing?"

"Yes," Nina answered. "Where will you be?"

Emma spun back to face Bobby.

"Carleton College," she said. "I have a midterm in the morning."

They discovered Chopper's geek-in-chief sitting behind Chopper's desk like he owned the place when they rolled into the office in Minneapolis. He pointed at Chopper's computer screen.

"You should see this," he said.

Chopper stared wide-eyed at him as if he already couldn't believe what he was seeing. Herzog chuckled.

"You expect he was gonna do the research you wanted on his phone?" he asked.

Chopper waved at the dozen computer terminals that were scattered throughout his office.

"He can't use the boss's computer?" Herzog said. "When did you start voting Republican?"

"Hey," the geek said. "You want to look at this, what?"

Chopper wheeled himself around the desk. The geek pulled away the chair he was using to give him plenty of room. He leaned down until his head was level with his employer's and pointed at the computer screen some more.

"Jenna King is one of *the* Kings. Charles King, her brother, he owns KTech Industries, creates artificial intelligence designs. AI, man. AI. AI is like . . ."

"I know what artificial intelligence is," Chopper said.

"These people are going to rule the world."

Chopper was looking at Herzog when he asked "How much are the Kings worth?"

"Hundreds of millions of dollars," the geek said. "Maybe more. Maybe billions."

"You don't just shoot a billionaire."

"Why would you do that?" the geek wanted to know. "AI, man. AI."

"Why would someone want us to do that, better question?" Herzog said.

"We could ask Jenna," Chopper said.

"Think she'd talk to us? Think we could get within a mile of her up at Lake Minnetonka? Puh-leez. We can't even walk through a shopping mall without being followed."

"She doesn't live on Lake Minnetonka," the geek said. "Her brother does, but Jenna, Jenna King, right? She has a place on Summit Hill in St. Paul."

Chopper gestured at Herzog.

"Whaddya think?" he asked.

"What do you think?" Herzog asked in return.

"If she thought she was in danger, if she thought Jamal and the doc-tor were fucking with her; that might be enough to convince her to tell us 'bout McKenzie. She might tell us a lot."

"How we gonna convince her of that; convince her that we're her friends?"

"Do you have Jamal's number?" Chopper asked.

"Yeah."

"I think we call him and tell him that we changed our minds. Tell 'im we thought about it and decided we're out of the thug life. See what he does."

"If you're right, if Jamal and the doctor were tryin' to make us their bitch—you know, they might go over t' her place and do her themselves. Jamal in particular, he's pretty ambitious."

"Maybe we should go over there and watch," Chopper said. "You know, just in case."

"Be the cavalry riding to the rescue?"

"Buffalo Soldiers, that's us."

Greg Schroeder was sitting in his office overlooking U.S. Bank Stadium when his phone rang.

"Schroeder," he said.

"This is Brian Wilson. You busy?"

"No."

"Still want to interview Jenna King?"

"I do."

"I'm in Brooklyn Park . . ."

By the way, Harry hated Brooklyn Park. That's the suburb the FBI moved to about ten years ago. Granted, the ultra-modern five-story building was so much better than the hovel they had worked out of in downtown Minneapolis. Still, Brooklyn Park. The chance of being a victim of either a violent or property crime was one in twenty-nine; its crime rate was higher than 93 percent of the cities and towns in Minnesota. Probably the reason why the FBI's campus was surrounded by an iron fence. Anyway . . .

"I'm still in Brooklyn Park," Harry said. "I can swing by your office or I could give you Jenna's address in St. Paul and we can meet there."

"Why don't you come here, first," Schroeder said. "Do you know where I'm located?"

"I do. ETA in about thirty minutes."

"I'll be ready."

The admin summoned Dr. Lillian Linder the moment that Nina entered the waiting area outside of the SICU at Regions Hospital. Less than a minute later, Lilly was by her side.

"So far so good," she said. "We've been slowly reducing the drugs in McKenzie's system. All his vitals are exactly where we want them to be."

"How long will it take for him to regain consciousness?"

"Like I told you before, it depends on the individual. It could take a couple of hours. It could take all night."

"Can I see him?" Nina asked.

"Of course. In fact, it's been shown that hearing the voices of family members helps patients come out of a coma sooner; it exercises the circuits in their brains. What I want you to do— tell McKenzie who you are. Hold his hand and stroke his skin; that can be a great comfort to him. Talk to him about your day; talk to him as you normally would. Remember, though. He can hear you. If you tell him he's a soulless jerk . . ."

"I'll wait until he's fully awake."

"Good idea."

Lilly led Nina into the room where they had been keeping me since Tuesday night; the glass wall had been rolled back. By then they had extubated me; the medical term for removing the tube they had pushed down my throat to help me breathe and the one they had shoved up my nose to draw out stomach contents. Lilly gave Nina a stool that she rolled as close to the bed as she could. She took my hand and brushed the hair off my forehead.

"McKenzie, it's Nina," she said. "In case you've forgotten, I'm your wife. We've been in love since the beginning of time . . ."

Always watch the eyes, Detective Jean Shipman had been taught at the academy and by supervising officers when she was a rookie. Watch the eyes when questioning a suspect or whenever anyone was holding a gun. The eyes were always the tip-off.

Marshall Sohm's eyes told her that he was anxious. They told her that he was angry. They also told her that he had been drinking. The combination made her wish that she had brought backup, Mason Gafford or Eddie Hilger, even Sarah Frisco. Only this was her case and she was going to solve it if it killed her—although she sincerely hoped that it wouldn't. That's why she adjusted the Glock she wore behind her right hip beneath her blazer when she settled on the sofa in Marshall's living room.

Marshall sat in a chair on the other side of a coffee table from her. Shipman was glad for the table. It would give her a couple of extra seconds if everything went sideways, she decided.

"Can I get you anything?" he asked. "Coffee?"

"Thank you," Shipman said.

Marshall left the room and went into his kitchen. That gave Shipman a chance to get up and examine the large collection of photographs that had been arranged on the living-room wall. They were all family photos—Marshall and a woman that Shipman guessed was his wife, an older couple that could have been his parents, group photos of a dozen or more relatives gathered together, more couples with and without children, two men and a woman with arms wrapped around each other.

Most of the pics, though, were of Elliot taken at various stages of her life, from infancy to college. In some she was alone, in others she was posed with her parents, in still others she was accompanied by Emma King. The shots Shipman found most riveting, though, were of a very young woman with long blond hair holding an infant that seemed to have been taken decades earlier plus a more recent photo of the same woman with her arms hugging Emma's shoulders from behind. In that one her hair had been cut short. Shipman recognized her instantly. It was the same woman she had seen in the video taken at my building.

She heard Marshall approaching and quickly returned to her perch on the edge of the sofa. He entered the room carrying two mugs. He crossed over to where Shipman was sitting and offered her one of them.

"I didn't ask if you wanted cream or sugar," he said.

"Black is fine," she said.

He grunted as if he disagreed and returned to his chair. He made himself comfortable and took a long sip from his own mug. Shipman didn't think it contained coffee.

"You accused my daughter of murder," he said, getting right to it, no chitchat, no Minnesota Nice.

"No," Shipman said. "I did not. But Elliot does know who delivered the message to McKenzie's building the night he was shot. So do you."

Marshall stood up straight; his eyes narrowed. Shipman's right hand went to the butt of her Glock. With her left hand, she pointed at a photograph on the wall. Marshall's head turned. He couldn't have known which pic Shipman was pointing at, yet he said, "Sonuvabitch," just the same.

"I'm not accusing anyone of anything," Shipman said. "I just want to get the answers to some questions in case McKenzie doesn't wake up and answer them himself."

"McKenzie."

"You spoke to him."

Marshall slouched against the back of his chair.

"Yes," he said.

"When you called that night, the night he was shot, did you tell him to come here?"

Marshall nodded.

"He sat right where you're sitting now," he said.

"What did you tell him?"

"I told him that I wanted him to go away."

"He refused, didn't he?"

"He was polite about it, but yeah, he refused."

"Did you threaten him?" Shipman asked.

"What? No. God no. I don't—I don't . . . We're not that kind of people. What happened to him later; that had nothing to do with us, what we were talking about."

"How can you be sure?"

"Because . . ."

Marshall took another pull from his coffee mug.

"Because," he repeated.

"Because what?"

"Because I told him the truth. The whole truth and nothing but the truth, what they say in court. Once I told him what happened there was no reason—ah, fuck."

"What truth?"

Marshall shook his head.

"So long ago," he said. "It should have been forgotten. It would have been forgotten if not for McKenzie."

"Mr. Sohm . . ."

"Look. It's about family and none of your damn business."

Shipman's eyes went back to the wall. So many photographs of Marshall's wife and parents and daughter and brothers and sisters and nieces and nephews and of his cousins, but not one photo of anyone who could have been identified as Gerald King. Her instincts—okay, they were good instincts, I admit it, although, you know what? I had figured it out, too, sitting on the same damn sofa as she was. That's why Marshall revealed his truth to me.

Shipman's instincts told her to say, "Gerald King."

Marshall flinched as if he had heard a loud noise.

"Is that what you and McKenzie discussed?" Shipman asked. "Gerald King?"

Marshall squirmed in his seat.

"What do you know about it?" he asked.

"Only what the Minneapolis Police Department told me. That he disappeared twenty-one years ago. He disappeared before Emma was born, didn't he? He disappeared, if I'm not mistaken, before Elliot was born."

"My wife had just told me that we were expecting. I remember being so happy . . ."

"What happened to Gerald King?"

"If you spoke to the Minneapolis cops, you know what happened to him. He got tired of being Gerald King and ran away from home. They found his car at a marina on Lake Superior. I think he took a boat to Canada and was eaten by wolves."

"That's one theory," Shipman said.

"You want another? Gerald fucking King was a sick pervert who assaulted his female employees, who raped them, and one of the woman he raped was McKenzie's mother and McKenzie's father found out about it and he hid in the backseat of Gerald's car and when Gerald was about to drive home after work, McKenzie's father strangled him and drove the car to Gitche Gumme and threw the body into the lake never to be seen again. How's that for a theory?"

"I like it. Do you have another?"

Marshall stared at her for a few beats while he wondered

what he could say that would make Shipman go away without causing any more trouble. He decided to tell her what he told me in just the way he told me.

"I'm just speculating here," he said. "Just telling a story."

"That's right," Shipman said.

"I'm not confessing to any crimes; I'm just making shit up."

"I understand."

"I think Gerald King raped his own daughter."

Marshall took a long pull from his coffee mug before continuing.

"I think he raped Jenna," he said. "After Charles and Porter went away to college and he was all alone with her. I think he raped her and she became pregnant and Gerald found out and he decided he was going to beat the baby out of her and during the fight he slipped and hit his head on the edge of a kitchen counter. Or maybe Jenna hit him with a baseball bat; Charles was always leaving his shit lying around. Or maybe she pushed him and he fell down a flight of stairs. Whatever, it was self-defense."

"I'm sure it was," Shipman said. "Why didn't she call the police?"

"I think—this is just me talking here—I think that the family didn't trust the system. That the police, the courts could have just as easily decided that Jenna was a little whore who killed her father when he tried to—when he tried to discipline her and charge her with murder. Being a cop you know, you know personally, that never ever happened, especially twenty years ago, putting it on the woman, the girl, right? Instead of taking that chance, though, the family—I think maybe a cousin just happened to come by while all this was going on. The cousin had studied agriculture at the University of Minnesota and decided afterward to stay in Minneapolis to work and get married instead of going back to the family farm in

Wisconsin. He came over to visit, came over to check on Jenna because his mother was always worrying about her because Jenna's own mother had died four years earlier and she knew that Jenna's father was a complete asshole. I think the cousin called his mother after he discovered what had happened and his mother and his father drove all the way from Shell Lake, a two-hour drive. Maybe they parked Gerald's car in the attached garage and with the door closed so no one could see, they put Gerald's body in the backseat and his father took it back to Shell Lake and buried it on the farm and afterward they drove Gerald's car to a marina they knew on Lake Superior not all that far from where they lived and after that everyone pretended that nothing happened. Except that it did happen and even though Jenna and her cousin are the only ones alive who know what happened, not her brothers and certainly not her daughter, and they don't ever talk about it to anyone much less to each other, it's haunted Jenna every day of her life which is why she sometimes suffers from depression, why sometimes she does drugs. 'Course, what do I know?"

Marshall finished his drink while Shipman watched.

"You told all of this to McKenzie?" she asked.

"Yes."

"What did he say?"

"He said he liked the first theory best—that Gerald King ran away from home, adding that he did it because he knew sooner or later people were going to find out about what he was doing to his female employees. He said if anyone asked, that's the story he'd go with."

"Anything else?"

"He also apologized. He said he was sorry for imposing on me and my family and he was sorry for dredging up an uncomfortable chapter in our lives but it didn't change anything as far as he was concerned. He was still going to help Charles."

"Then what?"

"He shook my hand and left."

"Did he tell you that Jenna had delivered a message before you called him?"

"No."

"Or what it said?"

"No."

"Or that he was going to RT's Basement?"

"I didn't know anything about that until I read it in the paper."

Shipman had a few choice words for me at that point, only she didn't speak them out loud.

"Do you know where I can find Jenna King?" she asked instead.

"Why? So you can accuse her of murdering her father?"

"So I can find out what happened to McKenzie. Mr. Sohm, the killing that may or may not have occurred in Minneapolis twenty-one years ago—that's not my case; that's not my jurisdiction."

The answer seemed to satisfy Marshall.

"She has a small house in St. Paul," he said.

NINETEEN

Jenna King was sitting in a stuffed chair in her living room and staring at nothing while she contemplated the universe and her place in it. It was not a happy place, she told me later.

She heard her front doorbell and decided to ignore it. The chimes were replaced by a hard knocking. She decided to ignore that, too. Only the knocking became incessant. She leapt angrily from the chair and crossed the room to the hallway. She disregarded the spy hole and instead just yanked the heavy door open. Jenna didn't even look to see who was standing behind it before she shouted, "What do you want?"

Jamal Brown was standing on her long porch. He smiled at her.

"Baby, you okay?" he asked. "You sound stressed."

Jenna attempted to shut the door but Jamal used his foot and a shoulder to keep it open.

"What's wrong, baby?" he asked.

"I told you that I didn't want to see you again."

"I know you were upset about the other night, saying things you didn't mean."

"I meant what I said."

Jenna tried to push the door closed again to no avail.

"Baby, let me in," Jamal said. "You know I have what you need."

Jenna kept pushing the door. Jamal pushed back. After a few seconds, Jenna gave up. Jamal entered the small house and quickly closed the door behind him. He tried to embrace the woman; called her "baby" again. Jenna shrugged his arms away and stepped deeper into her living room. Jamal followed her. He had always liked her house; ninety years old in the heart of Summit Hill as close to the James J. Hill House as it was to the Minnesota governor's residence—hardwood floors, built-in cabinets, ceramic tiles, glass knobs, coved ceilings, fireplace, porch. He had even entertained the idea of living there; brought it up to Jenna during one of their late-night sessions. She wouldn't even consider the possibility.

"My daughter lives here," Jenna said.

When she turned to face him, Jamal was right there, close enough to rest his hands on the woman's shoulders.

Again, Jenna pushed him away.

"Please don't," she said.

"Baby, I know we can get past this."

"Stop calling me baby. I'm not your baby."

"You'll always be my baby, Jen." Jamal stepped closer again. Jenna moved away. "C'mon now, don't be like that."

"You shot him. You shot McKenzie."

"I did it for you."

"For me? How is this for me?"

"You said you didn't want him prying into your past," Jamal said. "So I stopped him."

"No, no, no, God. That's not what I meant and you know it."

Again Jamal tried to embrace the woman.

"Stop it," Jenna said.

"Baby, what's done is done. It's time for us to move on. Time for us to have the life we talked about."

"What life? You're my fucking drug dealer."

Jamal didn't like being called that and had to work hard to keep his voice low and relaxed.

"Hey, hey, hey, you know I'm much more to you than just that," he said.

Jenna covered her face with both hands and turned toward the fireplace; her back to Jamal.

"You're not, you're not, you're not," she chanted.

"You know we belong together."

Jenna refused to respond.

"I get that you're upset about this guy, this McKenzie that you've never even met before. Only you don't need to worry 'bout him no more. We can go back to the way things were between us. Tell me that this doesn't change anything between us."

"It changes everything."

"Don't say that. Jenna? Jenna, look at me."

"No."

"Think about it, Jenna," Jamal said. "If you think about it, you'll see that you're as guilty about what happened to McKenzie as I am. You're the one who delivered the message. Even used your niece's name cuz you panicked when they asked you for yours."

"Don't you think I know that?" Jenna finally turned to look at him. "I know what I did. Why do you think I feel so—to talk, you said. We'll check him out, you said. Find out if he's legit, you said. Bring McKenzie to RT's Basement, a place I had never even heard of. Bring him down there because it would make him feel uncomfortable and he would be more apt to tell us the truth if he was feeling uncomfortable. Find out if he was really related to me, if he was going to hurt me or help me, help save Charles. You said."

"Don't kid yourself. *We* brought him down there because RT's was known as a drug haven. Cuz it was known for being a trouble spot; cops had to be called in a half-dozen times in the past few months. No one should've been surprised if he got shot down there."

"Not 'we.' You. You meant to shoot him. You meant to shoot him all along."

"*We* meant to shoot him. That's the way the police will see it; what you have to understand."

"You're just saying that because you're afraid I'll turn you in. Turn us both in. I should. I really should."

"Don't talk like that," Jamal said. "It makes me nervous you talking like that."

For a couple of heartbeats, Jenna remembered sitting next to Jamal in the front seat of Jamal's car just down the street from RT's Basement. They saw a man wearing an expensive sports jacket enter the club alone.

"Is that him, is that him?" Jamal asked. "I bet that's him."

Jenna made to open her door.

"No," Jamal told her. "Let's wait."

"Why?" Jenna asked. "I thought we were going to talk to him."

"Want him to be feel uncomfortable, remember what I said?"

So, they waited.

After about fifteen minutes, the man appeared just outside the entrance of the club. He glanced around. Jenna knew he was looking for them.

"Wait here," Jamal said.

He got out of the car and walked swiftly to where the man was standing. The man didn't see him coming. He was too busy gawking at a woman who looked like a hooker approaching from the other side.

When he got close, Jenna saw Jamal raise his hand and shoot the man in the back.

She wanted to scream, but no sound came out.

Jamal turned and started back toward the car.

He was smiling.

Jenna opened the door of the car. She started running, not even bothering to close the door behind her.

She didn't know why she had picked the narrow path between RT's Basement and the building next door except that it led away from the man lying on the sidewalk. She rounded the corner and nearly collided with Dr. Tucker Hammel. She was shocked to see him there. Her first thought should have been to ask for help. Instead all she could think was that he would recognize her. She turned and ran off in the opposite direction. Fifteen minutes later she was in a Lyft and heading back to her home in Summit Hill. She couldn't bear to return to Lake Minnetonka and face her brothers.

"Why, why, why?" Jenna asked. "Why did you do it?"

"I did it for you, baby. How many times do I have to say it?"

"He could have helped Charles."

"Once he's gone and we're rich, you'll feel better about it," Jamal said.

"I'm already rich. Wait. Once he's gone? Who? Charles? I don't, I don't understand."

"You told me about Charles, remember? Told me he was dying of some liver disease I can't pronounce. Remember?"

"I was crying and you wanted to know why I was crying and I told you."

"The way I saw it—what happened, I have connections, Jenna. I know people. Not just you. Customers most of 'em. They helped me get my hands on some KTech stock. Thousands of shares that I sold. Now, when Charles dies and the stock prices collapse . . ."

Jenna shouted at him.

"You shorted KTech?" she said.

"What I don't get is why the stock price hasn't kept going down; why it's going up instead. No one has seen him in weeks, right? They have to think Charles is sick. Have to think he has the COVID or something. You'd think the price would be going down at least a little bit."

"Oh my God."

Jamal saw something in Jenna's face then, a mixture of both sadness and contempt.

"Baby . . ." he said.

"This was never about me, about stopping McKenzie from looking into my past, discovering my secrets. You shot McKenzie to keep him from helping my brother. You want Charles to die so KTech's stock price will drop and you can make a killing. Only the stock price won't drop, at least not enough to make a difference. I've already seen to that."

Jamal moved closer to the woman.

"Jenna, what have you done?" he asked.

"We've been playing an investor named Justus Reinfeld, convincing him that the company was a prime target for a hostile takeover. He's been buying up shares, keeping the price high. If Charles recovers, we'll drive a stake through his heart. If he doesn't, then Reinfeld can have KTech. Let him be the white knight. My brother and I don't want to have anything to do with the company if Charles isn't there."

It took a few beats before Jamal realized what Jenna had told him.

"The stock price will remain high?" he asked.

"That's the plan."

"You did this?"

"It was my idea."

Jamal balled up his fist and hit Jenna.

She staggered backward.

"You fucking bitch!" he shouted.

He hit her again.

"Do you know what you've done? You've wasted me."

Jamal hit her a third time.

Jenna crumbled to the floor.

"I didn't want to do this," Jamal said. "I tried to keep it from happening and then . . . and then when I decided if it had to be done, I wanted someone else to do it."

Jamal pulled a gun out from where he had hidden it behind his back and pointed it at the woman sprawled across the floor.

"Why are you making me do this?" he asked.

Jenna gazed up at him.

"Not here, not here," she chanted. "This is her house. This is Emma's house. Please not here."

Jamal knew that Emma was Jenna's daughter. He had seen her a few times from a distance, yet they had never been introduced. That was Jenna's doing and Jamal resented her for it. At the same time, he felt a twinge of sympathy for the young woman he had never met. Emma shouldn't be the one to find her mother's body . . .

"All right," he said.

Jamal grabbed hold of Jenna's upper arm and yanked her to her feet.

"All right," he repeated.

A jinglejangle of chimes sounded around him and for a moment Jamal became convinced that he had somehow caused it.

"What is that?" he asked.

"The doorbell."

"The doorbell?"

"Someone's at the front door."

Jamal felt the icy fingers of panic seize his heart, yet he quickly brushed them away. He squeezed Jenna's forearm.

"Answer the door," he said. "Get rid of whoever it is."

Jamal showed Jenna his gun.

"I'll be standing right here," he said.

Jenna moved toward the door as another round of chimes sounded. Jamal quickly thrust the handgun under the waistband of his jeans behind his back and stood facing the door as if he were waiting for a bus.

Jenna opened the door.

Detective Jean Shipman stood on the porch in front of her. She immediately noticed the swelling on the woman's face, and knew someone had punched her. She smiled just the same.

Jenna smiled back, an odd thing to do all things considered.

Jenna was holding the door far enough open that Shipman could see a young black man standing off to the side, his hands folded across his belt buckle. He was staring at her so she stared back. Watch the eyes, an unheard voice told her. She kept smiling and kept watching the young man even as she spoke.

"Jenna King?" Shipman asked.

"Yes."

Shipman produced the wallet containing her badge and ID. "Detective Jean Shipman, St. Paul Police Department."

"What the fuck!" Jamal shouted.

He reached behind his back, found the handgun he had hidden there and brought it out.

Shipman watched him do it even as she dropped her wallet and reached under her blazer for the butt of her Glock.

She knew that the young man would get to his gun first. She crouched down, trying to make herself smaller.

"No, no, no!" Jenna screamed.

She slammed the door shut.

Shipman fell backward, yet managed to maintain her balance. She pulled her Glock, gripped it with both hands, and spun so that her back was pressed against the wall next to the door. She half expected to hear and see bullets ripping through the door, yet none came.

She could hear Jenna screaming inside the house.

"Stop it, please stop it," she said.

"This is all your fault," Jamal screamed back.

Shipman was shouting herself, hoping her voice could be heard inside.

"Nothing bad has happened yet," she said. "We can still make this go away."

She didn't hear a reply.

Shipman told me later that she experienced what she called brain freeze. For a few brief moments the many thoughts that swirled in her head paralyzed her into inaction—kick open the door and confront the assailant, run for cover, grab her phone and call for backup, reach down for her badge and ID; what were they doing on the floor, anyway? What brought her back to the world was the sight of Bobby Dunston strolling up the sidewalk. He stopped when he saw his detective. He looked at her as if he was having a hard time believing that she was there. Shipman, on the other hand, never questioned his presence, not for a second.

"We have a hostage situation," she said. "Unidentified black man, armed, semiautomatic handgun, five ten, hundred and sixty pounds, black slacks, white shirt, black suit jacket, black-rimmed glasses. Woman identified as Jenna King, five four, one twenty, short blond hair; face shows signs of swelling where she might have been struck several times."

Bobby reached into his pocket. Instead of pulling his piece, however, he withdrew his cell phone.

Only he dropped his phone and reached for his Glock the moment the front door opened.

Jamal had been thinking fast. He knew if he was going to get out of the house he would need to do it now. In just a few minutes the place would be crawling with police, he decided; St. Paul's SWAT team was probably already on its way. He gathered Jenna up, wrapped his arm over her breasts, pulled her tight against his chest, and pressed the muzzle of his handgun against her throat. He pushed her toward the door.

"Open it," he said.

She did.

He started to ease Jenna past the door when he saw Shipman. He spun toward her, using Jenna as a shield.

"Get back, get back," he said.

Shipman moved backward across the porch even as she trained the sights of her Glock on Jamal's head, hoping for a clean shot.

"Get back," Jamal repeated.

Shipman kept moving until the back of her legs hit the porch railing.

"Drop your gun," Jamal said. "Do you hear me? Drop your gun. Drop it or I'll kill her."

Shipman did not drop her gun. She was too well trained for that.

By then Bobby was in a classic Isosceles Stance, both hands gripping his Glock near the center line of his body, his arms extended, his elbows bent slightly to control the recoil.

Jamal's eyes went from Shipman to Bobby back to Shipman again and then settled on Bobby as if he was wondering where he had come from.

"Drop your gun," he told him.

Bobby replied calmly.

"You have nowhere to go, no way to get there," he said.

Jamal turned Jenna to face Bobby, then back again to face Shipman. He pressed the muzzle against her throat hard enough for her to cry out.

"Please, please," she said.

"What's your name?" Bobby asked.

"Fuck you," Jamal replied. "I'm leaving. You try to stop me and I'll kill her."

"You're not going anywhere," Bobby said.

"Don't try to stop me. I mean it."

Jamal edged Jenna forward, Shipman on their right; Bobby directly in front of them. Shipman was waiting for Jamal to move even with her so that if she was forced to fire, she wouldn't have to shoot around Jenna. She would have an unobstructed line of fire. One step. Another. Another. Only Jamal halted just as he reached the center of the porch.

It was the car that stopped him. A 2017 Ford Escape. It slowed directly in front of the house before the driver cranked the wheel hard, punched the accelerator, and drove on to the boulevard, the nose of the SUV touching the sidewalk, the rear hanging above the street. The doors flew open. Special Agent Brian Wilson came out of the driver's side, pulling his 9 mm SIG Sauer as he approached the scene in a crouch. Greg Schroeder came out of the passenger side. He, of course, was carrying a .45.

Harry circled to his right, putting himself at the corner of the porch so that Jamal was now covered on three sides. Schroeder moved to Bobby's left. Bobby was appalled to see a PI, a civilian, at a live crime scene.

"Stand down," he said. "I mean it."

Schroeder looked at him as if he had just been insulted. He didn't leave, though, merely rested his weapon alongside his leg, the muzzle pointing toward the ground.

Chopper and Herzog watched the scene unfold from the relative safety of Chopper's black van parked a few houses up the street. Herzog turned to speak to his friend.

"Don't let Jamal go int' the house, I said. Take him while we have the chance, I said."

"Oops," Chopper replied.

On the porch, Jenna was having a difficult time remaining on her feet. Jamal had to keep her upright with one hand while holding the handgun against her throat with the other.

"Please," Jenna said.

"No one needs to get hurt," Jamal said. "If you just let me go . . ."

He was staring at Harry when he spoke.

"FBI," Harry said.

"C'mon," Jamal said.

Herzog and Chopper kept watching through the front windshield of the van.

"Maybe we should get some popcorn," Chopper said.

"Fuck this," Herzog said.

He opened the driver's side door and slid out of the vehicle.

"Where you goin', Herzy?" Chopper asked. "Herzy, what are you going to do? Herzy? Ah, man."

Herzog walked quickly along the boulevard to Jenna's sidewalk, then up the sidewalk toward the house. Shipman and the others were so intent on what was happening on the porch that they didn't notice him. Jamal did, though. His eyes grew wide with both recognition and fear.

"You, too?" he asked.

The others finally saw Herzog when he reached the porch steps.

"What are you doing here?" Bobby shouted. "Get back, get back."

Herzog climbed the steps and stood directly in front of Jamal and Jenna.

"You done playin'?" he asked.

"I don't know what happened," Jamal told him. "This should have worked. I should be rich."

"I used t' think the same way."

Herzog held out his hand.

"This is what you're gonna do," he said. "You're gonna give me the piece. You're gonna release the woman. You're gonna let them arrest you. When you meet the county attorney, you gonna trade the doc-tor and his Oxy operation for a reduced sentence. Then you're gonna do your time like a man; finish that degree you talked about while you inside. Then you gonna come out and make something of your life while you still young enough to do it. You said you wanted t' go basic. A counselor I talked to when I was inside said sometimes it takes what they call a significant emotional event for you to get from where you at t' where you need to be. What happened to me. This is your emotional event. Ain't pretty. It is what it is."

Herzog made a gimme gesture with the fingers of his hands.

"Either that or you gonna be just another brother killed by the po-lice," he said.

Jamal slowly released the woman. Jenna collapsed to the floor of the porch and crawled away. Shipman shouted at her.

"Stay down, Jenna," she said. "Stay down."

Jamal set the gun in Herzog's hand. The big man glanced at it, recognized it as a .32 caliber Walther, and thought it was probably the same gun Jamal had used to shoot me; that forensics could match it to the bullet they took out of my back easily enough. Herzog could hardly believe that Jamal had kept it. You never keep the gun.

"You just ain't cut out for the thug life," he said.

"What am I going to do?" Jamal asked.

"Nothing. You don't say nothing. You don't even tell 'em your name. Me and Chopper know people. We'll send somebody t' help. 'Kay?"

"Thank you."

Herzog turned and walked back down the porch steps. Shipman and Harry surged forward.

"Put your hands on your head, put your hands on your head," Shipman chanted.

Jamal dropped to his knees and did what he was told.

Herzog approached Bobby who was still standing in an Isosceles Stance and aiming his Glock at Jamal.

When he reached him, Herzog held out the Walther. Bobby came out of his stance and took the gun.

Herzog stepped past him and started walking back toward the van.

"Where do you think you're going?" Bobby asked.

Instead of saying what was on his mind, Herzog just kept on moving.

While Jamal followed Herzog's advice and remained silent, Jenna King couldn't stop talking, which was fine with all the law enforcement personnel that had descended on her house. Under the Federal Rules of Evidence, "excited utterances" were admissible in a court of law.

Jenna explained how she had met Jamal and became emotionally dependent on him. She explained about Charles and how Jamal had shorted his company. She explained about the night I was shot. She even gave a brief tutorial on opioid addiction.

"I sprained my ankle while jogging," she said. "The doctor gave me OxyContin for the pain. I followed the prescription the first day, one tablet every eight hours, and then did the same the second day. I didn't take any the third day. The fourth day my ankle ached a little bit when I tried to run prematurely, so I took more pills. The same the fifth day. And the sixth. And the seventh.

"I understand addiction. Sixty percent is genetics; the body is predisposed to become addicted. The other forty percent is psychological. The brain wants what the brain wants. It wasn't like when I was on coke, though. I didn't take opioids for the rush, for the high. I took them to make the pain go away. Once I was hooked—I would try to go a day without using. That's what they teach you. One day at a time. Only I would become physically ill. My body would feel as if I hadn't eaten in three days. I went back to my doctor, partly to get off the drugs but also partly to stay on. His response was to hook me up with Jamal. I should have quit right then and there; book a room in a chemical dependency clinic. Only you can't defeat your demons if you still enjoy their company. My family didn't know anything about this, of course. People who are addicted to opioids can still hold down jobs; they can meet their responsibilities; maintain the appearance of stability at work and home. Until they can't."

Yet while Jenna talked up a storm, Bobby told me later that at no time did she incriminate herself; at no time did she utter a single word that could be used against her. It was always Jamal this or Jamal that.

"I was told that Jenna King is the smartest person in the room," I said, "no matter what room she happens to be in."

"I believe it," Bobby said.

Detective Jean Shipman was feeling a little depressed when she finally left the crime scene. She had been there first, she reminded herself. Yes, Bobby and the others eventually turned up at Jenna King's house, but she was the one who knocked on the front door; she's the one who broke the case. It was her cuffs that were wound around Jamal Brown's wrists.

She took pride in that. Only not a lot. Discovering who had shot me and why and then bringing him down hadn't given her nearly the satisfaction that she had hoped for. She didn't believe the case had tested her skills. It never gave her an aha moment.

While she was driving back to the Griffin Building, Shipman heard the sound of a bell coming from her cell phone. It told her that she had just received a text. She accessed it at the first stoplight.

The text had been sent by Officer Kyle Cordova of the Northfield Police Department.

"U up?" it read.

The question made Shipman shake her head. It was still early evening after all.

She replied when she was caught at the next stoplight.

"Your seduction skills are sorely lacking," her text read. "But since you asked, yes, I'm up."

IN CASE YOU'RE WONDERING

I wish I could say that when I finally opened my eyes for good I was gazing into the lovely face of my wife. Or Lilly Linder. Or Kate Beckinsale playing a nurse in *Pearl Harbor*. Instead, I got a male nurse who thought a three-day-old beard looked good on him. He shined a bright light into one eye and then the other, felt for a pulse even though a machine was counting my heartbeats for him, and said, "The doctor will be with you in a moment."

This had been the fourth time I had come out of the coma by my count. The first time, I woke with complete clarity about where I was and what had happened to me. I sat up and looked around the room; even saw Nina sitting there, before falling against the bed and drifting back to sleep. The second time, I couldn't move, couldn't speak, my vision was blurred, and I had no idea where I was or why. The third time, I was convinced that all of the doctors and nurses were attempting to kill me; that even the room fixtures and machines that surrounded me were encouraging me to die. Then there was

Dan—Dan being the name of the male nurse and with all due respect to him and his profession, goddammit!

This is not the way it would have happened in the movies, my inner voice told me.

Dan was correct about the doctor, though. Lilly Linder was by my side less than ninety seconds later, and Nina, too, who took my hand, kissed it, and pressed it against her cheek.

"I can't leave you alone for a minute, can I?" she said.

Lilly was intent on conducting a bunch of examinations then and there to test my mental status, cranial nerves, individual senses, motor function, and reflexes. She wanted to know where I fit in something called the Glasgow Coma Scale. Apparently, I scored high.

I have to say, though, I didn't care much for her bedside manner. She asked "What's your name?"

"Is that a trick question?" I answered.

"Do you know who you are?"

"It depends. What have you heard?"

Lilly whacked me on the shoulder.

"And you wonder why somebody shot him," she said.

"Wait. Somebody shot me?"

"It's a long story," Nina said.

Once Lilly deemed that I had recovered sufficiently enough to receive visitors, damn I received a lot of them—Bobby, Shelby and the girls, Erica after she completed her exams, Harry, Greg Schroeder, Riley and Mary Pat Brodin-Mulally, Mason Gafford, Emma King, Herzog, and to my great surprise, Chopper, who despised hospitals. I even received a call from Heavenly Petryk who was purposely vague about where she was at the time and what she was doing. They all helped filled in the blanks for me. Including Detective Jean Shipman, who was surprisingly forthcoming about her role in all of this—at least I was surprised. 'Course, she kept calling me "hotshot," which was infuriating. "So, how are you doing, hotshot?" And I kept calling her "Jeannie," which seemed to annoy her, too. "Pretty good, Jeannie, how are you?"

Despite what she had told Marshall Sohm about Gerald King's disappearance not being her case or her jurisdiction, she felt compelled to take her supplementals to Lieutenant Rask at the Minneapolis Police Department and tell him what she had learned. She was a cop after all and her instructors were correct—you can't choose the victim.

Rask hadn't known that Jenna was pregnant when he conducted his first investigation or he might have done things differently, he told Shipman. As it was, DNA testing—remember that? DNA testing proved that Emma was, in fact, Gerald and Jenna's daughter and that Jenna, Charles, Porter, and, yes, Dave Deese, were her half siblings. Rask confronted Jenna with the findings. Jenna was outraged yet also unruffled. She admitted that her father had raped and impregnated her. She suggested that's why he abandoned the family; why he ran away rather than take responsibility for his crime. I remember saying "Good for her" when Shipman told me that part of the story.

Still, armed with the DNA evidence and Marshall's semiconfession, Rask was able to convince a judge in the Fourth Judicial District Court to issue a warrant stating that "you, Lieutenant Clayton Rask, peace officer of Hennepin County in the State of Minnesota, and any other authorized person, are hereby commanded to enter and search between the hours of seven A.M. and eight P.M. the above-described premises, for the described remains of Gerald King, and to seize and keep said remains in custody until dealt with according to law."

Rask took the warrant to the Washburn County Sheriff's Office in Shell Lake, Wisconsin, and asked that he be allowed to use ground-penetrating radar to search Marshall and Mary Ann Sohm's farm for the body of Gerald King. The sheriff told him to stick his warrant where the sun doesn't shine. He had no intention of besmirching the sterling reputation of a good man and his darling wife on such flimsy, unsubstantiated, and unconvincing evidence.

"Sohm was a veteran," the sheriff said. "He served in 'Nam. He was a volunteer firefighter for Christ's sake."

Rask revealed all of this to an assistant Hennepin County attorney who told him that there was never a chance that he would have prosecuted the case anyway given the flimsy, unsubstantiated, and unconvincing evidence.

"Why are you wasting my time?" he wanted to know.

"Well, I did my bit," Rask said and closed the case.

"Good for him," I said.

"You understand why I called LT, though, don't you?" Shipman said. "Why I had to call him?"

I told her something then that I wish I hadn't; that I wish I could take back.

"You're a good cop, Jean," I said.

She seemed as surprised by the declaration as I was.

"So were you, McKenzie," Shipman said.

Still, I couldn't let it go at that, could I?

"All the crap I've given you over the years?" I said. "I wish I could go back and do it all over again."

"I wouldn't have it any other way," Shipman said.

Eventually, I summoned Dave Deese to my sickbed. By then I was feeling pretty good and getting anxious to leave the hospital. Yet when he arrived I made it seem as if I had about three minutes to live, cough, cough, and he needed to do me a favor before I, cough, cough, passed on. 'Course, Deese had known me for a long time, so he stood at the foot of my bed, folded his arms across his chest, and said, "What?"

That's when I told him about the King family. It was a long conversation and Deese ended up sitting for most of it. What hurt was my theory of how his mother became pregnant by Gerald King. He had a hard time accepting it and probably wouldn't have if not for the DNA evidence. He wondered aloud if his father, the man who raised him, had known the truth and decided he hadn't. Otherwise, Gerald would have "disappeared" a half dozen years before he actually did—the quotes were DD's.

That's when I hit Deese with the news about Charles King and his desperate need for an immediate liver transplant. I told him that I would have taken the tests myself to see if I was compatible even though we weren't related because, well, that's the way I'm wired. Unfortunately, my current state of health had made that impossible; the doctors had forbidden it. I asked Deese if he would help. He said no.

I don't think he was afraid of the risks associated with being a live-donor or because he was indifferent to his half brother's plight. He wanted to punish someone for what had happened to his mother and Charles was the closest someone at hand.

I told Deese that he wasn't Gerald King's only "victim"— this time the quotes were mine. He didn't care. So, I guilted him into it, telling him that he owed me one; reminding him that I had been shot in the back and had been clinically dead for four minutes and ten seconds and yet I had been willing to help the Kings.

Finally, he agreed to take the tests, hoping, I'm sure, that they would prove he was incompatible. Only he *was* compatible and that news alone was enough to convince Deese to go through with the transplant. If you know you can help save someone's life and you don't even try, that makes you an asshole. Deese was not an asshole. He was a "good guy" and in the neighborhood where I grew up that was considered the highest praise.

I was proud of him. DD saved Charles King's life and oh boy, did Charles appreciate it. Suddenly, this charismatic, billionaire entrepreneur was treating Deese as if he was, well, as if Deese was his long-lost brother from St. Paul, showering him with gifts. And he had plenty to give him, too. There had been a stunning dip in the KTech stock price when news of Charles's condition went public followed a few weeks later by a meteoric rise when his liver transplant was deemed a resounding success on every media platform known to man, most of it orchestrated by Porter. If Jamal Brown had played by the rules, he would have made a fortune. Justus Reinfeld, too.

It's really too bad that shortly after Charles King had his long-delayed meeting with the Securities and Exchange Commission—held in his hospital room the day before his surgery—the Enforcement Division of the SEC charged Reinfeld and three other traders with willfully violating Sections 17(a)(1) and 17(a)(3) of the Securities Act of 1933, Section 10(b) of the Securities Exchange Act of 1934 and Rule 10b-5, specifically "parking." And that Reinfeld, who "cooperated" with the SEC investigation, settled the charges by disgorging all of his profits estimated at over $200 million and agreed to being barred from the securities industry for a period of three years with the right to apply for reentry after six months. 'Course, it could have been worse. He could have been barred for life. He could have gone to prison for a couple of years. Like Jamal. Oh well.

Charles King's gratitude extended to Barbara, as well. And to T. Emma and Elliot had met her during the transplant ordeal and simply adored her. Apparently, T was the unfiltered, unabashed, and utterly unapologetic role model they had been craving all of their young lives.

Unfortunately, the rest of Deese's family wasn't as agreeable.

"My aunt hasn't spoken to me since it all came out," Deese told me. "Not being my father's son, it was a secret that she didn't want revealed; one that only she and my mother had shared. I've tried to talk to her only she won't talk. She won't even tell me if my father knew anything about what happened.

"At the same time, my other aunts and uncles and some of my cousins claim that I'm an ingrate. No, I'm not, I tell them. I'm grateful for everything. Others in my family think because of the gifts Charles had given me; the invitations to his place on Lake Minnetonka— A cousin said 'Isn't the Deese family good enough for you anymore?' Some of them still refuse to believe any of the DNA evidence. Either the science is screwed up or I am; that's their explanation. Except for T. If anything, all of this has brought us closer. Imagine.

"Still, I'm glad to know the King family, Charles and Porter, the girls, even Marshall Sohm, although he sometimes acts like a prick. It's hard for me to think of them as actual family, though. I suppose it's because we didn't grow up together; their experiences aren't my experiences, you know? But they're all very nice people."

This included Jenna.

After she kicked her opioid habit, she reached out to me. She told me about her unhealthy liaison with Jamal, the whys and wherefores; how victims of sexual abuse committed by a parent—that is, incest—are forever hopping from one abusive relationship to another as if they were trying to confirm their own worthlessness; as if they were trying to prove that they deserved the abuse.

And she told me what had transpired at her house in St. Paul that day. She was as apologetic as hell, too, only I don't think that's why she wanted to talk. Lieutenant Rask had buried the DNA evidence linking Emma to Gerald King and Jenna wanted to know if she could trust me to keep the secret as well. I told her that she could. I also told her that I thought her family, especially Emma, was strong enough to know the truth; that they probably already did and were waiting on her to admit it. She disagreed. I told her that at least she should seek professional help; try to heal herself. She said she already had on numerous occasions. Like many victims of incest, though, she had gone through counselors the way fashionistas go through shoes, discarding them at the slightest hint of abandonment or betrayal both real and imagined. Besides, she reasoned, she was at least as smart as they were.

"Ask me anything you want to know about betrayal trauma theory, trauma bonding, and disassociation," she said. "I'm an expert."

"I wish I could help you," I said.

"Why? We're not even related."

Oh, before I forget, I bought Nancy Moosbrugger a new dress. Mason Gafford told me about her, about how she had cradled my head in her lap until help arrived after I was shot. So, I bought her a new dress—a half-dozen new dresses, actually. I noticed that Gafford never left her side during the shopping expedition, but didn't say anything.

Later, Nancy asked how she could repay my generosity.

I told her she already had.

Still, she insisted that she should do something.

I told her to "Live well, be useful."

She asked me if that was my personal mantra.

I told her that it was.

Which brings me back to Nina Truhler.

We had our ups and downs after I left the hospital. One minute she treated me as if I were the most precious thing she owned. The next she wanted to slap me upside my head. I asked her exactly what she wanted from me.

"Tell me what to do and I'll do it," I said.

"I want you to say that you're done. I want you to say that you'll never do another favor for another friend forever."

"I . . ."

Nina quickly covered my mouth with her hand. After she was sure I wouldn't attempt to say anything more, she removed her hand, kissed me hard, and hugged me close, which I happily tolerated despite the pain it caused.

"You should never make a promise you can't keep," she said.